FAITH *of our* FATHERS

THROUGH THE PERILOUS FIGHT

Volume Three

OTHER BOOKS AND AUDIO BOOKS
BY N.C. ALLEN:

Faith of Our Fathers, Volume 1: A House Divided

Faith of Our Fathers, Volume 2: To Make Men Free

Faith of Our Fathers, Volume 4: One Nation Under God

FAITH of our FATHERS

THROUGH THE PERILOUS FIGHT

Volume Three

a novel by

N.C. ALLEN

Covenant Communications, Inc.

Cover photo © Al Thelin; Cover flag illustration by Joe Flores;
Endsheet Maps courtesy of Geography and Map Division, Library of Congress, Washington, D. C.

Published by Covenant Communications, Inc.
American Fork, Utah

This is a work of fiction. The characters, names, incidents, places, and dialogue are products of the author's imagination, and are not to be construed as real.

Printed in The United States of America
First Printing: September 2003

15 14 13 12 11 10 09 08 13 12 11 10 9 8 7 6 5 4

ISBN 13: 978-1-59811-665-6
ISBN 10: 1-59811-665-7

For all the in-laws who never made me feel like one:
Ed, Laura, Paul, Tammy, Peri Ann, Marylynne,
Jed, and Mariah.
Love you guys.

LIST OF CHARACTERS

The Boston, Massachusetts, Birmingham Family

James Birmingham, the father, a wealthy iron magnate
Elizabeth Stein Birmingham, the mother, abolitionist descendant of Rhode Island Quakers
Their children: Luke
Anne
Camille
Robert
Jimmy

The Charleston, South Carolina, Birmingham Family

Jeffrey Birmingham, the father (James's twin brother), married to plantation heiress
Sarah Matthews Birmingham, the mother, plantation owner
Their children: Ben
Charlotte Birmingham Ellis, married to William Ellis
Richard, deceased
Emily Birmingham Stanhope, married to Austin Stanhope
Clara
Elijah, their grandson, biological child of Richard and Mary (a slave)

The Birmingham Slaves

Ruth, head house servant, the "matriarch" of the majority of the slaves
Joshua, raised as Ben's companion
Mary, Ruth's granddaughter (Joshua's biological half sister), close friend to Emily; also Elijah's biological mother
Rose, Mary's little sister; companion to Clara

The O'Shea Family, New York City

Gavin O'Shea, the father
Brenna O'Shea, the mother
Their children:
Daniel
Colin, deceased

The Brissot Family, formerly of New Orleans, Louisiana

Jean-Pierre Brissot, the father, deceased
Genevieve (Jenny) Stein Brissot, the mother; sister to Elizabeth Stein Birmingham
Their children:
Marie Brissot O'Shea, married to Daniel O'Shea

The Gundersen Family, Cleveland, Ohio

Per Gundersen, the father
Amanda Gundersen, the mother
Their children:
Ivar
Inger, Ivar's daughter

The Dobranski Family, Salt Lake City, Utah Territory

Eli Dobranski, the father; baptized Ben Birmingham years earlier on a mission to the southern states
Ellen Dobranski, the mother
Their children:
Earl, their eldest son
The Dobranskis also have seven other sons

Other Fictional Characters

Isabelle Webb, Pinkerton operative
Abigail Van Dyke, fiancée to Luke Birmingham
Jacob Taylor, newspaper editor and acquaintance of the Boston Birminghams
Lucy Lockhart, Confederate spy

Nonfictional characters to whom reference is made or who play a minor role, interacting with the fictional characters

President Abraham Lincoln
Jefferson Davis, president of the Confederacy
P. G. T. Beauregard, Confederate general
Robert E. Lee, Confederate general
George McClellan, former Union general and presidential candidate
John C. Fremont, presidential candidate and former Union general
Alexander Stephens, Confederate vice president
William Quantrill, Confederate raider
George Thomas, Union commander, "the Rock of Chickamauga"
Patrick R. Cleburne, Confederate general
William Tecumseh Sherman, Union general
Ulysses S. Grant, Union general
Jubal Early, Confederate general
Andrew Jackson, Lincoln's vice presidential running mate
Salmon P. Chase, Union secretary of the treasury; Supreme Court chief justice
Horace Greeley, *New York Times* editor
Joseph Johnston, Confederate general
John B. Hood, Confederate general
Admiral David Farragut, Union naval officer
Roger B. Taney, Supreme Court justice
Edward Everett, American scholar and opening speaker at the ceremony where Lincoln delivered the Gettysburg Address
Allan Pinkerton, private investigator

TO THE READER

As I embarked upon the third volume of this series, I began to realize that, while in the beginning I had given myself many characters who, spread out, would give us a nice, bird's-eye view of Civil War events firsthand, we are now progressing further into the conflict. Many of my characters have been shoved out of commission, either through death or wounding. Thus, the advantage of having such a large cast of characters begins to diminish.

As a result, the reader will see in this volume that I have taken some liberties with the placement of my soldiers. It was not uncommon for soldiers to transfer from regiment to regiment, and in this book I not only make use of that fact, but also in the instance of Lincoln's speech at Gettysburg, I have placed two soldiers in attendance when there were not, in fact, soldiers present at the speech, except for a color guard. I felt it important enough to the plot, however, to take this liberty.

I would also mention again that this series focuses on the minority—the educated, literate black population and the "forward thinkers"—men and women who were years ahead of their time. I have chosen to write about them because they were bright, insightful, and different. My respect for those who dared question the status quo deepens with each volume.

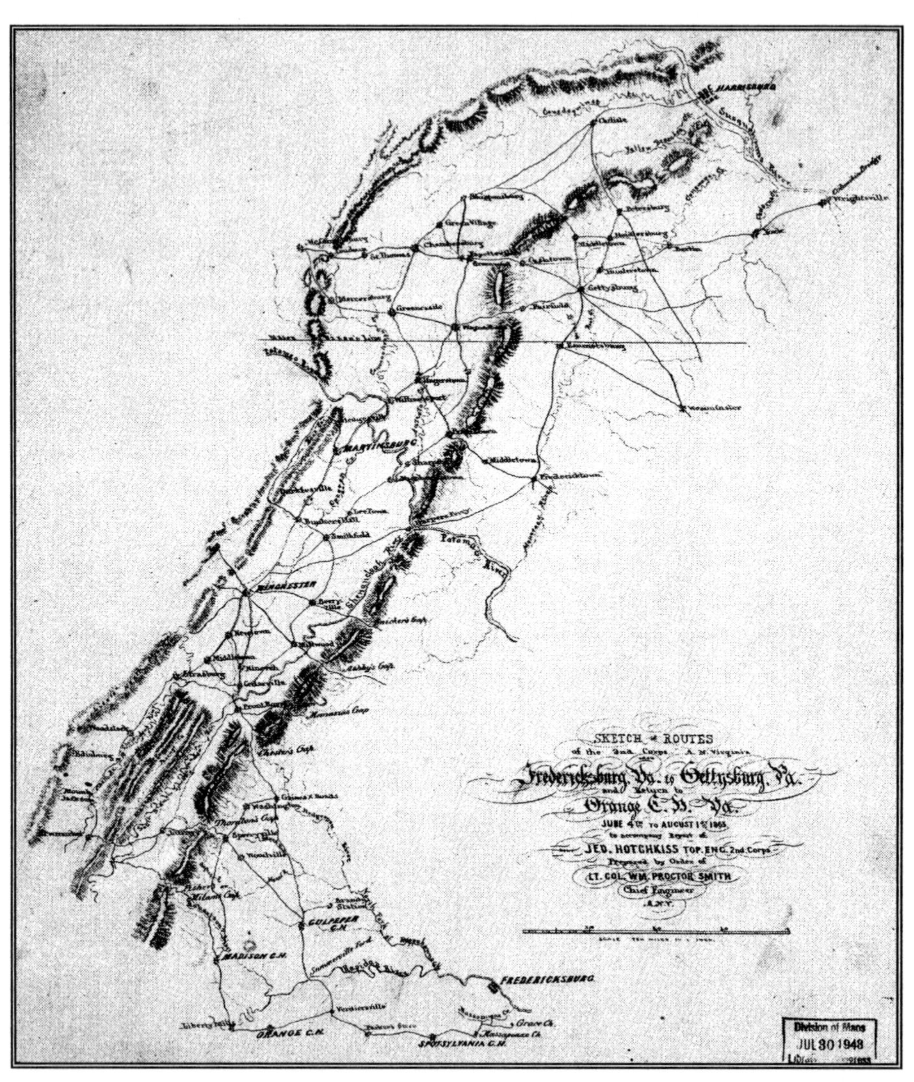

Hotchkiss's Sketch of the Routes of the Second Corps,
Army of Northern Virginia,
from Fredericksburg Virginia, to Gettysburg, Pennsylvania,
and Return, June to August 1863

Geography and Map Division, Library of Congress, Washington, D. C.

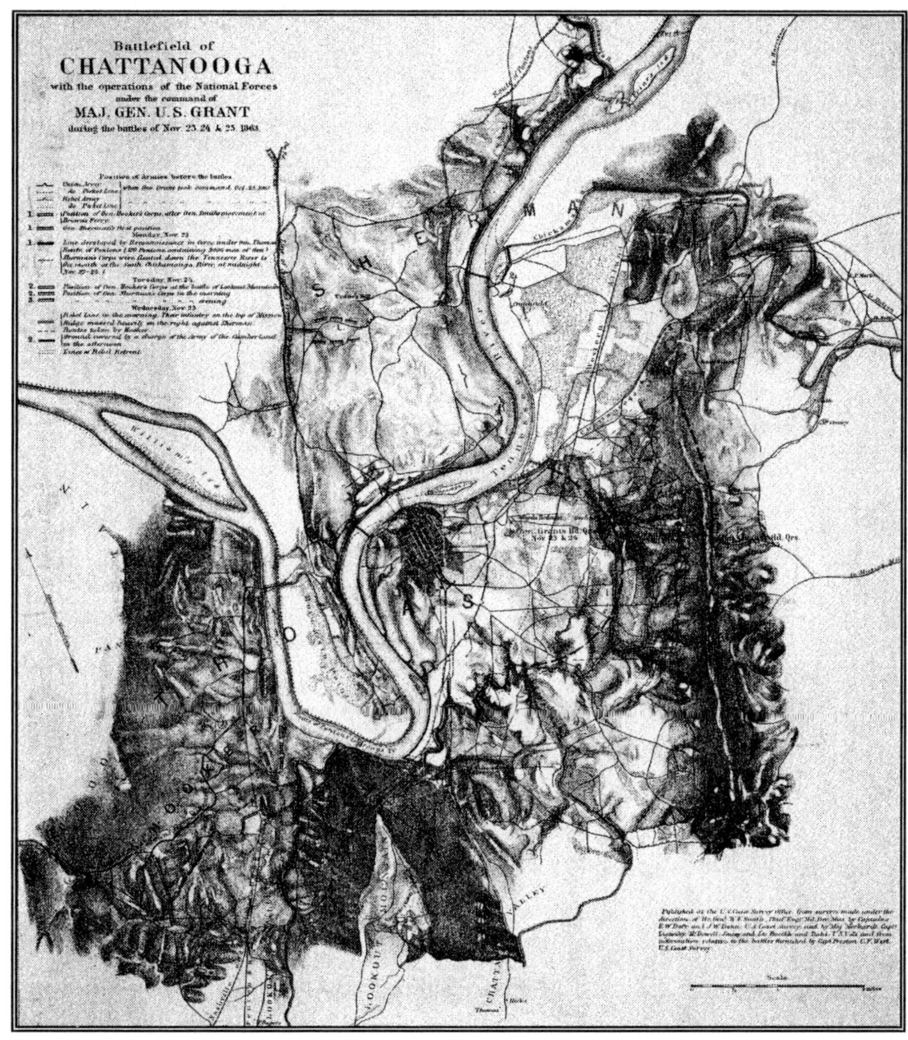

United States Coast Survey Map of the
Battlefield of Chattanooga, Tennessee
November 23–25, 1863

Geography and Map Division, Library of Congress, Washington, D. C.

Oh say, can you see, by the dawn's early light,
What so proudly we hailed at the twilight's last gleaming,
Whose broad stripes and bright stars, through the perilous fight,
O'er the ramparts we watched, were so gallantly streaming?
And the rockets' red glare, the bombs bursting in air,
Gave proof thru the night that our flag was still there.
Oh say, does that star-spangled banner yet wave
O'er the land of the free and the home of the brave?
—Francis Scott Key

CHAPTER 1

Dear Father:

Finally I came to poor Albert lying on the ground wounded under the left eye. . . . He also had a ball shot through his left leg. I had no one to help me bear him from the field. I then called a captain of another company to assist me. . . . We bore Albert six hundred yards through a dense swamp all bleeding and sore with pain before we could find any of the Ambulance Corps to bear him off to the hospital. . . . I assisted him in the stretcher. Dropping a tear of grief upon his bleeding face, I bade him goodbye.

—Charles Batchelor

* * *

1 July 1863
Boston, Massachusetts

Anne Birmingham rose from her bed and awkwardly stepped onto the floor. She moved to the window, her step slow and pained, and drew back the drapes. Her fingers tightened on the fabric until her knuckles whitened, and she leaned her forehead on the windowpane, which was warm from the summer air.

The black night held no answers for her—certainly no more than it usually did when she awoke from her nightmares. They were dreams, memories sometimes, of the battles she'd lived through, the horror she'd seen. And always, always by the end, just before her terrified mind called her forth from her restless slumber, she saw Ivar.

She missed him so much it made her sick to her stomach. The separation from him, given her feelings of intense affection, would have been painful under normal circumstances, but to know that he now languished in a Confederate prison camp drove her nearly out of her mind with worry. She loved him, knew that she had long before they'd been captured.

He was bright and compassionate, reserved and thoughtful. Her mind's eye pictured him perfectly to the last detail sitting near the campfire or outside their tent, reading letters from his parents or browsing through a newspaper from home, his plain, round spectacles perched on the bridge of his nose. So many times from that very pose he had looked up at her approach, his eyes flashing a sparkle of warmth. He would smile at whatever quip she delivered and offer a wry comment in return, which invariably would make her laugh. He had cautioned her once to drop the tone of her laughter a bit; he was certain she would give herself away as a woman if she didn't.

That he had waited so long to finally turn her in himself was a miracle. She had begged him on more than one occasion to keep her secret; she had been determined to finish her term of enlistment, and he had been as good as his word until the end when she was nearly dead. She knew of very few men who would have supported her cause, and his respect for her position and willingness to keep his nose out of her affairs were the reasons she had begun to feel so deeply for him. What kind of man supported a woman who enlisted as a man to get a good news story or two? The kind of man with whom she wanted to share the rest of her life, but such a dream might likely remain just that.

Anne took a shaky breath and gingerly drew one knee upward onto the window seat. She released her grip on the drapes and dropped her arm as she dragged herself onto the cushion with a wince of pain. Her thigh throbbed horribly where she had been shot, and her body was only now showing signs that it might regain its former strength. She had been so horribly depleted of liquids on her return home that her mother had sat by her side throughout the night more than once, awakening her on regular intervals to see that she drank.

She extended the wounded limb forward and pulled the other close to her chest, resting her cheek on her bent knee. The view outside her window eventually blurred with her tears and she felt a sadness in her heart that she had never before known. Anne had always been able to solve her problems. If she could think, she could develop a plan, and if she could develop a plan, she could then put it into action. It was a series of steps that had never failed her, but suddenly her old methods were useless. She could think, but her thinking brought her nothing but a sick, black sorrow and an inability to see beyond the moment and Ivar's inevitable and eventual death.

The thought of him wasted away and dying alone in the prison camp wrenched a choking sound from her throat, and rather than sensing the fire of fury she usually did when confronted with a problem, she felt what little strength she had slip from her limbs, and her hold on her leg loosened. Upon her arrival home, she had decided that planning Ivar's rescue would be the impetus that would propel her to her usual robust health; instead, she had fallen into a downward spiral unlike anything she had ever imagined.

Nothing was right—her world felt entirely skewed. She was weak and still nearly forty pounds shy of her normal healthy weight, her monthly cycle was absent and had been for months, and while she wanted to eat, it seemed that nearly everything she tried brought forth a gagging reflex that made it nearly impossible to swallow.

Her tears dampened her light cotton nightgown, and she tried to think of the one thing that would make her happy. It wasn't her writing—suddenly her obsession with the printed word had failed her—and it wasn't her family, although they were close by and solicitous in their concern.

It was Ivar Gundersen. He, healthy and by her side, was all she wanted. The dark night eventually gave way to the pale glow of dawn creeping over the horizon, and it was then that Anne, exhausted, finally fell asleep leaning against the window.

* * *

Northern Virginia

Ivar Gundersen sat apart from the other prisoners held captive with the Confederate regiment. His prison guard, whom he and Anne had named Bulldog, was ever vigilant, ever present. Ivar leaned his head back against the walls of the abandoned shack that was their temporary home and gave in to the luxury of a small sigh.

Bulldog didn't allow Ivar to communicate with anyone. The few times he had tried, Ivar had found himself on the wrong end of a shotgun butt. His head still bore the lump of the last assault. He was by himself in a roomful of people.

Ivar was still a bit puzzled as to the man's total and complete hatred of him. It might have been that upon their original capture, Ivar had treated Bulldog with cold disdain because of the man's idiocy. Or it could have been Ivar's physical stature—he was taller than Bulldog, and although he'd lost weight in his army tenure, he still maintained his Ohio-grown farm muscles. He never gave the guard the satisfaction of hearing him cry out in pain at his abuse, and he never rose to the verbal insults. He always met the man's eyes, and Ivar knew that his disgust was prevalent in every glance. If he had any smarts about him, Ivar often thought, he'd avoid looking at Bulldog altogether. He just couldn't bring himself to do it, though. He couldn't let the man think he'd broken his proud Norwegian spirit. He might die of disease, of starvation, of some future wound, but he would never, ever concede defeat.

Ivar thought of Anne for the thousandth time that day and closed his eyes. Her absence had affected him more than he could ever have imagined. He missed her companionship so very much, not only because she'd been a woman, but also because she was who she was. Anne Birmingham was an incredible person; she had made him laugh daily—no, hourly—and he missed the stimulating conversations that had become such a part of his life since enlisting.

She had more bravery than she had smarts—he'd always believed that. She should never have placed herself in danger by enlisting and pretending to be a man, although he had to grudgingly admit that she had done it well. The only reason she'd been sent home was because he had turned her in. She would have died, though, and he couldn't have borne it on his conscience. Anne had been reduced to little more than skin and bones, and at the end she hadn't had enough fluid in her body to summon tears.

Ivar wondered how long it would be until he lost so much weight he'd be unable to function properly. Food was scarce for the Confederate army; for their prisoners it was laughable. He determined to stay as strong as he could until the bitter end. He moved around as much as he possibly could in the course of a day, trying to keep his body mobile and healthy. What he wouldn't give for a good meal, though! It had been so long, but he hadn't forgotten the taste of his mother's cooking. His mouth watered at the memory of her boiled potatoes and gently fried trout.

Those thoughts turned his mind toward his parents at home and his young, motherless child. How old would she be now? Five years? Blonde, blonde curls and ocean-blue eyes—he doubted he'd recognize her when he saw her again. For sure she would have forgotten him by now. His mother had told him once in a letter months before that she showed Inger her father's picture every day and that they talked to it, but a picture wasn't the same thing.

And for what purpose? He had enlisted out of a sense of duty, watching his friends leave their families for the good of the country, and now those friends were dead. Soon, he too might be dead, and if the Confederacy succeeded in their rebellious cause, it would have been an enormous waste of life that ended in nothing.

He shook his head slightly, chiding himself for thinking such negative thoughts. He must keep his spirits up if he hoped to survive to make it home to his parents, his child, and eventually, Anne. God willing, she'd keep herself single until he could at least find her and court her the way most people did before the war had started. He smiled at an image of Anne in a ball gown with her hair long—or was he smiling at the fact that he couldn't really summon such an image? He had never seen her in anything but her army uniform, her hair short like a boy's.

What was she doing now? Had she healed? Was she well? Was she again writing for the newspaper, or had she taken on some other pursuit? He knew that she would have tried to write to him, to find him. The haunted look in her eyes and her whispered promise of rescue when they'd parted stayed with him still. He also knew, though, that even if she had written, the letters would never reach him. Should anyone know where to deliver his mail, Bulldog would never let him receive it—of that he was certain.

Where he would eventually end up, Ivar could only guess. The only thing he knew was that Bulldog had begun moving him and the handful of prisoners under his care farther south. With each passing mile, Ivar felt his heart slip a bit into discouragement, but it also hardened his resolve to stay strong so that when an opportunity presented itself, he could take it and escape. If he were calm and predictable, if he bided his time, somehow a door would open. Even if it was just a crack, it was all he needed.

CHAPTER 2

Up and down the line, men reeling and falling; splinters flying from wheels and axles where bullets hit; in the rear, horses tearing and plunging, mad with wounds or terror; drivers yelling, shells bursting; shot shrieking overhead, howling about our ears or throwing up great clouds of dust where they struck; the musketry crashing . . . bullets hissing, humming and whistling everywhere; cannon roaring, all crash on crash, and peal on peal; smoke, dust, splinters, blood; wreck and carnage indescribable. . . . Every man's shirt soaked with sweat, and many of them sopped with blood from wounds not severe enough to make such bulldogs let go—bareheaded, sleeves rolled up, faces blackened.

—Union cannoneer Augustus Buell at Gettysburg

* * *

2 July 1863
Gettysburg, Pennsylvania
Little Round Top

"We're supposed to hold them off for how long?" Luke Birmingham stared at Colonel Joshua Chamberlain's assistant as the shots continued to pop all around them.

"As long as we must. If they take this hill, they'll infiltrate the whole Union line."

Luke stared at the man for a moment and finally nodded once and gripped his weapon, crouching low beside the other men of the 20th Maine. Luke and his cousin, Ben Birmingham, had been sent with a few others of the 1st Massachusetts Cavalry to reinforce the troops fighting on the outskirts of a small town called Gettysburg, Pennsylvania.

Luke and Ben had been separated, as had Luke and his horse. The horses were in the care of his commanding officer of the 1st Massachusetts, and Luke and Ben both had received an extremely hasty education in foot soldiering. They were fighting as infantrymen for the first time since their enlistment, and although being without the animal caused Luke no small amount of anxiety, his separation from Ben affected him much more strongly. It galled him to admit that as a man of twenty-eight he was nervous to be without his cousin, but in the year since their enlistment, he and Ben had spent every waking and sleeping moment together, side by side. To now be under such ferocious fire without him was unsettling.

The Confederates had reportedly entered the town of Gettysburg looking for shoes. As Ben watched them swarm the hills and fight on the fields below his vantage point, he wondered how they managed to go onward, marching barefoot for miles up and down the eastern seaboard. Luke was exhausted much of the time, and he usually had a horse to ride, let alone shoes on his feet.

Now, as he tried to focus on the task at hand, time stretched ahead, punctuated by the continual pop of gunshot and boom of cannon. His head ached horribly from the noise, and fear lodged in his throat, choking him. He had swallowed his own bile time after time when watching men around him fall—sometimes dismembered, disemboweled, or beheaded—to the ground. The thought that he was inflicting the same on the men who charged the hill made him all the more sick, but self-preservation was a powerful motivator, and Luke forced himself to remember that it was better that the enemy fall than him, shoeless or not.

In his mind was a prayer that repeated itself over and over again. *Please, Father, please let this be over soon.* Could it have been only scant weeks before that Ben had baptized him so peacefully in the river? Luke had felt such calm then, such joy. A feeling of love unlike any he had experienced had enveloped him that day, and he had basked in it. Such a simple prayer it was too, yet poignant in its spiritual beauty. *I baptize you in the name of the Father, and of the Son, and of the Holy Ghost . . .* He had wanted to fly to the very heavens that day and proclaim glory to the Father for the entire world to hear.

And now he was in purgatory. How could two such events occur so closely together in time? How could one experience the glory of God one day and be thrust into the fiery depths so soon after? *Father, there are so many things I haven't done! I want to share Thy goodness with the world. I want to serve Thee, to love Thee. I long to see my sweet family again, my Abigail . . .*

For one brief moment, it was as if he were far away from the horror of the battlefield, and he felt silence, peace, and an arm about his shoulders, buoying him up and bidding him, without words, to be strong. Then, as quickly as the impression had come, it vanished with a loud crash and the acrid smell of death and gun smoke.

Luke looked quickly about him as Chamberlain shouted to his men, who now numbered less than five hundred. Their ammunition was nearly gone, and still the rebels pushed upward. The Union soldiers would surely be overtaken in a matter of minutes unless something drastic happened. Colonel Chamberlain was outlining that something drastic to the men as Luke strained to hear.

"What did he say?" he asked the man next to him.

"We're charging down the side of the hill."

"With *what?*"

"Our bayonets."

Luke looked toward Chamberlain in disbelief but found comfort in the grim determination on the man's face. Chamberlain was a college professor by trade. He was a gentle man who loved learning and loved his country. Luke took a deep breath and fell into place beside the others as they prepared to stampede down the hill.

And then they were running. Luke screamed with the rest of the Union blue as they charged toward the advancing gray-clad men. He was bracing himself for the worst when, to his complete surprise, the Confederate soldiers, who apparently assumed there were more to the 20th Maine's meager number than reality proved, turned and ran.

They ran! Luke stared ahead as the rebels ran back the way they had come only to be confronted and attacked from the rear as well by Chamberlain's Company B, whom Chamberlain had assumed had long since been demolished. As Luke and the others scrambled back into a defensive position atop the hill, he shook his head in disbelief. A passing man in blue slapped him on the arm and said, "Looks like we're not going to die today, eh, soldier?"

Luke released a shaky breath. "Not today."

* * *

3 July 1863

The shells came from nowhere and were suddenly everywhere. Ben stared in dumb shock as men around him dropped to the ground, some with food still clutched in their fingers. Many had been napping, only to rise up in surprise at the sound—a movement that had been their last.

Ben scrambled to the side and took cover behind the guns that were now answering with return fire. He looked around in vain for his commanding officer and shifted his attention instead on finding his cousin. After being separated for a day and a night, they had found each other in the early hours of the morning, and he had been loathe to leave Luke's side for even a moment. When he finally spotted the man who was the mirror image of himself, he saw that Luke was crawling along the ground, favoring one leg.

Ben rushed over to him and pulled him to relative safety far behind the guns. The sun was unmercifully hot overhead, the sky a beautiful blue. On more than one occasion, it had struck Ben as completely ironic that sometimes the ugliest, fiercest battles were fought on the most beautiful of days, in the most beautiful of places. He had seen more of the United States countryside than he ever imagined he would, and he wished it might have been under different conditions.

What had begun for him as a quest to right a wrong, to free the slaves, had grown from there and evolved into a fierce desire to put the country to rights, to unite it as it never had been before. But where the countryside itself was beautiful, the people who inhabited it hated each other with a virulence that drove men to slaughter each other like dogs.

The cousins now served as reinforcements for the men who held the ground at Cemetery Ridge. The first day's fighting had ended with both sides warily withdrawing to assess damage and plan for the next day's maneuvers. Some were saying the rebs had won the day, but only those who dared give voice to truth. The bulk of the soldiers Ben questioned insisted that the Union had emerged ahead at the end of the day despite the fact that they had been driven back into the town of Gettysburg itself, fighting in hand-to-hand combat before finally retreating to Baltimore Pike, southeast of the town.

He could only imagine what the citizens of the town thought as they watched the war being played out on their streets and yards, in front of their churches and places of business. Ben had seen women and children huddled behind their windows, viewing the drama that unfolded before their very eyes.

The second day of fighting saw losses on both sides, but by evening the Union still held advantageous, high-ground positions. Now, as the relentless barrage of Confederate cannon fire continued, answered in kind by the Union guns, Ben pulled Luke toward a ledge of ground that provided shelter for many men who were already gathered there, lying low in the oppressive heat and waiting with their rifles to rise up and fire.

The shells smashed into the ground well behind the small ledge, as well as in front, but the area just behind the rise of earth remained blissfully safe. "Are you hit?" Ben finally asked Luke, having to repeat himself to be heard above the noise of the shell exchange.

Luke looked at his cousin, his expression pained but sheepish. "Not with a shell, no. A man fell on me back there and landed hard on my ankle."

Ben laughed with relief, feeling slightly giddy. Fear had made him insane and lightheaded. "A broken ankle is easily enough fixed," he said, although they both knew that to trust a doctor was to take one's life in one's hands, even if it was an issue of only a small bone. If he weren't careful, a man having entered on complaint of a cough would leave without a limb.

The time Ben and Luke spent in the shelter of the ledge stretched interminably, shells exploding around them and the roar of answering cannon screaming as though it would never cease. Luke checked his pocket watch, wiping away sweat that dripped into his eyes. "Two hours this has been going on," he said. "Don't think I've ever heard of such a thing before."

Ben nodded his head in agreement. "I haven't either." He paused as one brave soldier next to them rose slightly above the line of the earth behind which they hid. The man's gasp was audible, even over the noise of the cannons.

"They're marching across that open field," the soldier shouted to them. "It's hard to see because of all the smoke, but they can't be more than a half mile away by now, marching shoulder to shoulder in perfect formation."

Ben stared at the young man. "Are they mad?"

"Their memories of Fredericksburg must be awfully short," Luke added. "*They* whipped *us* when we tried that."

The soldier shrugged and raked a hand through his hair, which was sodden with sweat. He replaced his cap, his attention turning to the Union artillerymen who were planning a different assault on the advancing Confederate lines. The artillerymen changed their shot to canister, which, according to the soldier who again raised his head to watch, rained shrapnel and balls upon the enemy, exploding on impact and taking large chunks from the rebel ranks as they continued marching across the open field. Each time a hole opened in the lines of gray, the men closed ranks and continued their forward assault.

The soldier sank back down onto the ground with a shake of his head and imparted his information to those crouched low with him. "They must know they're marching straight to their own deaths," the man said. "I think old man Lee has taken leave of his senses."

Ben leaned back against the earth, his thoughts spinning. From the direction of the advancing enemy, they had obviously been occupying Seminary Ridge, a position of high ground. Why on earth would the rebels abandon it for a foolhardy advance that could surely come to no good? Perhaps they assumed their two-hour cannon assault would have sufficiently weakened the Union advantage of high ground on Cemetery Ridge.

Ben looked around to assess the damage behind the wall and saw that while many had fallen, the majority remained unharmed and at the ready. He touched his own weapon for reassurance and readied himself for the command that was sure to come. He didn't have long to wait, for the shout to rise up and open fire rang out, and he and Luke, side by side and surrounded by a sea of blue, lifted their guns to their shoulders and took aim on the enemy.

The soldiers in gray were stopped up behind a fence along a road as they tried to cross, and they fell like toys knocked down in a child's game. Still, the men climbed over one another and marched forward, shoulder to shoulder, arm to arm, holding their fire and their customary rebel yell. They must have been instructed to do so until they were close enough for the effects to be fully felt, and Ben could attest to the chill that crept down the spine of a Union soldier at that awful scream. But the great majority of these men were never going to make it that far. They fell like flies, and Ben could only stare in wonder at their continued advance. How could they keep marching forward like that, knowing, *knowing,* they couldn't possibly escape with their lives? *I would never have believed this if I hadn't seen it with my own two eyes,* he thought as he emptied his gun.

He blinked repeatedly, grateful for small gaps in the smoke that gave him a quick glimpse of the enemy. It was like firing into a fog. He reloaded his weapon and took careful aim, knowing full well that if he didn't fire upon the men in gray, he would be killed himself. It was the only thought that kept him sane in battle; when he examined the matter too closely, his stomach turned and he wondered if God would forgive him.

To his surprise, in his mind flashed images of scripture—verses from the Book of Mormon and thoughts of Captain Moroni and Nephi. There were things that God understood fully that man did not, things that men did to each other that perhaps only God would be able to sift through when the dust settled. Ben knew he would never comprehend the whole of it. All he knew was that he had come to fight for a cause. He had never imagined the toll on both the body and the mind.

Ben gritted his teeth together and continued at the task before him, taking no joy in it but somehow not feeling estranged from his Eternal Father as he had on other occasions. It was for a greater good, a worthier cause than most would comprehend, and Ben could only pray to live out the day with Luke, healthy and well, by his side.

* * *

4 July 1863
Gettysburg, Pennsylvania

The gore of the aftermath was unimaginable. Nine brigades of Confederate manpower had marched on the hill in what was quickly being termed as "Pickett's Charge," and except for one quick break in the Union line, which was summarily stemmed, the brigades had fallen to their doom. It was estimated amongst the men in blue that only half of the rebels who had begun the charge returned to their former position on Seminary Ridge. Some said less than half. Luke overheard a man describing the aftermath as "ghastly heaps of dead men," and another claimed that "the dead to the front of us were so thick that it reminded me of harvest, like huge sheaves of wheat."

Luke had to agree—the piles of spent humanity were almost beyond comprehension. After a while, his conscious mind shut off, and he moved about mechanically, barely noticing the limbs and torn flesh visible on all sides.

The charge up the hill could only be called bravery; the Union men knew full well that as a soldier, one was meant to follow orders. There wasn't a man among them who didn't know how much fear must have settled into the hearts and minds of those who had continued marching while those around them fell to the ground, broken into pieces that could never be fixed.

Luke hobbled on an ankle secured with a makeshift splint and leaned heavily on a long, sturdy stick he had found to use as a cane. "This one's alive," he said to a pair of medics at his side who were walking the ground with stretchers. He knelt down at the side of a young boy in a gray uniform whose shallow breathing was visible in the subtle rise and fall of his chest.

The medics reached under the boy's shoulders and feet and hoisted him on the stretcher. Luke winced at the groan sounding from the soldier's throat and watched as the medics carried him off the field, slipping in puddles of blood and stepping over the dismembered bodies and limbs that littered the ground. More than once he saw those with him, searching for survivors, losing their lunches or heaving from stomachs that had been empty. Luke fell into the latter category; he and Ben both had been unable to eat that morning, the sights and sounds precluding any attempt at appetite their protesting stomachs might have made.

The Confederate army now marched away from the Potomac, slow and arduous the process. Someone had told Luke earlier that morning that the train of retreating soldiers was seventeen miles long. Ben had muttered that it would be wise to rally their forces and go after the rebels, ending the war once and for all, but General Meade had other ideas. The Union had sustained heavy casualties of its own; they needed to rest and regroup, according to the new Union commander.

Luke had agreed with his cousin's assessment—as would Lincoln, they were sure—that although difficult, it would be sound indeed to pursue the rebels while they were weak and put an end to the war. The Union soldiers were exhausted, however, and while in theory it would have been wise to finish Lee's army, Luke wondered how the men would have reacted had Meade given such an order.

Lincoln was far away, not present to give the order himself. There was nothing to be done for it now except to gather their own dead and wounded and try to help the doctors and medics handle the seven thousand Confederate wounded who had been left behind. The small, quaint town of Gettysburg had added to its constituency by thousands when the addition of wounded soldiers from both sides of the conflict were taken into account.

Nearly every available building, including homes, was transformed into a makeshift hospital. Carpets were soaked with blood and ruined beyond repair. Stacks of books, used as pillows, were sticky with blood that flowed from head wounds and severed limbs. As Luke looked around himself at the open fields of battle, he wondered if he would ever be able to banish the awful sight of ruined humanity that surrounded him on all sides. Rarely had he ever considered the fragile state of the human body, nor had he ever imagined he would see so many bodies mangled, destroyed, or ghoulishly bloated from the oppressive heat. Almost as an answer from heaven, the skies eventually opened and rained down a shower that washed away the puddles of blood that had collected on rocks and stone ledges.

Luke raised his face to the sky and closed his eyes as the rain pelted his face and cleaned some of his own grime. It soon was raining so hard that he was forced to duck his head as the pounding hurt his face. Blinding sheets of the moisture fell to the earth in a torrent the likes of which he didn't think he'd ever seen.

Luke didn't envy the retreating Confederate army their task of marching along in the mud, the wounded jarred at every bump or rock in the road as they sat listless in their wagons. He imagined them returning home to their families, who had since faced poverty in most quarters because of the cost of the war, trying to resume their lives and reclaim some sense of normalcy amidst missing limbs, broken bodies, and broken spirits. He felt a stab of pity and compassion that he didn't usually allow himself.

As for the military command, General Meade was pleased that the Union soldiers had kept themselves between the Confederates and Washington. Another attack on Union soil had been a brave attempt on the part of Lee and his men. If the Union had been defeated on their own ground, morale amongst the citizenry of the country would undoubtedly have plunged. As it was, according to the newspapers, cities across the North were celebrating the Fourth of July with renewed vigor and excitement. A major battle had just been won, and politically for Lincoln, it was crucial. If the rebels had been victorious in their assaults, they might even now be marching to the Union capital city, demanding a truce and recognition of the Confederacy. Then all hopes for reuniting the Union with her errant sisters would be destroyed.

The thought of sisters brought to mind an image of Luke's own sister, Anne. The crazy girl had enlisted and been fighting for the past year with a regiment from Ohio, and only just recently had she been discovered and returned home under a flag of truce. She had been wounded, his father wrote, and was ill and weak from time spent in a Confederate prison camp, but otherwise her wound was on the mend.

What had she been thinking? He had asked her as much in his last letter home, but had yet to receive a reply. She was brave and reckless, and he would wager his military pay that she had done it to provide fodder for her writing. Underneath his shock and worry, however, was a deep sense of pride. She had the bravery—or perhaps the foolishness—of ten men.

The rain ran across Luke's neck and shoulders in rivulets, and he leaned heavily on his cane for balance, thankful that he was standing and not lying prostrate, as were the men groaning around him on all sides. He envisioned his family, the people he loved back home in Boston, and wondered how long it would be until he would see them again.

* * *

Ben held the shoulders of a wounded man as a doctor proceeded to amputate the man's leg below the knee while the storm raged outside. The soldier screamed in anguish, and Ben's eyes burned and he looked away. Such an odd setting it was for surgery. They stood in the small library of a local citizen's home. Books lined the walls in stately elegance, matching in green- and burgundy-colored leather bindings. Men in uniforms, tattered and bloodstained, lined the floors.

The woman of the home moved about in stoic silence, bringing tea and portions of food around the clock. As she ventured into the library, Ben saw her blanch and look quickly away from the man who was losing his leg, stooping instead to offer a drink of water to a man who lay groaning on a once-beautiful Oriental carpet now soaked and ruined with blood. The man took a grateful sip of the water as the woman held his head and neck in the crook of her arm, much as she would a baby. He looked up into her face as though she were a godsend, and she managed a wan smile.

Ben winced at her in sympathy. She must have been exhausted; she hadn't had time to change her stained dress or see to her own comforts in hours. She pushed on with an energy that Ben was sure she probably didn't feel, and he wondered how long it would be until she would sleep well at night without fear of attack on her small town, as well as without images of dying men crowding her hallways and rooms.

Sometime later when all was dark and the only sounds were those of animals and wounded, dying men, Ben found Luke. They didn't say much to each other—merely found a spot of ground that wasn't occupied by another creature, either alive or dead, and tried to obtain some rest.

Ben lay on his back and looked up at the sky, imagining as he often did that this was a good time to converse with God, as at least half of the world was sleeping. *I can't help but think that somehow, someway, Thou couldst well have softened a few hearts and changed a few minds to avoid all this bloodshed and horror. Please forgive my impertinence, but Father, how canst Thou stand it? How dost Thou not hide Thy face and cry for Thy children?*

The answers spoke to his mind, as they often did, by way of scriptures he had read and thought he had forgotten. *Remember that ye are free to act for yourselves . . .*

Ben turned onto his side and tried to find comfort, soon wishing he hadn't. Not far in the distance he spied a body that lay in similar fashion to Ben's own position, but it was lifeless and spent. The man that it once had been wouldn't rise in the morning to face a new day.

He was tired, and he knew his mind was taking him places he didn't want to be. The man seemed to stare back at him with sightless eyes, mocking Ben with his lifeless presence. *This could be you . . .* The thought came unbidden to Ben's mind, and he closed his eyes. He didn't want to die alone on a battlefield, far from anyone who loved him, his body waiting on the compassion—or disgust—of a passerby for a burial. Alone—the dead man seemed so very alone.

Are not two sparrows sold for a farthing? and one of them shall not fall on the ground without your Father. But the very hairs of your head are all numbered. Fear ye not therefore, ye are of more value than many sparrows.

"Thank you," Ben whispered into the night sky. A tear rolled out of his eye and down his face, trailing toward his ear before it fell to the ground. Sleep was a merciful thing, then, and it came upon him, offering temporary rest.

CHAPTER 3

We are utterly cut off from the world, surrounded by a circle of fire. . . . The fiery shower of shells goes on day and night. . . . People do nothing but eat what they can get, sleep when they can, and dodge the shells. . . . I think all the dogs and cats must be killed or starved. We don't see any more pitiful animals prowling around. . . .

—Diary of a young woman who lived through Grant's siege of Vicksburg

* * *

4 July 1863
Vicksburg, Mississippi

"Gin." Isabelle Webb looked at Lucy with a triumphant grin and managed a laugh as Lucy Lockhart threw her cards onto the table in disgust.

"You cheat, Isabelle."

"I do not. You've been watching me the whole time. How could I have cheated?"

"I don't know. But you do, and I will catch you someday soon."

Isabelle sat back in her chair and regarded her card-playing companion with an objective eye. Lucy must have lost fifteen if not twenty pounds since their involuntary incarceration in the town of Vicksburg, Mississippi, and Isabelle knew she looked much the same herself. Her dress, stained with dirt and grime, hung loosely on her frame, and the constant grumble of her stomach bespoke her physical condition.

Isabelle was a spy for Allan Pinkerton, and in her pursuit of Lucy Lockhart, *Confederate* spy, she had become entrapped in the city that was currently under Union siege. General Grant seemed more than happy to wait until the citizens starved, and Isabelle was afraid they just might. There had been a buzz of surrender lately, and it was no wonder, really. The Confederate soldiers who guarded the city and tried to return fire on the Union troops that bombarded Vicksburg on a daily basis looked little better than the dogs, squirrels, and rats the people had been capturing and eating.

The soldiers' clothes hung in rags, their gaunt faces telling tales of starvation. Lice were their constant companions. Isabelle couldn't help but feel pangs of sympathy for the poor creatures who were trying their best to defend the town but before much longer would surely be forced to surrender.

Lucy's sister entered the cave where Isabelle and Lucy currently sat playing cards, and announced that surrender was closer at hand than Isabelle had imagined. Today it had been announced and was official: Confederate surrender in exchange for an end to the siege.

Isabelle breathed a huge sigh and stood, making her way to the entrance of the cave, one of many that had been dug into the hillsides of the town. The citizens of Vicksburg had dug in like small animals and had furnished their caves with items from their own homes. "Prairie Dog Village," the Union soldiers had renamed Vicksburg, and indeed it was.

Isabelle's surge of relief was tempered by shock when she took a good look at her surroundings. So bored had she become with the siege and so dangerous it had been to venture outside the caves with the constant Union shelling that she had stayed mostly in the cave and took pleasure in beating Lucy at a variety of games. The city, meanwhile, had been leveled. As she looked around, she saw others emerging from their caves and staggering toward their former homes to take stock of what was left.

"A bitter thing," one woman muttered as she passed, "to suffer such defeat on *their* Independence Day."

Isabelle stared at the woman for a moment before she realized the import of the statement. When she fully grasped it, she laughed out loud, long and hard until her weakened body threatened to collapse. "What is so funny?" Lucy hissed at her as she walked from the cave.

"It's the Fourth of July."

Lucy scowled. "I suggest you lower your voice unless you'd like to find yourself pummeled."

"Oh, but haven't you heard?" Isabelle gasped. "Grant is in town today!"

"You're mad. Lack of food has made you insane."

Isabelle's fit finally subsided, and she looked at Lucy, who had become a reluctant friend more than an enemy. "I do not mean to laugh at your pain," Isabelle said. "But it is well that this siege has ended. Better for everyone."

"We don't surrender to the Union, you know," Lucy said, her eyes flashing in a face that seemed too small for them. "We surrender to starvation."

"I know." Isabelle turned to make her way toward the center of town, where much noise was heralding the raising of the Union flag over the courthouse.

"Belle," Lucy called.

"Yes?"

"Why did you stay? You could have approached Union lines and identified yourself."

Isabelle made her way back to Lucy and grasped her in a quick hug, a gesture both women knew was completely out of her character. "Because you were here and couldn't get away."

"You didn't even like me! You came after me to confront me about my political activities."

"We're kindred spirits, Lucy—two of a kind, even though we don't see eye to eye. I couldn't very well let you starve alone. Besides," Isabelle said as she turned to go, "it was only a matter of time. I knew we'd outlast both armies." She winked at Lucy and went to find someone who could help her get back to Washington.

"After all that, and you aren't even going to turn me in?" Lucy called after her retreating form.

"'Twould be a shame to lose such a worthy opponent," Isabelle called back. She spied the Stars and Stripes as she made her way into the center of town and smiled.

* * *

Charleston, South Carolina
Bentley Plantation

Emily Birmingham Stanhope rested the newspaper on her growing midsection and read with interest. Beneath the Southern propaganda and bias lay some interesting facts. Lee had sustained heavy losses at Gettysburg. His second attempt at invading the North had failed, and Emily doubted the revered general had resources to try for a third. "The tide is turning," she murmured to herself, for she was alone in the Bentley library.

Bentley, although still alive due to Ruth's careful efforts, was showing signs of wear. Nearly half of the house had been closed off after being stripped of anything that could be traded for goods. The fields lay dormant for the most part—only a quarter of the former lands had been planted and was being worked this season.

Emily's mother, Sarah, was still out of her head with delirium; her father, Jeffrey, was lost at sea and presumed dead. Her older brother, Richard, was dead—not that she missed him—and her other brother, Ben, was fighting for the Union. The entire family was garbed in black, and she was tired of everyone looking so somber. Mourning was beginning to try her nerves, which were already stretched taut with the oppressive summer heat.

Perhaps one bright spot in Emily's faltering family was her sister. Charlotte had come alive with the birth of her son. She was suddenly warm and considerate, if not altogether chatty, and she was pleasant to be around. Emily couldn't remember a time when Charlotte had ever been pleasant to be around, although Ruth assured her she was often so as a child.

Emily winced as a small foot or hand—or maybe it was the head—shoved against her side. The child was turning circles inside her today. Such an odd sensation it was, to feel the life growing and moving about in her body. Not a day passed that she didn't think of the child's father and wonder how he fared. She hadn't heard of his condition after being wounded at Chancellorsville beyond the initial telegram that had arrived, a telegram saying he was gravely ill, that *something* had been amputated, and the final outcome of his overall health was yet to be seen.

In short, he may well already be dead and she wouldn't know it.

They hadn't had much time together as a married couple, but Emily relived the details of the memories whenever she had a moment to herself. Conversations she'd had with her husband played over again in her head. Every glance and whisper, things he'd said that made her laugh—they repeated themselves in her memory with clarity, and Emily was worried she might never have more than those memories.

Time and distance had worked their magic on her emotions, and Emily found herself completely in love with Austin. Although another had initially claimed her heart, and Austin had known of it, he had shown her a kindness and tenderness that had taken her aback. He had proven himself to be of strong character, possessing many of the traits Emily admired.

She wondered if the newfound intensity of her feelings was kindled or accelerated by the fact that Austin might die. If he were home safe at her side, would she admit to herself how much she cared for him, or would she continue to pine away for a love that she would never have? Joshua flashed into her thoughts, and she acknowledged him with a twinge of guilt. She could only hope he hadn't had feelings to the degree that she had. He certainly had given her the impression that her girlish love for him had been one-sided.

Emily worried for Joshua's safety, however. He had enlisted and would undoubtedly be moving his way south. The whole endeavor for black troops was fraught with danger. They not only were at risk in potential battle, but there were also slave hunters aplenty, and many a man wouldn't think twice before snatching up a black man and selling him into slavery. It even said right out in the paper that some free blacks near Gettysburg had been abducted and sold south, Lee doing nothing to prevent it.

Emily clenched her teeth together in frustration as she read back over the article in the paper. Lee was revered as a gentleman, a brilliant commander and strategist, and most importantly as a good person, a kind person. How, then, she wondered, could he stand by and watch as people were taken from their towns and cities—on free soil—and be sold like cattle?

I must be maturing, Emily thought. *A few years ago—one year ago even—I'd have been yelling and throwing things after reading something like this. Or maybe it's just being with child. I have no energy to move.* It was awfully hot, she acknowledged as she looked over to the long wall of windows that allowed in the glaring afternoon sun. The heat sapped her strength and will to do anything other than sit. It was so unlike her, and as fascinating as it was to be with child, Emily determined that she just didn't have the energy to bear as many children as had her mother.

"That may not be a problem if Austin doesn't come home," she muttered, and wasn't aware she had done so aloud until Ruth, who was standing in the doorway, interrupted her thoughts.

"Don't talk like that. Not yet. And what won't be a problem?"

"Having more children."

"Do you want more than this one?" Ruth smiled and sat next to Emily on a sofa that needed to see the talented hands of a reupholsterer.

"Maybe one more. Or perhaps these are twins and I won't have to do it ever again. It feels like I have two in there."

Ruth laughed. "Girl, you'd be a lot bigger if that were true."

"I feel like a house."

Ruth leaned back into the couch and laid a hand on Emily's. "You're nothing but belly, silly. Not an ounce of fat anywhere else. Now me," she said, closing her eyes in memory, "*I* was as big as a house. And not my slave quarters, either. *This* house."

Emily laughed and kissed Ruth's cheek. She smelled like the warm, clean, soapy scent that Emily always associated with the woman. A dozen images filled her mind—memories from when she was small. She wrapped her arms around Ruth's shoulders and gave her a gentle squeeze. "I love you," she whispered.

"Sweet Emily. I love you too." Ruth rested her forehead against Emily's. "If I ask something of you, would you do it?"

"You know I would."

"Your mother needs you. I would very much like it if you'd talk to her, spend some time with her."

Emily drew back and stared at Ruth, her mouth slack. She opened and closed it several times before finally finding her voice. "Why? She didn't like me when she was well!"

"Emily, your mother did like you. She loved you."

"I've never known you to be one to stretch the truth."

Ruth looked into Emily's eyes. "I'm not stretching the truth. I think you know that. Now I will not watch your mother waste away without trying every last option."

At that, Emily laughed. "I'm the last option."

"Yes. Not because you're not a good option, but I've avoided involving you because I knew you'd resist."

Emily sighed. "I tried when I first arrived here to speak with her. It made me very uncomfortable, and I'm sure she didn't enjoy it either." She looked at Ruth's expectant face and gave in. "Very well. What do you want me to say to her?"

"That would be your decision."

Emily sat for a moment longer after Ruth planted a kiss on her cheek and left the library. She finally decided that this was as good a time as any to visit and rose to her feet with some effort. Placing a hand at the small of her back, she walked slowly from the room and down the hall toward the spacious front foyer.

She climbed the stairs, one by one, and marveled that as a child she'd raced up that very staircase, skipping one and sometimes two stairs at a time. She'd always been sharply reprimanded by both her mother and Ruth. Making her way to her mother's suite of rooms, she pondered what she'd say to the woman with whom she had virtually no ties other than blood.

Her heart was not immune to compassion, however, as she looked into Sarah's sitting room. Sarah sat in her rocking chair next to the empty hearth. The room was neat as a pin, everything appearing as it should except for Sarah herself. She looked as though a stiff breeze would knock her flat.

Emily entered the room with a small knock on the door frame. Sarah looked up, her face registering nothing.

"Mother? I've come . . . to visit for a bit." When Sarah didn't reply, Emily gestured to a vacant chaise near Sarah's chair. "May I?"

Sarah nodded slightly but still said nothing.

"Awful warm July weather, isn't it?" Emily said, fanning herself a bit. "We must remember to open your windows tonight in hopes of a breeze off the water."

Sarah looked at Emily for a moment longer before turning her eyes back to the empty hearth.

"Would you like your sewing, or a book perhaps?" Emily was starting to feel foolish. "Are you thirsty?"

"I can't find my father."

"I'm sorry?"

"I can't find my father."

Emily stared at her mother for a moment. Sarah's father had died before Emily was born—before Sarah and Jeffrey had even married. "Oh," she said. "Oh, well . . ." What to say? Ruth had told them all that Sarah was like a child again. "I hate to be the bearer of bad tidings, but . . ."

Sarah's eyes widened in alarm, and she snapped her head toward Emily. "There's something wrong? Don't tell me there's something wrong with my father!"

Emily blew air out of her mouth and chewed on her lip for a moment. "No," she finally said, "no, it's nothing. Only that he won't be back for dinner tonight. He's, he's . . . in town."

Sarah visibly relaxed and nodded a bit. "He often does that. Leaves me here to take care of things."

Emily cocked one brow. This was news. "Do you *want* to take care of things?"

"I must. It is my responsibility as the only child. Father doesn't have a son, you know. Only me, and I must show him I can care for Bentley." Sarah frowned. "He will be most vexed to see that the fields are not fully planted."

"I don't think he's overly concerned with it," Emily muttered, wondering how long Ruth wanted her to stay in the room. Her mother's state of mind and strange statements were leaving her with a distinct sense of unease.

"Who are you?" Sarah asked her, as though suddenly realizing a stranger was in her room.

Emily rose more quickly than she had in weeks. "I came to see if you'd like to join us for dinner," she said, knowing full well that her mother would decline.

She did. "I must stay here and wait for my father to return," Sarah said.

"Fine." Emily fled the room and quickly made her way down the hallway and around the corner to her own former bedroom. She shook her head a bit as she reviewed the odd conversation in her mind. She fully intended to tell Ruth that there was no hope for Sarah, that the woman was mad.

She shuddered and fought a sense of sorrow. It had been easier pretending that Sarah wasn't there at all.

* * *

Northern Virginia

Austin Stanhope lay on a narrow bed in a soldier's hospital, his mind, despite a severe blow to the head, at rest and his body barely clinging to life. He had no realization that his wife, hundreds of miles away, was close to delivering their child. He didn't know that his leg was missing, that nurses gently fed him fluids and broth and rubbed salve into his burned flesh. The nurses wondered if he would ever awaken, but as long as his heart still beat, they would keep him alive until God decided otherwise.

CHAPTER 4

I can't write you a love letter today, my Sally, but for you, my darling, I would rather, a million times rather, sleep in an unknown grave.

—George Edward Pickett, following his disastrous defeat at Gettysburg

* * *

11 July 1863
Boston, Massachusetts

Anne sat curled in a window seat of the Birmingham family library and looked out into the gardens at the back of the house. Her fingers gripped a letter, wrinkling and crushing the words written on the parchment. How Bulldog had managed to keep Ivar from the prisoner exchange she might never know.

Alexander Stephens, the Confederate vice president, had negotiated a prisoner exchange on the second of July, and it had been Anne's first hope that Ivar might be transferred to a hospital—or at least back to their regiment—and away from the clutches of the sadistic prison guard and the deadly conditions of the prison itself. The letter she held in her hand was from a fellow prisoner who had become a friend to both her and Ivar during their capture. The letter writer was released to a Union hospital in the exchange; Ivar had been transferred to a prison farther south.

The prison exchange system was faulty at best, and rumor had it that it would be discontinued entirely because of disagreements over the treatment of the prisoners. Anne felt as though a thin thread of hope had slipped through her fingers and reaching for it was futile.

There were now no definitive answers as to Ivar's new whereabouts, no clue of anything, really, except that Bulldog had ensured Ivar was not released into Union hands. Anne closed her eyes in fear, leaning her head against the window. Time was critically of the essence. Ivar was a strong man, but in the two weeks they'd spent together in the prison camp, Anne had watched him lose weight before her very eyes. How long would he survive now at a different camp, under what kinds of conditions?

Anne barely registered the opening and closing of the front door. She heard a murmur of voices down the front hall and footsteps that eventually brought her father into the library. "Anne?"

She turned her head and tried to smile. At the sight of her father's concerned face, however, she felt her efforts melt and her eyes fill with tears. He crossed the room and pulled a chair close to the window seat. "What is it?"

"They've taken him farther south."

"Who?"

"Ivar."

James nodded. Anne had told the family about her friend, but she hadn't described the depths of her feelings for him. Camille was astute though, curse her. She had surmised that Anne was in love with Ivar within a day of Anne's return to family activity. James, though—Anne doubted he understood exactly how much Ivar meant to her.

James gestured to the paper in Anne's hand. "Who sent the letter?"

"A soldier named Williams. He was captured with us—from a different company in the regiment. I slipped him my address before I left so he could let me know if something happened to Ivar."

"Is he a trustworthy source?"

Anne nodded. "I believe so. My instincts tell me yes."

James smiled faintly and rubbed Anne's hand, capturing her fingers and giving them a reassuring squeeze. "Your instincts are rarely wrong."

"Now I find myself wishing they were—that Williams is just toying with me and that Ivar is really at the same hospital."

"That would be needlessly cruel though, wouldn't it?"

"I suppose so." A tear slipped from her eye, and she brushed at it with the mangled letter. "If only I weren't so tired. I've never been this weepy in my entire life."

"Anne, you were on the brink of death when you arrived here. You've lived through and seen horrors that make grown men cry. I should be very surprised if you didn't shed a tear or two."

"It doesn't help matters to sit and weep."

"No, but perhaps after the tears comes a clear head."

Anne smiled a bit. James gestured toward the letter and asked, "May I?"

She nodded and handed him the paper, taking a plain white handkerchief from a small pocket in her dress and drying her eyes. As her father silently read the letter, she folded the square piece of linen and traced her finger along the initials embroidered in blue thread. *IAG. Ivar Asbjørn Gundersen.* She had snatched it one day from his bag of belongings. When he had remarked later that he was missing a handkerchief, she told him that someone must have needed it more than he did, and besides, he had plenty. He had glanced at her askance with half of a smile, his expression telling her that he knew very well she had taken it. "Well then," he had said, "I hope the new owner appreciates it."

She could hear the conversation inside her head, and the memory brought forth a fresh rush of tears. They slid slowly down her face and dropped onto her wrist, where they rolled onto the embroidered letters.

James smoothed the wrinkled paper on his leg and glanced up at Anne. "All is not lost, dear. He's still alive."

"We don't know that."

"As of the writing of this letter he was. We can discover easily enough if he still is."

She looked up at her father, feeling a spark of hope. "How?"

He winked at her. "I have a few well-placed employees who maintain a good network of information. Let me see what I can do. In the meantime," he said, giving her a look that bore no traces of teasing or humor, "you will please not enlist."

"Of course not."

"Or go off by yourself trying to save this man."

"Father, I can barely move around the house."

"You're being evasive, Anne."

Anne looked into the depths of her father's green eyes and finally turned away. As a child she had always felt he could read her thoughts. She was chagrined to realize she still felt that way.

"I won't do anything without telling you first."

James regarded her in silence for a moment. "I suppose I should be grateful for that much."

"I'm not a child anymore, Papa," Anne murmured.

"That doesn't make me love you any less."

* * *

James walked down the hallway to his study at a brisk pace. If he moved quickly, if he worked hard enough, he could make things well for his family. Anne was back home, she was alive and safe; if she wanted information on a friend, she would have it.

Anne wasn't the only person on his mind. He also worried about his son Luke. It had been a few weeks since the family had received word from either Luke or Ben, and James suspected from the location of their last correspondence that they had been at Gettysburg.

As if his concern over his immediate family wasn't enough to fully occupy his thoughts, he had someone else to contend with as well. James had just received word only that morning that his brother, Jeffrey, was alive. Yet somehow, he had known all along. When his friends in the Senate had alerted him to Jeffrey's disappearance, he had told his wife, Elizabeth, that he knew Jeffrey would return.

"You can't be sure of that, James," Elizabeth had told him gently.

"But I am." James and Jeffrey shared a connection that time might have dimmed but hadn't diminished. Their mother had often said that because they were twins, they could hear each other's thoughts, and when they were children it had certainly seemed that way. Adulthood had separated them by both miles and ideology, but even now,

James had known he would have felt Jeffrey's absence from the earth.

James entered his office and closed the door quietly behind him. Sinking into his chair behind the desk with a sigh, he contemplated his responsibilities. First, he would draft a letter to an employee who had contacts south of the Mason-Dixon Line. He would try to locate Anne's friend, Ivar, and see what could be done to arrange some sort of prisoner exchange. Money spoke loudly these days, and gold to a Confederate went a long way when swapped under the table.

Next would be arranging a meeting with Jeffrey. Found at sea by a Union steamer, Jeffrey and three other Confederate officers were temporarily housed in separate New York homes under heavily armed guards. James knew that the situation might prove to be a bit trickier, as the powers that be would be suspicious as to his motives. After all, he *was* the prisoner's brother.

James tapped his finger restlessly on the desktop. He would have to think of something—a compelling reason to convince the Union officials that Jeffrey should be released to his care. He was a creative man; he knew that given a bit of time, he would devise a solution. Jeffrey's family and his country were falling apart at the seams, and when the sun set at the end of each day, blood was thicker than water.

* * *

Camille Birmingham lifted her hand to her brow, shading her eyes against the brightness of the sun. She stood next to her brother Robert, watching the crowd of people at the docks.

"I'm not sure this is going to tell us anything," Robert muttered under his breath to Camille.

"It probably won't," she agreed, "but I feel like we need to do something." As she watched, Olivia Sylvester and Olivia's mother greeted a woman who disembarked from one of the ships. "She hasn't changed a bit, has she?" Camille said as she watched Olivia's aunt embrace Mrs. Sylvester.

Robert shuddered. Olivia's aunt reminded both Robert and Camille of an ill-fated trip they had taken with the Sylvesters, where they had witnessed firsthand the carnage at the first battle of Bull Run just outside Washington. Olivia's brother, Nathaniel, was Robert's friend, and he had made vague references of harm coming to members of the Abolition Society in Boston, of which the Birminghams were ardent members. Mrs. Sylvester's sister had a reputation for causing trouble for abolition groups wherever she went, and Robert and Camille were left to wonder over the coincidence that she was now showing up in Boston, one of the strongest abolition-supporting cities in the Union.

Camille sighed. "You're right, you know. I don't know what good it's going to do, spying on them like this. I suppose I'm hoping she'll shout her intentions to the world."

Robert smiled. "Unlikely. But with Nathaniel in Austria now, I don't know how we're going to get any information out of the Sylvesters. Any chance Olivia will come to tea if you invite her?"

"Hardly! Her mother won't let her come within two feet of me." Camille scowled under the parasol she held above her head to block the hot sunlight. "Let's go home. We're not gaining anything from this venture. I'm sorry I dragged you down here. I do have one more stop to make, though," she said as they climbed into their open carriage.

Robert gathered the reins and snapped them gently, urging the horses forward. "Where to?"

"I need to drop something by Jacob's office. Another article."

By the time they reached the newspaper building where Camille's editor, Jacob Taylor, worked, Camille was wishing she could strip off a few layers of clothing and still be considered decent. She snapped her parasol closed and hopped down from the carriage with an exasperated sigh.

"I would have helped you down if you'd only have waited," Robert told her.

She waved a hand at him. "Stay put. It's too hot to be moving around much." She retrieved a handkerchief from a reticule that hung from her wrist and dabbed at her forehead and neck. "I'll be only a moment," she said.

Climbing the stairs to Jacob's office, she found herself sputtering in heated irritation by the time she made her way to his door. She knocked briskly and waited for a moment, hearing a chair scrape inside. Jacob opened the door, looking a bit heated himself. His shirt collar was open at the throat, his tie hanging limp and wilted around his neck. His hair looked as though he had raked his fingers through it numerous times, but he managed a smile for Camille.

"What a refreshing treat," he said. He opened the door wider, allowing her entrance.

"I don't feel refreshing in the least," Camille said, and sank down into one of two chairs on the far side of his desk. "I think it's time you considered having your office moved down to the first floor."

"They won't let me. I've tried." Jacob left the door open, as he always did when she visited, in an effort to observe propriety. He sat next to her in the other of the two chairs and motioned to a paper she held in her hands. "Very timely, Miss Birmingham. You're always punctual."

"Here you go." She handed him the paper and nodded. "I hope it meets with your approval."

"I'm sure it will," he said, not even looking at it. "How's Anne?"

"Not herself yet. But she will be." Camille nodded slightly, slowly, looking at Jacob. He seemed pained. "Are you sweet on my sister, Mr. Taylor?"

Jacob raised his eyebrows high before finding his voice. "I forget how direct you've become. You've abandoned the art of speaking in circles altogether. Proper ladies would mince and be coy and try to subtly pry information from me in a delicate manner."

"It takes longer and I find it irksome. You haven't answered my question."

Jacob's mouth quirked in obvious amusement. "You haven't always been so lacking in feminine convention. There was a time, I recall, when you would have played the game or perished."

Camille flushed. "That was a long time ago."

"That was less than a year ago."

She tipped her head to one side, her eyes narrowing. "I do believe you're avoiding my question."

He sobered. "I'm not avoiding your question, Camille, nor am I 'sweet' on Anne. I feel partly responsible for her injuries, and I would like to see her fully recovered."

"Oh." Camille felt an odd sense of relief. "Well, you've said it yourself—Anne makes her own decisions. You couldn't have stopped her from enlisting."

"True enough." Jacob nodded slightly, falling into a silence that encompassed them both for a time.

Camille glanced around the disorganized office with a shake of her head. "When are you going to hire someone to come in and clean this place?"

Jacob straightened in his chair, shaking the strange intensity of the moment. "What's wrong with it?"

Camille opened her mouth in amazement and laughed. "Look at it! You have piles of paper all over the desk, on the floor, against the wall—it's a disaster in here!"

"I know where everything is, thank you."

"If you say so."

"I do."

She sighed and rose from the chair, wishing she had another reason to prolong the visit just a bit. "Well," she said as he stood.

"Well."

"I should go. Robert is waiting for me outside."

"I'll see you at the next Society meeting, then."

She nodded, looking at him for a moment before finally turning and making her way out of his office and down the stairs. She turned back once to look at his open door and saw him standing there, leaning against the frame. He gave her a smile, an odd one that seemed to say he knew something she didn't.

* * *

New Orleans, Louisiana

Daniel O'Shea embraced Marie one last time before seeing her safely aboard a ship that would carry her north. "I'll see you soon," he shouted to her from the docks as she looked over her shoulder at him with a brave smile. Marie Brissot O'Shea waved at him and shifted her satchel, which held a few belongings. She hadn't much left to her name since her house and family's newspaper office in New Orleans had burned to the ground.

Marie blew him a kiss and strained against the tears she knew were forming in her eyes. They had been married for such a short time, and they were being separated by a war that had already done likewise to so many other families. She was on her way to New York to take up residence in Daniel's small home, which sat in the quiet outskirts of the bustling city. When he had asked her if she wouldn't be more comfortable going to stay with her mother, who was currently in Boston, she had given the matter careful consideration. While being with her mother would undoubtedly provide her with some comfort, especially given the recent death of her father, she knew that eventually she would grow restless, and she didn't want to be a visitor in someone else's house indefinitely.

"I want to go to your home," she'd told Daniel. "Our home. If you don't mind, perhaps my mother can visit me there."

"Of course I don't mind," he'd said. "You may do whatever you feel you need to do. My parents will be thrilled to have you down the street."

That, of course, was another issue altogether. Daniel had written to his parents the moment he and Marie had married, but mail was anything but predictable anymore, and Marie knew she might well reach the O'Sheas before Daniel's letter. Would they like her? Would they accept her? Would they think she was good enough for their son?

These thoughts plagued Marie as she stood on the deck long after the ship left port. It was a Union ship, carrying mostly sailors and a few civilians to New York. She glanced at the men who were returning to their wives and wished her own husband were with her. He was still several months from completing the terms of his enlistment, and she was already counting the days until his discharge. She hardly knew him, really, but she knew she loved him, and for now, that was enough.

* * *

Daniel wiped the back of his neck with his kerchief and cursed the sweltering Louisiana humidity. He had stood on the docks and watched Marie's ship until it was nothing more than a speck on the horizon. Letting her leave was more painful than he could have imagined, but she wasn't safe in New Orleans. Her father had made some powerful enemies, enemies who had ultimately been responsible for his death and now for the burning of his home and newspaper office. The Union officers currently dealing with matters of law would look into it, of course, but Marie had told him she doubted those responsible would ever be brought to justice; they were too strong, too powerful, and ultimately untouchable. Plus, she had added, the evidence against them was purely circumstantial. She had no proof that her neighbors, *her neighbors* of all people, were responsible for her losses.

Marie would be safe in New York. He would write to his parents again and beg them to care for her. Surely they would love her and welcome her with open arms. Gavin and Brenna were good people with good hearts, and besides, the thought of prospective grandchildren would have them giddy with excitement. Daniel was their only hope of extending the O'Shea family line, and Brenna had been after Daniel to settle down and marry since shortly after his fiancée had died many, many years earlier.

Daniel smiled a bit and wished he could see his mother's face for himself when Marie showed up on their doorstep. He imagined the squeal of delight at her arrival and didn't doubt for a moment that Marie would charm Gavin senseless. For a moment he begrudged the voluntary servitude that kept him from witnessing the meeting with his own eyes, but he ultimately had to be grateful for it because he had been here when Marie had needed him the most. That she had become his wife was more than he could have hoped for.

Still envisioning the happy meeting between his wife and his parents, he whistled as he made his way back to the small boat that would row him out to his ship stationed in the harbor. He would work hard and hope that the time would pass more quickly than usual. He looked forward to being home again in the arms of his wife and parents.

CHAPTER 5

Many men were killed and thrown into rivers, a great number hung to trees and lamp-posts, numbers shot down; no black person could show their heads but what they were hunted like wolves. These scenes continued for four days.

—Brooklyn, New York, correspondent for the Christian Recorder

* * *

14 July 1863
Gettysburg, Pennsylvania

"People are restless in cities all over the North," Ben told Luke as he returned from speaking with one of the senior officers. "New York looks especially volatile."

Luke nodded and winced as he shifted his ankle, which throbbed with a dull ache. He was grateful he suffered only a small injury at Gettysburg—so many had lost much, much more. "Because of the Conscription Act?"

"Yes. Most aren't willing to be called up to fight against slavery. That's how they see it. The major thinks we may be sent to New York if the situation there doesn't improve."

Luke leaned against a tree trunk and closed his eyes. "I wish people understood how important it is."

Ben smiled and tossed a frayed stick into a small fire pit. "You're a revolutionary, cousin. I'm sure it will be quite some time before the general populace embraces the abolitionist vision."

"Sometimes I wonder if they ever will." Luke was quiet for a moment, his thoughts wandering over familiar trails, and he found himself eventually thinking of his family. He wanted so much to tell them personally about his newfound faith in God and his baptism. Would they think him batty? What would they say when he told them he was now a Mormon? *It feels so right,* he wanted to tell them. *I've never felt so peaceful about anything in my life. God has spoken with people throughout the ages—ordinary men as well as kings. Why wouldn't He again answer the prayers of a young boy? He once helped David slay Goliath . . .*

He already had the argument framed in his head. Anne would be skeptical, as would Camille. Robert would analyze it from every angle, and Jimmy would sit quietly and absorb the reactions of the rest of the family. His parents—well, on that score Luke had to admit he was puzzled. They were both God-fearing people who prayed daily. What would they think if he told them the gospel of Jesus Christ had been restored in its fulness to the earth after dying off with the last of Christ's disciples?

He shook his head a bit.

"What are you thinking?" Ben asked him.

"Wondering what my family will think of my baptism."

"Well, if you're fortunate, they won't react the way mine did."

Luke winced. Ben's parents had thrown him out of their home. Ben's conversion, however, had been only one in a long list of events that had precipitated his departure.

"Your family respects you, Luke," Ben said, picking up another stick from the ground and breaking it into pieces, tossing each into the fire. It was a typical habit of Ben's; he was often restless. "They'll show respect for your religion too."

"Ben, I must know," Luke said suddenly, watching his cousin. "I'm more at peace now that I've been baptized than I've ever been, even knowing I'll go again into battle. You've known the gospel for years now. Why are you not more . . ."

Ben looked up, one brow raised.

"More . . ."

"More what? Peaceful?"

"I suppose."

Ben turned his attention back to the fire. "You and I do not come from the same place, Luke. And you were more at peace before either of us was baptized than I ever was."

Luke nodded slightly but remained silent, hoping Ben would say more.

"I have calmed considerably, but I still remember . . . everything . . ." Ben tossed the rest of the stick into the fire and watched as a shower of sparks shot skyward.

"You're waiting for the rest of the world to give you peace, I believe."

Ben shrugged.

"It never will, you know."

"I thank you for your encouragement."

"Ben, the world will never give you what you're looking for. You were raised on a plantation, hating slavery, and now you find yourself in love with a black woman whom I believe you hope to marry."

Ben looked at Luke in some surprise but eventually nodded slowly.

"And your community in Utah? Will they look kindly on such a union?"

"I hope most of them will."

"But for even the kindest and most intelligent it will be a struggle to understand."

Ben nodded. "I suppose."

"So you're going to spend the rest of your life being fitful and angry." When Ben remained silent, Luke continued. "Why would any woman want to be shackled to a man with a perpetual scowl?"

Ben took a deep breath and looked Luke square in the face. "Cousin, I'm a bit confused. Does this conversation have a purpose?"

"My purpose is this: you're going to have to find your own peace, Ben, and the rest of the world be hanged. If you love Mary, then go and make a life together and relinquish your hold on all of the bitterness. It's turning you into a very hard man. Your parents are who they are. Your past is what it is. Did you ever think that maybe you were placed on that plantation for a purpose? That your spirit would rise past the ugliness and be a force for good? Just consider it for a bit," Luke said, and rose, dusting his pants. Anything further he might have said was cut short by an officer who was mounted atop his horse.

"Pack up! We're going to New York."

Ben stood as the officer maneuvered his horse through the crowd of soldiers. "What's happening?"

"Riots. Looting. Mostly the working Irish—they've gone mad and are killing any blacks they can find."

* * *

The situation that greeted Ben and Luke late the next day as they rode into New York City was one of utter chaos and terror. Buildings were ablaze; shops had been vandalized; and, the cousins witnessed with mounting horror as they drew closer upon the scene, black men were hanging, lynched from lampposts and trees.

Meade's troops arriving from Gettysburg were weary not only from having ridden hard to arrive in the riot-torn city, but also from surviving a bloody battle only one week before. As they rode into town, rioters stood on rooftops and fired upon the troops. The tired soldiers returned fire, dropping the sharpshooters from their perches.

The troops began fanning out following hastily given orders. Where to even begin? The scene was an odd one, and Ben couldn't fix it in his mind. He had become so accustomed to fighting men in uniform, men there for the same reason he was. Now he looked upon a city street teeming with crazed, angry people who certainly had a right to their frustration but who sought to wreak their vengeance upon the innocent.

As the soldiers began reining in the citizens, calling order with their voices and their weapons, it became evident rather quickly that the trained and professional troops would carry the day. The disorganized masses of humanity roaming the streets were powerful and dangerous but ultimately no match for soldiers who had fought in battle and were trained to win at all costs.

Ben continued down the street, leaving the situation in the control of other soldiers, and urged his horse to a faster pace so that he might reach a crowd of people near the corner. They were screaming at a white man who stood at the center of the small mob, acting as a shield to a black man who stood behind him, bloodied, beaten, and barely standing.

"You must not do this thing!" the white man shouted, his Irish brogue thick, his voice hoarse and strained. "This man is innocent! I'm beggin' you to stop."

"Get outta the way, O'Shea," came an answering shout. "This don't concern you!"

"I won't!" The man called O'Shea spread his arms wide in protection of the man behind him. "Ye've beaten him, ye've mutilated him, ye've robbed him of his dignity—I will not let ye take his life!"

Ben turned his head over his shoulder to Luke, who rode closely behind, and motioned to the mob. He looked back seconds later and choked on his own shout as the white man recoiled from a bullet to his chest. O'Shea fell forward onto the ground with a look of utter disbelief upon his face. The mob converged upon the black man, stepping on O'Shea and crushing him beneath their feet as they attempted to fit a rope around the neck of the black man, who was only partially clothed and had been noticeably cut and mutilated.

Luke charged from behind and reared his horse high into the air, firing his weapon with a shout that had the heads of the mob turning in stunned surprise. Ben watched with a sinking heart as more rioters from around a corner converged upon the scene with guns, knives, ropes, and burning torches.

As Luke's horse made its descent, the man who had shot O'Shea raised his weapon. Ben pulled his own gun into the air, but his shot fired a fraction of a second too late. His bullet hit its mark, and the man fell to the ground, lifeless, but not before the man had fired a shot of his own that hit Luke in the center of his forehead.

Ben screamed and moved his horse as Luke slid from his saddle, his weapon falling from his hands. Ben caught his cousin and pulled him across his lap, looking in desperation down the street to see other soldiers, both mounted and on foot, approaching them.

The light from the sky was beginning to dim, and Ben saw that the faces of those surrounding him were mostly filthy, frightened, and crazed. The black man fell to the ground on his knees, and then lifeless to his side, his arms bound behind his back.

Soon, after witnessing the soldiers' overwhelming skill and firepower, the mob dispersed, leaving a battleground of dead and wounded in the streets. Ben clutched Luke's limp, heavy form, desperate to keep him from falling. His horse skittered near O'Shea, who lay upon the ground, one eye swollen shut, but the man was still breathing. Ben looked around, trying to find the path of least resistance so that he might escape, when he saw O'Shea weakly lift a hand and point a bloodied finger at Luke, whose face was visible to him from the ground.

"Birmingham." Ben saw O'Shea mouth Luke's last name. He then watched as O'Shea looked up at Ben himself, his eye widening slightly in surprise. It was no wonder, Ben thought as he made eye contact with the poor man. Ben and Luke looked so similar that people often mistook them for the same person.

Ben dismounted, grunting under the strain of trying to keep Luke lying atop the horse, and reached down to O'Shea. He put a shoulder under the wounded man's arm and hoisted him to his feet. Together, Ben leading the horse, they moved slowly away from the diminishing sounds of the mob.

They had gone some distance down the dusty street when O'Shea fell to one knee with a pained groan. "I can go no farther, young man," he said through teeth clenched in pain. He grasped at his chest and coughed, emitting blood from his mouth and onto his shirtfront.

Ben helped him onto a soft patch of earth under the leaves of a large tree and tugged the reins of the horse, which obediently came to his side. With some effort, he lifted and pulled Luke from the back of the animal and fell to the ground with him next to the dying Irishman.

"Are ye Luke, then, or is he?"

Ben held Luke's head and shoulders in his arms as the tears began to fall. They rolled down his face and splashed onto Luke's, which was frozen in shock, his green eyes open wide. Huge, coarse, racking sobs soon shook Ben's whole frame as he wiped his tears from Luke's face, the bullet hole in the center of his cousin's forehead mocking him with its small size and simplicity.

"He's Luke," Ben stammered to O'Shea, who laid a trembling hand upon Ben's arm.

"I met him once—he hired my son, Daniel, to work at the bank." O'Shea coughed and sputtered more blood. "A good man," he said, and then was seized by a fit of choking.

Ben looked up at the man, consumed with grief yet aware that O'Shea was close to death himself. Ben had seen it overtake so many men; he knew the signs well. He clasped O'Shea's fingers with his own and said through his tears, "Where can I take you, sir?"

"To my wife, Brenna. Tell her I love her. Tell her I will wait for her. I . . ." O'Shea coughed and doubled over Ben's arm with the effort. The smear of red blood pumping from the wound in his chest continued to spread until it flowed onto Ben's arm where he clasped the man's hand. His breath rattled once, twice, into and out of his lungs, and then ceased. O'Shea's grip on Ben's hand slowly slackened, and Ben sat in the dark under a tree, holding two dead men.

He raised his face to the sky and screamed as though his lungs would burst. The sound finally wound down, and he was left, instead, with sobs that burned his throat and eyes. "No, no, no," he cried in a low moan, rocking slowly back and forth as though the movement would somehow revive Luke, whom he still cradled in his arms.

It couldn't possibly be! How could Luke survive a battle like Gettysburg and then suddenly be cut down in a riot on a city street? Ben couldn't think of where to go, of what to do. He sat in confusion, rocking and crying and considering his own weapon at his side. He could end it all for himself too—a quick and simple gesture and he would be with Luke.

He felt Luke smile and somehow sensed he was at his side. He felt Luke's arms about him. "I love you, cousin," Luke's voice sounded in Ben's mind. "Live a good life. I'll see you again."

Ben closed his eyes, the hot tears continuing to seep from his eyelids. He cried as he hadn't for years, feeling like a child. He felt Luke withdraw, and then he was gone.

* * *

Boston, Massachusetts

"Why aren't they putting the fire out?" Abigail Van Dyke screamed over the noise as she approached Camille from the side of the burning Abolition Society meeting hall. She gestured toward the firemen who were adding to the mayhem.

"Because they aren't exempt from the draft anymore!" Camille yelled back to her, and watched in amazed horror at the people who looted the shops along the street. "They're just as angry as the rioters."

Abigail moved close to Camille and slipped her arm around Camille's shoulders. "We're not safe here," she said in Camille's ear. "We need to go back home."

Camille nodded but couldn't take her eyes from the complete and utter madness that engulfed the city. The women were standing to the side of the street, well out of the way of the carriages and horses that traversed it, and the riderless carriage, careening crazily and heading straight toward them, came as a surprise.

Abigail jumped back, pulling Camille with her, and as she did so, the carriage passing by was accompanied by the sound of ripping fabric. Camille looked at the back wheel of the carriage as it continued its mad dash. A long strip of Abigail's skirt went round and round with each turn of the wheel, caught on a jagged edge.

Abigail looked down at her torn dress, her face ghostly pale in the dark night. Camille grasped her arm and, without a word, guided her up the street and away from the chaos toward the safety of Abigail's home. "Jenny will wonder where we are," she said, trying desperately to wipe the haunted expression from her friend's face. It had been a carriage that had run down Abigail's mother and killed her. "We never should have come down here alone."

"We have to do something," Abigail mumbled, looking back at the burning buildings and the firefighters who refused to fight the blazes.

"We are," Camille answered her, frightened beyond words and desperate to get home. "We're keeping ourselves alive."

By the time Camille and Abigail arrived at Abigail's home, they were both trembling and walking as quickly as they could. Camille closed the door behind them both and leaned against it, feeling her eyes burn—a combination of smoke and tears. "How can they be so hateful?" she mumbled.

Abigail sat on the bottom step looking as weary and frightened as Camille felt. "It *is* unfair, though—the Conscription Act. It allows those who can afford to pay for a replacement a way to avoid the draft, while those who cannot simply have no choice."

"Fine, it's unfair, but so is burning the Abolition Society building!"

"You know, Cammy, I think the only consolation is that they were burning everything. I don't think the Society building was singled out intentionally."

"How about that carriage that nearly ran us down?"

"The horses were spooked." Abigail shrugged slightly and rubbed her eyes. She turned and looked over her shoulder, causing Camille to raise her gaze. Jenny Brissot, her widowed aunt, was descending the stairs in her night rail.

"Girls, I don't know if I even dare ask what you've been doing."

"The riots—do you hear them?"

Jenny nodded and placed an arm about Abigail's shoulders as she stood, then took Camille's hand as she descended the last step. "I heard them, yes. I can't sleep because of them. And here I thought you two were tucked away in your beds. Let's have some tea," she said as she led the girls to the kitchen. As Jenny went about the business of preparing the tea, she shook her head a bit.

"Girls, I must ask—what is it that made you believe you should go outside tonight?"

Camille opened and closed her mouth a few times, searching for a response that eluded her. Abigail finally answered for her. "It was stupid."

"That's not quite what I was looking for," Camille muttered.

"Well, it *was* stupid," Jenny replied, and glanced at her.

"You're going to tell my mother, aren't you?"

"And what would your mother do, do you suppose? You're a woman now, Camille. You can make your own choices. I'm sure she would say to you, though, that she expects you to use wisdom in your choices. Yes?"

Camille nodded and slumped in her chair. Her aunt had taken on the very tone her mother would have used had she been present.

"Now that I've done the proper reprimanding," Jenny said, taking a seat at the table while she waited for the tea, "tell me what you saw."

The girls looked at her in silence for a moment before Abigail spoke. "Mayhem."

Camille nodded her agreement. "They're burning and stealing everything."

Jenny nodded and traced a pattern on the tabletop with her finger. "We're on the brink of tremendous change. I wonder how it will resolve itself."

Camille snorted. "I wonder if it ever will. Feels like we've been at war forever."

The teakettle hissed, and Jenny rose, pouring three cups. As she carried them to the table, Camille was suddenly very grateful she was there. She sometimes wondered if she'd ever be too old to need a mother.

* * *

15 July 1863
New York, New York

Ben held the hand of the woman and looked at her through eyes that felt like sand. "I'm so very sorry for your loss," he said, knowing that the words were not enough.

The woman gazed at her husband, who lay in the back of a farmer's wagon. She moved to his side and looked at his form, so still in death. Ben had done his best to clean the man and dress him in a fresh albeit slightly torn and dirtied shirt. Brenna O'Shea looked back at Ben, her face drained of all color, and he watched in alarm as her eyes rolled back in her head. He caught her just before she hit the ground.

Ben cradled her in his arms and turned to the two soldiers and farmer with him. "I'll take her inside. Tie my horse to that post and move Mr. O'Shea to the side of the house."

"I have to be goin'," the farmer told him. "I can't stay here all day."

"Fine. Lay him there on the ground then."

Ben carried Brenna inside the house and turned to a room on his left. It was a small parlor, and he laid her on a sofa near a front window. Her eyelids eventually fluttered, and she focused on Ben's face in confusion. He saw the exact moment when her memory returned, and her eyes filled with tears. She rolled to her side on the sofa and covered her face with her hands.

He moved back a bit, taking a seat on a footstool near the sofa. He couldn't leave her alone; as far as he could tell there was nobody else in the home, and he wasn't sure where the son, Daniel, was. Ben sat quietly as the tears continued to flow and allowed the woman the time and space she needed to accept the news of her husband's death.

Brenna O'Shea eventually sat up on the sofa and took the handkerchief Ben offered her from his pocket. "How did this happen?" she finally mumbled. "And where was he? I was out lookin' for him."

"There was a mob in the city. He was defending a black man. He was shot once in the chest."

"Were you with him when he died?"

"Yes, ma'am. I was."

"What did he say to you?"

"He said to tell you that he loves you and that he'll wait for you."

Brenna's tears fell afresh. "That man!" she said. "I begged him to stay home. He was such a foolish man sometimes—he believed in the good nature of people."

Ben smiled, pained. "Probably because he was of such good nature himself. I was . . . my cousin was . . ." Ben paused, his own grief still so raw. "I was with my cousin when your husband died. Luke was already dead. Your husband wanted me to know he thought Luke was a good man. He died wanting to ease my pain."

Brenna looked at Ben and nodded through her tears. "That sounds very much like him. How did he know your cousin?" Her lovely Irish brogue was like music, even in sorrow. She sniffed and wiped at her nose, her tears still falling.

"He met Luke through some bank business. Said Luke hired your son, Daniel."

Brenna looked at Ben with new recognition. "Oh, of course," she said. "Birmingham, is it?"

He nodded.

"Oh, I am sorry. Danny spoke most highly of your cousin. Ah, my boy," she said as though just remembering Daniel. "I wish he were here. He sent word that he's married a girl with whom he'd corresponded." She talked as though to avoid silence. Ben nodded politely in response, and then she looked at him again with a sort of recognition or connection.

"His wife is Luke Birmingham's cousin, in fact, from New Orleans. She would be your cousin then as well?"

Ben cast his thoughts about on his and Luke's relatives until he finally realized of whom she was speaking. "Oh, no, the cousin in New Orleans is from Luke's mother's side of the family. I'm a cousin on his father's side."

Brenna nodded, silent, and seemed at a loss for any further conversation.

"What can I do for you?" Ben asked her softly.

She smiled a bit, although her eyes still flowed with tears. "You're a dear boy, you are. Just lost your cousin and you're thinkin' o' me."

"I'm not being noble. I suppose I figure if I keep myself busy, I won't have too much time to think."

"And wise you are too. Where are you from, then? Your voice doesn't sound like it should be wearin' blue."

"I'm from South Carolina. But my heart is in Boston."

"I see. Well then, young man, since you offered help," Brenna said, standing, her tears still flowing unchecked, "I'd much appreciate it if you'd help me bury my husband."

* * *

In her head, Marie composed a letter as she rode in a hired hack through the bloody streets of New York City. *Dear Daniel,* she imagined writing, *I think I might have been safer in New Orleans.* The aftermath of the rioting was horrific, and the city looked like a war zone. She began to breathe a bit easier when the conveyance moved away from the noise and crowds.

The streets became less congested, the buildings and homes spaced farther apart, and it was with a sense of relief that when the hack came to a stop, she was looking at a relatively small, well-kept farmhouse on the outskirts of the city. She climbed down and accepted her bags from the driver, paying him for his services, and then watched as he turned back to the city and disappeared from sight.

Marie drew up her shoulders and sucked in her breath, wondering how on earth one approached one's parents-in-law when they were total strangers. She picked up her bags and was approaching the front door when a movement to the side of the house caught her eye.

She dropped her bags in surprise and ran toward the figure that was digging in the earth with a shovel. So great was her shock she didn't even register the crude box at his side. "Luke!"

He looked up as she threw herself into his arms. He slowly returned her embrace, and she wondered at his reluctance. Pulling back, she looked at him carefully. Something wasn't quite . . . right. "Luke?"

He winced, his red-rimmed eyes moist. "I'm Ben," he said.

Marie gripped his shoulders uncomprehending.

"I'm Ben, the southern Birmingham. Do you remember?"

"Oh . . . oh!" She stepped back, horrified. "I'm so sorry—you look just like him." Marie squinted her eyes at Ben.

"You must be Marie. Your new mother-in-law is expecting you."

"She is?" They had received Daniel's letter, then. Well, that was good. She was relieved that she wouldn't be forced to try to explain herself. "I've been worried about meeting them. They weren't expecting Daniel to marry, and . . ."

Marie finally took a good look around and slowed her thoughts. "What has happened?" she finally asked, sounding foolish even to her own ears.

Ben cleared his throat a bit, and it was then that she noticed the strain apparent on his drawn face. His black hair was disheveled, his uniform unkempt, and he looked as though he hadn't slept in days.

"Perhaps you should go inside," he said gently to her. "Much has happened in the last day or so."

"You tell me, please, before I meet my husband's parents." Marie swallowed past the knot that had suddenly formed in her throat.

* * *

Brenna O'Shea stared into the empty hearth, wondering why she had allowed Gavin to leave the house. She should have tied him down in his sleep. She knew he had been determined on going into the city to see if he couldn't talk sense into some of their countrymen. The fear in the hearts of the working Irish was real and beyond "sense." Gavin had known it too, and still he had gone ahead.

The Irish had only just escaped the potato famine in their own land, and now, racial hatred was strong in the city where black workers replaced the Irish who were striking for better wages. "If we go and fight for the Negro," was the common cry of recent days, "he'll come up here and take *all* the work!" When the first draft had been issued—had it been only three days ago?—the citizens of the city stormed the draft office and tore up the notices. When they had been unable to break open a safe in the office, they set fire to the building instead.

And then, the looting, rioting, torturing, and murdering had begun. Black families all over the city fled for safety while their homes were burned and the men were hacked to pieces, dragged through the streets, and lynched from light posts. Some of the rioters had even set fire to an orphanage for colored children. It was at that point, when word reached the O'Sheas, that Gavin had determined he wouldn't stand by and allow it to continue. Brenna had begged and pleaded, but Gavin had stolen away in the early morning hours while she slept. He had been gone all day and all night, and then had been brought back home to her in a wagon.

Brenna looked up from her position on the parlor sofa as a small knock on the door sounded, followed by a creak as the door opened. A beautiful young woman with black hair and violet eyes entered quietly and looked around the corner. "Mrs. O'Shea," she said, standing uncertainly in the doorway and sounding very southern, "I am Marie."

Marie's eyes were wet. She had obviously spoken with someone, probably Ben. "I am so very, very sorry," she said, and bit her lip as though to stop its trembling. "I've recently lost my father, and I understand your pain. Daniel will be so upset—he doesn't know. We didn't know . . . of course, when I left New Orleans everything was fine for you and your husband, but . . . and Luke, my cousin Luke . . ."

Marie clutched her fingers together, and Brenna's heart lurched. She rose from the sofa and approached the young woman. Without saying a word, she enfolded the girl in her arms and together they cried.

CHAPTER 6

My dear son Albert. . . . I received your affectionate letter yesterday. . . . I had not heard one word from you since Barlow Rogers returned home, hearing of so many battles in Virginia. . . . May God bless you, my dear Albert.
—Your devoted father, Thomas A. G. Batchelor.

* * *

20 July 1863
New York, New York

Jeffrey Birmingham sat on the small bed in the sparsely furnished bedroom. He was currently the uninvited guest of a local politician, and the spare room upstairs was better than he'd hoped for when he had been rescued at sea some months before. His time had been divided since that fateful day when the ship he sailed on had gone down to a watery grave. Plucked from the water by a passing Union vessel, it was almost as though the boys in blue hadn't quite known what to do with him. His brother was revered and wealthy, and by that relation alone he had avoided a jail cell. Jeffrey himself held a fair amount of status, however, and as he was considered a senior diplomat for the Confederacy, he had been under some pressure to give up whatever information the Union thought he might have.

For weeks now, he had been transferred from one home to another without explanation. So much time was passing, so many things occurring. He was desperate for news of his family. Perhaps that was the thing that shocked him the most. He had always thought that if he had plenty of money and the financial security he'd lacked as a youth, then life would fall nicely into place and he would be happy. He was a husband and a father, though, and his regrets over his lack of participation in those roles were too numerous to count.

Someday, somehow he would have to be set free. When that day came, he would make things right. He had made a pact with himself, a promise while seated in a small lifeboat in the middle of the immense Atlantic, that if he were rescued and given a second chance at life, he would do something with it. He would make a difference for the people in his life, rather than be a puppet that danced on the end of a string.

Sarah was showing signs of strain. He had seen it in her before he left for England. She had never allowed herself to falter in all the time he'd known her, had never given herself the luxury of sharing her burdens with another. She had taken a stern approach with him and with the children, and he'd blithely accepted it because the plantation, the money, and the status had all been hers. He never once considered that she might have welcomed the support. He didn't know because he had never tried.

The scraping of the key in the lock interrupted his thoughts, and he turned his head as the door to the bedroom opened. His voice was rusty from disuse, and it sounded very strained when he started in surprise at the vision of his brother, James, standing in the doorway.

"You don't look too much worse for the wear," James said, and entered the room, the guard posted outside closing the door behind him.

Jeffrey stood and watched his twin for a moment. The face was so familiar, in part because it bore a mirror image of his own, but also because there had been a time when the two were closer than most siblings. What a waste the past several years had been. There were so many things Jeffrey wished he could go back and do differently. But the time for wishing was past.

He looked at James, saying nothing. In truth, words failed him as he searched around for something that wouldn't sound completely idiotic. James must have sensed his discomfort because he moved forward and embraced Jeffrey, thumping him once, firmly, on the back. Jeffrey's arms rose of their own accord, and, stunned, he returned his brother's affection.

James pulled back, his hands gripping Jeffrey's shoulders. "I hope you're well."

Jeffrey nodded, clearing his throat. "I am."

"And what are your plans?"

"I plan to look out this window until nightfall and then dine on whatever the family has left over from supper. Then I suppose I'll go to sleep and arise in the morning to look out the window some more."

James's lips twitched. "You've not even tried to contact your support in Virginia?"

"Oh, I've tried. I have yet to hear."

"More likely than not, your correspondence was never delivered." James motioned to the window, which was barred on the outside by iron. "I suppose climbing out was never an option."

"I'm not thin enough to fit through the bars."

"I've made arrangements for you to come home with me."

Jeffrey stared at his brother. "Why would you do that?"

James cast him a look that hinted of scorn. "You think I would allow you to languish away in someone else's house if I had a say in the matter? Jeffrey, when I received word that your ship was lost, I felt very . . . I had many regrets over time lost in recent years. I didn't feel that you were dead, though, and I decided I would change things in the future if I could."

Jeffrey nodded slightly, absorbing the words and the unspoken feeling behind them. "I appreciate that. Very much."

"Do you have any personal belongings with you?"

Jeffrey gestured to a small satchel he had been given, courtesy of a Union officer who took pity on him as they had reached port. "Just this."

"Well, then—we're off. Unless you have other plans?"

Jeffrey smiled. "No, I believe my schedule is clear."

* * *

James and Jeffrey came upon the Union encampment as it was preparing to move out. "I don't know if the boys are actually here—I was told that part of their regiment came here earlier last week to help subdue the riots," James said.

Jeffrey nodded. The city still showed signs of wear; even the citizens themselves looked weary. The rioting over the Conscription Act had affected cities all across the Union, and he supposed that fact probably had his associates in the Confederacy dancing in their offices and streets. He had watched the rioting, in fact, from afar in his little room—the screaming, shouting, and flames visible and audible from his point at the window. "It was madness," he said to his brother. "Utter lunacy."

"Boston was much the same," James told him. "Although I understand not to the degree it was here. Excuse me," he said, interrupting himself and catching the attention of a passing soldier. "If I were looking for someone specific, how might I find him?"

The soldier asked which company and regiment were in question, then pointed the Birmingham men in the right direction. After considerable wandering through rows of tents and men, Jeffrey spotted a familiar face, and it shook him to his core.

Ben.

His eyes stung with harsh tears and his mouth hung slack at the vision of his son, now a man grown. He had matured, thinned, and there was a look of strain about his eyes and face that made his heart hurt. Ben had often looked angry in the time before he had left Bentley years earlier, but the appearance of such raw pain was new.

Jeffrey knew the moment when Ben looked up and recognized the two men. His eyes flashed upon James's face with a sense of subtle joy, and then he looked at Jeffrey with an expression of complete shock. Casting his own personal reservations aside, Jeffrey moved forward and grasped his son, clutching him and never wanting to let him go.

Regret, regret. It coursed through his thoughts as he considered all the time lost, all of the experiences he should have had with his oldest son. That he should have taken the initiative but hadn't was a bitter pill to swallow.

"Father?" Ben's voice was incredulous as Jeffrey pulled back and looked at his son. "What . . . what . . ."

"I'm vacationing." Jeffrey smiled at Ben's bafflement.

"I don't understand."

"I'm actually James's prisoner."

"For the time being," James interjected, and reached to embrace Ben when Jeffrey released him. "He'll be on his way soon enough, but we'll keep that to ourselves."

As Ben moved back from his uncle, his face twisted a bit, and a muscle moved in his jaw, displaying his agitation. "There's something you don't know," he said, his eyes filling with tears. "I sent a message to Boston nearly a week ago, but the telegraph lines were down here. It's probably only just now reached your house."

"What is it?"

"Luke."

James looked at his nephew in dawning comprehension. Jeffrey closed his eyes briefly and bowed his head, already feeling his brother's pain.

James looked around for a moment as though searching for his son. He stumbled back a bit and sat on an overturned barrel, looking up at Ben with pleading eyes. "When? Where? Gettysburg?"

"No." Ben gruffly cleared his throat. "Here, in the city. He was attempting to defend a man the rioters were about to lynch. He was shot once—he was gone instantly. He didn't suffer."

James hung his head, looking burdened and confused with grief. He took a few deep breaths that shuddered through his frame, and then he looked up again and asked in a voice harsh with strain, "Where is his body?"

"I'll show you where I buried him. He can be moved to Boston if you wish."

* * *

James stood at the foot of the freshly dug grave in the O'Shea family garden. There were two graves, actually—his son's and Gavin O'Shea's. Mrs. O'Shea had graciously offered the small plot of ground in Luke's honor, and James looked at it through burning eyes, his arm around his wife's niece. He wondered at that point which of them was truly the one offering support. He leaned heavily on Marie and considered how he was going to go home to his wife and tell her their child was dead.

Marie leaned her head into James's shoulder, and he felt her reach up to wipe at her face. "So much death," she whispered, and he planted a gentle kiss on her head, closing his eyes. It hadn't been long since Marie's father had passed away under James's own roof in Boston. The bitter truth was that both Jean-Pierre and Luke were dead because of other people's hatred, and it made James's heart burn with fury. How easy it would be to return that hatred measure for measure.

Marie sniffed and lifted her head. "Will you move him to Boston, do you suppose?"

James shrugged a bit. "I'll ask which Elizabeth prefers. This is beautiful here—it's a fitting resting spot for him."

"He was a good, good person, Uncle James."

"Yes, that he was. He was a good man. I admired him greatly."

* * *

Ben sat with his father under the shade of a tree near Luke's grave and gave his uncle some time to absorb the news of his son's death. He wasn't exactly sure what he should say to Jeffrey. They had never been close, and time and distance had done nothing to help the relationship. It had, however, given Ben a sense of longing for something he had never had with his father. He was too weary to feel the familiar rage.

Jeffrey saved him from searching for conversation by opening it himself. "I owe you so much, Benjamin, that I will never be able to give you."

Ben stared at him. "I'm not sure I know what you mean."

"I think you do. I know it too—have known it for a long, long time. I owe you support. Years ago, you did something brave, something you felt was right . . . and in truth, it was right. I wasn't there with my support for you. I let you go, and it was your choice, but I let you go believing I cared little for your future. That wasn't true."

Ben held his breath, then released it. "I'm not sure what to say."

Jeffrey held up a hand and shook his head. "You don't need to say anything at all. Just know that I haven't shown it, but I have always loved you, son." He looked over at his brother, standing in grief at Luke's graveside, and then looked back to Ben. "I should hate for you to be gone and not know that."

Jeffrey untied the bow tie at his throat and opened his shirt collar. He leaned back against the trunk of the tree and closed his eyes as a soft breeze blew his hair across his forehead. Ben closed his mouth, not realizing until that moment that it had fallen open. "Sir, I . . . I . . ."

Jeffrey opened his eyes and smiled slightly at him. He waited for a moment, then said, "If you should ever feel it in your heart to return the sentiment, I'll be glad to hear it. In the meantime, have you heard any news at all from home?"

"Which home?"

Jeffrey winced, almost imperceptibly. "Bentley."

"I have heard, actually, quite a few things." It dawned on Ben as he mentally counted the months his father had been away that much had happened in his absence. "Richard—had you heard?"

Jeffrey shook his head, sitting up slightly.

"I'm the bearer of bad tidings for all today." Ben wished he could spare his father the news. "He's gone."

Jeffrey stared at him much as James had earlier. He finally nodded slowly, swallowing several times before finding his voice. "Where?"

"Chancellorsville. Carrying Jackson off the field of battle."

Jeffrey looked off into the distance. "He would have wanted to die doing something . . . something . . ."

"Honorable?"

Jeffrey looked at Ben with an inscrutable expression, one brow slightly cocked. He looked back into the trees with a sigh. "Something impressive, I suppose. There are many things about Richard of which you probably aren't aware. After you left home, Richard grew to be rather, rather . . ."

Ben watched in sympathy as Jeffrey searched for an inoffensive term to describe his own flesh and blood.

"Rather dogged, I suppose one might say, in the pursuit of a meaningful life. He did some dishonorable things along the way. You have a nephew, I'm told."

"Oh?"

"Yes. A slave baby who was sold to the Charlesworths."

Ben sucked in his breath and felt a stab of rage at his dead brother. Richard hadn't been someone Ben had liked before he left home, and Jeffrey's news that Richard had become unscrupulous came as no surprise. "I don't know anyone at Bentley who would have willingly lain with Richard." The old, familiar anger was back.

Jeffrey glanced at him with an open face, free from defense or guile. "Nobody would have—willingly."

"Does it not—" Ben broke off and wiped at his forehead, lowering his voice. "Does it not bother you that you have a *grandchild* living a mere two miles down the road, and that child is someone else's *property?*"

Jeffrey nodded, still meeting his eyes. "It bothers me a great deal. I've done many things and allowed many things as an adult that cause me no small amount of shame, Ben. I decided as I floated in the frigid waters of the North Atlantic that if I received another opportunity to be a person of integrity, I would do everything in my power to do so. You are my first step in that direction."

Ben felt the anger abate and was vulnerable in its absence. His shoulders sagged and he leaned forward, bracing his elbows on his knees.

"I want to live a good life. I haven't been the companion your mother might have appreciated in years past."

Ben glanced up. "She wouldn't let you."

"I never tried."

Mother. Ben briefly closed his eyes. Jeffrey probably didn't know of Sarah's condition. Ben himself had only just recently learned of it through a letter from Emily. "Mother is not herself."

"What do you mean?"

"Emily writes that when she learned of your death, the news—compounded with the effects of the falling South—pushed Mother into a state of mind such that she believes she is a girl again and is constantly watching for her father."

Jeffrey's mouth hung open and he squinted at Ben. "Is she well otherwise?"

"Emily says she doesn't eat much."

Jeffrey looked over at his brother, who had kissed Marie on either cheek and now walked toward them, his step slow. "I must go home," he murmured, and Ben barely heard him. "I must get her away from there."

"Where will you go?"

Jeffrey shook his head. "I don't know."

A thought struck Ben, but he dismissed it as ludicrous. As he watched his father's haunted face, however, he decided it was perhaps not a bad suggestion. "You might take her out west, if she's well enough to handle the trek."

His father looked back at him as though he'd grown two heads. *"Where?"*

"To Utah. Or California, perhaps. Away from the South. It will never be the same again, you know."

Jeffrey nodded, slowly. "I know. Perhaps . . . perhaps . . . if it seems as though it might be to your mother's benefit, I'll come to you for further advice—contacts in Utah."

"I'll be happy to share whatever I know. I have many, many good friends who would be willing to help you once there—and a friend who might not be averse to coming out this way to escort you back. He's a good man—I'd trust him with my life."

"Will you keep in contact with me, then? Will you write to me and tell me of your whereabouts as you move with the army?"

"I will. I . . . that is . . ." Ben stood as James drew closer and rubbed the back of his neck as his father stood and dusted the seat of his pants. "I'm glad to have had this time with you, sir. I'm very . . . gratified to see the changes in you." He awkwardly leaned forward and gave his father a hug, which was warmly returned.

"I'm glad for this time too, son," Jeffrey murmured in Ben's ear, and thumped him on the back. "Glad, indeed."

CHAPTER 7

I . . . am now quite certain that the crimes of this guilty land will never be purged away but with Blood.
—John Brown, December 1859

* * *

22 July 1863
Boston, Massachusetts

Robert Birmingham sat in his bedroom and listened to the harsh sounds of his mother's sobs. His own tears had fallen, and in copious amounts, in the privacy of his room throughout the evening since his father's return from New York. James had gathered the family and told them that Luke was gone, and although Robert had always thought they were a strong family, it seemed that they each broke down at the news.

Things weren't the same anymore, and they never would be. Camille had been the most vocal in her grief, leaving the parlor in an angry rush, eventually ending up in the library where Robert heard her throwing books against the wall. Anne had sat in the window seat, tears coursing down her face in earnest. Before the news of

Luke's death she had cried every day anyway but never would discuss her reasons. It was so unlike her that it had even young Jimmy worried.

Jimmy himself had perched on a window seat in the far corner of the parlor, his knees drawn to his chest. He was nearly twelve years old now and had always been withdrawn and quiet. Robert presumed that this further disruption to his world would pull him inward even more so.

Elizabeth, though—her anguish had been the most difficult for Robert to witness. Such a strong, refined, and elegant woman she was. It broke Robert's heart to see her in pain. She had borne the news with her usual grace and dignity, but now that the hour was late, Robert heard her in her room, next to his, crying with huge, gasping breaths that he was sure would never leave his memory.

Every so often, Robert heard the low timbre of his father's voice as James made attempts to comfort his wife. In an odd way, that soft, rumbling sound was a soothing balm for Robert. He remembered a time when he had been very young and ill, and James had taken it upon himself to see Robert through the worst of it. That low, gentle voice had nursed him through long nights of fever and nightmares.

Robert thought of all the people who would be affected by the loss of Luke Birmingham. He was well respected in his career at the bank and well loved by members of the Abolition Society. He had been a faithful member since his youth, following his parents to the meetings and eventually adopting and living the life of an abolitionist to the very letter. He had *loved* the cause, had fought for it here at home, had supported it financially, and had in the end, given his life for it.

Robert groaned as he remembered one person who would most definitely feel pain at Luke's death. Abigail Van Dyke. Surely she would know by now. That night after she had calmed herself a bit and through her tears apologized for making a mess of the library, Camille had insisted on going back to the Van Dyke home, where she had been living since Dolly Van Dyke's death several months back. She would have told Abby, and now Abby would be grieving for not only her mother, but also her fiancé.

Robert had adored Abigail for some time and now felt a tremendous amount of guilt for it. Luke was cold in the ground, and his brother was coveting his fiancée. Shame flooded through him as he envisioned Abigail crying, and he wanted so much to take away her pain.

He moved from his bed where he'd been lying on the quilt, dressed in his shirtsleeves and trousers. Tomorrow he would wear a black armband that would signal his state of mourning over the loss of a family member. He never imagined he would wear that armband for Luke. He had worried a bit, but in the back of his mind he couldn't fathom that everything wouldn't eventually return to normal after the war.

Pacing the length of the room, he raked a hand through his hair and for a moment covered his ears with the palms of his hands, wanting to block out the sounds of his mother's grief, of the memory of Camille's pain, the image of Anne's tear-streaked face, Jimmy's haunted expression, even his own terrible anguish. Luke was gone, and he was never coming back! At his memorial service, the preachers and ministers would say he was in heaven—wherever that was—and was with Jesus, who was everywhere and nowhere, in the clouds or on the face of the earth—who really knew anyway? There was nothing solid for Robert to grasp, and he felt a panic clench his chest and set his heart to racing.

Luke is dead, Luke is dead, Luke is dead . . . The voice in his head wouldn't stop, and he dropped to his knees, his hands now fisted in his hair. He bent forward and touched his forehead to the cool floor, the tears again coming to his eyes. He stayed that way long into the night and didn't remember finally crawling, exhausted, to his bed.

* * *

Anne limped into the kitchen, fumbling in the darkness for a match. Finally lighting a lantern that sat on the wood surface of the worktable, she sank into a chair and gingerly stretched her leg. She winced in pain and frustration, elbows on the table, burying her face in her hands.

The melancholy that had settled over her since her return home had steadily worsened until she wondered each day how she would pull herself from bed in the mornings. She thought constantly of Ivar, wondering if he were still alive, and now, tonight, her father had brought the news of Luke's death. It made her throat hurt just thinking of it. How could he possibly be dead? She had worried about it in the back of her mind since his enlistment, but somehow she had assumed he would survive—that he would make it home alive and they would grow old sharing family stories together.

It hurt so very much! She could never have imagined that it would feel so horribly painful to lose someone she loved. In her life she hadn't experienced much death—only that of her elderly grandparents when she had been a child. This, though, this was vastly different. Luke had been young, handsome, and had such a future ahead of him! He was to have come home to marry Abigail and raise little black-haired babies with green eyes.

Anne rested her head in her arms on the table, the tears rolling out of her eyes and down toward her right temple. She looked at the countertops and the shelves that flickered in the lamplight, sideways to her view. *Just like my life right now,* she thought. *Sideways. Mad.*

A rustle at the doorway caused her to raise her head slightly. She wondered who else in the home was unable to sleep. To her surprise, it was Mary Birmingham, one of the family's seamstresses who had come north from her Uncle Jeffrey's plantation. She was a free woman now, and in the past weeks and in spite of Anne's sadness, Anne had noticed with a spark of satisfaction the glow about Mary's face and in her demeanor.

"I'm so sorry, Miss Anne," Mary said as she backed away from the door. "I didn't know you were here."

"No, please," Anne said, straightening her back a bit and motioning to an empty chair.

Mary retrieved two mugs and went about filling them with cool water from the kitchen's pump. She sat at the table, placing one mug in front of Anne, and wrapped her fingers around the other. Taking a small sip, she whispered, "I'm so very sorry."

Anne reached for Mary's hand and clasped her fingers. Her tears continued to fall, and she said nothing, just held the hand of the compassionate young woman. Eventually she wiped at her tears and took a sip of her water, enjoying the refreshing feel of the liquid as it trickled down her throat. It was all she had wanted since her return. At every meal, she drank water. She had often been so thirsty during her time with the regiment that she swore that when she returned home, she would drink water forever until her body would hold no more. It was tender of Mary to remember that. She could just as easily have brewed some tea or poured her a glass of brandy.

"He was so, so good," Anne murmured. "I know of very few people who share his integrity."

Mary nodded and sipped her water, letting Anne talk.

"I'll miss him so much. Things will not be the same again—ever. Just for a moment, I wish we were all here together."

Mary took a crisp, white handkerchief from the folds of her robe and offered it to Anne. It smelled clean and fresh, like life itself. "Why am I still here? How did I survive and Luke did not?" She dabbed at her eyes with the square of material. "I saw horrible things, awful things. I saw bodies . . ." Anne shuddered and felt the bile rise in her throat. Had her brother's body been torn to pieces like so many she'd seen fall in the field of battle? Did they desecrate him in the riots? Had he been dragged through the streets? James hadn't offered any details, and amazingly, nobody had asked. All her father had said was that he hadn't suffered. That didn't mean that what was left of him hadn't become something unrecognizably ruined.

She gagged, then, on the memories, and Mary stood. She moved to the pump, and Anne barely registered the sound of water being wrung from fabric. There was a brief pause, and then Mary returned, placing a cool, wet rag on the back of her neck. Anne laid her forehead on her hands, and Mary gently smoothed her hair, which was still short from her time as a soldier.

After a moment, Mary turned the cloth over, again placing the cool side down on Anne's skin. She felt Mary's slender fingers gently massage a tight spot between her shoulder blades that ached under her constant state of sadness and stress. The young woman's fingers worked at the knot in her muscles until Anne exhaled a shuddering sigh of relaxation. She wanted to stay in that moment forever—someone kind caring for her, working away her troubles and her pain. The tears continued to flow, and she said, "Mary, I don't know how I'll ever be happy again."

Mary's soft voice answered her as she continued to work gentle circles on Anne's back. "You will. But let yourself be sad first."

* * *

It was nearly dawn by the time Mary helped Anne to her bedroom on the second floor and then made her way up to the top floor to her own small room. Entering her bedroom always gave Mary a surge of joy, and tonight was no different, although the entire house seemed cloaked in pain. The smooth, wood floor and braided red rug, the neat bed and table—they were such comforts to Mary despite her troubled state of mind.

Luke Birmingham had indeed been a good person. She remembered him well from his visits to the plantation back when they were all young. He and Ben had been inseparable, looking alike, sounding alike except for the difference in accents, and showing a fun affection for each other that clearly suggested the two boys would have been friends even if they hadn't been related. It was a hard thing for the family to lose him, and she understood the reason for their grief.

She thought of Ben and wondered how he fared. It had been some time since she had received a letter from him—well before the battle at Gettysburg, Pennsylvania. When word had reached the other states—and it hadn't taken long—of the huge losses of life on both sides, she had feared for Ben's life. How ironic it was that both Birmingham boys survived that atrocious battle but that Luke should die such a short time later in a riot.

Mary tried to imagine what Ben was feeling, how he would react, what bearing Luke's death would have on his future. She could presume the answers to those things, but the truth was she didn't know him well of late. She had known his habits, his personality, everything about him when she'd been a young girl and he a young man, but all she knew of him as an adult was that he was extremely angry and frustrated with the social conditions in the South and that he fought for the Union to ensure some sort of justice.

Additionally, she knew Ben adored his cousin Luke. As much as she felt sorrow over Luke's death, she felt more fear for Ben's future. Would he be able to continue to go into battle with his mind focused on the task at hand? Would he keep his temper in check in his relationships with others in his regiment? Would he still value life enough to keep fighting, or would he take a nonchalant attitude toward death?

She climbed into her bed and chewed on her lip in worried contemplation. What a blessing it was that today was her day off. She had planned to go into town with some of her friends—other household servants—but would plead a headache instead and sleep as late as her tired body needed. In truth, although she had genuinely wanted to comfort Anne Birmingham in the kitchen when she had seen her sitting there, forlorn and grief-stricken, she had been grateful for selfish reasons that Anne was there. It gave Mary something else to think about rather than stewing over her own worries for a moment.

As she drifted off to sleep, her head aching with worry over Ben, she felt a tear seep from the corner of her eye and roll onto her pillow. It seemed she wasn't entirely immune to the family pain herself. Luke Birmingham had been a good, good man.

* * *

James Birmingham sat slumped over his desk in his study, a glass of untouched whiskey at his elbow. His family's grief left him feeling as though his heart had been torn from his chest. He had known it would be hard, yet it had been worse than he imagined. Finally, though, the sounds of anguish coming muffled from behind closed doors had subsided, and the household rested. It was James's turn to release his own torrent of emotion.

His head fell forward onto his arms, and the sobs erupted from somewhere deep inside, causing his shoulders to heave. Images of Luke's life flashed through James's mind, and he remembered his son as an infant, as a child, a young man, and finally an admirable adult. To know that Luke wouldn't walk through the front door and join the family for dinner ever again tore at him deeply.

James hadn't slept well since his visit to New York, and he was beginning to wonder if he ever would again. He had spent the better part of the night holding Elizabeth in his arms, and when she had finally fallen into an uneasy slumber, he had checked in on Jimmy, whose tearstained face rested against his pillow.

Now, as his own tears fell, he couldn't help but be grateful he'd been blessed with a son whose life had meant much to many people. To lose a child, however, was a new experience for James, and one he hoped never to repeat.

* * *

Across town, another household was finally settling into an exhausted sleep after spending a long night in misery. Abigail Van Dyke's eyelids fluttered for a moment, and she jerked awake, aware that something was wrong, but she couldn't remember what it was.

Camille's dreadful news returned to her mind, and she groaned, turning onto her side. The first rays of light were beginning to streak into the room through the open curtains. In the shadows she saw Camille, sprawled fully clothed minus only her shoes, sleeping fitfully next to her on her bed. The covers were not drawn back, the young women not dressed for bed. Abigail's attire was the same as Camille's, and even though she knew she was falling asleep, she couldn't summon the energy to rouse herself from the bed to change.

Camille's eyelids were swollen from crying, and she sighed in her sleep, as would a small child. Abigail reached for Camille, holding her best friend's hand tightly within her own. Camille unconsciously squeezed her hand in return and Abigail again fell into a troubled sleep, tears wetting her pillow as she dreamed of the man she was to have married.

* * *

Later that evening, miles away from Boston, Ben sat alone in the dark of the warm night, slowly pulling things from Luke's haversack. The campfire burned low, and he was forced to hold the items down close to it for thorough recognition. The first thing he retrieved was Luke's small grooming kit. He then pulled forth a small, leather-bound book that he momentarily set aside. He proceeded to pull out cooking utensils, a cup and tin plate, a bundle of letters from home, some fresh clothing, a Bible, and Ben's small, black copy of the Book of Mormon.

Inside the Book of Mormon was a picture of Abigail Van Dyke. Ben ran a finger over the picture in sad sympathy and wondered how the young woman would take the news. The whole family would be reeling in shock by now, and he felt their grief across the miles. It blended with his, and for a moment, it felt too heavy to bear.

He opened the small leather book and recognized it as Luke's journal. It was with a sense of guilt that he began to read it. It didn't seem right to intrude on his cousin's personal thoughts. Yet that was part of the purpose of keeping a record—so people could read it when one was gone. That Luke was actually gone still didn't seem real.

Ben angled the book toward the fire and read the words his cousin had written in a neat hand. Luke had written of his anxieties about going into battle, worries for the safety of his horse, concerns that he remember the drills and perform well. He wrote about his love for Abigail and his excitement when she had accepted his proposal. He detailed his continued devotion to the Abolition Society and his hope for the ultimate outcome of the war.

He wrote of his affection for Ben, of his concern for his safety, and also of his gratitude for baptizing him into the gospel of Christ. He had hoped to share his newfound knowledge with his family upon his return home and hoped they would find the joy and peace in it that he had.

Ben closed his eyes with a sense of dejection. Luke had allowed the joy of the gospel to seep into his soul even in the midst of all the horror. He had been right. Ben continually challenged it to comfort him; he was ever fighting feelings of anger and resentment toward his family, the South, everything that was unfair and unjust in life. Luke had taken the time to appreciate the joy but still maintain his concerns and ideals. He had balanced his responsibilities with an ease that Ben envied. Luke's final words to him rang constantly in his head; that last conversation at the fire replayed itself with clarity throughout his thoughts at all hours of the day.

Ben didn't want the companionship of the others in the regiment. They offered him condolences, shock at Luke's death, and expressed their sorrow, and while he was grateful for the support, he wanted solitude. Just for a while, he wanted time to be sad and alone—he didn't want to have to explain to anyone why he was upset, and didn't want anyone telling him they felt his pain. He was sure they did—everybody had lost *somebody* lately—but he wanted a few precious hours to feel his grief and somehow try to say good-bye.

Tears fell when he didn't think he had any left. He clung to his knowledge that Luke's separation from earth was a temporary one, that someday, somehow they would meet again in a better place.

CHAPTER 8

Use all the Negroes you can get, for the purpose for which you need—but don't arm them. The day you make soldiers out of them is the beginning of the end of the revolution. If slaves will make good soldiers our whole theory of slavery is wrong.
—Howell Cobb, former governor of Georgia

* * *

22 July 1863
En route to Morehead City, North Carolina

Joshua Birmingham looked out over the blue expanse of water and sky, wiping the sweat from his brow. His mind wandered again over the details, as they had many, many times in the past few days, of the battle that had engaged the 54th Massachusetts colored troops in Charleston, South Carolina.

Had Joshua enlisted earlier, he might well have been among their doomed yet heroic ranks. As it was, the 55th, of which he was currently a part, had joined with the nucleus of those left over from the 54th. He wondered if he'd have a chance to prove his bravery as those other men had.

Led by Robert Gould Shaw, the 54th Massachusetts had stormed Fort Wagner in Charleston, and the loss of life had been staggering for the volunteers who were among the first officially raised and recognized the colored troops in the North. Shaw had given his life as well, and in his mind's eye, when Joshua thought of the white man who had been of a wealthy, staunchly abolitionist Boston family, he saw Ben. He was certain Ben would have done the same had he been in Shaw's shoes.

It was such a victory for the black man! Those brave souls had proven that they could not only learn and take orders, but that they could act with decisiveness and valor, that they were worthy citizens of the United States. Joshua's heart swelled with pride when he thought of them, relishing in the right to defend themselves. Frederick Douglass had long called for the Union government to allow the Negro to enlist and fight for his own rights; now it was a reality, and though the deaths were sad, what those men had done that day in South Carolina was much bigger than they knew. Joshua felt it in his heart.

His regiment was ultimately headed for Folly Island, just south of Charleston. How ironic that only a few months before, he had escaped to freedom from this very place. He knew he must be insane to revisit it, to risk capture and death or slavery, but he had no choice in the matter. His reasons for enlistment were ones he scarcely understood but by which he felt compelled nonetheless.

Protect me, God, he thought as he squinted against the sunlight, *and I will do good things with my life. I promise it.* He felt at peace even though he might well be sailing to his own death. He hadn't lied, however. If his life was preserved, Joshua had made up his mind that he would work to make life better for his countrymen, to see that his black brothers and sisters in the South learned to live lives of freedom side by side with their white counterparts. He did not delude himself for a moment that the task would be simple. But it was a worthy one, and well worth his time.

* * *

3 August 1863
New Orleans, Louisiana

Daniel O'Shea stared at the words Marie had written him nearly three weeks before. He only now had received her letter; he should be grateful, really. The mail traveled by ship, and because he was with the navy and easy to find, he wasn't forced to wait out interminable delays the Union army did when anticipating mail. For this particular letter, however, he almost wished it *had* been delayed.

Gavin, dead. He closed his eyes against the pain and felt the tears form. First his brother, Colin, and now his father. And Marie's first day with his family—the glorious meeting he had imagined with such joy—was the very day that Gavin's body was brought home to his mother. He scanned through the rest of Marie's letter, loving her all the more for the obvious pain she felt at having to deliver the news to him. She was no stranger to the loss of a father; she mentioned to him in her letter that she knew full well how much it hurt.

He was grateful, so grateful, that Marie was in New York with Brenna. Daniel hated to imagine his mother living in her grief alone. The neighbors were friendly, but truly her best friend had been her husband, and Daniel wasn't sure to whom Brenna would have turned for comfort. Tears of tender gratitude for his wife mixed in with his tears of agony over the news, and he tried to keep quiet. He was one of just a few who were taking advantage of a free afternoon aboard ship down in the area where he and many other men hung their hammocks for the night. He didn't want to attract attention to himself, though. He didn't want to have to say aloud, "My father is dead."

He hadn't died in battle, hadn't even been an enlisted soldier! How very like Gavin it was to lose his life in defending another. Daniel shook his head and gritted his teeth together as he imagined the scene. His father had always been so idealistic, so full of hope in mankind. He believed in people's inherent goodness and in the ideals of the United States of America more than anything else. The rioting would have been entirely too much for Gavin to stand by and watch; in his own way, he defended his country as much as Daniel did in his sailor's uniform.

"Da," Daniel whispered aloud as his tears fell onto Marie's letter, smudging the ink. He watched her neat script feather and spread in the moisture. *I never told you good-bye! Couldn't you have waited until I got home? You'll never see my children! They'll never know their grandfather—either grandfather!*

People were ignorant and cruel—Gavin's death reinforced what Daniel had come to believe as a young Irish child growing up in New York City. There were some who possessed good hearts, but the rest were self-serving and when pushed, murderous. Daniel had always depended on his father to supply the optimism and faith in people that Daniel so very much lacked. Now he was gone. Who would help him?

Without thinking, he looked back down at the letter from his wife and felt a measure of peace. Marie might not possess

Gavin's naïveté about people as a whole, but she waited until she knew a person before she judged him. She was solid and strong, and as she was now lending her strength to Brenna, Daniel knew she would be a strength for him as well.

* * *

Boston, Massachusetts

Jenny Brissot closed her small traveling case with a snap and turned to the two young women who had been her strength in the months since Jean-Pierre's death. "I do believe I have everything," she said with a sigh. "I hate to tell the two of you good-bye."

She stretched her arms toward Abigail, who embraced her and smoothed her back.

"I will miss you, Aunt Jenny," Abigail said. "You filled a void my mother left."

"And I will miss you, Abby. Thank you so much for opening your home to me." Jenny released the woman with a misty smile and turned to her niece. "Cammy," she said, hugging her, "you behave yourself."

"Oh, I like that. You tell Abby you'll miss her. You tell me to behave myself. Why is that, I wonder?"

Jenny laughed and pulled back, running the back of her finger along Camille's cheek. "You have a look in your eyes, young lady, that makes me wonder what you're thinking. Something mischievous, I'm sure. I love you." She pulled her sister's daughter close for one more quick hug, then turned and retrieved her traveling case.

"The rest of your luggage is already aboard the carriage," Abigail said, folding her arms across her midsection. "It's waiting outside."

"Thank you." She kissed each young woman on the cheek and made her way down the stairs of the classic colonial home and out the front walk. Climbing into the carriage with the assistance of the coachman, she waved out the small window. She had bid her farewells to her sister and the rest of the Birminghams earlier in the day; she had saved her good-byes to Camille and Abigail for last. "I'll write to you as soon as I get to New York," she called to them, and watched out the back window of the carriage until she turned a corner and the sight of them, arms around each other's waists and waving, was no longer visible.

Jenny settled back into the seat then, marveling once again at her sister and brother-in-law's generosity. James and Elizabeth surfaced from their grief over Luke's death long enough to insist that one of their personal carriages and coachmen accompany her to New York and her new home with Marie and Brenna O'Shea.

A week earlier, Jenny received a letter from Marie stating that not only had she married the man with whom she'd been exchanging mail, she was now living with his mother in New York. Jenny felt an instant kinship with this woman she'd never met, who had just lost her husband because of other people's cruelty. She had been touched as well by the fact that Brenna very generously offered her home to Jenny. She seemed to feel that there was no reason the three of them shouldn't spend time together and help one another.

As Jenny reviewed the past two years in her mind, she couldn't help but feel a sense of loss. Marie hinted at something that had happened in New Orleans to their home; Jenny could only assume her husband's enemies had taken their final revenge and destroyed it. She had no home and no husband. She was dependent upon the generosity of family, and generally being a woman of independent nature, this gnawed at her. She had always assumed that when the war was over, she would return to her home in New Orleans. But now not only did she not have a home, Marie wasn't even there anymore.

There was nothing for her in the South but memories of her tender husband and child. Somehow she would have to build a new life for herself and make herself useful to someone. There still had to be a purpose for her. God had seen fit to leave her on the earth instead of taking her home as He had Jean-Pierre. She couldn't wallow in self-pity forever. The time had come to find someone or something to serve.

CHAPTER 9

It is heart-sickening to see what I have seen here. . . . A desolated country and men and women and children some of them almost naked. Some on foot and some in old wagons.
—Union officer and eyewitness to the exodus of the Burnt District

* * *

23 August 1863
Charleston, South Carolina
Bentley Plantation

Emily's eyes jumped again to the top of her cousin Anne's letter with a sense of sadness and horror, ignoring the pain that stretched across her abdomen. She had thought to lose herself in mail from up north to avoid growing consumed by the discomfort that signaled her child would soon arrive, but, according to Ruth, not quite yet. "Here," Ruth had said. "Distract yourself with this." She had handed her Anne's letter, and Emily had looked forward to a bit of good news.

It was anything but that. Luke was dead, and Ben was fiercely mourning. Anne didn't seem herself either. She hadn't been, of course, since returning from the battlefield, and Emily couldn't blame her. Anne's letters contained a sense of melancholy that was completely unlike the Anne of former years.

Emily continued reading and came upon Anne's account of recent news concerning a raid in Lawrence, Kansas, that had seen over 150 unarmed men and boys ruthlessly murdered in front of their wives, sisters, and daughters. William Quantrill, a man who had begun his raiding first as a Union supporter and now as a Confederate, had led the raiders. He and his men had apparently been seeking revenge for the deaths of some of their women supporters who had died in Union captivity, crushed in the collapse of a dilapidated old house. The town had been summarily looted and burned, all except the saloon, whose inventory they plundered before riding on.

In retaliation, the Union general Ewing ordered the evacuation of nearly four counties' worth of citizens near the Kansas-Missouri border in an effort to stem the support given to Quantrill and his band of marauders. The citizens' homes were looted and burned to the ground, leaving ten thousand people homeless and living on the plains.

Emily's head reeled as she read the news that Anne had dutifully shared, a sense of her own sorrow infused in each line. Madness! The whole of it seemed utterly inhuman to Emily. The war had drawn from the woodwork people of differing degrees of brutality and evil, and the chaos that had abounded for a long time now in both Kansas and Missouri was staggering. People were being murdered by lawless bands of crazed men for crimes as small as feeding Union soldiers—or Confederates, for that matter. It was with a sense of sadness that Emily had read the newspapers in recent months only to realize that many in the North were every bit as ignorant and cruel as many in the slaveholding South. She had come of age believing the Union citizens were all of a like mind with her Bostonian relatives.

With a sigh, she ran a hand across her burgeoning midsection and winced a bit as the pain increased in intensity. It was happening with more frequency now—she'd have to find Ruth and tell her. As she contemplated rising from her chair in the parlor, she scanned the rest of Anne's letter, the final paragraph sending her a jolt of shock so great she completely forgot she was about to give birth.

And now, Emily, I finally have some good news to share with you, Anne wrote. *Your father is not only alive, but is on his way home to you—he was picked up by a Union ship somewhere in the Atlantic. Father arranged his release from imprisonment in New York and has helped secure him transportation home. I thought you might appreciate the news so that you might anticipate his homecoming.*

Emily read the paragraph three times before she knew what to make of it. Jeffrey was actually alive? And on his way home? Wonders would never cease, she mused as she stared, openmouthed, into the hall visible through the open door of the parlor. And then, the final surprise of all, Emily felt tears form in her eyes. Her father was alive and coming home. Maybe he could help somehow—help them all stay alive and safe until the war was over. She still hadn't heard from Austin, and it had been months since she had received word that he'd been wounded in battle at Chancellorsville. The thought that Jeffrey was coming home somehow made her breathe a bit easier despite the fact that she had never found comfort in his presence before.

A cry escaped her lips as the pain intensified, and she rose awkwardly to find Ruth. She tried to fight a sense of panic at the coming ordeal, and thoughts of Jeffrey and Austin faded from the forefront as she slowly made her way from the parlor.

* * *

2 September 1863
Boston, Massachusetts

Abigail Van Dyke closed the front door behind the back of the retreating private investigator. She watched Camille descend the stairs without really seeing her. "What is it?" Cammy asked, approaching her in some concern.

"The man I've hired to investigate mother's death," she said. At Camille's nod, she continued. "They have someone in custody who admits he was hired to inflict harm on some of the Society's more influential members."

Camille gripped Abigail's arm and led her into the sitting room on the left. "Who hired him?" she asked, drawing Abigail onto the sofa.

"He won't say."

Camille's expressive face gave away her every thought. She looked frustrated and disgusted. "They should *make* him say!"

"How are they going to do that?" Abigail asked her, looking out the window at the leaves on the trees, soon to turn colors and fall to the ground. "They can't very well torture him."

"I would."

"That's why you're not a policeman."

Camille snorted in a derisive huff, and Abigail could feel the energy radiating from her friend. Camille was so full of life. There was something about the young woman that lit up a room, even when she was angry. Abigail looked back at her and tried to summon a smile.

"Perhaps with the right inducements he'll eventually admit who hired him." She examined the drawn expression about Camille's eyes and imagined that her own looked much more severe. "I feel old," she admitted to her friend. "Death is making me feel old."

Camille's face softened, and she winced a bit. She pulled Abigail forward into her arms and rocked her much as would a mother with a young child. "I am so sorry," she whispered in Abigail's ear. "I would give you the moon if I could."

"I know." A knock at the front door drew Abigail from the tender embrace, and she sighed, making her way to the entrance and waving the young parlor maid aside. "I'll answer it," she said.

On the other side of the door stood Robert Birmingham, looking young and yet somehow bearing the same aged expression about the eyes and in the small, drawn lines near his mouth as Camille now wore. Abigail managed a smile for him and held the door wide. "Well," she said, forcing some levity into her voice. "To what do we owe such a pleasant surprise?"

Robert's lips twitched into a bit of a smile as he entered the home carrying a small box. "I have something for you," he said.

She gestured for him to enter the sitting room, where Camille turned to see who had arrived. A look of surprised pleasure lifted her features, and she smiled at her brother. "Hello, Robert," she said, and rose to plant a kiss on his cheek. He settled into a chair opposite the sofa and laid the box he carried on the low coffee table between them.

"These are some things Ben sent home, things of Luke's," he said, clearing his throat gruffly, "and we thought you might like to have them." He glanced up at Abigail, his face at once apologetic and kind.

Abigail lifted the simple wooden lid and found inside letters she had written to Luke, a photograph of herself, and a simple, small ring of her own she had given him to remember her by when he'd enlisted and left for war. Tears formed, burning her eyes, and it surprised her. She didn't think she had any more to cry. Neatly folded, at the bottom of the box, was one of Luke's handkerchiefs, embroidered with his initials in dark blue thread. She took it and held it to her face, her tears falling all the more when she realized it still carried slight traces of his scent.

"I'm sorry," Robert whispered. He leaned forward, his elbows on his knees, and looked into her face. "We're all so very sorry, Abby."

"Oh, Robert," she sighed, trying to pull her emotions into check. "Your whole family is grieving, and yet you all apologize to me as if it were my pain alone."

"We feel . . . I feel . . ."

"Responsible? That's silly," Abigail sniffed, wanting to ease the burden for him.

"Something that was a part of us was . . . promised to you . . . and now it's gone." Robert spread his hands as though trying to make sense of what he was saying, and yet somehow she knew what he meant.

"You Birminghams are all so noble," she mumbled into the handkerchief and closed her eyes hard. On a pained, shuddering sigh, she opened them again and smiled through her tears at Robert, who looked grim and much too mature for a boy just turning eighteen, and at Camille, whose eyes were filled with her own tears. "I love you both very much," Abigail said. "You give me comfort, and I do appreciate it."

Robert nodded but still looked as though there were things he wished to say.

"Are you not well?" Camille murmured toward him, dabbing at her tears with a lacy handkerchief she had kept perpetually tucked into her dress since the news of Luke's death.

"No less than you, I suppose," he answered with a bit of a sigh.

"There's something else."

He sat back in the chair, running an agitated hand through his hair. "I'm enlisting," he finally said, and the silence following his pronouncement roared.

"Pardon me?" Camille finally asked, her tone flat. "I don't think I heard you correctly. I'm sure you meant to say that you're going to spend three hundred dollars to hire a replacement for yourself. All the wealthy men in the North have done that very thing—there's no reason for you not to as well."

"Cammy, really. You don't expect me to take the coward's way out. The Conscription Act is unfair, and you well know it. This city still smolders from the aftereffects of the rioting. I can't ignore it, nor does Father expect me to. He wanted me to take advantage of Senator Crompton's offer to see me 'well placed' with a regiment. Something about mustering me in as a quartermaster."

"What are you going to do instead?" Abigail asked, her mouth suddenly going dry.

"I'm signing on in Luke's place," he admitted after an obviously reluctant pause. "I'll join Ben by the end of the month."

Camille rose from the sofa in one swift, angry movement. "You are insane," she stated, the full force of her reaction directed toward her brother, who watched her warily from his chair. "Absolutely insane! Have you forgotten Bull Run? Flying limbs, dead bodies?"

"I haven't forgotten."

"Then how can you do this thing?" she demanded, her tears flowing freely. Abigail hurt for her. "You'll put Mother and Father through the death of yet another son? It's selfish! You're being selfish, Robert!"

"Cammy . . ."

"No! Don't try to explain this to me," she choked out. "I won't hear it! You are sending yourself off to die without even considering the effect it will have on this family. I cannot comprehend why, when it can be avoided, you won't do it!" She turned and rushed around the sofa, out of the room, and up the stairs. Abigail heard a door slam above them.

She closed her eyes for a moment and then opened them, looking at Robert, who seemed stricken. "I thought she would understand," he mumbled.

"She doesn't want to lose another brother," Abigail told him quietly. "Camille is a passionate person. Once she thinks things through, she'll calm herself a bit. Give her time to accept your news."

"I'm sorry," he said, his face reddening.

"Robert Birmingham, if you don't stop apologizing to me I'll be offended."

"Right," he said, moving to stand. "Sorry."

She couldn't help but laugh a little, and she stood, moving to embrace him. She gave him a small squeeze and said, "Come back in a week or so. She'll have forgiven you by then."

Robert surprised her by placing a kiss on the top of her head. "Thank you," he said.

She walked him to the front door and saw him out, hoping with all her might that he would not meet the same fate as had his brother.

CHAPTER 10

I . . . do order and declare that all persons held as slaves . . . are, and henceforward shall be free; and that the Executive Government of the United States, including the Military and Naval authorities, thereof, will recognize and maintain the freedom of said persons. . . . And upon this, sincerely believed to be an act of justice, warranted by the Constitution . . . I invoke the considerate judgment of mankind and the gracious favor of Almighty God.

—Text from Lincoln's Emancipation Proclamation

* * *

6 September 1863
Charleston, South Carolina
Bentley Plantation

As Jeffrey rounded the corner and proceeded down the long drive toward his home, he could only stare in shock at the state of the grounds. The fields were empty and forlorn, the flowers wild and overgrown, and as he neared the house itself he could see patches where time and weather had beaten away at the exterior walls.

The horse plodded slowly along, a pace somehow appropriate for Jeffrey's dampened mood. It wasn't as though he hadn't anticipated this very outcome; he had known from the start that the Confederacy was doomed to fail. Fevers still ran high in some areas, true, as people refused to admit defeat, but the South was slowly being strangled to death, and the fact of the matter was that there just were not enough resources—time or men—to continue the fight much longer. He had no doubt that they would keep hurling everything they had at the Union, but in the end, it would be to no avail, he was sure of it.

The road home from New York had been long and cumbersome, and he felt weary to his bones. He acknowledged a sense of defeat as he brought the horse to a stop in front of the wide, palatial porch with its magisterial columns and soaring windows. He was not defeated because of the war, though—he had been a beaten man for years.

Jeffrey had five children, one now dead, and no relationship to speak of with any of them. After conversing with Ben, he had allowed a small spark to kindle a flame of hope that things might become different with his oldest son, that somehow he might be able to capture some of what he had allowed to slip away when the children were small. As for the immediate future, he had a wife who had disdained him for the bulk of their marriage and who was now completely unaware he even existed, and a home that had never been his.

His mind flashed back to the first moment he had seen his future wife. Sarah Matthews was petite and fiery, beautiful and captivating. She held court with a gaggle of suitors at every social event she attended, always remaining aloof when the inevitable proposals rolled around. She said she was waiting for "the right man," and she finally settled on Jeffrey Birmingham, a man of no means but plenty of charm. He had been a Yankee, true, but Sarah was willing to overlook that irritating fact. They were everything to each other that they felt they needed; Jeffrey needed money and status, and Sarah needed a man she could control.

* * *

"She's not herself, Mr. Birmingham," Ruth told Jeffrey quietly as they roamed the halls of the mansion, slowly making their way to Sarah's suite of rooms on the second floor. "She hasn't been since we received word of your disappearance."

Jeffrey nodded. "I know. Ben told me."

Ruth paused for a moment, her eyes lighting up at the mention of his son. "Is he well?"

"Seems to be. He's mourning the loss of his cousin, though."

Ruth nodded. "Anne sent word." She paused then, seeming to search for the right words. "Sarah's but a shade of her former self. She eats only when I sit with her and insist. She occasionally walks the grounds, but it's never apparent to me what she's thinking. When she does speak, she's in another world. She's a young girl again, asking for her father."

Jeffrey tried to absorb the woman's words, but he couldn't form a reply.

"Perhaps seeing you will help her. I've tried everything I can think of, but she just won't respond."

"What of my children? Emily is in Savannah, I presume?"

"No, actually, she's here. She just gave birth to a healthy little girl."

Jeffrey felt another surge of hope in his chest. Emily was at Bentley—it was another chance at absolution. He would see her as soon as he'd visited Sarah.

"And where is Charlotte?"

"She is at the town house this week with her son. Said she needed to escape for a bit. She grew rather melancholy one day, but won't explain why."

Jeffrey took in this news, wondering how to reach his oldest daughter, whom he knew even less than Emily. "Is she still devoted to the Confederacy?"

"She doesn't seem to be, not as she used to. Little Will keeps her busy. Charlotte has improved much in spirits in spite of the war. Although worried, she seems much more at peace than I have ever seen her. Clara is well also. She and Rose both."

Jeffrey glanced askance at the woman who walked beside him, tall and composed. "I appreciate your efforts, Ruth. Things have changed—I know full well that you could have left this place by now." He gestured toward the walls bearing portraits of Sarah's ancestors. "This house has been a prison for many of us. I once mentioned to you that in my adult life I have been as much a slave as you. You seemed to resent the comparison."

Ruth looked back at him but remained silent, her expression giving away nothing.

"Please. I would know of your opinion."

"Very well. Yes, I do remember the occasion, and I did resent the comparison. You could leave any time you chose. I've never had that option."

"True. But I have come to realize that I was a slave of my own making. I lacked the courage to leave or to challenge my wife for an equal share in our family's doings. I have failed as a father, as a husband, and as an individual. I felt I had nothing in this world without Sarah and this plantation, and she knew it."

"Yes, she did. It was to your misfortune and hers as well that she used it against you. Sarah did not do herself any favors by denying herself the equal companionship of a good man."

Jeffrey let the comment fall without responding. His mind wandered over events and places of the past, coming to rest on the present. "I am a grandfather now."

"Yes, three times over."

A weight settled heavy in Jeffrey's heart. "Yes. Sarah spoke of it briefly before I left for England. I don't suppose . . ." Jeffrey rubbed a hand across his brow. How did a man ask a woman if his son had forced himself upon her granddaughter? "Was Mary a willing . . . recipient of Richard's attentions?"

The look of scorn upon Ruth's face was answer enough. Still, she replied, "No. Mary did not care for Richard in the least. Do you suppose that because she was a slave, she placed so little value on her virtue?"

Jeffrey flushed. "Is Mary here? I should very much like to speak with her—to somehow . . ."

"Mary is in Boston."

Jeffrey stopped walking and faced the woman he'd known as long as and almost as well as his own wife. "Ruth," he said, reaching for her hand. "I am so very sorry. For a lifetime of ills, I am sorry." His eyes and throat burned. "Mary's child—have you ever seen him? Is he well?"

"I haven't seen him in some time. I hear he is well enough."

"We share blood then, Ruth—my grandchild and your great-grandchild. I shall visit the Charlesworths tomorrow."

Ruth looked back at him with an inscrutable expression, but she remained silent.

"Do you miss your husband, Ruth?"

"Every day."

Jeffrey looked again at Ruth for a long moment, contemplating her fine, strong bone structure, clear skin, and neat, black hair pulled into a bun. There were a few strands of gray hair streaked into the black, and it made her appear all the more wise. "You're a beautiful person. In another life, we might have been fine friends."

The corner of her mouth quirked up in half of a smile. Her brown eyes took in his face and seemed to see much more, clear into his soul. "Yes. In another life."

"I might not have been strong enough for you either," he murmured.

"I would have allowed you to be." Ruth turned and walked the few remaining steps to the threshold of Sarah's sitting room. "Your wife, sir," she said, gesturing within.

"Thank you, Ruth." Jeffrey looked inside the room to see Sarah's silhouette against the window. Her back was to him, and she looked out over the plantation fields that were now barren and bereft of their former meticulous care.

Jeffrey stood at the doorway and listened to Ruth's retreating footsteps as she left and made her way back to the main floor until he heard nothing but silence. He took a deep breath and wondered at his trembling. The Sarah who occupied the room was not the woman he'd grown accustomed to in past years, and he was unsure of how to approach her.

"Sarah," he finally said, softly so as not to startle her. She made no answering gesture, but remained as she was. He worked his way into the room, glancing down at the carpet, once fine, and now shabby and threadbare. When he reached her side, he placed a hand on her arm.

"Sarah, I've come home."

She finally turned her head to look at him, and he swallowed once, hard, at her appearance. Never a very large woman, she now couldn't have weighed more than one hundred pounds. Her skin was pale, and the circles under her eyes testified of distress and inadequate sleep. "Jeffrey," she whispered, and he felt a spark of hope at her recognition of him. "I can't find my father. He's been taking ever so long with his errands in town."

His hope sank at her words. "It's all right, Sarah. I'm here to care for you. Would you like that?"

She seemed confused. "Yes, yes, I think I would. Just until Father returns. Then he will take care of me and of Bentley."

"Of course."

* * *

Emily stared at the man in her doorway. It took some time before she could think of anything to say.

"May I sit down with you for a moment?"

She nodded, still unable to form any words. She cradled her tiny, sleeping daughter in her arms. Jeffrey sat in a chair opposite hers, near the empty hearth, and motioned to the baby.

"She's beautiful, Emily, as are you. You look well."

"Thank you," she finally said. "I . . . Welcome home. I'm glad you're not sitting at the bottom of the North Atlantic."

He smiled. "Now there's the Emily I remember." He motioned to Emily's baby. "What is her name?"

"Mary Alice. Mary for my best friend, and Alice for Austin's mother."

He nodded. "Very nice."

There was silence, then, and Emily was at a complete loss as to how it should be filled. She felt tears form and bit her lip to stop the trembling. Since the birth of Mary Alice, she had been nothing but a crying puddle.

Jeffrey looked slightly alarmed. "Do you need something? Shall I summon Ruth?"

"No, no." Emily waved a hand at him. "I cry all the time lately. Ruth tells me it will pass."

Her father visibly relaxed, as though grateful he wasn't the cause of her distress. "I seem to remember your mother being much the same."

Emily laughed. "I cannot even envision such a thing."

"It's true. She never let me witness it, though. I only heard it through the closed door."

"Very fitting."

"Yes, I suppose it was." Jeffrey smiled, but Emily saw a hint of sadness. "You always did understand this family much better than I ever imagined."

Emily shrugged, trying to shake off a stab of emotional pain. Years of resentment tried to surface, and it was only with a valiant effort that she shoved them back down.

Jeffrey shifted a bit in his chair, changing the vein of conversation. "I hope to help your mother," he said. "Ben offered a suggestion I've been considering."

Emily examined Jeffrey's trail-worn, dusty clothing and imagined he must have had quite a bit of thinking time as he'd traveled home. It had been weeks since he left New York, according to Anne's letter.

"Ben wonders if a change of scenery might do Sarah some good."

Emily's curiosity was piqued. "Oh?"

"He thinks I should take her west to the Utah Territory."

Emily felt herself staring. "Leave Bentley?"

"Leave Bentley." Jeffrey nodded, his expression firm and resolute.

"Mercy," Emily murmured to herself. "Are you thinking this will be a permanent situation?"

Jeffrey sighed. "I don't know, Emily. The only thing I'm sure of is that I need to get Sarah away from here. Whether or not we'll ever return is something I don't have an answer for."

"What will happen to Bentley?"

* * *

Ruth was restless. She couldn't sit still wondering how Sarah had received her husband after believing him dead. The old Sarah would have remained composed, taking everything in stride. She would have been angry she had been misinformed and demand that someone apologize.

And now that Jeffrey had returned, what did that mean for Ruth? Should she stay? Keep running the plantation until the Union blue swarmed over the land and burned everything to the ground? It wouldn't have bothered her so much on a sentimental level, she mused as she studied the library she now stood in, except that this had been her home for nearly her whole life, and she wasn't sure where she would go if it were gone.

Later that evening, Jeffrey sat at the dining room table with Ruth, Emily, and a handful of servants. "Please," he had said, waving a hand in their direction when they realized the lord of the manor was home again and would probably not want to dine with his slaves, "carry on as you have been. I would be happy for the company." He paused for a moment as he examined his plate. "This is impressive fare for such dire times, Ruth," he said as he sliced a knife through a boiled potato. "How have you managed?"

"We've been resourceful," she answered, casting a scrutinizing glance at Jeffrey. He appeared tired, but there was a strength to him she wasn't sure she'd ever seen—a set to his jaw, perhaps, that spoke of resolve. "How did Sarah receive you?"

His nod was curt. "Well enough—she recognized me, but is still waiting for her father to materialize. Perhaps if I can spend some time with her—draw her out of her sitting room—she may improve."

"Will you be called on to make any more diplomatic missions?"

Jeffrey shook his head. "Mr. Davis has sent me home to 'see to matters on a local level.' There's not much here for me to do."

"Will you enlist?"

Jeffrey looked at her with a flat expression. "Do you believe in this cause, Ruth?"

Surely he couldn't mean for her to answer his question.

"Do you believe in the Confederate cause?" he repeated.

"Of course not," she finally said.

Emily remained uncharacteristically silent.

"Neither do I." Jeffrey took a swallow from his glass and set it down again with a definitive *thump*. "I never have. I see no need for further pretense. My heart has never supported this conflict. I thought it madness from the very beginning."

Jeffrey continued eating while the rest of the table's occupants watched him with slack jaws, forks midair. When he glanced up again and noticed their stunned reactions, he looked a combination of amusement and chagrin. He said nothing further, however, and they all resumed the meal in comfortable silence.

* * *

Later that evening as he lay exhausted in his bed, Jeffrey couldn't help but wonder if he weren't morbid to the core to be feeling such . . . such . . . he couldn't put a finger on it, and *happiness* certainly wasn't the right word. He felt that all would be well, though, and he knew that he would be the one, with the merciful help of Providence, to bring it about.

His family's welfare was in his hands, and the urge to find a way to get them away from Charleston was overwhelming. He knew he needed to find a fresh start for Sarah, and he also knew that he loved her. He loved the woman at the root of who she was. He had seen glimpses of her through the years, and he hoped to bring her out in the remaining time they had together.

He hoped for a continuing improvement in his relationship with Ben, and he hoped to achieve a closeness with his daughters. They were good people, all of them, and he wanted to know them better, to spend the rest of his days being a better father to them.

The moonlight shone through a gap in the curtains and cast his surroundings in a gentle glow. He looked at the objects in the room that had been his companions from the first days of his marriage. They were things that had belonged to Sarah's father, and before him had belonged to *his* father . . . there was little in the room, except for clothing, that belonged exclusively to Jeffrey.

It was time for a change. Time to fully admit to his family and to the world that the Confederacy would never stand on its own and that trying to divide the United States had been not only unfortunate but also very, very sad, from the beginning. It was time for Jeffrey to claim a life of his own and take care of his family. He could think of no better way of doing so than by beginning anew and afresh.

As he drifted into much-needed sleep, he realized it was contentment he felt. Contentment with who he was, with who he was working to become. He hadn't been proud of himself in a long, long time.

CHAPTER 11

The world has seen its iron age, its silver age, its golden age and its brazen age. This is the age of shoddy . . . the new equipages at the park, the new diamonds which dazzle unaccustomed eyes, the new silks and satins which rustle over loudly, as if to demand attention, the new people who live in the palaces and ride in the carriages and wear the diamonds and silks—all are shoddy. From the devil's dust they sprang and unto the devil's dust they shall return.

—New York Herald

* * *

10 September 1863
New York, New York

"Over here, Jenny, I think," Brenna's voice called across the room. "I believe I saw someone putting them away in these cupboards."

Marie smiled as her mother made her way to Daniel's mother's side and withdrew a clean sheet from one of the cupboards in the large, dormitory-type room that served as an orphanage for many of the city's orphans, both colored and white. Jenny made a comment to Brenna that had the

Irish woman laughing. Brenna was beginning to smile more—something she'd rarely done since Gavin's death when Marie had first met her—and to live again with her own mother and see her regain some of her own happiness as well was all Marie felt she could ask for. Once her husband came home, she would finally and fully relax.

Brenna and Jenny worked alongside a few other women who had taken it upon themselves to see to safe housing and schooling for the young orphans, especially in the aftermath of the draft riots. The children were innocent, and it had broken Marie's heart to see their tattered conditions and forlorn expressions shortly after the rioting masses had burned their only home. Since opening the new orphanage, many more young orphans of all nationalities had surfaced, and the building was near to capacity.

Marie sorted through her school bag and retrieved the items she'd planned to use for the day's lessons. Then, picking up the bag and calling to the children, she led them into an adjacent room that housed supplies purchased with money donated from some of the city's wealthier citizens. She settled the children into their places at the small, wooden desks and began the day with a storybook. Soon, the young faces were enthralled with the tale, and for a moment their concerns appeared to melt away. They were just children with nothing more required of them than that they attend school and learn as much as their fertile minds would absorb.

For the time that Marie taught them, there was no war, no rioting, no hunger, no pain. It was as much a blessing to her as to the children. To be teaching again warmed the place in her heart that had suffered when she'd been forced to stop instructing her young pupils in New Orleans.

Some days, when Brenna and Jenny had finished with their duties of straightening and cleaning clothing and bedding, and the other rooms of the orphanage shone and smelled fresh to their satisfaction, they crept quietly into the back of the classroom. When the time came for the children to work individually at their studies, the older women walked from desk to desk, helping when asked and praising regardless of the level of achievement.

Later in the day, toward evening, when the children had been fed and bathed, Marie and her two mothers left the orphanage in the capable hands of the young women who stayed the night with the children. They made their way toward home in an open carriage pulled by two horses.

As they traveled through town, Marie took note of the extravagance of many of the other carriages and their contents. It seemed that riches had become the order of the day. The more money one possessed—and soon spent on extravagant things—the more popular and admired that person became. Marie glanced at the two women by her side and hid a smile. For all that Marie thought people were behaving ridiculously with their money, Jenny and Brenna were downright disgusted. They had each spent a lifetime married to men who worked hard for the money they earned and had learned to be frugal and careful with that money. To see it tossed willy-nilly on carriages, horses, furs, and diamonds set their teeth on edge, the both of them.

Marie had seen an article in the *New York Herald* calling this new worship of money the "shoddy age." When Marie thought of her own husband working hard to finish his enlistment and of all those soldiers whose lives were in peril daily, she had to agree that the showy lifestyles many of the citizens were embracing were in poor taste indeed.

As if thinking along the same lines, Brenna said, "I met a woman when we were in town this morning. Her home is in Gettysburg."

Marie and Jenny were instantly attentive, as many were at the very mention of the town in Pennsylvania.

"How is she faring?" Jenny asked.

Brenna's face twisted in a grimace. "They *still* must contend with the aftermath of the battle. You remember that many of the dead were buried shallowly in the first days?"

Marie and her mother nodded.

"This woman told me that many people come from out of town trying to find their dead and take them home for burial. They disrupt the other graves and leave them in a worse condition than they found them. There are often body parts, if you can imagine, protruding from the ground." Brenna's face took on a slightly green shade but she continued talking as though the thought of keeping the awful details to herself would weigh too heavily on her mind.

"That's awful," Jenny whispered.

"Yes, and there are farmers who have had to work around bodies buried in their fields—there are large lumps everywhere—on personal property, in open fields, every place one can imagine."

Marie groaned. For days, they had heard, after the battle was over, the stench of death in and around Gettysburg, Pennsylvania, coupled with the horrific sight of corpses whose conditions worsened in the summer heat, burdened the citizens of the small farming community. It was rumored that they buried bodies, retched, and then got back to the business of burying more bodies. Dead horses were also burned, adding to the awful smell.

"War is not a glorious thing," Marie murmured as they passed a woman who laughed a little too loudly and whose diamonds sparkled a little too brightly in the waning sun.

* * *

Confederate prison camp, Tennessee

Ivar Gundersen took stock of his surroundings as he walked the perimeter of the temporary prison camp. The word buzzing among the men was that they were moving into the deep South—somewhere with better resources and far removed from the North. He sighed to himself and looked upward into the trees visible on the other side of the stockade.

He was a long way from home.

Bulldog kept his usual obsessive vigil—the fact that Ivar was allowed to walk around and stretch his legs for a bit was a miracle in itself. Bulldog usually commanded him to sit in a corner somewhere, most often with his back to the others. As a result, the other men who didn't know him well watched him with curiosity—who was this man that the crazy prison guard kept under such close scrutiny? Ivar wanted to laugh. If they only knew he was but a humble Norwegian farmer from Ohio, they'd be mighty surprised.

He heard snatches of a conversation on the other side of the blockade as he strolled along, his hands in the pockets of pants that were in desperate need of a good washing. ". . . is scouting out a place in Georgia," the voice said. "There's a little town called Andersonville—somethin' like twenty citizens." Laughter. "They can't put up too much of a fuss about a prison camp in their backyard."

Ivar furrowed his brows as the voices of the guards moved away from the stockade wall, and he began strolling again, his eyes trained thoughtfully on the dirt. Georgia. What were his options? So far, the thought of escape had been nothing but a dream. The opportunity had never presented itself, and as they made their way farther south, his chances for survival, should he manage to elude his captors, were slim.

He summoned a private dialogue, one that he had begun a few weeks before and continued in light of the fact that he wasn't allowed to speak with anyone else. *I've just overheard an interesting development. I trust that if an opportunity for escape comes along, Thou wilt help me see it.* He glanced up again at the sky and squinted at the brilliance of the blue expanse. *I have nobody else. Please do not forsake me.*

Ivar looked around at the men who were mirror images of him: tired, dirty, in clothing spattered with mud and sometimes the blood of a fallen friend. Why would God bless him—Ivar—above any of the rest of those men? Surely there was nothing more special about him, nothing that would endear him more to that paternal deity than somebody else in need.

And yet his dialogue continued, often late into the night, and it became his lifeline, his one remaining tie to hope. He had never been one to relish an active social life, had never needed crowds of people or numerous friends. He had surrounded himself with loved ones and a few close acquaintances he trusted. Ivar supposed that had he been more of a social creature in his life before the war, his current isolation might be a heavier burden. As it was, he contented himself with talking to God and keeping his eyes open, all of his senses alert for a possible opening in the prison system, a chink in the armor. He had yet to find it, but he was a patient man. Something would turn up.

* * *

Northern Virginia

Ben watched the shadows of the flames flicker across the face of his young cousin. Robert's eyes had been active the entire day as Ben had shown him the routine of their current camp life and introduced him to the other men. Nonstop they moved, Robert taking in the surroundings, the details, working to remember the names of those he met. Only now as the day drew to its close did those eyes begin to slow a bit. Robert's fatigue showed, and Ben figured it was probably a good thing they were about to turn in for the night.

As for his own opinion, Ben wasn't sure how he felt about Robert coming to take Luke's place. It had been Robert's idea, Ben read in a letter from his Uncle James some weeks back. Robert wanted to try and finish what Luke had started. When Luke had died, Ben thought back to the day they had enlisted together and tried to forget the fact that it had been Ben's idea in the first place that they do so. It was awfully hard not to blame himself or at least take some measure of responsibility for his cousin's death.

And now, here was the younger son, following right along where the elder had stopped. Ben had the feeling, watching Robert's resolute face and the set of his jaw, that Robert had something to prove, but whether it was to himself or his family Ben didn't know and didn't ask. He braced his elbow on one knee and rested his forehead in his hand. Robert was barely eighteen. How on earth was Ben to keep him safe?

He glanced up at his young cousin and found him looking at Ben with an unguarded expression of pain. Robert glanced away from Ben's raised brow and shook his head slightly. "It's like looking at a ghost," he muttered, and Ben barely heard him.

"I'm sorry, Robert, that he's gone," Ben said in a low voice. "Sometimes I think I'd trade him places if I could."

Robert shook his head. "I can't even remember the last time I wrote him a letter. I just assumed he'd be coming home, that I'd have plenty of time to talk to him then." He examined his fingernails by the firelight, picking at one, probably trying to find a distraction.

Ben cleared his throat, wondering how to broach his next subject, wondering if it was even necessary. "Robert, I don't know if you've braced yourself for what you'll probably see here," he began. "It's not . . . it's not pretty."

Robert laughed, sounding much too jaded for as young as he was. "All my delusions of battlefield glory were finished at Bull Run."

"The first or second time?"

"First."

Ben nodded. He spread his hands apart, searching for something further to say. When nothing substantial came to mind, he finally said, "We may as well turn in. Morning comes early."

CHAPTER 12

The standing rain water breeds a dense swarm of animalculae. . . . The whole contents become a turgid, jellified mass of waggle tails, worms, dead leaves, dead fishes and other putrescent abominations. . . . The smell of it is enough to revolt the stomach . . . to say nothing of making one's throat a channel for such stuff.
—Confederate prisoner of war at Fort Delaware

* * *

26 October 1863
Boston, Massachusetts

Anne Birmingham slowly approached the circle drive at the front of her family's home, noting with a fierce sense of satisfaction that the pain in her thigh had been absent for the bulk of her two-mile walk. Her spirits jumped a bit in the brisk autumn air, and she turned her face toward the sky, taking in a deep, cleansing breath that filled her lungs. Slowly releasing it, she closed her eyes and for the first time in weeks, she smiled.

Her soul had been wallowing in the depths of a place she didn't care to further examine. It had been as her strength returned and she was able to get out of the house and move around that she had felt the darkness begin to lift a bit. As she thought back on the time that had passed since her return from the regiment, she barely recognized herself. She had been in a sad, cold place, in much pain, bad health, and then deeply sorrowful over the death of her older brother. Her fear for Ivar had put her into such a state of anxiety and gloom that she barely dared think of him.

Only that morning, however, James had come to her in the parlor and told her he'd finally received information that Ivar could be in Tennessee. "It's not entirely reliable information, or may be dated at this point," he cautioned her. "I hear talk of a new prison for Union soldiers being constructed, most likely as far south as they can manage. Word is the Confederacy wants to clear the Union prisoners out of Richmond."

Anne had absorbed the information, the cogs in her brain shaking off the dust and beginning to churn. James must have seen it for himself because he'd sat next to her on the sofa. "Anne," he began, sounding hesitant. "It's good to see a spark of your old self. I would caution you, though . . ."

"You think I'm going to enlist again?"

"Are you?"

"No."

"However?" Darn the man. Anne had always felt he could read her thoughts, and her growing older apparently hadn't protected her one bit from his all-seeing eye.

"However, I would very much like to find a way to get him home before he dies. You've seen the newspaper reports—more soldiers on both sides are dying in prison camps now than on the battlefield, almost."

"Do you have feelings for this man? Affection?"

"He's a good friend—surely it makes sense to save the life of a good friend."

"I daresay you had more than one good friend in all the time you spent in that regiment, yet the only one I hear you mention is this Ivar."

Anne had glanced down at her hands, twisted tightly in her lap. "I care for him very much," she finally admitted. "Very much. And it's my fault he's a prisoner of war."

"How can it be your fault?" James reached forward and clasped one of her hands in his own, squeezing it gently. "I think you may blame yourself unnecessarily."

Anne had finally unburdened her heart, sharing what she'd kept inside for some time. "I insisted he remove the bullet from my leg so the surgeons wouldn't touch me with their filthy instruments. We lost ground in the time it took for him to dig the bullet out—by the time he finished we'd been overrun by the rebs. He had known we were retreating quickly and suggested we go to the hospital tents set up at the back of the action." She paused, feeling her eyes well up. "I made him stop where we were."

James squeezed her hand again. "He could have insisted you keep moving, Anne. He knew what he was doing."

She shook her head. "You know how I am. I bend people to my will . . ."

"Sweetheart, he must return your affection. As your father I can only be grateful he wanted to help you."

"I doubt he returns my affections," she had murmured, giving voice to another, deeper fear. "He's very much a gentleman. He knew I was a woman from the beginning, and he was always very chivalrous, sometimes to the point I was afraid he would give away my identity with his actions and comments."

James had smiled then, and Anne was left to wonder what he was thinking. He finally released her hand and patted it. "I'll keep working at it," he promised her. "And in return, I'll ask that you do not take any action on your own without consulting me and your mother first."

"Fair enough."

Now as Anne reflected on the conversation, she was grateful for an understanding father. He had changed through the years. Whereas he had always been what others termed as "radical" in his views on women's rights and abolition, a few years ago he would have absolutely forbidden her to take any action toward seeing Ivar freed. Now, he "asked" that she not.

Unfortunately, although she had been mulling the issue over the bulk of the day, she wasn't any closer to a solution. The answer must lie just beyond her reach, she thought as she made her way to the home's entrance. Her fingers itched for a pen and paper. She needed to make a list of all her resources—people and things—on which she may be able to draw. The house was quiet, and she climbed uninterrupted to her bedroom, her brow furrowed in thought.

* * *

Camille stood beside Jacob in the smaller hall that had become a temporary home to the Abolition Society since the burning of the original during the draft riots. As she talked, she ticked off several items on her fingers. "I have articles on reactions to Lincoln's proclamation of a national yearly day of thanksgiving and on Grant being named as the head of the western armies. I have yet to find a reliable source for reaction to the battle at Chickamauga in Tennessee, however. I know of a few who have sons that probably were engaged there, but I'm reluctant to intrude . . ."

Jacob nodded. "I understand."

She glanced at him in surprise. "You do? I thought a newspaper editor wanted the story, regardless of circumstances."

He looked down at her with eyes half closed. "You think so little of me, Camille?"

"Well, I . . . yes, I suppose so."

He laid a hand over his heart. "You wound me, fair lady."

She snorted. "I doubt that. Most likely you're not overly concerned with the content of my pieces as they're all editorial in nature anyhow."

"Most of the newspaper articles across the nation have become editorial in nature," he said with half of a smile. "The location of the city determines the opinion."

Camille cut him off with a slight gasp, and without realizing she had done it, she grasped his arm, digging her nails deeply into the fabric of his suit coat. "I cannot *believe* that woman dares to show her face here!"

Jacob winced at the pressure on his arm and laid a hand over her fingers, gripping them into submission. "Who?" he asked, looking around and trying to follow the direction of her gaze.

"Aunt Helena! Come with me," she stated, moving forward and pressing through the crowd, her fingers still gripping his in her fury.

"Camille," he said when she had thrown him forward and he stumbled, off balance. "Do you suppose we might try this in a civilized fashion?" He pried her fingers loose from his and instead tucked her hand into the crook of his arm. When she moved to rush forward again, he held her back, walking at a more leisurely pace, nodding slightly to people they passed.

"She'll leave before I have a chance to find out why she's here," Camille hissed at him.

"If you cause such a stir," he muttered to her under his breath, "she'll avoid you like the plague. Now," he continued with an absent smile at another Society member, "this is the woman you've spoken of? The one from Washington?"

"Yes! She and Olivia's mother are up to absolutely no good when it comes to the Society—they hate us!"

"Does she remember you?"

"Apparently, yes," Camille said as they approached the woman who viewed them through eyes that had narrowed to slits.

"Helena, isn't it?" Camille said to the woman when they reached her side. It was disrespectful to use the older woman's first name, and they both knew it. Jacob looked at Camille with his eyebrows raised, but refrained from comment.

"It is," the woman answered. "And you are Olivia's former acquaintance."

Camille bristled at the woman's flat tone. "Why are you here?"

Jacob cleared his throat. "Miss Birmingham, I don't believe you've introduced me to your friend."

The older woman examined Jacob from head to toe before again turning her attention to his face. "I am Helena Smythe. And you are?" she asked, extending her hand.

Jacob took it and bowed slightly over her fingers. "Jacob Taylor."

"Taylor . . . Taylor . . . Would I know of your family?"

"I doubt that sincerely. My father keeps a lighthouse in Maine."

"Oh."

Camille glared at the woman. Jacob might as well have told her he had leprosy that spread when he looked at people.

"And what brings you to Boston, then?" she asked.

"I'm a newspaper editor."

"Oh."

Camille wished she had fangs to bare at the woman. "Why are you here?" she repeated again, ignoring Jacob's warning grip on her hand.

Helena looked at her with some amusement. "Does your mother realize you're so comfortable with a working man?"

Camille drew herself up to her full height, feeling a cold fury settle into her limbs. The look in her eyes must have been fierce because the woman took a nearly imperceptible step backward. Camille placed her other hand atop Jacob's arm and moved slightly closer to his side. "My *father,*" she murmured to the woman in an icy tone she didn't recognize as her own, "is a working man. And incidentally," she added, "you might watch more closely those you so obviously disdain. If I were you, I should hate to see my name appear in print."

Camille moved against Jacob's side, urging him away from the woman who stared after them in openmouthed outrage. When he would have stopped some distance away, she exerted pressure on his arm and led him to the doors, instead, and out into the cold night air.

"Let me get your cloak," Jacob said, but Camille held fast to his arm.

"Get me away from here," she said, feeling her eyes burn.

"Very well. I walked here tonight, though. I don't have my equipage."

"I walked as well. I don't mind." She turned her face away as tears fell, hot and angry down her face. The sounds of the door opening behind them signaled someone else leaving the building, and she began walking quickly in the opposite direction.

"Are you still staying with Abby?"

Camille nodded. "It's just around the corner."

"I know. I'll walk you there. Here," he said and lowering his arms, he shrugged out of his jacket. He draped it over her shoulders and drew it close under her chin. "We'd better hurry. When people see us together unchaperoned, with you wearing my coat, your reputation will be in shreds." The tone of his voice held only the slightest amusement—he spoke the truth and they both well knew it.

They began walking again, and Jacob reached for her hand. He found it under the folds of the coat, and he gave it a gentle squeeze. "I must say, this has been a first for me."

She glanced at him, her tears still falling.

"I've never had such a fierce—or small—defender before."

Camille shrugged, wishing she could think of something to say. She was so upset she was afraid all she would manage would be unsuitable for civilized ears. Her voice hitched on a sob. "I hate that woman," she choked.

Jacob paused to reach inside the folds of the coat she wore and pulled out a handkerchief. He handed it to her, and she mopped her eyes and nose with it, willingly returning her hand to his when he sought it as they began walking again.

"Tell me again how you know her."

"I met her when Robert and I went with the Sylvesters to Washington. She was with us at the first Bull

Run." She shuddered involuntarily at the memory. She had shut it out for so long that she was surprised when the images came rushing back in full force. "And now she's here, of all places, and Robert's gone, and Luke is dead." Camille knew that in a saner moment, she'd have been mortified that she was crying in public. "She is so awful! Did you know she was among the hecklers in the crowd when the Society building was burned to the ground? And now she has the audacity to show her face at a *meeting*?"

Jacob paused again, halting their forward, albeit slow, progress. "Are you certain?"

"Yes! She's made veiled threats for years—she's always present every time there's a major upheaval in any city where abolition societies meet. I cannot *believe* she has the unmitigated gall to actually appear here now!"

"I think perhaps I should speak with someone from the police force. They may want to observe her for a while."

Camille felt somewhat mollified at his statement, but still wanted very much to scratch the woman's eyes out herself. "And she was rude to you! Looked you over like a racehorse she found wanting. And her comment! But the most ironic part of all," Camille finished on a tear-filled hiss, "is that she and Olivia's mother do *not* come from money! Their mother was a seamstress and their father worked the rails!"

Jacob threw his head back and laughed long and hard. Camille looked about, her tears slowing a bit, her senses finally returning. She tugged on his hand while he continued to express his mirth—doubled over and gasping for air.

"What is so funny?" she demanded in a whisper.

He finally stood and, to her surprise, wrapped her in his arms, still laughing. Her arms hung limp at her sides, her face against his shirt. She rolled her eyes upward, confused.

"Camille," he finally managed, and held her out from himself a bit, his hands gently grasping her shoulders, "may I please call on you sometime? Soon?"

"Call on me for what?"

"May I call on you?" A smile still lingered on his handsome face, his eyes intense in the approaching darkness of the evening.

"Call . . . call on me?"

"Yes. I would very much enjoy your company for tea. Or perhaps a ride in the park."

Her breath quickened a bit as he wiped the traces of her tears with his thumb. "Please say yes," he whispered.

She nodded dumbly. "Yes."

"Good." He smiled and, reaching for her hands buried in the coat, lifted them to his lips, kissing first the knuckles of one, then the other.

"Mr. Taylor," Camille murmured, her old flirtatious habits rising to the surface and saving her from an awkward moment, "you're behaving most scandalously." She sniffed and realized her anger had abated in the presence of Jacob's good nature.

"I know." He looked fully into her eyes and tugged a bit on her hands playfully. "Miss Birmingham," he said, and straightened, placing one of her hands in the crook of his arm. They again began their walk to the Van Dyke home, which was now in sight. "You do not currently have any other suitors, do you?"

"Not at the moment, much to my eternal regret."

"It's just as well. If you did, I'd tell you to dismiss them all."

She glanced at him through her lashes, still wet from her tears. “You’re awfully sure of yourself, Mr. Taylor.”

“A necessity for a working man, Miss Birmingham.”

CHAPTER 13

The world will little note, nor long remember what we say here, but it can never forget what they did here. It is for us the living, rather, to be dedicated here to the unfinished work which they who fought here have thus far so nobly advanced.
—Abraham Lincoln

* * *

19 November 1863
Gettysburg, Pennsylvania

"In a larger sense, we cannot dedicate—we cannot consecrate—we cannot hallow—this ground . . ."

Robert listened to President Lincoln's voice as the man, ever tall, erect, and sad about the eyes, delivered a speech to dedicate the cemetery for the fallen soldiers at Gettysburg. The narrative itself was poetry, capturing the solemnity of the moment in beautiful eloquence.

"He's aged," Robert whispered to Ben, who stood at his side.

"When did you see him last?"

"His first inaugural address." Robert turned his attention back to the man who bore the weight of democracy on his shoulders. *I don't envy him his task,* he thought as he studied the man who engendered such passionate feelings in the hearts of the citizenry. People usually either loved him or hated him, and often with an intensity on both sides.

When Lincoln's remarks were finished, Ben stretched a bit and looked out over the landscape. Robert watched him unobtrusively, wondering what his cousin was thinking. The day had gone fairly long—the crowd of people standing for quite a time, listening first to Edward Everett, the distinguished American scholar who spoke for two hours, and then to the president, whose appearance at the event was one of invitational generosity on the part of the State of Pennsylvania. This was officially a state affair, not a federal one. Robert was glad, though, to see Lincoln in the flesh. He offered a quick, mental prayer for the president's health and turned his attention again to his cousin.

"I imagine you don't relish being here," Robert said to him as they made their way through the crowd.

Ben shrugged, but the haunted look in his eyes betrayed his otherwise casual demeanor. "It's necessary," he said. "This needs to be done." As they neared the edge of the people clustered in large and small groups, Ben looked out over the peaceful scenery.

"Bodies," he said under his breath, "as far as the eye could see."

Robert swallowed a knot in his throat and followed Ben's gaze. Robert shook his head at the strangeness of it all. When the battle at Gettysburg had erupted, he had read a piece in the paper that said the peaceful countryside had already been the subject of paintings and prints depicting the area as an ideal in American life. Would it now be remembered forever as the place where purgatory had unleashed its awful fury?

The two men moved down a gentle slope and away from the people, preparing to return to their camp some miles away. "So, tell me about this religion of yours," Robert said.

Ben looked at him for a moment and then laughed gently, his features softening for a moment. "Your brother," he said, smiling at the memory, "did the same thing hoping to change the subject and guide my mind to greener pastures." He shook his head. "You'd best watch yourself, Robert. Luke found himself baptized as a result."

"He did?" Robert couldn't contain his surprise. Luke had said nothing of a baptism in his letters home.

"He did. It was shortly before Gettysburg," Ben said with a gesture to the landscape. "He probably didn't have time to draft a good letter. I think he wanted to take his time and explain himself well so the family wouldn't think he was next in line for bedlam."

Robert absorbed the information carefully. Luke had never been an overly religious person—he claimed to believe in God and went to church occasionally with James and Elizabeth—but to be baptized into the very religion that had taken Ben thousands of miles from his home?

"You don't approve," Ben observed.

"I'm only surprised, I suppose." Robert glanced at Ben, wanting his cousin to feel his sincerity. "Anything good enough for you would have been good enough for Luke. He loved you very much. As much as he did me or the rest of my family." Robert turned his head and blinked rapidly a few times. It wouldn't do at all to cry like a baby in such a public place.

Ben clasped the back of Robert's neck with his hand and pulled him close as they walked to their horses. "I appreciate your thoughts," he said, his voice gruff. "How is Luke's fiancée faring with her loss?"

Robert felt his heart hitch at the thought of Abigail. "Well enough. She recently lost her mother in a bizarre accident—Luke's death only compounds her grief, I'm afraid."

Ben nodded. "I remember him writing to her—he had such plans for the future." He paused for a moment and managed a smile. "But enough talk for now of Luke. He is well and wouldn't want us blubbering like this."

Robert stopped when they reached their horses and turned to Ben. "You're sure he's well? Do you know where he is?"

"He is well, Robert. I do know where he is. And I know we'll see him again."

Robert untied his horse's reins and mounted the saddle with practiced ease. "I envy you that knowledge. Perhaps I'll pursue my inquiry into your religion after all."

"Perhaps." Ben smiled at him and mounted his horse, and they set off together at a comfortable pace.

* * *

Boston, Massachusetts

Mary sat upright in her bed, her heart pounding. She pressed her hands to her ears to still the inner voice that had plagued her of late, screaming at her for abandoning her child. *But I didn't . . . I didn't . . . Sarah Birmingham sold my baby.*

You didn't want the baby . . .

Mary closed her eyes against the last vestiges of the dream that still clung to her memory. A child, nearly three years old, was crying inconsolably for his mother, a child forced on her by a selfish boy who thought little of causing others pain. She drew her knees to her chest beneath her warm quilt and hugged them. Why now, when she was too far away to even check on the child, to ask after his welfare, were the dreams coming?

Mary knew that her son was probably loved. Families were broken and separated so often in slave life that many times a new child managed to *almost* replace one who had been lost. She couldn't be sure, though, and until lately she had been able to dismiss the whole painful episode as something in her life that almost didn't seem real anymore.

She had been but sixteen when the baby was born and had not been in a position to care for the child. She laughed, and it turned into a moan. Nobody who was enslaved was in a position to properly care for a child. It wasn't as though she had made a willing choice to share her child with a loving family who would cherish him. Her baby had gone from her arms to the arms of another who may not have been able to love him or feed him much of anything. His care and well-being were solely dependent on the master of the plantation and his attitude toward his human chattel. She wondered if *she* would have been able to love him had he stayed at Bentley.

She would never know because Sarah had taken her freedom to choose. A surge of white-hot anger stabbed through her chest, and she coughed with the pain of it. Sarah had sold her baby because she knew Richard had fathered him and she couldn't bear the reality of that fact living on her property and staring her in the face, day after day.

Perhaps now that Mary was older and possessed a life of her own, perhaps because Richard was dead and her memories of him were fading, perhaps those were the reasons that Mary's thoughts turned to her child, living far away on a plantation down the road from Bentley in South Carolina. She would write to Ruth—see if she had heard anything regarding the boy, how he fared, who cared for him.

Then, maybe, the nightmares would cease.

* * *

Charleston, South Carolina
Bentley Plantation

Emily smiled and reached down to tickle the tummy of her nearly three-month-old baby. Mary Alice gurgled in response, drawing her knees in and hitting herself in the mouth with her fist. She saw so much of Austin in the little girl and was glad to have a piece of him in her life. The child was growing so quickly it amazed Emily. If the war didn't end soon, Mary Alice would be of marriageable age when she finally met her father. Emily's heart thumped at the thought of Austin, and she shoved her despair aside, concentrating instead on the beauty of her young daughter. She could never have imagined her heart would be capable of holding so much love. The child would be spoiled if her mother wasn't careful.

A joyous shriek called her attention from Mary Alice, and as she watched the antics ensuing at the other end of the nursery, her smile broadened until she laughed out loud. Clara, her younger sister who was growing into a delightful young woman, nearly thirteen years old now, was tickling and wrestling about on the floor with a small child of three.

He was a strikingly handsome child, with thick, curly short black hair and enormous green eyes framed in a face whose complexion was a gentle golden-tan. As she laughed at the sounds of his merriment, she marveled again that he was even with them.

Upon Jeffrey's return and after speaking with Ruth and Emily at some length about Mary's child, who had been purchased by the Charlesworths, he had opened a private safe in his office—the existence of which nobody had had any knowledge—withdrew a handful of gold coins, traveled to the neighbors, and bought the child back. He had asked Emily, before leaving, what she thought of his intentions.

"My only concern might be disrupting the child himself," she had told him once she recovered from the shock of his pronouncement. "If he's living with people who are kind, if he has adopted a mother of sorts among the other slaves, it might do him harm to separate him from her."

With a promise to examine the situation closely, Jeffrey had departed only to return a scant thirty minutes later with the child in tow, a child dressed in a filthy shirt that was little more than a rag. His eyes had appeared even larger than usual in a face that was gaunt from lack of adequate nutrition. The bulk of the Charlesworths' slaves had abandoned the plantation, and the child had been left behind with an old woman who was blind and near death. The plantation was in worse condition than Bentley, the Charlesworths themselves living from day to day in a state of shock and dismay over the escape of so many of their slaves and the general shape of ruin flowing over the South. Efforts to recapture their runaways had ended in failure, and Emily was unashamedly grateful.

Upon seeing the condition of the old woman, Jeffrey had purchased her as well, dropping several more gold coins into Mr. Charlesworth's outstretched palm. In the privacy of her own room, Emily had shed tears of grateful surprise at the new sense of philanthropic humanity her father seemed to have embraced. If she lived a thousand years, she never would have believed it if she hadn't seen it with her own eyes. The old woman, Constance, now spent her time with Ruth, resting in the kitchen, talking with the cooks of hard days gone by and the uncertain shape of things to come.

According to Constance, the name of Mary's son was Elijah. Clara and Rose, Mary's younger sister, had taken the boy instantly to heart, and he now trailed after them all day long. He was a bright child; he had even begun to mimic some of the signs the girls used because of Clara's hearing problem.

Emily's eyes clouded for a moment when she thought of Mary. She hadn't yet found the courage to write to Mary and tell her Elijah was with them. The conditions of his conception had been so awful, and she wondered if seeing the child again someday would bring to light memories Mary would rather leave buried.

If the time ever came, though, Mary should be given the option to choose whether or not she wanted to raise Elijah herself. The decision should be hers to make, and Emily felt like a coward for avoiding the issue. The family so adored the little boy that it was altogether too easy to put it off for a time.

Elijah escaped from Clara's teasing fingers and ran the length of the room, laughing, his eyes bright. Emily, seated on the floor next to Mary Alice, who lay on a blanket, spread her arms wide. "Come to me, Elijah! I shall protect you from the ogre!"

He ran full force into Emily, wrapping his arms around her neck and laughing so hard she was afraid he'd start crying. Clara pursued him, tickling his ribs while Emily pretended to fight her off. Finally, Clara subsided and placed a kiss on the boy's soft cheek. His laughter eventually calmed and he relaxed, sitting in Emily's lap, limp for a moment before finding his energy and again jumping up to run back to the other side of the room.

It was amazing that he had adapted to them, but then, children were prone to versatility, Emily mused as she watched her young nephew. Upon his arrival, he had been afraid of everything and everyone, clinging to Constance for reassurance. Eventually, however, they had won his love with affection and attention, Clara and Rose keeping him occupied with toys and games, Ruth and Emily seeing to his physical needs and clothing. Even Jeffrey appeared at least once a day in the nursery to spend some time with the little boy and rediscover his youngest daughter, who barely knew him at all.

Jeffrey's return had been a blessing for all of them, even Sarah, who seemed to slip into moments of lucidity every now and again. As conditions in the South continued to worsen, however, he mentioned a westward move with more frequency. Emily figured the day would not be long in coming when he would finally make the decision and pack up his wife, taking her far away where they could start over in a place untouched by the ravages of war and painful memories of a lifetime filled with regret.

Emily's mind wandered over the details then. What of Clara and Rose? Would they take both girls with them? They were much like twin sisters—a separation would be extremely hard on both. How logical was it, though, for Clara and Rose to live with Jeffrey, a man who had paid little attention to either child until recently, and Sarah, a woman who had no idea who they were at all?

The most logical solution, really, would be for the girls to live with Emily. It wasn't an imposition on her, and her only reservation with that kind of arrangement was that she hated to take Ruth's only remaining granddaughter away from her when they eventually left for Willow Lane in Savannah.

Emily sighed. The future was uncertain, and she wished for just a moment that she had the talent to read tea leaves or something magical that would give her a hint as to coming events. She wished she knew whether or not her husband was alive and well. She wished Joshua hadn't enlisted, because as proud as she was of him, she worried for his safety. She missed Mary horribly and wished they lived closer. She wished her cousin Luke hadn't died. She wished Ben were home again.

As had become her habit of late, she again focused her attention on the children, losing herself in Elijah's simple joy and the world of discovery before Mary Alice. She leaned forward and stretched herself along the floor on the blanket next to her baby and kissed her soft head, inhaling the sweet scent and smiling at the whisper of a tickle from the young girl's fuzzy hair.

CHAPTER 14

The immense slaughter of our brave men chills and sickens us all.
—Gideon Wells, Union navy secretary

* * *

24 November 1863
Chattanooga, Tennessee

Ben glanced over at the face of his young cousin, grateful to see the grim determination still apparent. Six short days before they had been in Virginia. A whirlwind trip by boat and rail had deposited them in Tennessee with speed in transport heretofore unparalleled.

The beleaguered Army of the Cumberland, after taking Chattanooga, Tennessee, in a bloodless battle, had summarily lost ground afterward at a creek called Chickamauga. The Confederate victory, although extremely costly to the rebels, had forced the Army of the Cumberland back to Chattanooga, where the Confederates, under General Braxton Bragg, began a siege intended to starve out the boys in blue, much as Grant had the Confederates in Vicksburg.

Grant himself had come to the rescue, drilling a hole in the Confederates' defenses and establishing a route on which food and supplies could again find their way south to the Union troops. Seeing the desperate situation in which the Army of the Cumberland had fallen, Washington ordered men from Meade's troops in the North to travel south under Joe Hooker as reinforcements. It was for that reason that Ben and Robert found themselves now fighting to take Lookout Mountain, a thousand-foot-high piece of earth on the Tennessee River just south of Chattanooga.

Ben had wondered how Robert would handle the intense fighting that had become so familiar in the year since his own enlistment. He knew the young man had seen his share of gore at Bull Run, but watching a battle from a relatively safe distance and participating in one were two different matters altogether. Much to Ben's proud surprise, Robert was holding himself together extremely well, following orders, pushing forward when necessary, and handling his weapon with admirable ease.

Ben wiped at the grime coating his face and took a moment in the dark night sky to check his timepiece. The glow of battle provided the illumination necessary for him to see that the clock showed the hour approaching ten. The battle had begun at eight o'clock that morning. He suddenly wished he hadn't looked after the time—he felt all the wearier when he realized how late it was.

As if reading his thoughts, Robert looked at him as Ben replaced his pocket watch and said, "Don't tell me what the time is. I don't want to know." He removed his cap for a moment and ran a hand through his hair, which was coated with dirt.

Ben managed a weary smile. "Welcome to the United States Army, my friend. Perish the thought that your first battle should be less than a twenty-four-hour experience."

Shots continued to pop around them as the fighting continued into the darkness, and as they advanced up the mountain, the action stretched for another two hours before the Union finally claimed victory.

* * *

It was early the next morning that the United States flag could be seen from the top of Lookout Mountain, appearing to those below to be floating in the clouds. The fighting nearby, though, was far from over. Sounds of battle—the crack of bullets fired from guns, the blast of cannon, the groans of the dead and the wounded—continued to assault the ears of all present.

Ben stood away from his prior position on Lookout Mountain, having descended in the early morning hours with Robert and the rest of his company. They were separated from the bulk of men holding the ground they'd gained and were to be used as reserves should they be needed elsewhere as the fighting continued. They were tired, filthy, and hungry, and the nip in the air was chilling in their weakened state.

He watched with a slight sense of awe as General Grant stood in conference with his military advisors and colleagues, most notably Major General George Thomas, who had stood his ground at Chickamauga, earning him the affectionate nickname of "The Rock of Chickamauga" from his admiring men. The generals conversed in even tones, and Ben watched closely, wondering for just a moment how it would be to see inside Grant's head. The man was a gifted tactician and a boon to a grateful president who had been forced to wade his way through men who were either lacking in military wisdom or the courage to act.

The men of the Army of the Cumberland, whom Ben currently observed, had been dispatched to root out the Confederates who had secreted themselves in rifle pits at Missionary Ridge, east of Lookout Mountain. Ben smiled as he thought of the men of the Cumberland, who had to endure much ribbing from those in his regiment for having lost ground at Chickamauga and being forced into a siege in the city. The taunts had been a combination of mild jesting and downright rudeness, and although they took it as well as could be expected, Ben wondered if they weren't feeling they had something to prove, if not to others, then most definitely to themselves. He couldn't say he blamed them.

Ben inched his way closer as Grant and Grant's aides moved toward Missionary Ridge for a better angle of inspection. As he swung behind the men, Robert on his heels, Ben saw the men of the Army of the Cumberland situated near the Ridge, having overtaken the rifle pits. Ben spied a man he had met on one occasion, General Phil Sheridan, who currently led the men who sat poised and ready for further orders.

He shook his head, remembering the man's sense of humor and reckless courage. As Ben watched, Sheridan retrieved a flask from his coat and toasted the rebels situated on the slope above him. He shouted at them as he lifted the flask, "Here's at you!"

The resulting gunfire had Ben wincing as he expected the wiry little man to drop dead. He wasn't hit, however, but outraged. "That was ungenerous! I'll take your guns for that!"

The men, almost as one, roared with him and began charging up the hill. Ben turned, openmouthed, to Grant, who had also been observing the events unfolding before them.

"Who ordered those men up the hill?" Grant asked one of his aides.

"No one," the aide answered. "They started up without orders. When those fellows get started, nothing can stop them."

Ben turned his gaze back to the ridge, watching as the men swarmed upward, most groupings in V formation, pointing toward the rebels. They moved continually, some falling, but ever pressing onward with a fervor born of a desire to avenge a loss.

Robert was at his side, muttering something under his breath as his eyes flew over the scene. "There must be, roughly, . . ." he paused for a moment, counting, "close to sixty flags on that hill. And look, not one has touched the ground yet."

Ben squinted his eyes at the men in blue, his fingers tightening unconsciously on the barrel of his weapon. As he watched, he saw one of many flag bearers sustain a wound and fall to his knees, but before he fell completely to the earth, the man next to him willingly took the flag and pressed onward. Robert's assessment was correct—the flags were never given a chance to fall.

"They're not going to make it," Ben murmured, watching as the men approached sections of the slope that were so steep they were forced to drop to all fours and climb toward the top. The frantic Confederates were scrambling to keep shot raining down upon the blue-coated soldiers who swarmed over the hill in an unrelenting tide. Some Union men grabbed tree branches for leverage as they continued in their upward progression.

"I wouldn't be so sure of that," Robert said as he watched, wide-eyed. Many of the Confederate soldiers, terrified in the onslaught, were throwing down their arms or turning to flee in the opposite direction.

To Ben's amazement, the Union boys, who had acted entirely on their own without orders from the high commanding officers, had taken the ridge. They reached the top, fighting and taking prisoners, and before their eyes, a young man bore his colors to the top, shouting, "On Wisconsin!"

"I don't believe it," Ben said, shaking his head. "They actually made it." He and Robert moved forward to the ridge with scores of others who had witnessed the amazing feat. A man rushed by, his face flushed, tearing his way through the crowd to reach the men who, it soon became apparent, were under his direct command.

"It's General Granger," Robert said, watching the man attempt to reach his soldiers.

Ben looked at his cousin in amazement. "How do you know that? I've been doing this for over a year, and I think you know more about all of these people than I do."

Robert flushed a bit, but smiled. "I follow things closely," he said, but broke off as they heard General Granger shouting at his men who had just taken the hill.

"You ought to be court-martialed, every man of you. I ordered you to take the rifle pits, and you scaled the mountain!" The general had tears rolling down his cheeks.

Ben couldn't help but nod at the man's condition. He didn't find it the least bit odd for Granger to be so overcome. It had been an amazing thing, and Ben had feared for the soldiers himself as he had watched their insanely brave attack. They had acted on their own, without orders, and had, in the end, done themselves proud.

"That's probably all the chastising they're going to get for this," Robert said, a grin stealing across his face and transforming him into the young boy that Ben had known years ago. "They made a decision on their own and followed it."

Ben grunted his reluctant agreement. "I'm not altogether sure they took the time to actually make a decision," he said, "but they did achieve the ideal result."

Robert shook his head and looked to the top of the mountain, where the colors of the Wisconsin regiment waved in the wind. "Crazy fellas. Good for them."

* * *

Robert lay on his bedroll that night, exhausted but unable to sleep. They had been awake for over thirty-six hours, and the sleep the men had managed to catch before the battle on Lookout Mountain had been sporadic at best. He was a long way from home, missing the comfort of his own bedroom, and perhaps for the first time, Robert fully comprehended just how many blessings filled his young life. His childhood had been one of comfort, his material needs always met often to excess, and his relations with his family were affectionate and warm. Men in the regiment often spoke fondly of home, of loved ones and comfortable habitations, but many also spoke of hardship, poverty, and loss.

Robert and Ben now lay under a hastily erected tent, and the flap in the material afforded him an unobstructed view of the starlit sky. Never in his wildest dreams had he imagined he'd one day be sleeping on the ground in Tennessee. He wasn't the only one—often the other soldiers spoke of never having been more than a mile or two from their homes until their enlistment with the Union army.

Ben's breathing was deep and even. He lay on his back under his blanket and rested with the talent of the dead. Robert envied his cousin his peace. Ben usually slept well with the occasional fits of tossing and turning. There was a haunted look about the man's eyes in his waking hours, and Robert knew he often thought of Luke. It was a comfort, in a macabre way, that someone else shared the pain of his loss. Ben had never said one way or the other whether he was happy to have Robert in Luke's place, but they got on well enough, and Robert was grateful for the older man's presence in his life. He was a constant reminder of Luke—he looked so much like him—and while it was painful, it was also comforting.

Robert shut his eyes and dug the heels of his hands into them, breathing deeply and trying to shake the images of the past two days from his mind. They would never go away, though. He had known the few gruesome things he had witnessed at Bull Run would pale in comparison to being in actual, full-blown battle, and he had been absolutely correct in his assumptions. He would never forget the faces of the wounded and the dying. He would never forget the fact that the human body could be so completely and utterly destroyed, transformed into something mangled and lifeless where only moments before there had been vitality and relative health.

Regarding that state of relative health, Robert had noticed coughing around the camp increasing daily in intensity and volume. There were many illnesses that quickly spread from one soldier to the next; it was inevitable living in such close quarters and being in constant exposure to the elements, which were often not friendly. If battle didn't take the lives of many soldiers, the illnesses would. They already had, in fact.

He turned on his side, trying to find a comfortable spot and wondering why, as tired as he was, he couldn't sleep. It was cold—that may have been part of the problem—and the ground wasn't very forgiving. It wasn't just that, though. He was startled by every little sound outside the flimsy walls of the tent. Every footstep, the scuttle of small animals curious or rabid enough to venture into the encampment, all was amplified in light of his new awareness born of mortal fear.

He was afraid to go to sleep. He checked his gun for the third time in as many minutes and settled his head back down onto his haversack. Robert looked again at his sleeping cousin and wondered how he managed it. How did one finally overcome the fear? What if they were ambushed in the middle of the night? What if the sentries on picket duty fell asleep? What if the shadows against the material of the tent proved to be the enemy, bent on killing them all while they slumbered?

Robert groaned and closed his eyes again, feeling like a fool but unable to rectify it. *Please, God, please keep us safe so that I can go to sleep. I can't go this whole war without getting any sleep. I'm afraid. I'm so afraid . . .*

They were his last thoughts as he drifted into a merciful rest.

CHAPTER 15

If a fellow has [to go to the] Hospital, you might as well say goodbye.
—Union soldier

* * *

2 December 1863
Boston, Massachusetts

Anne briskly walked the length of the library, her limp barely noticeable. She had perfected her stride by taking long, daily walks around the city, and even those who knew of her injuries were hard-pressed to see them. She still felt the pain, and in bad weather specifically her thigh throbbed, but she was determined that it not control her life any longer. She was very nearly as healthy as she had ever been. She even noticed when she turned a critical eye to her upstairs mirror that the color in her cheeks was high, and the fire in her blue eyes, though a bit more world-weary, was back in place.

Her hair was still extremely short for a woman. It curled just at her earlobes, brushing against her skin as a constant reminder of what she'd chosen to experience. She felt as though she were only half finished with her task, though. Ivar was still in enemy hands, and until she could somehow secure his release, she wouldn't rest.

It was for this purpose that she now paced, considering her options in approaching her parents. She had no wish to cause them further distress; they worried constantly over Robert's health—she saw it in their eyes—and she often saw the both of them tear up a bit at the mention of his name before looking away and changing the topic of conversation. Anne knew they thought of Luke, and truth be told, so did she.

James and Elizabeth eventually entered the room, their faces red from having just come in from the cold. "Griffen said you were in here pacing," Elizabeth said, rubbing her hands together and moving to stand near the hearth. "I don't suppose you're hatching a plan?"

"What would make you think such a thing?" Anne tried to paste an innocent expression on her face, but doubted she succeeded.

"I know you too well, Anne. You move around excessively when you have something churning in that brain of yours."

"Very well, I see no need for pretense then." Anne glanced at her father and took note of his expression before proceeding. He appeared outwardly calm, as was his usual demeanor, but she noticed a tightening of his stance, almost a physical manifestation of a hardening of his resolve.

"I want to go south to visit Emily."

After a moment's pause, Elizabeth ventured, "Your cousin Emily?"

Anne nodded. "I want to use her resources to see if I can't find Ivar. She has told me I'm welcome to visit anytime."

James released a breath of air. "Your use of the word *visit* is amusing, Anne." He placed a hand beneath Elizabeth's elbow and moved to a sofa. They both sat, and Anne noticed James's protective arm around Elizabeth's shoulders, almost as though he willed her some of his strength. Anne took a good look at her mother, satisfied to see the familiar lines of determination around her mouth. Elizabeth still had much fight left in her, and Anne was glad for it.

"How on earth are you going to travel and be safe?" Elizabeth asked her with a brow raised.

"Uncle Jeffrey made it home in one piece. If he can do it, so can I."

James briefly closed his eyes. "Sweet girl, you are going to drive us to an early grave."

"I surely hope not. That is not my intention. Please understand though, Father, I need to do this."

"Only you would reverse the roles, Anne—the damsel rescuing the hero in distress." Evidence of a smile hovered around the corners of Elizabeth's mouth.

James glanced at his wife in some surprise. "You approve of this?"

"She'll do it one way or another."

"I made her promise she wouldn't."

"No," Anne interjected. "You made me promise I would tell you and Mother of my plans."

"And now you've told us, so you're going to just up and go. Is that right?" Elizabeth asked her.

Anne flinched a bit at the tone in her mother's voice. Elizabeth had always been able to hone right in on her children's intentions. "You know I wouldn't cause you unnecessary worry, Mother. Not at this time, after all that's happened. But the death rate in prison camps all over this country is climbing—the men are sick from the conditions they live in. I should know, I've seen them myself."

Elizabeth sighed a bit and settled more securely into the crook of James's arm. "What is your plan then, sweetheart? How are you going to find this man, and then how are you going to secure his release?"

Anne spread her hands a bit. "I have no other choice, really, but to travel from camp to camp and see where he is."

"And you think the men who run these prisons are just going to tell you whatever it is you need to know?"

"It's all I have. I don't know what else to do."

"Fine, then. Let's suppose you find Mr. Gundersen. How are you going to get him out?"

"Money."

"Whose?" James asked, interjecting for the first time in a few minutes.

"Mine."

"You saved your army pay?"

"I'm not speaking of my army pay."

James's eyes widened fractionally. "Your inheritance?"

Anne nodded. "I'm old enough now to claim it. The stipulations were that if I remained single, I would be unable to claim the funds myself until my twenty-fifth year." She lifted her chin a bit. "My birthday is next week."

"Anne, this is important to you, and a man's life is at stake. I wouldn't have been so callous as to deny you your money had you come to me earlier," James said in a gentle tone.

"I didn't think of it as an option until just recently," Anne admitted. "But it's just as well. I needed this time to heal, and I feel very near to my old self."

"Well, then, I suppose the only question is would you rather travel by ship or by rail?"

* * *

Charleston, South Carolina
Bentley Plantation

Emily read her cousin Anne's telegram with a leap of joy. It would be so wonderful to see her again! The purpose of her extended visit was a grim one, but Emily relished the prospect of having a purpose beyond mere survival. She scanned the contents of the briefly worded telegram once again, this time watching for details. Anne would arrive in a few weeks' time by Union ship and would sail into Charleston Harbor.

Emily was glad to have an excuse to stay longer at Bentley. She knew her place was probably at Willow Lane. Were she a proper plantation mistress she would be at home in Savannah, but truthfully, the thought of leaving her family was painful. Little Elijah, her newfound nephew, was thriving on the abundance of love and attention he received daily, Clara and Rose were happy despite the wretched conditions of the war, and Ruth was entirely in her element, calmly running Bentley with expertise born from years of experience.

Perhaps most of all, however, Emily would miss her father. She had never really had a father in her youth; he had always been mentally absent even when he'd been at home. But often, he hadn't been home—he'd been blending with politicians and securing Bentley's place in high society while Sarah had run the plantation itself. Now, Jeffrey's focus was entirely different. All he cared about, it seemed, was the family. He and Emily had made it a tradition in the last several weeks to sit together in the library after dinner while Clara and Rose played card games. Emily and her father had many long discussions on the war, on things political, and on other issues completely unrelated to anything at all, really. Emily had come to greatly enjoy the time spent with him.

Now that Anne was on her way, Emily had an excuse to stay longer at Bentley, awaiting her arrival.

* * *

Northern Virginia

Austin Stanhope focused his gaze on the far wall of the infirmary, grateful that his vision was clearing. For months he had languished in the hospital, but he couldn't complain of boredom. Until a scant week ago, he hadn't even known where he was or who he was. The nurse who had been sitting at his bedside when he came out of his stupor was so surprised she had dropped her knitting on the floor.

He had raged with fever, she had said, for months, kept alive only because the nurses fed him broth. When he had been injured in battle, his leg had been in need of amputation. As she mentioned this to him, the memories, hazy images of pain and suffering had returned tenfold. Following his surgery, he had contracted the fever, compounded by a coughing in his lungs that had very nearly claimed his life.

"You just babble all the time," the nurse had told him wide-eyed, so excited to see him coherent that she came near to babbling herself. "You talk about someone named Emily, you talk about slaves, and you moan and cry out."

At that, he had straightened himself a bit against his bed, trying to rise and exhausting himself with the effort.

"Emily is my wife," he gasped. "Has anyone written to her, contacted her?"

The woman frowned a bit. "We didn't know who you were. We would have contacted her if we could, but in the confusion of transferring the wounded, your name was lost."

Austin fell back against the bed. "What is today's date?" he asked.

"November 29."

"She probably believes me dead." And then another thought struck him. "I'm a father," he whispered. "She would have had our child by now." A dozen worrisome images clouded his mind; women often died in childbirth, as did the children themselves. He wondered if all was well with Emily and their baby. He felt sick that he had missed so much time, that if Emily was well and whole she had no knowledge of her husband's condition or whereabouts.

She hadn't wanted him to go, had been extremely angry at the threats on his life that had necessitated his enlistment. He saw her face as he had seen it that last day; she had been even paler than usual, her red hair standing in stark contrast to her face and enormous green eyes. "I love you," she had whispered almost shyly, which was so unlike her. They hadn't been married long, indeed hadn't even known each other long, but he returned her sentiment with his whole heart. He had despaired of ever finding a woman who would delight him as Emily did, who would understand his life's cause and not only support him in it, but be willing to risk all for it.

"I have to get home," he said to the nurse. "Surely I won't be required to return to my regiment. I don't even know where they are."

The nurse had looked at him with an expression he couldn't read. Finally, she had said, "This Confederate cause will fail without the support of every person available."

Austin held a hand toward his left leg, which was missing below the knee. "I have no leg, ma'am. Should I hop into battle?"

Her face softened a bit. "Of course not, it's just that . . . well, much has happened since you came here . . . you'll be shocked when you hear of conditions in the South. Things are not necessarily going well," she said, lowering her voice and glancing over her shoulder. "I wonder if President Davis knows what he's about."

Austin nodded, knowing full well that if he told the woman he felt the whole Confederacy doomed from the beginning, she would find him shocking. She eventually obtained from him his name, place of residence, and his regiment. She had returned later that evening to tell him he was free to return home, as his injury rendered him "useless to his regiment."

He would never have believed he'd be grateful to have his leg cut off. The woman then told him she had taken the liberty of sending a telegram to his wife at Willow Lane in Savannah, Georgia, to alert her to his condition and tell her that when he was well enough, he would be home.

"Thank you so very much," he had said to the woman, grasping her hand, wincing in pain at the bedsores and stiff muscles that desperately needed movement. "Truly, I owe you my life. You've kept me alive all this time . . . I am so grateful to you."

His eyes had clouded and to his surprise, so had the woman's.

"I've been watching you die for a long time now, young man. I think it's time you go home to your wife. You eat and get yourself strong."

A week or so later, his vision was clearing and the awful pain in his head was subsiding, so he was actually able to walk the length of the room with the use of crutches and without falling to the floor more than twice. The nurse had told him to eat so that he might heal, but unfortunately, the food wasn't sufficient to feed a healthy person, let alone one who had hovered so near death.

Austin found himself caught somewhere between gratitude and frustration. He wanted so much to go home to Emily. He wanted to take her somewhere far, far away so that they could just spend some time in one another's company without thoughts of war or slavery or battle or illness.

The nurse who had been near his side since his recovery appeared with a tray of food. He slowly moved himself into a sitting position and groaned with the effort. She let him do it himself, and he appreciated her resolve to help him regain his own strength.

"I have a surprise for you," she said, and placed the tray on his lap.

"New food?" He tried to swallow his disappointment when he spied the usual fare of dried bread and broth.

"No, something better."

Austin glanced up at the woman and noticed for the first time the way her eyes were sparkling.

"Better than food? I can't imagine." He smiled a bit, her happiness contagious.

"A telegram came for you." She pulled a chair close to his bed and showed him the piece of paper she held in her hand.

He was almost afraid to take it. "What does it say?" he asked, hating the way his fingers shook as he reached for the paper.

"Read it yourself!" The woman gestured at him to get on with it.

Austin's eyes blurred as he read the message from Gwenyth, his housekeeper. Emily was well and healthy, spending time at Bentley with her family and Austin's new daughter, Mary Alice. He glanced up at the nurse, his throat raw. "I have a daughter," he whispered. "I'm a father!"

"I know," the woman said in obvious glee, wiping at her eyes. "I read it already! I couldn't very well just hand you a telegram that contained awful news now, could I? I took the liberty of opening it myself."

He was so happy he didn't care who read it—he wanted to tell the world! "Mary Alice," he murmured, his throat clogging further still.

"Does the name have special meaning?"

"Mary is my wife's bosom friend who lives in Boston, and Alice was my mother's name. She remembered," Austin murmured, wanting so desperately to hold his wife and child. "Let's see," he said, rubbing a fist across his eyes and looking again at the telegram. "She was born at the end of August. That would make her now . . . three or so months old."

The nurse leaned forward and touched the back of her fingers to Austin's cheek, sniffling. "You get yourself strong so you can go home to them."

"I want to go now," he said, clearing his throat and folding the telegram.

"Dear man, you know you can't do that yet. You'll have to make much of the journey either on horseback or in a carriage, and you just don't have the strength."

"How bad are the railways?"

She shrugged. "Depends on where you are. In some cities they're still sound. In others, the blue bellies have torn them to shreds. Still in other places, we've destroyed them ourselves to keep the invaders from making use of them. When you're ready to go home, you'll have to take it one stretch of travel at a time."

Austin was quiet for a moment, thinking. "If I could book passage aboard a ship, I could sail right into Charleston Harbor. That's where Emily is now."

The woman nodded slowly. "Yes—provided we could actually get you aboard a ship. Might prove a bit tricky unless we could find you a Union uniform . . ."

"Miz Hampton, ma'am," Austin drawled, "you mean to tell me you'd help me attempt a serious case of subterfuge?"

She blushed and slapped at his arm. "It's not subterfuge. It's helping a man get back home to his family."

Austin settled down to his meager meal. "I would be most kindly obliged," he said and, with new purpose of heart, attacked his food.

CHAPTER 16

You say you will not fight to free Negroes. Some of them seem willing to fight for you. [When victory is won] there will be some black men who can remember that, with silent tongue and clenched teeth, and steady eye and well-poised bayonet, they have helped mankind on to this great consummation; while, I fear, there will be some white ones, unable to forget that with malignant heart and deceitful speech, they strove to hinder it.

—Abraham Lincoln

* * *

12 December 1863
Boston, Massachusetts

"No, no, I can manage," Camille said to her mother, and climbed the stairs to her bedroom in her parents' house. "There's a dress I meant to take last time I visited but forgot. I'll need it when we're out of mourning."

"Very well," her mother called up after her, "but at this rate, you're going to be permanently moved out!"

Camille paused on the second floor landing and leaned over the railing, looking down into the foyer at her mother's upturned face. "No, I can't bring myself to do that just yet. This is still home."

Elizabeth smiled. "I confess, I'm glad. I've missed you."

Camille's throat tightened a bit. "I've missed you too." Before she allowed herself to get weepy, she turned and fled down the hallway to her bedroom, the soft sounds of her mother's chuckle drifting upward. It was good to see Elizabeth smile. The entire family still wore black, but she was slowly recovering from Luke's death, as they all were, and Elizabeth had always been the family's foundation. Where she went, the rest were likely to follow.

Camille entered her bedroom with a sense of peace and satisfaction. Her eyes lingered over familiar objects, each tied to memories of her girlhood. She was now becoming a woman, and by society's standards, had been of marriageable age for nearly two years. As she looked around her bedroom, she felt aged.

With a sigh, she wandered to her armoire and made a pretense of looking for the dress she'd told her mother she wanted. In truth, her motives were not so pure, and her heart jumped a bit at the reason for her visit. She made a show of clunking about in her room for a moment before silently stealing down the hallway to Robert's bedroom, her valise in hand.

She padded across his room on tiptoe, ignoring the sting in her eyes at his familiar scent and treasured belongings. The room was so very Robert, full of models of ships and military figures, books and newspapers. She reached his wardrobe and opened the doors, wincing at the resulting creak.

Plunging her hands into the darkness, she flipped through shirts and trousers, looking for something she knew she may not find. Finally, when she was about to admit defeat, she opened the door slightly wider to allow more light into the dark interior. There, toward the back, were some of Robert's older clothes—slightly smaller pants and shirts that Elizabeth had yet to go through and donate to charity.

Looking quickly over her shoulder, she yanked a pair of pants and a shirt forward and held them up briefly for examination. Yes, they would do, although they were still a bit large. She balled them up together and shoved them into her valise, closing the doors to the wardrobe and preparing to leave the room.

Satchel in hand, she gave the room one more glance and turned to go only to be caught short at the sight of a figure in the doorway. She let out a shriek and placed her hand on her heart. "Mother!"

"My apologies," Elizabeth said as she entered the room, looking about much as Camille had been doing. "It still feels like he's here, doesn't it?"

Camille couldn't make herself look at her mother. With a guilty pang, she realized Elizabeth thought she was in Robert's room seeking relief from the nostalgia for her brother. "Yes," she agreed, inching her way toward the door.

"Do you miss him?" Elizabeth asked her as she slowly followed her out of the bedroom.

"I do," Camille admitted honestly. "I miss him very much. I want him to come home in one piece."

Elizabeth nodded, folding her arms across her middle. "That would be nice, wouldn't it?"

Camille narrowed her gaze on her mother's face, feeling a fissure of alarm. "Don't you think he *will* come home?"

Elizabeth hesitated, examining her daughter's face for something, and Camille wondered if she found it. "I don't know, Cammy. If he doesn't get wounded, he may well get very ill." Elizabeth turned back to look into Robert's room, her arms tightening their hold on her middle. "He didn't need to go," she murmured. "If we were Southerners, he would have had to go. But we have more than enough . . ."

Camille moved to her mother's side and put an arm about her shoulders. She pulled her mother close and laid her cheek against Elizabeth's. "Hope deferred maketh the heart sick," she said. "Proverbs. You taught me that one."

Elizabeth turned her head and winked at her daughter, visibly pulling herself out of her temporary melancholy. "You listened! I didn't think you ever heard anything I said."

"Well, I heard some of it." Feeling guilty again for allowing her mother to believe her falsehood about the dress, she tightened her grip on the valise and kissed Elizabeth's cheek. "I must be going. I promised Abby I'd be back in time to take a walk down the street."

"It's almost dark, and it's cold outside. I've a feeling I'm better off not knowing what you two do with your time."

"Abby needs fresh air. She says a walk in the evenings helps her sleep better at night."

Elizabeth nodded. "Have you written to Robert yet?" she asked, leaning forward to close Robert's bedroom door.

"No. I'm still angry with him."

"Camille," Elizabeth began, then hesitated. "If something should happen to Robert, you might regret that decision."

"You're doing it again." Camille scowled at her mother, knowing she was right.

"Doing what again?"

"Just as you did when we were small. If we were angry about something and dared to go bed without kissing you good night, you found us and told us we'd be awfully sorry if you were dead in the morning."

Elizabeth threw back her head and laughed. "I did say that, didn't I?"

"Yes, you did. You're a cruel, cruel woman. But I'll bet you don't do it to Jimmy."

"Jimmy is an angel. The rest of you were heathens."

"Of course Jimmy is an angel," Camille said with a roll of her eyes, but sobered. "How is he doing?"

Elizabeth shrugged a shoulder as they strolled down the stairs to the foyer. "As well as can be expected. He doesn't say much, but then he never did. He misses Luke, but I think he misses Robert more."

Camille nodded. "I'll pick up something special for him the next time I'm in town." She reached the front door and waved a hand at Griffen to indicate she didn't need the aging butler to see her out.

"How is Mr. Taylor?" Elizabeth asked Camille as she turned to leave.

"Why do you ask?" Camille responded a bit too quickly.

"I understand he's been calling on you. He asked your father for permission some weeks ago."

"I . . . he . . . we've only just been a few times for a ride in the park. And sometimes he comes over for tea or a game of hearts with Abby and me. I've been extremely circumspect, you know. My reputation is still as fine as ever."

Elizabeth laughed. "Camille, I never suggested otherwise. I merely wondered how he is doing."

"Oh, fine. He's fine."

"Do you enjoy his company?"

"Shouldn't I?"

"Certainly you should, if you like him."

Camille wrinkled a brow in perplexed frustration. Why was she so utterly flustered? "I like him just as well as the next man, I suppose."

"I like him too. I think he's a good person."

"You do? But what about the way he didn't tell us Anne enlisted? I didn't think you liked him because of that."

"I understand his reasons. He did what he thought was right, and he knew Anne as well as the rest of us. He knew she'd do it anyway."

"Oh. Well, good-bye!" Camille blew her mother a quick kiss and left the house in a hurry, wanting desperately to escape her mother's scrutiny but strangely feeling light on her feet, as if a burden she didn't know she carried had lifted. She shivered as she entered the carriage and pulled the lap robes close about her as the curricle rocked with movement and made its way back to the Van Dyke home.

She looked at the satchel containing Robert's clothing and wondered if she'd lost her mind. And why hadn't she told her mother about the reason she needed those clothes? The small lamp in the carriage gave off a soft glow, and reaching into the folds of her cloak, she pulled forth a piece of paper and read it again.

It had arrived at the Van Dyke home early that morning by messenger, and Camille had recognized the spidery, wispy handwriting upon sight. It was from Olivia Sylvester, her former bosom friend whose mother had forbade them further acquaintance because of the Birminghams' ardent participation in the Abolition Society.

Watch Jacob Taylor's house tonight, eleven o'clock, the message had said. That was all of it. Nothing more, not a signature or reason for the note. Alarmed, Camille had shown the note to Abigail and had tried in vain to reach Jacob. He was out of town for the day, she had been told, and couldn't be reached. She and Abigail had walked together to the police station and had told them of the cryptic message, but had received no guarantees in return that someone in uniform would investigate. They suggested without exact words that it might be something vindictive on Olivia's part, as the two were no longer friends and Olivia might harbor jealousies or ill will.

Camille kept her eyes trained on the bag, shaking her head slightly at the memory. It wasn't that Olivia was jealous—Camille knew it. Olivia was brainless and irritating, but they had once been quite close, and Camille knew that deep down Olivia had a pure heart. Her message that morning had been a warning, pure and simple, and although she knew it was folly, Camille had decided to take matters into her own hands.

* * *

"You're really going to do this?" Abigail asked, sitting on Camille's bed and watching as Camille fastened Robert's trousers around her trim waist.

"It appears that way," Camille said as she stood at a full-length mirror, studying her frame in the boys' clothing. Experimentally, she stretched her legs and took large, lumbering steps around the room. "I'm beginning to see why Anne was so enamored of these things," she muttered and came again to a stop before the mirror. "Complete freedom of movement."

Abigail laughed, and Camille met her eyes in the mirror, grinning. It had been a long time since her friend had laughed, and if she would keep doing it, Camille vowed to dress in boys' clothing every night for entertainment.

"And tell me again why I'm not going with you?" Abigail asked.

"Because I don't want to be responsible for your reputation as well as mine, and should I be caught, I may as well label myself a harlot. Or a crazed person."

"I think that should be my decision to make, not yours."

"Probably. But someone should stay here anyway."

"Why?"

"I don't know, in case the police come by wanting to take another look at the note."

"Camille, none of this makes sense to me. I think I should go with you."

"It's not safe, Abby, to be out at night and you know it." Camille sat next to Abigail and took both of her hands. "At least people will think I'm a boy. If they see you out in your dress, something could happen . . ." Camille let out a small, frustrated puff of air. "Do you see?"

Abigail leaned forward and kissed Camille's cheek. "I see that you're trying to protect everyone in your life from harm, and I think you're taking too much on yourself."

"I'm not. I know what I'm doing."

Abigail held Camille's hands out wide to the sides and studied her odd attire. "That, my dear friend, is entirely debatable."

"Just stay in the house and watch for me to return. If I don't come back in, say, an hour, send for my father."

"An hour?" Abigail's face registered her alarm. "Camille, Jacob's house is a five-minute walk from here. Why would you be gone so long? And what are you going to do if you see someone up to no good?"

"I'll scream the neighborhood awake, but not until I get a good look at who's doing this. I'll bet my life Mrs. Sylvester's sister is behind all of it."

"Well of course she is, but you can also bet she's not going to do the dirty work herself. She will have hired someone."

"Fine. I'll make sure I see who that someone is so I can identify him later if I need to, and then we'll torture him until he confesses who hired him."

"Torture, how?" Abigail asked, her lips twitching.

"I don't know," Camille muttered. "We'll make him sit with Aunt Helena and Mrs. Sylvester for an entire afternoon in the parlor. That ought to have him screaming in agony."

Abigail sighed and followed Camille down the stairs. Her eyes followed Camille's to the large clock on the wall in the entryway. "I have fifteen minutes before they arrive," Camille whispered, finding herself already spooked. "I need to go now."

"Very well," Abigail said. "You promise you'll scream?"

"I promise." As Camille ventured out into the cold night, pulling her cap more firmly down on her thick hair that was bunched up inside, she wondered why she was compelled to take such lengths for Jacob's sake.

She looked down at her clothing, marveling at the lightness of movement, the sense of freedom. She felt as though she could fly. Camille suddenly remembered the time her family had discovered that Anne had been dressing as a boy so she could investigate for her newspaper articles. Camille had been scandalized, of course, and completely embarrassed to be related to such a hoyden.

A groan escaped her lips as she scurried quickly down the street, and she realized that the ultimate irony had come full circle. "Jacob," she muttered to herself, "you've now had two women dressing as men for your sake. I hope you appreciate it."

The air was cold and crisp, invigorating her lungs and escaping her lips in a frosty cloud. She approached Jacob's street quietly and noted with satisfaction the absence of people. Most of civilized society would be either out entertaining or being entertained into the wee hours of the morning. All others who cared little for such pursuits were probably already asleep.

She approached Jacob's house and saw that all was dark inside. It was a small, stately colonial, similar in structure and style to Abigail's home. Camille knew it from the outside because she had driven past it on many occasions, sometimes with Jacob himself. She had never seen the interior, however, and she wondered how Jacob would decorate his home.

As she hunkered down in the bushes near his porch, she imagined the rooms inside would most likely be plain yet tasteful, much like the man who owned them. She was losing herself in rich colors of browns and burgundies when she heard the muffled sound of footsteps approaching.

Peering through the branches, she saw what appeared to be a male figure stop in the street and reach about in his pockets for an object. He slowly approached the house and studied it for a moment. He then looked into his hands, and the glow of a small flame appeared as he fumbled for a moment with something he held. His face was illuminated in the darkness, and it wasn't a face Camille recognized.

Before she knew what was happening, the man hurled the object straight through Jacob's front window, followed quickly by something else that flamed in its arc and settled in the house, catching the drapes on fire. Camille stood, gasping in outrage and completely forgetting her precarious position. The man jumped back in startled shock upon seeing her and tripped over his own feet when he moved to turn and run.

Camille finally found her voice and began using it to scream for help. She ran to the house and jumped toward the front windows, catching the ledge and using the drapes inside the broken window to pull herself up. She stood on the brick window ledge and reached repeatedly and quickly with all her might for a good handhold on the curtains themselves. Grabbing a fold that wasn't yet aflame, she yanked and pulled until the curtains gave way and she fell on her back into the bushes and shrubs, pulling the burning curtains out with her.

Twisting and turning in an effort to disentangle herself from the drapes, she eventually fell onto the snow-covered front lawn, rolling and smashing the burning drapes into the white, cold expanse. Her hands stung as she smacked repeatedly at the flaming fabric, gasping in alarm to see the hem of her pants smoking. She sucked air into her lungs and sputtered, the beginnings of panic settling in as her legs became completely entangled in the smoldering drapes.

When she was nearing the sobs of the truly desperate, two hands appeared out of nowhere and smothered the sparks on her pant hem, smearing snow into her burning ankle. She looked up in shock to see Jacob in his trousers and shirtsleeves, his tie undone and hanging limp, his shirt collar open at the throat. Camille had lost her cap in the fall from the window, and her hair now tumbled around her shoulders and down her back. When he got a good look at her face, his mouth dropped open in shock.

"Camille Birmingham, what are you *doing?*"

Camille remembered the rock-thrower and whipped her head around, spying his form now tiny in the distance. "He's getting away!" she shrieked and tried to stand, unable to disentangle herself from the heavy fabric. She stumbled and fell, landing hard on her hands and knees.

By now a crowd was gathering, and questions echoed in the night as Camille scrambled to stand and give chase to the figure that had now all but disappeared. Jacob grabbed her wrist when she would have sprinted down the street, and she cried out in pain at his touch.

"Camille, you can't catch him now," Jacob said, and pulled her close, trying to shield her from prying eyes. "Look, he's gone."

"I could have run after him," she wailed, sounding much like a child in her frustration, and she heard it herself. She looked back at the house and the ruined drapes in the snow and began to acknowledge the pain that throbbed in her hands clear to the bone.

The tears finally formed in her eyes, tears that spoke as much of her frustration and fear as her pain. "Come with me," Jacob said, and, holding her close against his body, began walking her to the side of the house where his carriage stood. She knew he was trying to hide her from the onlookers, but it wasn't long before she heard the whispers.

". . . Birmingham . . ."

". . . James Birmingham's daughter . . ."

Jacob called to his neighbors over his shoulder, "Everything's fine, now. Thank you for your concern, but you can all go home. Thank you."

"Mr. Taylor, who did this?" someone called.

"I don't know yet, but we'll find the man," Jacob answered, and maneuvered Camille into the cold seat of his open carriage. "Just a moment," he murmured to her and went into the small stable for his horse. She sat quietly, trying not to whimper, and watched the crowd slowly disperse while Jacob hitched a horse to the small curricle.

"Hold this," he said as he climbed in next to her and took up the reins. He dumped a large lump of snow into her cupped hands and she gasped in pain. "Don't drop it," he said when she moved to heave it over the side of the carriage. "It will take away some of the sting."

"It's not working very well," she said, trying to talk past the hitch in her breath. "I didn't even know you were home. When did you get home? Am I babbling? I feel as though I'm babbling."

Jacob glanced at her, his face drawn in concern. "Earlier this evening. I hadn't turned in for the night, though. I was in the back study reading. I heard the crash in the front, and by the time I made it to the parlor, I saw the burning drapes disappear through the window. Camille, how did you know to be here?"

"I received a note from Olivia this morning," she said, and in halting, shaky tones described the message and the events of the day. "I don't think I was very effective," she rambled when she described the police officers' ambiguity and her decision to act on her own. "Anne would have handled this so much better! What was I thinking, really—I'm no good at this boy thing—I never wanted to do this boy thing. I wish Robert were home. I would have made *him* do this. He would have too, you know. We're quite good friends now. And would you look at all the neighbors who came outside! Now everyone will know I've been following in my daft sister's footsteps. It wasn't for my own entertainment, however, I'll tell you that much."

Jacob rubbed his face and leaned forward to rest his elbows on his legs, the reins held loosely in his hands. "You Birmingham women are going to be the death of me," he muttered.

"Where are you taking me?"

"Home."

"Good. Abby is waiting, and I'm afraid she was worried when I left."

"She should have been worried! Do you understand how foolish it was for you to try to confront this danger on your own? Why didn't you ask your father for help if you thought the police were ignoring you?"

"That's Abby's street," Camille said, using both her hands, still cupped around the melting snow, to point to their left.

"I'm taking you home. To your home."

Camille's mouth dropped open, and her tears now fell in earnest. "Oh, no, you can't! My father will have an apoplectic fit!"

"I surely hope so."

"Jacob, please, I am begging you, do not take me to my parents. They have so much worry in their lives right now—one son dead and the other off at war, and now the second of their only two daughters running around town in trousers."

"Camille," Jacob said, his tone gentling, "your hands are burned and so is your . . . your . . . lower limb. You need to be seen by your family doctor, and I owe it to your father to see you safely home."

"No, no! My parents have absolved you of all responsibility for Anne's enlistment—I even spoke with my mother earlier today about it! You needn't feel obligated to somehow atone for that mistake."

He looked at her with an expression of amusement and exasperation. He did not, however, stop the carriage or attempt to change his course of direction. With a sinking heart, Camille realized he fully intended to take her to her parents.

"I was trying to do a good thing for you," she raged. "Is this how you're going to thank me, then? Take me to my poor, beleaguered parents?"

He glanced at her askance, his eyes full of amusement. "Your 'poor, beleaguered parents'? Your poor parents will be just fine. I'll be a lucky man if your poor, beleaguered father doesn't shoot me on the spot."

"This isn't your fault. In fact, it has nothing to do with you."

"You appeared on my front lawn in the dark of night and tried to stop a vandal from burning my house down! It has everything to do with me!"

Camille fell silent as her family home came into view, and they eventually came to a stop on the circular drive before the wide front doors. "Let's just go back to your house," she said in a hushed whisper. "We can send for my family doctor from there."

"Are you so determined to have the good people of this town think you a ruined woman, then?"

"Jacob Taylor, you are a man without a heart." Camille leaned over the side of the carriage and dumped what remained of the snow onto the ground and, with a grunt of pain, lifted herself from the seat and jumped to the ground without waiting for Jacob's assistance. She heard him curse under his breath and descend from the carriage behind her, trotting to catch up to her by the time she reached the front porch, her head held high. She rang the bell without looking once in his direction and waited until she heard a scurry of footsteps.

"Camille," Jacob began, but Camille silenced him with an imperious raise of her blistered hand.

"I begged you *shamelessly,*" she muttered.

"Camille, be reasonable . . ."

"*Shamelessly!* And still you wouldn't hear me."

The door opened and James stood on the inside, wrapped in a robe and slippers, his hair rumpled. His jaw dropped as he viewed his daughter and the newspaper editor on his front porch, his daughter looking much like his sons.

"What in *blazes* is the meaning of this?" He reached for Camille's arm and glared at Jacob as he followed them inside the house.

"James?" Elizabeth appeared on the landing above the foyer, her hair hanging in a long braid down her back. "Camille!" When she spied her daughter, she flew down the stairs and, upon reaching her side, grabbed her shoulders and shook her. "What are you doing? What is this?" She looked toward Jacob for answers.

He winced a bit and put a hand on the small of Camille's back, hovering close to her. "Her hands are burned, ma'am. You might send for the doctor. In the meantime, I think she should sit with her hands in a bowl of cold water."

"Are you responsible for this?" James turned the full blast of his green-eyed fury on Jacob, who removed his hand from Camille's back but stubbornly stayed close.

"I would like to speak," Camille said clearly, holding her hands up at her mother's insistence. Elizabeth gasped when she saw them and began tugging on her daughter's arms, leading her into the parlor.

Camille explained herself as the small group entered the room to the right of the foyer, and James lit the lanterns, which bathed the parlor in a gentle glow.

"You might have mentioned this message to me," James said as he bent over her hands for a closer look. "Why did you not?"

"I don't know." Camille felt miserable. Why had she insisted on trying to save the day for Jacob all by herself? Once the police had dismissed her concerns, she had assumed command of the situation and hadn't looked back. She couldn't bear the thought of another family member standing in the line of fire, though—she just couldn't! It was easy to say she would have asked Robert for help because Robert wasn't there. She realized, once she considered it, that she would have gone forward with her solitary plan even if he had been home. "I didn't want you to be hurt," she mumbled miserably to her father, knowing how childish she sounded. "I only wanted to see who would be there so I could perhaps identify him later . . ."

"Camille, I owe you my thanks," Jacob said, and managed not to wither under James's and Elizabeth's glares. "Because you were there and acted so quickly, my house didn't burn, and I am alive."

She felt herself flush, and for a fraction of a second, she wished her parents would go away.

"Mr. Taylor, I am beginning to believe you are a hazard to my daughters," James said, and looked back at Camille's hands, taking one gently into his own and tilting it toward the light.

"It's not his fault," Camille said, leaning against the back of the chair and closing her eyes. "I was just trying to help."

"You did help," Jacob said softly, and Camille opened her eyes a bit to see him looking at her from behind her worried, hovering parents. The corner of his mouth turned up in a slight smile, and he winked at her.

She returned his smile and again closed her eyes.

CHAPTER 17

My heart aches for these poor wretches, Yankees though they are, and I am afraid God will suffer some terrible retribution to fall upon us for letting such things happen. If the Yankees should ever come to southwest Georgia and go to Anderson and see the graves there, God have mercy on the land!

—Southern woman allowed to climb a guard tower at Andersonville

* * *

4 January 1864
Charleston, South Carolina

Anne squeezed Emily tight, marveling at how much her young cousin had changed. Emily was no longer a spitfire little girl, but a woman grown. As they made their way out of the city toward the plantation, Anne listened with interest while Emily described the effect the war was having on the city. The Confederate dollar was so inflated that the simplest of items cost two hundred times their worth.

Anne shook her head. "People up north are living the fancy life," she said, "to excesses you wouldn't imagine."

"You know," Emily said as the carriage rolled along, no longer the well-sprung vehicle it had been in its glory days, "there was a time when I was so hateful, so vindictive, I would have reveled in the suffering here."

"What has changed your mind?"

"My daughter. And my nephew Elijah. They're innocent, and many, many other people in the South are innocent as well. I never considered that fact."

Anne turned her full attention on Emily. "Is Elijah Charlotte's son?"

"No." Emily paused for a moment, deep in thought. "He's Richard's son."

Anne hesitated, feeling the need for sensitivity. "I see."

"Ah, but it grows ever more . . . complex. You recall Mary, I presume? She now works in your household as a seamstress."

Anne's eyes widened in comprehension. "Oh, my."

"Yes."

"And I would venture to guess that Mary needed to put some distance between herself and the child?"

"Well . . . she doesn't know we have him, precisely."

"And do you plan to tell her?"

"At some future point, yes. You see, Elijah was not conceived under the most ideal of . . . circumstances. And his paternal relation is most unfortunate."

Anne remembered well the unpleasant child Richard had been. "I had assumed as much."

Emily nodded slightly without any apparent regret for maligning her brother's name. "So you see the cause for my reluctance. Mary is building a new life for herself, and I'm not sure Elijah would fit well into it. I hate to mar her happiness with unpleasant memories."

"Yet it should be her decision to make," Anne said gently.

"Should it?" Emily looked at Anne without any guile or pretense. "Should I force her to abandon her child permanently? A child born of rape is still an innocent child, and if Mary cannot bear the sight of him, she is still turning away from her own flesh and blood." Emily looked out the carriage window and the passing landscape. "Mary is a woman of enormous heart. She would suffer endless guilt, so if I remove the decision from her hands, isn't that the kinder thing to do?"

"Perhaps," Anne said, considering the situation carefully and remembering her own night of pain over Luke's death when Mary had been so gentle and kind to her. "But what if she would love her son? Suppose she would relish the thought of being with him? The choice was never hers to make initially, but now . . ."

"Now I'm no better than my mother, taking away a person's right to choose for herself."

Anne smiled. "You seek to protect a friend, not dictate her life."

Emily shrugged, her expression troubled. "I'm sorry to burden you with this upon your arrival, cousin. You lend a good ear."

"It is my pleasure, Emily. I've much enjoyed our correspondence of the past few years. I've looked forward to your letters immensely."

"You'll find that things here are not at all the way you'll remember them from your visits when you were young. The whole shape of the family has changed—I hardly recognize it myself and yet I've been a personal witness to it." She turned and faced Anne squarely. "Now, then. How can I help you? What are your plans?"

Anne sighed, her heart taking a leap when she again remembered the purpose for her visit. She rubbed her wounded thigh absently, thinking. "I need to know where Ivar is. The only information I've received is that he has been taken farther south. I may be too far south at this point. The frustrating thing is that I simply do not know." She spread her hands apart. "This is the first step of my journey. I usually have a much more concise plan, but unfortunately, this time I find myself having to structure it as I go along."

Emily pursed her lips in thought. "My father," she said. "He holds an impressive amount of political influence. We'll see if he can't uncover something useful."

* * *

Camp Sumter
Andersonville, Georgia

Ivar looked around the prison yard, studying the layout. It was a plot of ground, rectangular in shape and sixteen and one-half acres in size, surrounded on all sides by a fence made of pinewood logs that stood roughly fifteen to twenty feet high. A small stream ran through the center, and Ivar surmised that this was probably one of the reasons the new prison had been built there, combined with the proximity to the railroad. Upon their arrival in Georgia two days before, the prisoners had marched one-quarter mile to the new site from the depot—Ivar had been grateful the walk wasn't any longer.

The prisoners had been busy since their arrival, erecting makeshift tents from whatever materials were at hand and trying to adjust to the fact that this place was to be their new home. They used scrap wood, tent material, and some even dug holes. Bulldog, Ivar's personal guard, had left him with the newly appointed prison guards at Camp Sumter with a sneer. Apparently he was satisfied with having drug Ivar as far away from home as possible and felt his work was finished. Watching the man leave had been a relief; it was almost worth it to be so far south if it meant he would no longer have to contend with him.

How long, though? He walked and walked around the prison yard, feeling a sense of desperate unease settle into his chest. It tightened as he moved until he felt as though a huge rope were squeezing the very air out of his lungs. How long could he survive? The water source seemed good enough, but that would remain so only as long as there were a manageable number of prisoners in the camp. He had seen places in his trek southward that were so overcrowded the stench was unbearable—and those had been outside!

His health was stable at best, but he worried over the nagging cough that had settled into his chest. He had lost much weight but tried daily to move about and preserve what strength he had left in hopes that he might last long enough to either see the end of the war or perhaps, if a miracle occurred, a prisoner exchange. The latter was an extreme improbability, however, since word was that this prison had been built as a direct result of the failure of the prisoner exchange system.

A rowdy scuffle among the prisoners ensued in the middle of the camp near the stream, and it took several threats and finally warning shots fired into the air to break the feuding men apart. They had been prisoners for a long while, and tempers ran high as personalities clashed. Ivar halted his progress, taking care not to step too closely to a wooden rail situated around the camp approximately twenty feet in from the outer fence. The dead line, it was called, and the penalty for crossing it was instantaneous death administered swiftly and without question from one or more prison guards who sat watch high in sentry boxes atop the prison walls. The prisoners had taken to calling the sentry boxes "pigeon roosts."

Slaves had built the prison itself, he had heard, and Ivar wondered how long the system would remain in place. It had only been two days ago that the Confederate general Patrick Cleburne had suggested slaves be freed and trained to fight for the Confederacy. The high command over Cleburne had reportedly called the idea "revolting" and dismissed it. With Lincoln's Emancipation Proclamation official for a year now, the focus of the war had shifted to reveal total emancipation as the eventual goal for the Union. Not everybody supported it, and if the papers were to be believed, often those who did supported it only as a logical way to break the South. Regardless of the reasons, change was in the air, and everyone felt it.

Ivar sighed a bit as he watched the men who had been fighting break apart and retreat to separate corners of the prison, putting as much distance between themselves as possible in the confines of the yard. One prisoner passing close by Ivar was talking to another, and Ivar caught a few of his remarks. "You know why we're getting less food these days—in December the rebels in Richmond ordered that supplies coming from our people up north to feed us be stopped."

"We're gonna starve in this place," the second man answered. "Those durned rebs don't get any food hardly at all! They're sure not gonna give us any more than they get!"

Ivar's thoughts turned to Anne, his solace, his secret angel who came to him in his thoughts and brought a measure of peace to his troubled mind. He clung to her memory so fiercely, so frequently, that he wondered if he were imagining things—conversations they'd never actually had, smiles she'd never really given to him. If she were smart, she'd find herself a husband and settle down. While he knew her to be a woman who flouted convention, he wondered if her experiences in battle hadn't calmed her somewhat, made her long for a conventional life.

The thought of her with another man made him wince, so he pretended she loved him, that she would wait for him to either die or appear on her doorstep in Boston. He imagined taking her home to meet his parents and Inger—they would love her, he was sure of it. Her strength matched his mother's, and he envisioned them getting along famously.

Ivar closed his eyes and shivered against the brisk day, folding his arms across his chest for warmth. His clothing hung loosely on his frame where it used to fit him to perfection. The material bunched under his fingers, and he clenched his teeth at the tremor of nervousness that had him wondering how much weight he could afford to lose before his life would be forfeit. To slow the rapid beating of his heart and level his breathing, he again pictured Anne smiling at him, Anne waiting for him.

* * *

New York, New York

Daniel walked the two miles outside the city to his home, carrying nothing save his knapsack. His clothing was worn, his appearance weary, and he had seen more than his share of blood and death in the battles he had engaged in during the year of his enlistment with the navy. His heart now, though, was as light as a feather. Despite the death of his father, the memory of which still often settled into his mind with a sad sense of gloom, he was so thrilled to be returning to his home, to Marie, and to his mother, that he felt nothing could mar his happiness. Not on this fine day.

The road home was familiar, and as he rounded a corner, his heart thumped in his chest as he spied his parents' home. A little bit down the hill from theirs was his own, small and neat and waiting for his return. The earth slept in winter, but he was grateful it would soon be spring—it was his favorite time of year.

His step slowed a bit, and he stopped in front of his mother's home, taking in the welcome sight of the neat little farmhouse, nothing changed in its appearance. His happiness faltered a bit when he thought that Gavin wouldn't be there to welcome him home. *You would be so proud of me, Da. I did it. I finished my obligation to my country, just as you would have wanted.*

For a moment, for just a small moment, he felt his father's presence, featherlight in his mind, brushing his thoughts like the touch of a warm blanket. It was enough. He knew Gavin was proud.

His thoughts were interrupted as the front door burst open accompanied by an ecstatic shriek. Marie was there, looking even more beautiful than he remembered. She ran to him and threw her arms around his neck, crying in her excitement. "You didn't even say you were on your way home!"

He laughed and hugged her to him, reveling in the moment and never wanting it to end. She fit so perfectly in his arms, as if she'd always been there. "I wanted to surprise you," he said in her ear, and as she pulled back, he wiped at the tear that trailed down her cheek.

"You even claimed you'd be delayed," she said, smacking at his chest with a closed fist. "That's not funny!"

"Forgive me?" He kissed the tip of her nose and laughed when she continued pounding on his chest.

"I suppose so," she finally said and made a show of pouting, looking up at him through her lashes. "I've missed you."

He closed his eyes and touched his forehead to hers. "And I've missed you." He turned his head to the right and looked down the hill at his small home. "You've seen the house, then?" he asked, feeling himself tense a bit as he waited for her response. His home didn't match the splendor of the Brissot family home she'd lived in all her life.

"I love it," she said, and nuzzled his neck. "It's wonderful. I wanted to stay there once my mother came, but she and your mother insisted we all stay together up here. They grew worried thinking of me living there alone—as if I wasn't alone in New Orleans."

"You had the Fromeres with you in New Orleans."

"My mother didn't know that." Marie shook her head with a sad smile and looked up at Daniel, her violet eyes large and expressive. "She and your mother both are a bit . . . well, they worry excessively these days. Having both lost their husbands recently . . ."

Daniel nodded, his throat constricting.

"Daniel, I'm so sorry about your father. I just missed meeting him, you know. And I felt awful having to tell you through a letter—I wanted to be with you when you received the news."

"Your letter was just fine," he said, touching a finger to her cheek. "It was a comfort." He glanced toward the doorway and saw his mother standing with her arm about the waist of Marie's mother. He grinned and motioned toward them with a nod of his head. "They get along well, then?"

Marie looked back at the door and smiled. "They do. They've been good company for each other. Your mother has asked mine to stay with her when we move to your house. I'm so happy—it could have been awkward, but they've become good friends. Your mother's a very generous woman."

Daniel released Marie long enough to retrieve his knapsack, which had fallen to the ground, and then, holding her closely against his side, moved toward the door to greet the two mothers who looked at them with teary eyes. Much to his chagrin, his eyes felt suspiciously wet as he embraced Brenna, loving his mother so much and missing his father terribly.

"Welcome home, my boy," Brenna said to him as she clutched him close.

"I love you," he whispered in her ear, and planted a kiss on her cheek.

"Your Da was so proud of you, you know," she said. "So proud."

CHAPTER 18

Will the slave fight? If any man asks you, tell him No. But if anyone asks you will a Negro fight, tell him Yes!

—Wendell Phillips, ardent abolitionist and associate of William Lloyd Garrison

* * *

22 February 1864
En route to Jacksonville, Florida

Joshua whipped his head around at the sound of a loud crash and stumbled until he nearly fell over his own feet. Nobody laughed, though, because he hadn't been the only one to react strongly to the noise. "Sorry 'bout that," someone down the line murmured. "Dropped some things."

When he finally was able to slow the wild beating of his heart, Joshua turned back and fell into line. He had become especially susceptible to anxiety over loud, sudden noises or calamities. He hated things happening behind his back especially. There had never been a time in his life when he would have thought of himself as jittery or nervous—not even when the overseer had been present and threatening.

Battle had done it to him. Battle and spending six months working detail on Morris Island, just south of Charleston, under constant fire from Fort Wagner and Fort Gregg. Noises, especially loud ones, drove him to distraction. And the events of two days before plagued him continually until he wondered if he'd ever forget.

His regiment had been sent into Florida earlier in the month to act as support for General Seymour, and on the twentieth had found themselves embroiled in the battle of Olustee. The 55th Massachusetts's involvement was minor, but the sights and sounds of that horrific and bloody scene had haunted his every hour, waking or sleeping, since.

He felt a slight tremor in his left arm and clenched his fist, holding his arm close to his side for a moment. The tremor had begun on Morris Island, when the constant barrage of gunfire had stretched his nerves taut, and had continued intermittently for weeks. It had stopped for a bit when the 55th had left for Florida, but it had recurred with increasing intensity since the battle.

Joshua didn't want anyone to notice; it was bad enough that the public and even other soldiers verbally attacked the colored regiments, suggesting that they would never perform to the same level as white regiments, that black men were not capable of the same achievements. The colored regiments had proven themselves time and again, but it seemed that anything they did they must do twice as much and twice as well to be seen as worthy in the eyes of the world.

He had heard stories of other men, white men, who had suffered many maladies both physical and mental from the strain of battle. Some had nightmares that never stopped, some imagined illnesses, and the number of soldiers who deserted on a daily basis was staggering. He was certainly no less cowardly than they! He couldn't, though, allow anyone to see that something was troubling him, that something had happened to him although he hadn't been wounded. He didn't have the luxury of asking for help or advice because he felt it would reflect badly on the regiment. It was a weight that grew heavy to bear.

How long they would stay in Jacksonville was anyone's guess. Rumor had it that they would continue to stay in the Deep South, perhaps progressing back again to South Carolina and her surrounding islands. As familiar as the countryside was, Joshua found himself missing Boston. He had just begun to carve, quite literally, a wonderful new life for himself when the urge to serve and do his part became most persuasive. He thought of Ben, as he often did, and wondered how he was. It was Ben's example that had prompted Joshua's decision and precipitated his enlistment, and while he ached to be far away from the sounds of battle and the now-familiar rhythm of the regiment, he knew he must stay and finish.

Joshua's thoughts turned to those he loved as he thrust his trembling hand into his pocket. Mary was well, and he was glad to hear it. Her experiences in the North had agreed well with her. She had written him recently of Emily's new baby girl, and he thought of them fondly. Emily, while once the sincerest object of his hidden affections, had become a tender memory. He knew she had grown to love her husband, and for that he was very grateful. Joshua had once harbored a secret dream of someday living a life of love with Emily, but the dream had faded from his mind and now, slowly, it was fading from his heart. He relinquished his mental hold on her for his own sake, and found that, amazingly enough, it didn't hurt anymore. He would always love her, but in releasing her, he had found a freedom of his own.

Please, God in heaven, he thought as he plodded along the dusty road, *please let me live to see a new day. Let me build my life again, help me be whole. Heal this thing that ails me.* The tremor in his arm still continued, and he felt a stab of disappointment. God had taken the children of Israel to the promised land, had parted the Red Sea, had drowned the Egyptians. Surely, if He were a God of miracles, He could stop the shaking of one arm.

Patience, my son . . .

The thought echoed in his head, and he glanced up, wondering if someone had spoken aloud. It hadn't been a voice, though. The sound of talking continued to buzz around him as the soldiers conversed one with another, but nobody seemed to even be looking his way, let alone speaking with him.

Patience . . .

The word pierced his heart with its softness, yet it was as direct as the shot of an arrow. Joshua drew his brows together in thought and pondered it, knowing of the source and yet amazed to be answered directly. *Patience.* That had been the mantra following him his entire life. It was a hard thing, to want something and not receive it. He had felt the bitterness of denial many times, and patience was not an easy virtue for him.

He felt a measure of peace, however, as he continued the march, as well as an increase in energy, almost as though a hand were placed upon his back, urging him forward with a gentle nudge. *Yea, though I walk through the valley of the shadow of death,* he thought, *I will fear no evil: for thou art with me; thy rod and thy staff they comfort me . . .*

* * *

Charleston, South Carolina
Bentley Plantation

"Surely goodness and mercy shall follow me all the days of my life: and I will dwell in the house of the Lord for ever." Ruth's gentle voice finished the scripture reading, and Anne closed her eyes as the woman concluded the small, informal worship service with prayer.

It had become customary each week for the odd assortment of family and servants to gather together in the parlor for some spiritual thoughts and prayer led by Ruth. Anne had come to enjoy those gatherings, but today she found herself especially restless. *I mean no offense, Father, but I'm not yet ready to dwell in Thy house. Please, I just want to find Ivar.*

Her Uncle Jeffrey had been spreading the word among his associates that he was searching for a particular Union prisoner of war, but as of yet they had turned up nothing. Anne was beginning to feel a restless panic to pack her bag and set out on her own if something didn't happen soon. It had been nearly two months since her arrival in Charleston, and with each passing day, she envisioned Ivar starving that much more or becoming that much more ill with some dreadful disease.

As Ruth finished her prayer, Anne rose and left the room, not feeling especially social. She wandered down the wide hallway to the front foyer, her head bent in thought. It was here that Emily found her a few moments later, Charlotte close behind.

"What is it, Anne?" Charlotte asked her. Anne glanced up at the woman and regarded the frank, blue eyes that studied her. Her cousin, Charlotte, Anne's same age, had become a woman of quiet strength. Anne had always remembered her as slightly shrill and demanding, yet

Charlotte's child and the condition of her own mother, it seemed, had wrought a change in her personality that was interesting to behold.

Anne looked from Charlotte to Emily. She placed her hands on her hips and took a shaky breath. "If I don't find him soon, he's going to die. I don't know what to do. I hate not knowing what to do."

Charlotte nodded. "I understand. Until I received word of William's death, I was nearly beside myself."

Emily gasped and moved closer to her sister. "What is this? When did you receive word of William's death?"

"Several months back."

Emily sputtered and stopped, trying for a comment she couldn't seem to form, which was entirely a rarity for Emily. "Charlotte," she finally managed, "why did you never say anything?"

Charlotte moved to a tall, straight-backed chair that sat along the wall next to a polished mahogany side table, one of the few items in the house that hadn't yet been traded for practical goods. "I didn't want to." She folded her hands in her lap and looked up at Emily, who stood close beside her. "I didn't want to tell anyone. I didn't want the sympathy."

Emily gaped at her. "I'm . . . I'm not sure what to say, then. Do you still not want the sympathy?"

Charlotte shrugged her shoulders, looking much like a little girl.

Emily kneeled beside her and grasped both of her hands. "Charlotte, I'm very, very sorry. William was . . . he was decent to me. Not everyone was."

"I wasn't, you mean."

Emily regarded her frankly. "No, you weren't. But you didn't understand me. I wasn't an easy girl to understand. And this was not an easy family for any of us to live in."

"That much is true," Charlotte said, not pulling her hands from Emily's grasp. "I'm sorry I didn't understand you, Emily." Her tone was stiff, but something in her expression spoke of her deep unease, of a desire that her apology be accepted despite her embarrassment.

"And I'm sorry I wasn't kinder to you," Emily answered, her eyes bright. "And I'm dreadfully sorry that William is gone."

Anne watched the scene with a sense of wonder. In the midst of the war, the family was somehow managing to heal some of the hurts created in a lifetime of pride and misunderstanding. There was a spirit in the home that had never before been there, even in the early years when money abounded and the plantation ran at full production, all members of the family hale and hearty.

Suddenly Anne's own worries were shoved aside as she regarded her cousin, having lost her husband and the father of her child. "I regret that William will never know his son," Charlotte was saying to Emily. "It was the reason he finally made his peace with me, you know. He wanted something to leave behind—almost as though he knew he was going to die."

"He felt affection for you, Charlotte. His motive wasn't only for the sake of having a child."

"Maybe not entirely, but you needn't pretend with me, Emily. You were here. You saw firsthand how it was between William and me. It was a marriage in name only."

"Toward the end it was more."

"Yes, perhaps. And now he's gone. He hadn't really wanted me in the first place. I don't delude myself into thinking there will be anyone else—which is why I am happy to have my son." Charlotte glanced at Anne, who looked her with an expression of chagrin. "Anne," she said, releasing her hands from Emily and standing, "I'm sorry. I stole the conversation."

"Not in the least," Anne said, and she meant it. "I'm sorry to hear of your loss as well. My troubles pale in comparison."

"Certainly not," Charlotte said, and took Anne by the elbow, leading her into the empty parlor. "I am at peace with my life. I don't regret anything. Now we consider you."

Emily stared at her sister with open amazement. Charlotte noticed and commented on it.

"Well," Emily began, "I'm not certain how to explain myself without offending."

"Don't worry about offending. You never have yet."

Emily's mouth twisted into a wry smile. "In that case, Charlotte, I am amazed to see you tending to another's problems. It's entirely unlike you."

"Most everything about me is entirely unlike me these days."

Emily nodded and took a seat opposite the other two women. "True enough." She patted Anne's knee. "Father will be home this afternoon from Atlanta."

"So soon? I had thought he was to be gone for at least another week," Anne said, wrinkling her brow in thought.

"He sent word of an early return. I don't believe he found circumstances there to be better than here. I could have told him as much, but he wanted to see for himself."

"He knows people, Emily. Most likely he wanted to examine every possibility before dismissing it entirely," Charlotte said.

"Would he really have moved your mother to Atlanta?" Anne asked the women.

Emily shrugged. "He seems determined to get her away from here. We have property in Atlanta. I think he considered it an option, but from what I understand, the stability of the city is in question." She glanced at Charlotte. "I believe he'll do as he mentioned when he first returned home and take her out west."

Charlotte nodded. "It may actually be good for her. But at any rate," she said, turning back to Anne, "he did say he would ask about your friend. If anyone can find information, it would be our father."

As though speaking of him had commanded his presence, the front door opened and Jeffrey stepped inside the entrance, visible through the open parlor door. The three women stood and moved to greet him, and Anne was touched to see the gentle beginnings of warmth between the father and his daughters.

"How did you find things?" Emily asked him.

Jeffrey shook his head as he shrugged out of his coat and laid it over a chair. "Disastrous. And now Sherman is on his way."

"Sherman is on his way?" Charlotte echoed.

"A few weeks ago he captured Meridian, Mississippi, and he has destroyed all supplies, buildings, and railroads. Word has it he's working his way east. Atlanta will most certainly be on his list of places to visit."

Charlotte's hand fluttered to her throat. "And then he will come here?"

Jeffrey hesitated.

"Think not to spare our feelings," Emily said in a dry tone. "'Twould serve no purpose at this point."

"I'm certain he will come here. This is where it all began."

The silence hung heavy in the hall, punctuated only by the consistent tick of the clock. Emily was the first to find her voice. "Well, then, it's only right that it be finished."

"Will they burn the homes?" Charlotte asked her father after glaring at her sister.

"Yes. They'll burn everything. That is exactly why we're going to leave. I have money; we'll be safe."

"I've never known any home but this one," Charlotte murmured, glancing about the hall.

"Wouldn't it be nice to have a new one, then, with new memories? Fond memories made with your child?" Emily asked her, and Anne had the sense that Emily was being as gentle as she knew how. "There are precious few good memories in this place, Charlotte—for any of us."

Jeffrey guided the women toward the center of the house, including Anne in his gesture with a gentle hand upon her elbow. "I have one bit of good news in all of this," he said, and Anne's heart took an enormous leap. She knew his news was for her.

"Ivar?" she asked, looking up at the man who was so very like her own father.

Jeffrey nodded. "He's near a village called Andersonville, Georgia. A new camp they've named Sumter."

* * *

Charlotte sat in her room that night long after she had tucked her son into bed. They would soon be leaving the only home she had ever known, and Emily was right, of course—it was a home full of conflicting memories. But wasn't a less-than-perfect familiar better than the unknown?

She had harbored dreams as a young girl, dreams that somehow, miraculously, Ben and Richard would tell Sarah that they had no need for Bentley, that surely it should fall to Charlotte's capable hands. After all, Sarah herself had been a young girl at the time of her inheritance, and she had run the plantation admirably through the years. Charlotte would do no less.

Those dreams had fallen flat, however, and she had become a person she didn't like. Yet it was easier and safer to be harsh and self-absorbed. Then she wouldn't have to think about how many suitors found her boorish, about how the only way she had snared a husband was because her father had paid off his debts.

She thought of William and began to cry. He had shown her great affection at the end before his enlistment, and although she fought it with all her might, she had begun to melt under it. He was dead now, and she would never know if it had been genuine. If she pretended he had been sincere, a little voice in the back of her mind taunted her for being a fool. And if she acknowledged that it might have been an act of a man who knew he was doomed an early death, then it made her as pathetic as she had always been.

How she wished for a nice man! A gentle man who wouldn't expect more from her than she was; a man who would acknowledge that she wasn't daring and exciting like Ben or Emily or cousin Anne; that she wasn't a plantation mistress like her mother; that she wasn't a favorite amongst the servants because of her benevolence or engaging personality or even a favorite amongst children and small animals.

She was just Charlotte, a woman who was a master at the domestic arts of the day—who now, because of straitened circumstances, could not only mend clothing but could cook an impressive meal as well. Those should have been qualities to draw men like flies, but compared with the fiery and brave women who lined her family tree, both living and dead, they only made her feel . . . matronly. Dowdy. Boring.

Charlotte enjoyed sitting before a fire at the end of the day and reading a book of poetry or perhaps a novel. She would never, *ever* admit it to anyone, but she quite enjoyed a good romantic story. She didn't even want to be part of a social whirl anymore—not that there was a whirl to be found south of the Mason-Dixon these days—but all those things that she used to think she wanted desperately she now realized she never really wanted at all.

What she had wanted was for Sarah to love her, to look at her as Charlotte worked with a needle and thread or played the pianoforte and smile. They were things Sarah had insisted Charlotte perfect, but when she had, it still didn't seem to please her mother. So Charlotte had decided to become as much like Sarah as possible. But Sarah still hadn't noticed or appreciated it, and in the meantime, Charlotte had slowly killed that which was *her.*

She had been afraid, too, she acknowledged as the tears quietly fell. She had been worried as a young girl that if she remained her peaceful, conventional self, that she would never find a man content to stay home in the evenings. It wasn't spoken of in polite circles, of course, but high-society wives frequently turned their heads while their husbands chased other pursuits. Charlotte had read fairy tales as a child, and she decided long ago that if her prince turned his interests elsewhere, it would break her heart.

So she had hardened her heart instead.

The casing around it had begun to melt, however, just as William enlisted, and it softened completely as she held her young son in her arms. It left her vulnerable, however, and she cried now more than she had in years. She cried for William's short life, cried for her own status as a widow, and cried for the fact that her prince never really had come along after all.

And now they were leaving the only place she knew in favor of something she might entirely detest. What were her options, though? Stay here and watch Sherman burn the place to the ground? Live at Willow Lane on Emily's generosity? Most likely Willow Lane would be burned to the ground as well. She had no options other than to go with her father and mother, but she didn't like it. Perhaps it wasn't too late for the family to consider something else.

CHAPTER 19

Grant is certainly a very extraordinary man, [but] he does not look it and might well pass . . . for a dumpy and slouchy little subaltern, very fond of smoking. Neither do I know that he shows it in his conversation, [he] doesn't seem to be a very talkative man, anyhow.
—Charles Francis Adams

* * *

8 March 1864
Washington, D.C.

James and Elizabeth Birmingham stood in the midst of the crowd at President Lincoln's weekly White House reception. The object of the attention of nearly every person in the room was a short man with a scruffy beard who currently stood on a couch so that he might better reach the many hands that were clamoring to grasp his.

"I doubt Mr. Grant knew he'd be so sought after this evening," Elizabeth murmured to her husband. "At the Willard this afternoon, nobody even knew who he was. I was in the lobby when he signed in."

James glanced at his wife. "You were?"

"I was. You were upstairs napping."

"It's not a sin to take a midday nap, dear," James said in low tones to his wife, fighting a smile.

"It's a waste of time," she said, slapping his arm with her fan. "And as I was saying, the clerk nearly turned the general away. Didn't realize until Mr. Grant signed the register who he was."

"He doesn't look . . . comfortable," James said, watching the general.

"I don't imagine he is. His place is on the battlefield, not at a reception." Elizabeth was quiet for a moment. "I feel bad for him that he must endure this."

As the evening wore on, Ulysses S. Grant was bestowed the rank of lieutenant general, a rank re-created especially for him and not in use since the title had belonged to George Washington many years before. Later, when Elizabeth wandered close to the general and the president, she heard Lincoln tell the man, "I wish to express my entire satisfaction with what you have done up to this time, so far as I can understand it. The *particulars* of your plans I neither know nor seek to know."

As the Birminghams returned back to the Willard Hotel later that evening, Elizabeth tried to express her feelings to her husband. "Lincoln has great faith in Grant. I believe we are seeing the beginning of the end," she said.

He nodded. "Grant is unafraid to use our resources. He knows we have more to spare than the South."

Elizabeth's lip trembled, and she drew it between her teeth. She had shed enough tears in recent months to last a lifetime. "I wouldn't mind so much if my son weren't one of those resources. I've already lost one. It's the only way to finish this thing, isn't it?"

James nodded and put an arm about her shoulders, pulling her close. "He knows the men are expendable, but

I don't think he finds joy in it. It's the one thing that helps me like the man. He's not driven by hatred, but by practical knowledge."

Elizabeth sniffed. "I'm finding that slim comfort."

"We must have faith that Robert will return home."

"And if he doesn't?"

James hesitated, then closed his eyes and placed his cheek against his wife's hair. "Then he goes with Luke to a far better place."

* * *

12 April 1864
Fort Pillow, north of Memphis, Tennessee

Ben rode hard with a portion of his cavalry, Robert close behind him, the miles disappearing beneath the horses' strong hooves. The message had been urgent: Fort Pillow was under attack by no less than Nathan Bedford Forrest himself. Forrest was a Confederate general who struck horror in the hearts of every Union soldier. He was a brilliant man, gifted in the art of war and utterly ruthless in his treatment of the enemy both before and after surrender.

Help was supposedly on the way in the form of Union steamers on the Mississippi, but the call had gone out for any available troops to come to immediate aid. It was with a sinking heart that Ben neared the fort, for Forrest had obviously lived up to his reputation. Down near the river lay the prostrate bodies of over two hundred dead Union soldiers. The Confederates had taken the fort, and the wounded had left a trail of blood that Ben turned to follow.

"Should we make a move on the fort?" Robert asked their commanding officer, who rode with them.

"No. We're not nearly enough in number. Something must be done soon, however. That fort is a direct part of our supply line." His face was grim as he turned his horse toward Ben's direction and took up the lead. It wasn't long before the small group of cavalry came upon what was serving as a temporary hospital for the wounded. A few questions proved the occupants to be survivors of the massacre at Fort Pillow.

Ben and Robert dismounted as the men in their regiment, coming down off their horses to stretch their legs and ask questions, circled the group of wounded. One man who had sustained a gunshot wound to his shoulder sat on an overturned log, awaiting his turn in the hospital tent. Ben approached him and, when asked, lit the man's cigar that was clamped between shaking fingers.

"It was murder, pure and simple," the man said. He cleared his throat repeatedly and rubbed the back of his hand across his eye. "He sent out the flag of truce, then repositioned his men under it. We asked for an hour to consider the truce because we knew the steamers were comin'. He gave us twenty minutes. When we refused, he stormed the fort."

The young man swiped at his eye again, smearing grime and telltale signs of tears across his face. "When they breached the fort, we knew we were had. He drove us to the edge of the river." He brought his cigar to his lips and managed to take a pull on it before continuing. "Most of us tried to surrender, but they started shooting—on his orders."

Ben didn't have to ask whose orders the man made reference to. Forrest was brilliant, clever, fearless, and hateful.

"I saw at least twenty-five Negroes shot down within ten or twenty paces from where I stood. They had surrendered and were begging for mercy. The slaughter was awful. General Forrest ordered them shot down like dogs."

The man clutched his shoulder where blood seeped through his shirt and onto his fingers. "I finally ran—ran like the devil."

Ben glanced at Robert, whose face was pale. Robert licked his dry lips and reached for his canteen. Withdrawing it from where he'd hooked it to his saddle, he uncapped it and then considered the wounded man who sat trembling on the log. He offered the man his canteen, holding it for him and placing a gentle hand on the back of the man's head as he drank.

"There must be a better way to spend time," Robert said to the soldier, who looked at him dumbfounded before finding a ghost of a smile. He laughed then, his drawn, haunted face showing the first signs of levity. "Me," Robert continued, "I think I'd like to take up fishing."

"Fishin's good," the man said, nodding his thanks for the water. "I fished all the time back home."

"Where are you from?"

"Chesterville, Vermont. Miss it somethin' terrible." For a moment the man seemed to be far away, in another life. "Those men were my friends," he said, his eyes glazed over. "Shot down like dogs."

Ben noticed Robert looking over the clearing and wondered what he thought. There were at least one hundred wounded men in varying states of pain, either waiting to be seen or having just exited the temporary hospital. Robert shook his head slightly and turned his attention back to the wounded man from Vermont.

"Forrest is notorious for repositioning his men under a flag of truce. He's done it before."

"It's not the thing to do," the man said, still clutching at his shoulder, which was obviously causing him increasing pain. "There are rules of war, rules to follow."

Ben looked at the man in quiet sympathy. The rules were changing, being broken all over the country. Nothing was as it once was, and what had begun as a war between gentlemen was swiftly evolving into something far more ugly. Ben had thought himself quite jaded when he had left his home in Utah to enlist with Luke. Occurrences in the past year caused him to feel as if he had lost what remained of his innocence entirely.

"Nobody follows the rules anymore," Ben murmured, and pulled a handkerchief from his pocket. He moved the man's hand and placed the cloth against the wound.

* * *

Boston, Massachusetts

The air was crisp and clear, the sky beginning to darken. Camille unconsciously shifted closer to Jacob as they made one final turn around the park in his open carriage. "They found him breaking into the clock shop," Jacob said in answer to her question.

"Are they sure it's him?"

"He admitted he was hired to throw the rock and burning stick into my house."

"Did he say who hired him?"

Jacob shook his head. "Not yet, but he was frightened. I believe he'll tell them soon, if the man at the police station is to be believed." He glanced at her for a moment before turning his attention back to the horses. "It's not at all the thing to be seen this time of day riding in the park, you know," he said.

"I am well aware of this."

"And yet you've ridden with me this time of day every day for two weeks now. Why is that, I wonder?"

"Because you're a working man and not available for the more fashionable morning rides."

"You could ride in the mornings if you chose. I know for a fact there are at least three young men clamoring for your hand."

Camille shot him an annoyed glance. "They want my father's money."

"Mmm. And yet they are gently bred men, entirely suitable for someone of your station. What would entice you to ride with me? I am a working man—as you so justly noted—and I have no family of consequence. Might I not be chasing your father's money as well?"

"You don't want my father's money."

He laughed. "And how do you know this?"

"You have your own."

"Well, yes, there is that. Newspaper editors make a copious living."

"You make enough."

Jacob was silent for a moment. "I do make enough—enough to satisfy me. But I often wonder if it would be enough for a woman accustomed to living with, well, much more."

Camille looked at his profile. "I'm sure if she were a woman worth her salt she would be more than satisfied to be your . . . your . . ."

"My . . . ?"

Camille glared at him. "What are you saying, Jacob? Where is this conversation leading? I grow tired of your double entendres, of your hints and odd comments. You've been seeking my company for several months now, ever since I saved your house from complete and utter ruin—"

He laughed long and hard, but she continued talking as though he hadn't interrupted.

". . . yet you still are cryptic and most exasperating! I sometimes think you like me only because I write for you, and—"

"If you will recall," he said, placing a finger to her lips, "I asked permission to court you long before you saved my home from 'complete and utter ruin.'"

"Is that what this is? Are you courting me?"

"I am. I rather thought that was clear by now."

"It would be, but you don't . . . you don't . . ."

"I don't what?"

Camille's nostrils flared. "You don't touch me beyond kissing my hand at greeting and parting. You don't give me any declarations of affection or tell me of your feelings for me."

"I don't write you poetry."

"Exactly! I've never been courted in such an odd way! I declare, if I didn't know better I would think these rides through the park are nothing more than business meetings!"

"Camille," Jacob said, drawing the horses to a stop beneath a secluded bend in the path. "I am not your other suitors. I will not bend and scrape and grovel. I write newspaper articles, not poetry. I will not declare my love for you a moment before I should because it would sound hollow and false."

She looked at him through narrowed eyes. "Why would you assume it would sound hollow and false?"

"Because other young men who approach you declare their love for you on the first or second acquaintance."

"How do you know that?"

"I've heard them. At balls, at soirees, at dinner parties—I can't count the times I've heard it."

"You've been *listening?*"

"I have."

"For how long?"

"Two years."

Camille felt her eyes widen. "You've been listening in on my conversations with other men for *two years?*"

"They haven't been men," he said in a flat tone. "A man in his thirties—that is a man."

"Well, I am so sorry that I haven't been courted by *men,* according to your exacting standards."

"Actually, you have been."

"Ah, yes. This, this thing we've been doing," Camille said, waving her hand at the park, "this is courting. I've been courted by a *man* in the park who would rather write articles about politics than poetry and would rather talk in circles than be clear in his intentions. A man who will only hold a woman close if her hands have been blistered by flames, and . . ."

Jacob placed his hand under her jaw and pulled her face to his, kissing her first to silence her, then prolonging the contact. When he pulled back, her eyelids fluttered open and she looked at him in silent, stunned shock.

"Now is the time for me to tell you," he said, his voice hushed. "I love you, Camille. I love you and have loved you for a long time. I want to marry you and make you happy. I have no doubt you would make me happy—as well as protect my house from invaders."

Camille felt her eyes burn with tears. "What on *earth* took you so blessed long to tell me that? I was beginning to think you were playing a perverse game with me! Would it have hurt you to grovel just a little?"

He smiled and kissed her again, threading his fingers into her hair at the back of her head. "I would have groveled if I'd had to. But," he said, releasing her and gently taking one of her healing hands into his own, "I wanted to be sure you returned my affections."

"I leaped into a burning drape for you, Jacob! And I defended you publicly to that odious woman. How could you not have known?"

"You are beautiful and well sought after. I wanted you to be sure. When I saw you continually rebuffing other men of late . . ."

"*Young* men."

"Yes, *young* men, I knew, well I thought I knew . . ."

"Jacob Taylor," she said, enjoying his discomfort. "I do believe you're flummoxed."

"I am. Now let's go ask your father before I lose my nerve entirely. He frightens me."

"I haven't said yes. You haven't even properly asked me."

"Camille Birmingham, will you marry me?" He brought her hand to his lips and kissed her knuckles, closing his eyes.

"Yes, I will. I saved your house from ruin; it's only proper that I should live in it now."

* * *

Mary read the letter from Emily three times, her heart pounding. She sat hard upon her bed, hearing the blood roar in her ears, and she wondered if she were about to faint. She'd never fainted before—it would be a first. She put a trembling hand to her forehead and read the name penned in Emily's careful hand.

Elijah. Her son. Her child, her flesh and blood. And Emily had him; the Birminghams were caring for him, loving him as their own. He *was* their own. Perhaps the most amazing thing of all was that Mr. Birmingham had been the one to seek after the child, to find him and bring him home.

It was divine Providence, it must be. The awful dreams Mary had endured for many weeks—they all pointed to this day, to this letter. Mary's son was alive and living with Emily's family. She closed her eyes as she remembered when the baby had been born—the awful, searing pain, no loving husband to comfort her afterward, and then, a ridiculously short time later, no baby at all.

She couldn't remember the pain of the baby's delivery without remembering the pain of events surrounding his conception. It was odd; she hardly thought of it anymore. At first those memories had haunted her viciously, never letting her sleep in peace at night. After a while, when Emily had forced the truth from her, somehow her bond with the girl and the fact that they both hated Richard helped ease her torment. It had been wonderful to know she wasn't alone.

When she had learned of Richard's death, it was as though her soul felt a measure of release—as though somehow by dying he left her and the awful memory he had given her. Slowly, slowly she had begun to think of her child, although she usually shoved the memory far beneath the surface. How could she think of him without crumbling? There had been nothing, absolutely nothing in her power she could do to be with him.

But now, now she held in her hand news that could change her life. What could she do, though? Her baby didn't know her, and how could she take him from the only family he knew outside of his slave quarters at the Charlesworths'? Furthermore, she couldn't very well bring him up north to live with her in Boston. She couldn't afford a place of her own and work and care for her child at the same time.

She slowly began to rock back and forth on her bed, fighting a low moan. Her throat felt thick, and she wondered if she were about to lose her supper. Placing a hand over her mouth, she read the letter again, wondering why now, of all times, God had chosen to free her child.

Mary read the things that Emily *didn't* say as well. Emily's grief and guilt over keeping the news from her for so long was evident, and Mary ached to hold her friend. It was so very like Emily to want to protect her for as long as she could. Emily wrote of her love for young Elijah, of his beauty and his bright little personality. *Clara and Rose have taught him all of the animals and the sounds they make,* she wrote, *and he now knows his colors and some of his letters!*

Mary looked out of her small window and into the evening sky. What on earth should she do? She wanted God to come down from the clouds and tell her which path to follow. If she stayed in Boston and wanted Elijah to come to her, she would take him from everything he knew. If she tried to return to Charleston, she would most likely be captured and sold into slavery yet again.

It was unfair, she thought, as she set the letter on her small table. Now when she was breathing free air and enjoying a free life, entanglements from the past rose like specters from a grave. She felt selfish. Little Elijah was innocent, and he would grow into adulthood knowing that his mother could have come for him but didn't. And what of herself? She would be denying herself a relationship that she currently shared with no one else on earth.

Mary squeezed her eyes shut when she remembered the one element she hadn't yet considered. What of Ben? What would he think of her son? What would he think of her? She hadn't been intentionally promiscuous, hadn't gone seeking for a relationship unsanctioned by God. Richard had forced himself upon her, and she had been sick with fever and in no condition to fight him. What if Ben didn't believe her? What if he believed she'd pursued his brother in an effort to gain leverage with the master's family? He had been gone from Bentley for so many years when it had happened that he might feel he hadn't known her well at all.

She felt crushed. Ben had expressed a tender interest in her, had hinted at desiring a permanent relationship with her when he returned home—she still kept the letter with his sentiments close by in a carved, wooden box that held a few of her treasures. Thinking of the box, she slowly pulled it from under her bed and opened the lid. She reached into the center and lifted a small swatch of material that was once part of a larger blanket. It was the blanket she had wrapped her baby in before Sarah Birmingham had taken the child from her arms and sold him. She had told herself at the time that it was for the best, that she hadn't wanted him, yet something through the years had insisted she keep the bit of blanket. She couldn't let him go.

CHAPTER 20

I have heard Captain Wirz swear that he is killing more —— Yankees with his treatment than they were with powder and led [sic] in the army. . . . Another old friend of mine . . . was shot dead by a rebel guard for reaching under the dead line for a drink of water, and another was shot dead at my feet for reaching under the dead line for a piece of mouldy bread.

—Henry Hernbaker, Union soldier and Andersonville prisoner

* * *

5 May 1864
Andersonville, Georgia

Ivar Gundersen stared numbly at the men who had fallen into the stream at some point in the night. They had undoubtedly tried to reach the water, hoping in some way to quench the thirst if not satisfy the awful wrenching in their stomachs. They lay dead in the only source of water the prisoners of Andersonville had.

I would venture to guess that drinking from such a stream will not be good for my health, he said to the Anne he had stashed permanently inside his head. *It's bad enough that we use it for a latrine.* He winced and stepped back at the voice he and all of the other men in the prison had come to dread.

"Get them out, along with the eighty other dead carcasses," Captain Henry Wirz barked in his heavy Austrian accent. He laced the order with a foul stream of swearing and cursing. He was the keeper of the prison and a man who relished in the number of dead found each morning, afternoon, and evening.

The conditions in the camp worsened the weakened state many of the men were already living with when they entered Andersonville. They were given the same amount of food each day as were the guards: one and one-quarter pound of cornmeal, and on occasion, one pound of beef or one-third pound of bacon. On extremely rare occasions, they were given beans, peas, rice, or molasses.

Dysentery was rampant among the men, as was scurvy. Ivar suffered pains in his abdomen so horrible that there were times he wished for the release of death. The chill of cold and the continuous rain with no protection from the elements evolved into a warm spring and summer. The men sat in the hot, blistering sun, most with no shoes. The sun burned their feet so badly, they blistered and cracked, and the conditions of the stream turned them gangrenous. Once the gangrene set in, the feet were amputated. Ivar had yet to see a prisoner survive the amputation in such a weakened condition.

Wirz took extreme pride in the death toll the camp exacted, and even greater pride in the reputation the camp was gaining for itself. Formally called Camp Sumter, for Sumter County in which the camp was housed, people now far and wide simply referred to it as Andersonville. The very mention of the name was enough to cause a shudder in the bravest of soldiers. Those who were transferred in knew they probably wouldn't leave.

"Grant did this to us as sure as any reb," a fellow soldier once complained to Ivar. "He's insisting the rebels exchange black and white prisoners the same or no exchanging at all! You know darn well the rebels aren't going to give the colored prisoners the same treatment as the whites. I think he does it for his own purposes too! He knows it's a strain on the Confederacy to keep us here!"

A strain it was indeed, Ivar thought as he watched Wirz approach and make arrangements for the morning body disposal. The man was ghoulish in his delight over the dead, and he would have many more to glory over if the current conditions didn't soon change. The prison yard teemed with people and was near to bursting at the seams. There were close to twenty thousand prisoners in a place designed to hold no more than ten thousand. The stench was unbearable, the shelters built early on all but destroyed, and tempers ran hot as small gangs formed among the prisoners themselves. One particularly harsh group of men had terrorized the others, creating a swath of havoc in their wake.

Only a week before, however, the rest of the men who had become victims banded together and put a stop to the marauders, and Wirz allowed the prisoners to hold court and execute those most offensive. As Ivar watched the bodies hang, he turned and retreated to a far corner, closing his eyes and wondering how much longer he would live to witness the madness. He couldn't say he was sorry to see the lawless men hang, but it so fit the craziness of his current world that it was merely one more instance in a long line of events sure to drive him to the brink of his own sanity.

He watched as Wirz's henchmen pulled the bodies from the stream and threw them atop a cart, then make their way around the camp looking for other lifeless forms, some missed from days before and in various states of decomposition. As he looked around at his fellow prisoners, he saw a sea of gaunt, sunburned, sickly people who were often little more than skin stretched over bones. He wondered how he appeared, wondered if the others winced inwardly when they looked his way.

* * *

Anne nearly stamped her foot in frustration. "I have been to see you three times, sir, and you have refused my request each time. My cousin and I have offered food and drink for your men, and we've been here with others from the local towns offering goods to feed not only your men but the prisoners as well. You refuse every offer." She considered the man for a moment and then moved closer to him despite her screaming instincts.

"I wonder if we might have a moment alone," she said to him.

His eyes widened a bit, and with a jerk of his head, he cleared his office of the other prison guards. Anne nodded once to Emily and Jeffrey, who hesitated but left her alone with Captain Wirz. "Other than my life or my virtue," she said to the man once they were alone, "what is it you want from me? I'm asking for one man. One man, nothing more. I'm sure he means nothing to you."

Wirz looked her over with shrewd eyes. "What does this man mean to you?"

Everything. "He's a very good friend." She drew in a breath. "I've offered you nearly all that I have, and my uncle has offered you contacts in high political places."

"I have contacts in high political places."

"What if Jefferson Davis himself were to request the release of this particular prisoner?"

Wirz's eyes hardened. "I don't like taking orders, and this is my domain, not Davis's."

Anne motioned toward the desk, where a bag full of gold coins sat. "What would you say if I offered you twice that amount?"

"No."

"Three times."

He paused. "Why didn't you offer it in the first place?"

"Do you take me for a fool? Why would I begin a negotiation with all that I have?" And indeed, it was all she had. If he didn't accept the money, she would lose Ivar forever.

"I don't believe you have it."

"Bring me Ivar Gundersen and I'll give you the gold."

"No."

"Bring him here to this room and I'll pay you. You'll still have him here—if I don't have the money, you'll still have your prisoner."

He looked at her for a long moment before speaking. "I'll have him brought to this room. Nobody else enters. Nobody else sees the money you pay me. Is that understood?"

"Yes. But if you somehow impede our departure or attempt to harm him, I will scream the entire Confederacy down around your ears and I will see to it that my family fortune goes toward your ruin. Is *that* understood?"

"I don't take orders from presumptuous women!"

"Three times that amount, Mr. Wirz," Anne snapped at him, pointing to the bag of gold on the desk. "Take it or leave it! It's a significant amount of money to a man whose Confederate bills aren't worth the paper on which they're printed!"

He ground his teeth and looked at her with such venom she very nearly stepped back. The moments ticked on into an eternity, and she wondered if she'd said too much, pushed his pride too far. He finally opened the door to his office and muttered an order in low tones to a subordinate.

While the minutes passed, Wirz took a seat behind his desk, watching her, never inviting her once to take a seat. His hard, glinting eyes raked insolently over her frame in what she knew was an attempt to intimidate her. Anne stood her ground, forcing herself to refrain from fidgeting. Her hands remained folded gently together, not clenched, her shoulders straight. The minutes stretched past ten, then fifteen. When nearly twenty minutes had passed in the interminable silence and Anne felt she would collapse from the strain, the door slowly opened.

The sight before her nearly did provoke that feared collapse. Ivar was but a shell of his former self. He was so gaunt and thin that his cheeks were hollow, with great circles under his eyes. His clothing hung on his body in rags, his feet bare, blistered, and bleeding from the exposure to the sun. His once thick, blonde hair was matted and filthy and beginning to fall out from lack of nourishment.

The only thing about Ivar that she recognized was the piercing blue of his eyes and the proud bearing of his shoulders. Even so obviously near death, he didn't slump. His eyes stared at her in disbelief, but he didn't utter a word as she looked at him, and she was so grateful to God that he remained silent. *Please, just stay quiet,* she thought as she looked at him. *Don't say a word, not one word.*

"He doesn't seem to know you very well," Wirz said to her, snapping her attention away from Ivar.

"I don't think it matters to you one way or another now, does it, Mr. Wirz? I'm about to make you a very wealthy man." She reached for her cloak and hugged it tight to her body, thrusting her hands into its folds. "Before I do, however, I want Ivar released to my uncle's custody."

"Show me your gold first."

I will fight you, Anne thought as she looked at the cruel man. *I will fight you and claw your eyes out and stab you through your vacant heart with the knife in my boot should you try anything.*

On some level he must have felt her unspoken threat because he barked an order to his assistant. The door again opened, and Wirz told the man to summon Jeffrey Birmingham. Anne pulled a bulging reticule from her cloak and allowed the coins to clink together as she did so. When Jeffrey appeared at the doorway, she opened the purse.

"Take Ivar to the first carriage," she said. "Have Emily take him to our lodgings." To Wirz she said, "When my cousin and Ivar are out of sight, Mr. Birmingham and I will leave you with this." She raised the purse and opened it widely for his perusal. He glanced inside and then at her face. Nodding once, he acquiesced, and Jeffrey disappeared with Ivar.

Some long minutes later, Jeffrey reappeared at the door. "They're gone," he said.

"Fine. Uncle Jeffrey, will you please close the door and wait for me in the outer office?"

He hesitated, then looked at Wirz. "You should know, Captain, that Jefferson Davis will have your head on a platter should anything untoward happen this day to my niece or to the man you've just released. I want papers signed in your name stating Ivar Gundersen has been released into my care and is no longer a Confederate prisoner."

Wirz eyed Jeffrey with contempt and then retrieved a paper from his desk. Dipping a quill in a jar of ink, he scrawled a hasty note of release and stamped it with his personal insignia. He handed it to Jeffrey with a scowl and dismissed him with a flick of his wrist. Jeffrey looked at Anne once, and at her nod, he withdrew and closed the door quietly behind him.

Anne watched Wirz's face as she dumped the contents of her reticule on the desk. Gold coins spilled forth as would a flowing waterfall, covering the desk, some clanking to the floor. To her immense satisfaction, his eyes widened.

"We won't be followed, correct? And you won't remember the name of Ivar Gundersen any longer?"

He looked up at her. "What's one prisoner more or less?"

* * *

By the time Anne reached the carriage, her uncle was supporting her weight against his own by holding his arm beneath hers. "Can you make it?" he whispered.

She nodded and climbed into the carriage, shaking from head to toe. Jeffrey climbed in after her and motioned to the groom and two of the four footmen he'd hired to act as guards on the journey. The carriage rolled forward with a small jerk, and Anne released her pent-up emotions.

They flooded from her in a torrent, racking sobs that had her choking and gasping for breath. Jeffrey braced her with an arm about her shoulders and held her close until she was spent, offering her a handkerchief, at which she laughed. "I'll make a mess of this in no time," she said, wiping her face and nose.

"Did you see him?" she said, tears continuing to fall but the horrible sobs spent. "I don't know if he'll live. What can I do?"

"Shhh," he said. "Hush now. We'll care for him. When he's well enough to travel, we'll get him home to Ruth. She can mend just about anything."

Anne blew her nose and chewed on her lip, fidgeting and shaking so badly she was sure the carriage rocked more from her agitation than the ruts in the road. "Poor Emily," she murmured. "He looks frightful and smells . . ."

Jeffrey laughed, and Anne looked at him in confusion. "How well do you know Emily, my dear?"

"Well enough, I suppose."

"She will be fine." Jeffrey continued chuckling and patted Anne's shoulder for reassurance.

Thirty minutes later saw them at the small farmhouse Jeffrey had secured for their purposes. Anne leaped from the carriage before it rolled to a stop, spying the identical carriage that had carried Emily and Ivar. The groom and guards were outside, but her cousin and Ivar were not. "Where are they?" she demanded breathlessly of the men.

"In the chicken coop," one answered her, motioning over his shoulder with his thumb.

Anne ran for the small outbuilding and, upon reaching it, slowed only enough to keep from tripping on the small ramp leading up to it. "Don't be silly," Emily was saying with shears in hand to Ivar as he sat in a chair. "I was raised on a plantation. I've smelled plenty of interesting things in my day."

"Ivar," Anne cried, and fell to the floor on her knees beside the chair, clasping him to her, chair and all.

"Anne." His voice was low in her ear. "I'm a wretched mess. Don't touch me, love, I'm swarming with lice and filth."

"I don't care." Her tears fell afresh onto his neck.

"Anne, move," Emily ordered. "I'm about to cut off his hair."

Anne reluctantly released him and looked at his beloved face. "Are you well? Will you heal?"

"Anne! Stop this instant or I'll have my father take you into the house. There will be time enough for talk later."

Anne glanced at Emily, grateful for her presence and practicality. She wasn't as gruff as she wished the others to believe, however. Anne caught a suspicious glint of moisture in her cousin's eyes as she made quick work of Ivar's filthy hair.

Anne glanced over her shoulder at a noise from the entrance of the coop to see her uncle enter. "Once Emily's finished with her shears," he said to Ivar, "I'll help you with the rest. Ruth anticipated your condition, God bless her, and sent some interesting medicinal concoctions along."

As Anne watched, Emily clipped Ivar's hair as close as she could with the shears and then stood back to examine her work. "My father will handle the rest with a blade," she said, "once you've been bathed. The men outside are warming water for you to soak in after my father smears Ruth's smelly medicine on you."

Ivar looked at the people surrounding him in the small chicken coop, and he swallowed several times before finding his voice. "I can't thank you all enough," he managed, and looked at Anne, his eyes filling with tears he hadn't let himself shed. "I was hoping to come to you," he said.

"I saved you the trouble."

* * *

Much later that evening, Anne sat in a chair beside a plain bed in one of the farmhouse's small bedrooms. The room held two beds, one of which Jeffrey would occupy. The other held Ivar, and Anne clutched his hand, afraid to let go. He looked strange to her, and yet wonderful. He was bald. Jeffrey had shaved his head completely to rid him of the lice that had swarmed about in his hair and had rubbed him down completely with Ruth's lice-treating medicine.

When all the vermin were killed and their nits banished, Ivar had bathed in hot water and scrubbed from head to toe with a bar of Ruth's lye soap. He had then rinsed and bathed again, repeating the whole process until Jeffrey felt sure he was clean and free from the parasites.

Emily had fed everyone then, a simple meal of stew and vegetables, and on Ruth's advice, a simple meal of broth and bread for Ivar. He had protested, albeit weakly, but Emily had held firm to Ruth's orders, knowing that to feed the starving man too much at the onset would be sure to kill his poor body.

Ruth had also sent along some herbs meant to help in curing dysentery. After taking them, Ivar admitted the pain had lessened somewhat, but Anne had to wonder how long he would suffer from the illnesses he'd contracted in the camp, and even before, when he was with the regiment.

"Ivar," she murmured, "I am so sorry. Your condition, your imprisonment, it's all my fault."

"Do not," he said, closing his eyes. "Do not say that to me, Anne. You made my life with the regiment bearable, and your memory kept me alive after you left. I won't hear you taking responsibility for this again." He opened his eyes. "Do you understand me? I won't hear it again."

"Very well." She rubbed his knuckles with the tip of her forefinger, gently smoothing the rough skin that had seen so much exposure to the elements. "I wonder if your hands need more oil," she said absently, and reached for a vial on the night table.

He reached forward and caught her hand, the crisp white of Jeffrey's nightshirt standing in stark contrast against the brown-red hue of his skin. "Be still, sweet Anne," he said.

"You don't understand," she said, her sore eyes filling yet again with tears. "I've thought of nothing but you since I returned home. I missed you so much I could hardly stand it! I didn't want to leave you there, but then you insisted and told them about me, and I didn't know if I'd ever see you again. I loved you so much by then that it broke my heart, and I was sure you would be dead before I could find you."

He closed his eyes briefly and brought her hands to his lips. "I love you as well, dear woman."

"Oh, I'm so glad. Then we can be married."

He laughed, and it subsided into a cough that had her wincing. "Yes, although I do believe I should be the one to suggest it. It shouldn't surprise me that you would take the initiative. But we will not wed until I'm well."

"No. I'm not waiting until you're well."

"Anne," he said gently, "I could die. I'll not tie you to a dead man."

"If you die, then I will have been happy for at least a short time. Ivar, if you make me wait I'll cry every day. Do not make me beg. Allow me a shred of pride."

"Are you certain this is what you want? A husband at death's door who can hardly stand to recite his vows?"

"I don't care if you lie here to recite your vows. I'll not wait to spend time with you, to be with you and care for you. I want to hold you and comfort you," Anne said. "I do not have the patience to live like this, worried about proprieties and not being able to spend time with you alone. I've waited long enough, and now you're alive and free. It's almost more than I dared hope for."

"Very well," he said quietly, closing his eyes again. "I'm in no position to argue with you anyway."

Her lips twitched. "You never were."

He opened one eye. "Is that so? Well then, someday I must prove you wrong on that score."

"I look forward to it."

* * *

The wedding was a simple, quiet affair. The following morning, Anne sent Jeffrey off to find a man of the cloth and clothed herself in a simple dress of ice blue. When he returned with a confused yet moderately cheerful minister, Jeffrey had helped Ivar dress in one of his own suits, which hung on him like a child playing in adult clothing.

Emily pinned Anne's short hair into a small, braided coiffure that flattered her face, and with a handful of wildflowers plucked from the ground outside the farmhouse, she and Ivar were married before her uncle, her cousin, two grooms, and four footmen.

Later that morning as he rested again in bed, exhausted from the strain of the ceremony and a small breakfast party, he looked at the woman who lay asleep beside him atop the quilt, still dressed in her beautiful gown of blue. Even in her slumber, she held to his hand as though it were the only thing anchoring her to the earth. He smiled and winced as his lip cracked. He needed more of this Ruth's magic oil. He looked forward to meeting the woman who was saving his life with her bag of herbs and medicines.

He had much for which to be grateful, and he began his list to God. *I thank Thee most fervently for sending me such gracious people, for Mrs. Stanhope, who cut my hair and helped me without a thought to her own discomfort, for Mr. Birmingham, who has treated me like a son, and for Anne, my angel.*

Ivar had no illusions about the fortuitousness of her timing; another week or two, certainly no more than a month, and he would have died. He should have known she would come to his rescue—she, a woman who posed as a man to enlist and go off to battle. She was strong and capable, and he loved her.

The war could rage on forever; in that moment, he was happy.

CHAPTER 21

It is well that war is so terrible, else we should grow too fond of it.
—Robert E. Lee

* * *

5 May 1864
Charleston, South Carolina
Bentley Plantation

Jeffrey stood on the mansion's front porch and looked over the long, tree-lined drive. The time had come to take his family and leave. He had received word only that morning that Grant was moving toward Richmond, Virginia, with his 120,000 troops to meet with Lee's 60,000. Even more imminent in terms of their own circumstances was the fact that General Sherman was marching his way toward Atlanta with his 110,000 men, burning, looting, and destroying everything in his wake. The Union had waged total war upon the South, and the time for illusions was long past.

Jeffrey leaned his shoulder against a pillar and took a deep breath, releasing it slowly. The house, the outbuildings containing the kitchens and pantries, and the stables and fields—he didn't believe Sherman would be so struck by the beauty of Bentley that he might stay his hand and spare it, especially once it became known that Jeffrey had close ties with the Confederate government.

So very much was changing—even the fragile routine the little family had been clinging to was altering. Rather than continue north to Charleston from Andersonville, Emily and Anne, judging Ivar to be in improving health, had gone south to Emily's home in Savannah. She had been away long enough, Emily felt, and should word come regarding Austin, she wanted to be there to receive it. Making Jeffrey promise to write often and keep her apprised of the situation at Bentley, she had kissed him farewell with a tear in her eye. "I'm very glad you've come home," she said, and he rather thought her meaning was layered.

Before his journey to Andersonville, Jeffrey had taken Ben's advice and written to his son's friend in the Utah Territory. In one of his letters to Ben, Earl Dobranski had expressed an interest in serving as a guard and lead for small groups wishing to head west. Only the week before, Jeffrey had received the young man's response; he would be glad to bring Ben's family to safety. As the mail had been severely delayed, Jeffrey expected that Earl would appear within days if not sooner.

Ruth approached behind him, walking out onto the porch with her arms folded around her middle. He had enlisted her help in selling what he could in the home itself, and together they had packed the most practical of personal necessities for themselves, Sarah, Clara, Rose, and Elijah, and sent the packages to the Dobranskis via the railroad and Pony Express. Whether or not the packages would survive the trip remained to be seen. The railroads ran only to the western frontier, and many had been destroyed by the Union.

As for Ruth herself, he could only say prayers of gratitude that she had possessed the heart to stay at Bentley when she so easily could have left. He'd have been lost without her help and expertise. "I figure we're about as ready as we'll ever be," she said to him, joining her gaze with his down the long drive, pausing to internalize the scene. "The trees are mighty pretty this time of year."

He nodded. "They surely are. I will miss them. Will you?"

"I suppose I will—they're all I've ever known."

"Ruth, I'm . . . I'm grateful you've consented to join Sarah and me. The girls, well, you've been more of a parent to them than anyone has, and Elijah adores them. They'll be so much more at ease with the changes, and . . ."

"I understand." She turned her face into the gentle breeze and inhaled the scent of the blossoms. "It will be safer for me as well. What do you suppose Sherman would say to find a Negress running a plantation?"

Jeffrey shook his head and looked at Ruth, who had turned to regard him with frank, assessing eyes. "I don't suppose he'd much care for it. Not many would. Are you sad about leaving?"

"I'm . . . anxious. I don't know what to expect."

"That puts us exactly in the same boat then." He paused and gestured toward the house. "Can you think of anything we might have forgotten?"

She shook her head. "I suppose we have everything we can manage. We'll take as much with us by way of supplies as we can; the rest we'll purchase in Nebraska. You did say our guide will be here soon?"

Jeffrey nodded. "Barring any trouble, he should be here right soon. If he doesn't materialize, why, I suppose we'll just have to start without him and hope for the best." He tried to inject a note of optimism into his tone, but wondered if he'd succeeded. To his own ears, he sounded flat and worried.

"This is a sensitive matter," Ruth said, "and it isn't my place or my business, but I'm wondering what resources you've secured by way of money—useful money."

"You don't believe our Confederate currency would take us far?" He smiled. "When I was in the North with my brother, I told him of the investments I'd made in his company through the years. He graciously arranged for me to obtain gold. Provided we aren't robbed along the way, we'll be fine."

She looked troubled.

"I've placed it in different locations, hidden it in luggage and will keep some on my person. I intend to give you some as well, should something happen."

"Thank you for reassuring me," Ruth said. "I am most . . ."

"Anxious."

"Yes."

He smiled at her. "Ruth, I have one consolation for you."

"What might that be?"

"We won't be here when Sherman marches through."

* * *

Earl Dobranski figured he was just a few minutes' ride outside of Charleston. The road had been long and hard, but he was a clever man. It also helped that he had been able to secure uniforms of both Confederate gray and

Union blue. Depending on the state, the countryside, sometimes even the city, he changed and blended in much like a chameleon.

It was a pleasure to be able to do a favor for Ben Birmingham. His family needed to leave South Carolina, and Earl was happy to oblige. According to the letter from Mr. Birmingham, Mrs. Birmingham was not well. There were also three children—two young women and one small child to consider. Mr. Birmingham's daughter was also to be a part of the traveling party along with her infant son. A woman named Ruth who had been with the family for years was the final person moving west.

As he followed the directions given to him in town, he marveled at the beauty of the countryside. In the day of riches and former normalcy, the plantations and fields must have been glorious. He neared what he believed to be Bentley Plantation and took in the sights and smells of the property.

He led his horse slowly down the path that pointed to the large mansion, the trees overhead serving as an enormous canopy, shielding him from the bright sun. He couldn't help but look up—it was an amazing sight. From the distance he could see three people standing on the spacious front porch, and to the side of the house he saw two carriages standing out and apart from the carriage house.

The voices were raised in a fair amount of agitation, one woman sounding decidedly more distraught than the other two people. As he neared the porch, he caught the eye of a gentleman who could only have been Ben's father; the resemblance was striking. Earl dismounted from his horse and, removing his glove, extended his hand to meet Mr. Birmingham's.

"You would be Earl?" the older man said.

"I am. And you would be Mr. Birmingham."

Ben's father nodded and gestured to the two women who stood with him, one a black woman of regal bearing and simple beauty, the other a younger woman with blonde hair and blue eyes, also a beauty. She held a baby boy braced upon her hip, and the expression on her face was flushed and uncomfortable.

"This is Ruth Birmingham," Jeffrey said, his hand on the elbow of the black woman.

Earl took her hand in his and shook it in the same greeting he'd given Mr. Birmingham. Ruth's eyes widened slightly, and a small smile graced her lips. "A pleasure," she said to him.

"And this is my eldest daughter, Charlotte Ellis, and her son, William."

Earl shook the hand of the other woman, who seemed uncomfortable with the exchange. Her hand had extended itself, of habit most likely, with her knuckles up, slightly cupped. Belatedly he realized that she probably had expected him to place a kiss on her hand, or at least bow slightly over it. He mentally cuffed himself, grateful his mother wasn't present to do it.

Jeffrey broke the silence. "It is wonderful to see you've arrived safely, Mr. Dobranski."

"Please, I'd appreciate it if you'd call me Earl."

"Earl it is, then. Won't you come inside? We were just discussing the particulars of our journey."

As the small group crossed the threshold of the mansion, Earl was suddenly conscious of his filthy attire. He was dusty and grimy and in desperate need of a bath. Mr. Birmingham smiled at him and said, "Allow me to show you to your room. We weren't certain when to expect you, but I presume you'd like to rest for at least a day or so before we leave?"

"That sounds very good," Earl said, suddenly remembering he still wore his hat. He quickly pulled it from his head, embarrassed to his toes that he'd forgotten to doff it when introduced to the women. Ellen Dobranski would have groaned if she'd seen his sloppy manners firsthand. With a firm decision to make his mother proud, he vowed to remember how to behave like a gentleman.

"I'll have some water drawn for a bath, if you'd like, and when you're feeling refreshed, we can discuss our travel plans further. We were just about to have afternoon tea. I hope you'll join us?"

The three faces looked at him expectantly; Jeffrey pleasant, Ruth kind and amused, and Charlotte disturbed. "I would love to join you." How was it that these folk managed niceties like "afternoon tea" in the midst of a war?

He later learned, as he sat with them in the parlor, that the meal was a sparse affair. Assuming they were stretching their resources as thinly as possible, he was grateful to them for sharing what they had. A closer inspection of the home revealed furniture that had seen some wear, carpets that were also rather threadbare, and a general scarcity about the house where there was probably once an impressive amount of abundance.

Jeffrey began the discussion by detailing to Earl exactly what he had shipped to the Utah Territory, what he had sent to his brother in Boston for safekeeping, and what they were planning to take with them once they reached Nebraska and purchased a wagon and team of oxen. Earl was pleased to note that his instructions and suggestions for travel had been followed to the letter.

"Now we have just one minor issue," Jeffrey said, taking a sip from his cup. "Charlotte isn't certain she wants to go."

Earl looked at the woman in some surprise. Throughout the meal she had been silent and appeared thoroughly irritated. He ventured to guess that she was seated in the room only at her father's request. Earl cleared his throat a bit and placed his teacup in its saucer, his large hand dwarfing the small piece of china.

"Are you apprehensive about the journey, Mrs. Ellis? I can assure you I will care for your needs—"

"I have no qualms over the journey, Mr. Dobranski," she said stiffly, barely looking at him. "I find that I . . . I do not wish to leave my home."

Earl nodded slightly. "I understand your hesitation."

Charlotte chewed on her lip and looked out the window, ignoring her food altogether. "I just do not wish to leave."

Earl glanced at Jeffrey for direction. The older man sat thoughtfully in his chair, looking at his daughter with a soft expression. "It won't be so very awful, Charlotte," he said. "I understand the folk in Utah have very nice cities and homes." He looked at Earl with his eyebrows raised.

"Oh, yes, yes indeed," Earl said. "Very nice indeed. We've built ourselves a jewel in the desert." Wondering if perhaps he'd spoken a bit too enthusiastically when Charlotte glanced at him with an inscrutable expression, he faltered. "Nice, wide streets," he mumbled. "Plenty of room to stretch . . ." When she merely continued to look at him, her expression giving away nothing, he fell silent.

Earl had some time to himself for the remainder of the afternoon, and he spent it roaming the house and grounds. Dinner proved to be a simple but adequate affair, and as the day grew dim and he considered preparing to bed down for the night, he passed the library on his way to his room.

Feeling guilty for stopping to listen to the voices coming from within, he found he couldn't help himself. "This is all I've ever known, Ruth. I love this home! Ben and Richard—they didn't care for it a bit, but I've always loved Bentley." The voice was Charlotte Ellis's, and she was crying.

"I know you do, Charlotte," came Ruth's answering tones. "But it isn't the same. Nothing is the same, nor will it ever be."

"I can stay here and run it myself! I've watched my mother for years—she never once considered leaving this place in my care, but I can do it. She never noticed that I wanted to; she never thought I could."

"Of course you can, but you must ask yourself if you *should.* Where will you find the hands necessary to continue production? You know the staff have left slowly until there are so few of us left we can barely manage the vegetable garden. And there is a threat, sweet girl. You know as well as I do this house won't be standing much longer."

"If I stay here and show that it's still inhabited, they wouldn't dare to take it from me. What will they do, burn it down around my ears? I have a child!"

"Charlotte." Ruth's voice took on the firm quality that Earl recognized in his mother. "They will not care a hill of beans that you have a child. This is a *war.* They are bent on destroying the South so that this will never happen again. Do you understand that?"

Silence met Ruth's statement, and Earl heard the creak of a chair, then sniffling. When he heard Charlotte's voice again, it was muffled as though buried in Ruth's shoulder. "It's unfair, Ruth," the woman cried. "This is our home."

"We will build a new one," Ruth answered, and Earl imagined she might be swaying back and forth, just as

Ellen did when one of the boys was hurting. "We're luckier than most, you know. The bulk of the South will be left with nothing."

CHAPTER 22

His soldiers do not salute him, they only watch him, with a certain sort of familiar reverence. [They] observe him coming and, rising to their feet, gather on each side of the way to see him pass.

—New York Times, *in reference to Ulysses S. Grant*

* * *

15 May 1864
Ashland, Virginia

"I wasn't comfortable being so close to Lee's army," Robert said to Ben as they sat close to their campfire under a dark sky. "Wouldn't have believed a disagreement between Meade and Sheridan would result in us chasing after ol' Bobby in a raid."

Ben looked at Robert. "How did you learn that bit of news?"

"I listen." Robert grinned. Despite the moments of sheer terror when the shots flew and cannons exploded, he found himself adjusting to military life. The nuances and intrigue fascinated him, as did deciphering the complexities of the personalities behind the men who made momentous decisions.

Ben shook his head. "Never fails to amaze me. You always have the news first, and the most details. What else have you heard?"

"Hmm. Well, I've heard that the Wilderness was again the site of a battle—raged for two days. Hundreds of wounded men were killed in a brushfire."

Ben nodded. "That seems to happen frequently. If the battles had been fought on open ground, they might have stood a chance, but in all those trees and undergrowth . . . Any other news?"

"Spotsylvania, Virginia. Grant tried to go around Lee—supposedly a good eleven days of fighting. Men still alive, barely, and trapped—buried under piles of their comrades' corpses. One place so bad in particular that the others called it the 'Bloody Angle.'"

"I managed to hear about that one myself. Such a waste when it ends in a stalemate. Grant knows we have more men, though, and will outlast Lee if only in sheer numbers."

"Oh," Robert added, "and I did hear of news right off of the telegraph wires today—Union offensive in the Shenandoah Valley."

"And were we victorious?"

Robert shook his head. "Jubal Early stopped it cold."

Ben winced and tossed a small stick into the fire. Robert had noticed it was a habit of Ben's. "Hard to believe you've been in the army for nine months?" Ben asked.

Robert sat back against a fallen log with a sigh. "Has it been so long?"

Ben nodded. "The terms of my initial enlistment are up in October. You're signed on for a year?"

"Yes. But I'll wait out the extra month with you."

Ben laughed. "Very generous, cousin. Much like your brother." Ben's smile lingered, and Robert was glad. Ben spoke more frequently of Luke, and when he did so it was without the extreme sense of sadness that had pervaded those first few months of Robert's enlistment. "So what do your listening ears tell you now? Any idea about what happens next?"

Robert shrugged and tried, unsuccessfully, to fight a yawn. "No more than you have, I suppose. We rejoin the Army of the Potomac. With any luck, October will arrive before any more battles."

"Highly unlikely, that."

"Doesn't hurt to dream a bit, though. Wish those darned rebs would just give up and go home."

Ben shook his head. "They won't give up, not while there's breath still left in 'em."

"Don't you ever sympathize with them, even a little? What with you being raised Southern, I might expect you to."

Ben sighed. "I don't like the Southern system, but I do feel mighty sorry for the average person who just feels like he's being invaded." He rubbed the back of his neck. "One of our boys who transferred into the company some time back had been fighting down in the Deep South. His regiment took some men captive, and he asked one of the rebs why he was fighting. The reb said, 'Because y'all are down here.'"

Robert laughed a little, nodding his head. He looked into the crackling flames, mesmerized by the bright sparks. "So what are we to do then? What if this just goes on forever?"

"We stay the course."

Robert glanced up at Ben, whose face was half in shadow. "Stay the course," Robert repeated, and Ben nodded slightly. "And if we make it to October? What will you do then?"

"Go to Boston, ask Mary to be my bride, see if she'll consent to going west with me."

Robert turned his gaze again to the flames. The woman of his dreams loved his dead brother. Abigail had written to him twice, as Camille was still angry with him for enlisting. He cherished those letters from Abby—she would never know how much. At the thought of Camille simmering, he smiled.

"What are you thinking?" Ben asked.

"Cammy is still vexed. Abby says she refuses to write to me."

Ben laughed. "Have you written to her?"

"Faithfully, every week. Abby tells me Camille is engaged to marry Jacob Taylor. It would have been nice to hear the news from Cammy herself."

"She's frightened. With good reason."

"I'm not going to die."

"How are you so sure?" Ben was studying him with slightly narrowed eyes.

Robert shrugged, feeling sheepish. "I just know. Doesn't keep me from being afraid, though. I could very well get wounded."

Ben cocked his head to one side with a shrug. "I hope you're right, Robert, that you won't die. It would be a hard thing for me to bury another cousin. And I hope for your sake you don't have to bury me." He paused. "I didn't enjoy putting Luke in the ground."

"Still, you feel his soul is . . . somewhere . . ." Robert said, motioning to the air.

"Yes."

"So why is it so hard for you when you have this sure knowledge? Forgive me, but I would think you would be more at ease."

"I am at ease, but it's taken some time. Just because I know where he is doesn't make me miss him any less. Death is hard only for the living."

"I'd like to know more about your religion. Anything Luke embraced so fully interests me."

"I have a book you should read, then." Ben stood and walked to the tent, pulling a small black book from his sack. "It's mine, but it was with Luke's belongings when he died. I'd like you to have it."

"What is it?"

"It's an account of Christ's visit to the people of this continent after His resurrection."

Robert studied Ben for a moment and then took the book he held outstretched in his fingers. "That's very odd, cousin."

"I know. But read it before you judge."

"I will."

* * *

Savannah, Georgia
Willow Lane Plantation

Emily watched through the glass doors that opened from her library out onto the back lawns as Ivar and Anne sat on a double-swing chair suspended from a large tree. It was the very swing in which Emily had been sitting when Austin had proposed to her.

She placed her forehead against the glass and closed her eyes, wanting so much to know where Austin was. When she had returned home to Savannah after being gone for so many months, Gwenyth, the housekeeper, had welcomed her with open arms and the news that Austin was alive and recovering at a hospital somewhere in Virginia.

Emily had been ecstatic at the news, but grew more frustrated as first days and then weeks passed by with no further word. She was grateful that Anne and Ivar had elected to stay with her for a time. They kept her blessedly distracted, and with her concentration on helping Ivar continue to heal, the only time she usually allowed herself to mope about was late at night, alone in her bed.

Mary Alice was growing, and what a joy the child was! She moved about on her own, crawling and rolling and laughing. She, also, was a welcome distraction. Between caring for her loved ones and trying to keep food growing in the garden and served on the table, her life was full.

Savannah was slowly being strangled to death. The simplest of supplies were impossible to come by, and the women of the South had to be creative in their efforts to stretch thin resources, wringing every last drop from what they had. Emily had made clothing for Mary Alice from table linens and bedsheets. She mended her own dresses repeatedly and washed them carefully. She cared for her daughter and largely left the dealing of household finances to Gwenyth, who had been running the plantation since before Emily and Austin had married. It was easier, she realized, to allow someone else the worry, although she often felt a pang of guilt at letting Gwenyth shoulder so much.

Every scrap of paper she could come by she used front and back, every inch and corner when making lists or keeping records. They had taken to chopping up some of the older, less sentimental furniture for firewood on the few winter nights when cold became excessive. Even the local newspapers were printed on smaller sheets of paper in an effort to conserve.

Emily thought often of Mary and wondered if her friend hated her now that she knew of the Birminghams' interference with Elijah. She hadn't heard from the woman, and it gnawed at her. There was no hope for any kind of reconciliation now unless Mary went west to find him.

Her heart troubled and her thoughts swirling, Emily was lost in another world when an arm stole quietly around her waist from behind. Caught by surprise, she looked over her shoulder, her heart thudding in her throat. Austin's dear, familiar, and entirely too thin face regarded hers with a soft smile.

"I made it home," he whispered.

With a strangled cry, she turned and reached her arms around his neck, holding him close as though she'd never release him. He held her tight with one arm, his face buried in her hair, letting her sob until she felt weak. When she finally pulled back, she placed both hands on his face and said, "You are never allowed to leave again. Too much happens when you go away."

He smiled and wiped her face with his thumb. "I'm staying right here. Or wherever you are." He leaned down to kiss her cheek. "You kept me alive."

Emily glanced down at his hand, which supported his weight by leaning on a crutch she hadn't noticed positioned under his arm. She then saw a second crutch that had fallen to the floor—presumably she had disrupted it with her embrace. "Oh," she said, pulling back a bit. "You should sit . . ." She broke off as she noticed fully the reason for the crutches—his leg was missing below the knee. She glanced up at his face, and saw him watching her warily. She knew her reaction was important to him, as if he were afraid she'd now think him less of a man or be too horrified to touch him.

"Austin," she said, looking back down at the empty space below his knee and shaking her head. "What on earth have you done? And how in blazes did you get into this room without me hearing you approach?"

He laughed then, and she felt him relax. "I've become quite proficient with these things," he said, and she moved to pick up the crutch that had fallen.

As she straightened and handed it to him, she asked, "Does it hurt?"

"Not anymore."

"How did it happen?"

He shrugged. "A couple of lead balls shattered my bone. Then I caught on fire—was in some trees that were burning. A Union soldier pulled me out and saved my life, probably the same darned one who shot me."

Emily closed her eyes and pulled him close, resting her head on his chest. "I'm so glad you're home," she said in a whisper. "So very glad you're home."

* * *

Austin held his wife with a huge sense of relief. He should have known Emily was of more substance than one who might shrink in fear at the sight of his leg. He also should have known it wouldn't matter to her whether he had two legs or no legs, but he had worried much on his trip home, which had consisted of exhausting rides on trains, farmers' wagon beds, and a tired old horse that had carried him the last fifty miles.

Emily looked up at him through a sheen of tears and said, "Come with me. I need to introduce you to someone." She watched him maneuver along beside her out of the room and into the hallway. "Very impressive, Mr. Stanhope. You get along quite well."

"I've had some practice by now," he said. "My only regret is that we'll never dance again. That ballroom upstairs will now be useless."

"That's silly," she said. "Of course we'll dance. If you can walk, you can dance. And besides, we can get you one of those wooden contraptions—people will never know the difference."

He nodded thoughtfully. In his concern over Emily's reaction since he regained consciousness and began to rebuild his strength in the hospital, he hadn't even considered the possibility of a false leg. "When I was young, there was an old man in town who had fought the redcoats in the Revolution. He had a wooden leg, and he used to like to make us laugh by poking himself with sharp objects, nails and such."

"I think that's rather morbid, but very well. When you're old and gray, you can be the town's silly old man who sticks nails into his leg." She stopped when they reached the entry hall. "It doesn't matter to me one way or the other," she said. "If you prefer your crutches, use those. If you want a false leg, we'll find you a false leg. I wouldn't care if you'd lost both legs—I'd push you around in a special chair. I'm just glad you're alive."

He touched a curl that had escaped her bun. "Thank you," he murmured.

She gestured toward the stairs. "Can you climb to the second floor, do you suppose?"

He nodded. "I may take awhile, but I'll make it."

The process was a slow one, and Austin paused once to catch his breath. He shook his head at the memory of spending a lifetime bounding up and down those very stairs only now to be struggling with one leg and two sticks. When they reached the top, he smiled at his wife, who winked at him through tears and waited while he positioned his crutches under his arms. She then led the way down the hall, and his heart increased in rhythm as she stopped at the door next to their bedroom.

He believed he knew whom he was about to see, and found he was correct in his assumptions as Emily tiptoed into the room and led him to his childhood crib. Inside the small bed lay a little girl, beautiful in her slumber, a head of riotous red curls surrounding her head.

"This is Mary Alice," Emily said, and laid a hand on his shoulder. He glanced at her and she sniffed, overcome. "I've been waiting anxiously for you to meet her."

"Emily," he breathed, "she's beautiful. My daughter . . ." He reached a hand inside the crib and stroked her soft little cheek. He felt a surge of anger that he'd missed the momentous occasion of her birth, of seeing her as a tiny infant, of watching her first smiles and movements. His throat was thick with emotion as he looked at the little girl and ran a hand down her arm and then her leg.

"Is she healthy? Were there any problems with the birthing?"

Emily shook her head. "Hurt like the very devil, but we were both fine."

He smiled at her blunt speech; from Emily he expected nothing less. "Where were you? In Charleston?"

Emily nodded. "With Ruth. We telegraphed Gwenyth in hopes the news would eventually reach you. Austin," Emily hesitated, "I've been worried over your property in Atlanta. He's not there yet, but General Sherman is . . . well, he's . . ."

"Burning everything in his path?"

"Yes. You've heard then." At his nod, she continued. "I had hoped to travel to Atlanta and try to save as much as possible from your town home, but I'm afraid we're out of time."

He waved a hand. "We have all we need, Em." He looked down at his sleeping child. "We don't need anything else."

She laughed a little through her nose. "As noble as that sounds, sweet man, I'm afraid we can't eat the drapes."

He glanced up at her, feeling a smile slip onto his mouth. It was funny—he had forgotten how much he had always smiled in her presence. "I've learned some things this past while. We'll manage. As long as I have you and this little one, I can do anything."

She looked at him closely, carefully. "I do believe you may be right. I didn't doubt, really, but I'm trying to think practically. Conditions are horrid down here."

"I know. I saw it myself on my way home."

She flushed. "Of course you did. I'm just . . . I'm very concerned. I don't know what we'll do."

He motioned to her, and when she moved toward him, he reached to place his hand on the back of her neck and pull her close. "We'll manage," he repeated. "We'll find a way to last through the remainder of the war, and then we'll rebuild the plantation. You know I never did use slave labor to support this place; I've always paid my workers. I won't have to adjust to the strain of trying to afford employees—I've always operated under those conditions. It won't be as difficult as you might think."

At her dubious expression, he added, "It will be work, yes, and it will require that we continue to scrape by and be frugal, but it can be done."

She shook her head. "It just doesn't seem right, in some sense. You worked for the abolition cause and never made your fortune on the backs of other people. You've labored and earned the increase your properties have seen—and I've looked over your books, believe me." He smiled, and she continued, "I can't stand to think of your home in Atlanta and all of your belongings looted and destroyed."

She gave a little laugh, but it was without mirth, and he soon saw she directed it at herself. "I used to be so smug, so very sure I would be dancing in the streets as the South fell. And I admit, there is a part of me that thinks of Ruth, Mary, and Joshua and feels such a sense of satisfaction I can hardly stand it. But when I consider the devastation, all the innocent lives affected—people like you . . ."

She faltered for a moment, and he remained silent, allowing her the time to sort her thoughts. "You very nearly lost your life for this ridiculous cause. It makes me wonder how many more thousands there are who are fighting because they've been bullied into it or who have been led to believe their freedoms depend on the Confederacy, who don't trust the Union or Lincoln because of what the wealthy have told them."

He nodded slightly. "I spoke with many, many who believe that Lincoln is bent on bringing big, industrial cities to the South and destroying the slower pace down here, or that the Union is fighting to take away individual freedoms. They see it as the second American Revolution."

A small, stirring sound from the crib turned their attention toward Mary Alice. Austin watched, charmed, as the little one opened her eyes and looked around, spying her mother and breaking into a tired grin. The child rolled to her side and began pulling herself up by grasping the bars of the crib. Emily reached in, lifting her high and then holding her close.

"Sweet girl of Mama's," she murmured, Mary Alice's cheek against her own, "this is your papa." Emily placed her hand on Austin's chest. "We love him very much."

Austin's throat constricted as he looked at his wife and child, the one but a smaller image of the other. His girls, his life—that he was alive to see them together was nothing short of a gift from God.

CHAPTER 23

I had seen the dreadful carnage in front of Mayre's Hill at Fredericksburg . . . but I had seen nothing to exceed this. It was not war, it was murder.

—Confederate general Evander Law, eyewitness to Cold Harbor

* * *

31 May 1864
Boston, Massachusetts

"Who said that to you?" Camille demanded of her husband as he dressed for work.

"A clerk. Wants to know if I'm one of the rich who paid for a replacement or if I somehow bribed my way out of conscription." Jacob's tone was light, but Camille noticed a look about his eyes that set her teeth on edge in his defense.

"Jacob," she said and moved to his side, brushing his fingers away and fixing his tie. "You're serving your country here. Where would we be, all of us, if we didn't have the papers to keep us abreast of things? We'd be in the dark, that's where, and I dare anyone to say you're unpatriotic when I'm around."

Jacob shrugged. "I haven't felt too bad about it before, but maybe he's right."

"Stop. You were advised by United States senators to stay put. You know you're needed here, and if you *don't* know, you should." She patted his tie into place and looked up at him. "Besides, I would be dreadfully bored if you were to go off and leave me here by myself. And we've been married for only two weeks. What will people think if you leave?"

Jacob pulled her close and planted a kiss atop her head. "I don't want to leave, Cammy. Sometimes, though, I wonder if I should have."

"I don't want to think about this anymore. Tell me something new instead."

"Hmm. Something new . . . well, it officially goes into print today—the Radical Republicans are nominating John Fremont as their presidential candidate."

Camille wrinkled her nose and pulled back from Jacob's embrace. "Ugh." She frowned for a moment, thinking. "And the Democrats have chosen McClellan."

Jacob nodded. "Little Mac, himself."

"This is no good. The Fremont nomination will split the Republican vote, and we may well find ourselves speaking about President McClellan."

"True."

"I don't like that, not at all. That little man is still as arrogant now as he ever was!"

"Do you feel inclined to write a small piece about it?"

Camille tapped her finger against her lip. "Perhaps, perhaps . . ." She followed Jacob downstairs, where he hastily ate a muffin from the bread box and chased it down with a cup of black coffee.

"Are you going into town today?" Jacob asked.

"I may—I believe Abby is looking to purchase a book and a new bonnet."

"If you're about the office, stop in to say hello."

Camille smiled. "You don't mind your wife infringing on your place of business?"

Jacob grinned at her, settling his cup on the kitchen table and moving to place a quick kiss on her mouth. "It never stopped you before we were married."

"I didn't stop in on you more than a handful of times!"

"And with every single visit, I wanted to kiss you senseless."

Camille blushed. "You didn't!"

"I did. And now I can." The gleam in his eyes was decidedly wicked.

"Jacob Taylor, you will do no such thing. What would the office staff think?"

He tried for an innocent expression that she knew all too well was patently false. "We'll close the door. They'll never know."

"Absolutely not," Camille said as she shoved her husband down the hallway toward the front door. "I don't think I'll be visiting after all."

"Don't you trust me?"

"Ha! Not as far as I can throw you."

"That may not be such a feat, you know. I've seen you hauling burning drapes out of a broken window, remember?" He nodded with his head toward the room at the left of the door, a room that had been repaired and fixed so that one would never know anything out of the ordinary had occurred.

"Drapes are one thing. Tossing you around is an entirely different matter."

"If only that were true," he muttered, and kissed her one more time. He lingered, and, flustered, she finally shoved at his chest.

"Go," she whispered. "Everyone will wonder why you're late."

"Would that be so bad?"

"It's unseemly and you know it."

"It is unseemly. I also don't care if the whole world knows I'm in love with my wife. I waited for you for a very long time."

She couldn't help but smile. "Go. I'll be here when you return."

Camille closed the door behind him and walked into the parlor slowly, watching as Jacob left the house on foot. She kept her eyes trained on his back until he walked around the corner, turning back once to wave in her direction. She smiled. He knew she'd been watching him.

Her life had taken amazing turns, and she had become the woman she never imagined she would. She had always assumed she would marry well, for status and hopefully affection, if not outright love. It was what girls in her social circles did—made advantageous, convenient matches and lived lives of relative ease.

Instead, she had married a man who worked for his income, who was unconventional in the extreme, who believed firmly in abolition, and who supported the blossoming women's rights movement. He believed a woman had the right to equal wages for performing equal work, and he also believed women should be allowed to vote—such radical, unthinkable concepts for much of society, highborn and lowborn, to accept! Yet he never apologized, never equivocated, always maintained his ideals, and Camille loved him for it. She was also afraid it would someday get him killed much as it had Dolly Van Dyke.

With a sigh, she turned away from the window, letting the sheer curtains fall back into place. She would have to watch him carefully, protect him from himself. The threats to the Abolition Society hadn't overtly continued, but as long as Helena Smythe was in Boston, Camille couldn't breathe easy.

She placed her hands on her hips and looked at the small writing desk in the corner. The piece of paper and pen she had placed there the night before were waiting for her, and she knew the time had come to write Robert a letter. Her brother had been gone for months now, and she was finally starting to feel the guilt of having made him suffer. Not that he had, really. He wrote to her faithfully as though nothing were amiss. It had been childish of her to ignore him. She was so hopelessly terrified for his safety, though, that she hated to even think about him for very long. Each letter from him she received, however, sent a surge of relief coursing through her veins. She and Robert had grown close, and she loved him. She wanted desperately for him to return safe.

With a small shrug of resignation, she went to the desk, sat down, and began to write.

* * *

7 June 1864
Cold Harbor, Virginia

Ben Birmingham lay on the battlefield, surrounded by roughly seven thousand dead and dying Union men. He had been hit in both legs, one bullet still embedded near his ankle, the other having passed through his thigh. Shots still fired, the chaos and cacophony of battle still raining down around him so much that he didn't dare stand or raise his head.

By his count, this was his sixth or seventh day on the field. Generals Grant and Lee had both raced to this place just a few miles away from Richmond, and Lee had made it first. He dug in and waited for the Union troops to arrive, and when they did on the first of June, Grant ordered attacks that led blindly to the entrenched Southern soldiers. Ben had watched with horrified eyes as most of the men currently covering the five acres of land had fallen within the first eight minutes of battle, one of whom had been him. Since then, both sides had hunkered down, dazed and shocked, neither giving an inch.

Ben had also watched as another assault had been launched the third morning, and had groaned in sympathetic pain as Grant had ordered another attack, resulting in terrible losses. *They'll have your head for this in the press, General,* Ben thought. *Lincoln will be glad you fight, but I doubt many more will.*

In the days spent on the field, Ben had dragged himself over the bodies of the fallen, some he recognized and some he didn't. The movement was slow and painful, and he expected to feel a bullet piercing his skull at any moment, the final piece of lead that would claim his life.

He had finished the water in his own canteen and had taken water from other dead men wherever he found it. The wound in his thigh burned and throbbed, but for the most part it was actually a healthy-looking tear. The wound that had him most worried was the one in his ankle. If the bullet wasn't somewhere near the surface, his foot would be amputated. While there were those who survived an amputation, Ben had seen many who hadn't.

It doesn't matter. I'm going to lie on this field forever. I'll never be free—I won't even die—I'm doomed to stay here in the stench, crawling around dead bodies that are bloated in the heat and blackened with death and decay. I can't find Robert . . . he's gone . . .

He had been separated from his cousin in the first moments of battle. They had charged in with the infantry, leaving their horses behind. He had felt extremely vulnerable without his mount. Now he held himself responsible for his own wounds and for Robert's demise, wherever he was. Ben at least had his Gettysburg experience to guide him; Robert had been trained only as a cavalry soldier. Ben knew he should have insisted they wait behind with their company rather than act as reinforcements.

He cautiously raised his head and looked for movement on the field. Nobody else even twitched a finger. He lay in a sea of dead men—not all of whom had died in the initial onslaught but who were certainly gone now. He had even watched, shocked and sickened, to see one of the fallen finally take his own life to end his agony.

Just as he resigned himself to an eternity of utter madness, ready to pray and beg the Father to take him home, he heard Luke's voice in his mind. *They're coming to find you, Ben. They'll take you to safety.*

"Luke," Ben groaned, his voice hoarse. "I can't find Robert. He's dead." The tears came, then, at hearing his thoughts finally spoken aloud. "I've lost him too. What will your parents think?" When Ben failed to hear a response, he buried his face in the blood-spattered ground and cried.

The silence on the field was sudden and, in a way, offensive after the constant barrage of popping and exploding shell. Ben lifted his head to see men bearing stretchers coming from opposite sides of the field. They picked over the dead, beginning the attempts to bury them, and looked for survivors. Finally, a pair in Union uniforms ventured into earshot, and Ben called to them.

They looked up, shocked, and then hastily made their way over to him, eyeing him in amazement. "One more," one soldier said to the other. "I wouldn't have believed it."

"How many other survivors?" Ben managed to ask as they maneuvered him onto the stretcher.

"One."

* * *

"Folks will never believe it," Robert said to Ben as they lay on the ground in the makeshift hospital later that night. Robert's left arm was missing below the elbow, he'd been shot once through his right shoulder, and a bullet had grazed his neck, cutting him open but narrowly missing his artery.

"*I* don't believe it," Ben said.

Robert looked up at the stars, hearing the hush that followed the conclusion of the battle. "When the surgeons were trying to repair what was left of my arm, I listened in on their conversation. Would you like to hear an interesting detail?" he asked Ben.

He heard Ben chuckle. "Absolutely, I would. I've missed your 'interesting details' over the past days."

"Maybe I won't share this one, on second thought," Robert said. "It's rather ghoulish."

"Nothing can be more ghoulish that what we've just lived through."

"True. Well, here it is then—in the past thirty days, Grant has lost fifty thousand troops, dead or wounded.

That's half of all the men lost in the first three years of this war combined."

Robert heard Ben's quiet exhalation, but otherwise he made no response.

"What lies in store for us now? Do you know?" Robert asked.

"Of the two of us to 'know' anything, I rather expect it would be you."

Robert shook his head, and it bumped against the ground as he moved. "The only thing I know for certain is that Grant is moving on toward Petersburg."

"Then we're going with him. We're not staying here—we can't risk being taken prisoner."

"Then on to Petersburg it is." Robert paused for a moment, trying to shake the horrors of the past week and fighting against sleep although he knew he desperately needed it. "I don't want you to think me strange or that I've lost my head, but something happened earlier today. On the field."

"Go on."

"I thought I was going mad. I was feeling so crazed from lying among all the dead for so long that I thought I might leap up and scream for the Johnnies to just shoot me and end my torment. I heard . . . I heard . . ." Robert faltered for a moment, his eyes burning. "I heard Luke."

Robert heard Ben shift beside him and out of the corner of his vision, saw his cousin propping himself up on his elbow. "I heard him too, Robert. You aren't losing your mind."

Robert turned his head and looked at Ben. In the darkness, the experience fresh on his mind, Robert could almost imagine that Ben was Luke. "I miss him. I didn't want him to leave me."

"He didn't. He's still here. They all are—can't you feel them? It was the same for me when we were at Gettysburg. They are all still there."

Robert nodded slightly. "I don't understand it, though."

Ben was silent for a moment. "You're a man of science, Robert, a man of exacting facts and figures. There are some things our understanding of science can't explain. There are things we may not comprehend until later—much later. It's just a fact of life."

"I want to understand it, though. I want to know how, if my brother is dead, I could hear him."

"Because only his body is dead. The spirit lives on until Christ returns, at which point the body and spirit reunite." Ben winced and settled back down, leaving Robert to ponder his words.

"Eventually you'll have to explain the whole of it to me," Robert said, sensing Ben's desire to sleep.

"Mmm hmm," Ben murmured. Within moments, the rhythmic breathing signaled his rest, and Robert envied him his momentary peace.

As for his own sleep, it remained elusive for another hour as he thought of his brother, somewhere on the other side of life, until his exhausted body could no longer sustain being awake. He fell into a blissfully dreamless state where his mind took a reprieve from the horrors of the prior battle.

CHAPTER 24

I am holding my breath in awe at the vastness of the shadow that floats like a pall over our heads. It has come that man has no longer an individual existence, but is counted in thousands and measured in miles.
—Clara Barton

* * *

10 June 1864
New York, New York

"I'm not altogether certain I'm comfortable with this," Marie told Daniel as they walked away from the bustling noise of the city toward their home. "I'm proud of you for wanting to help people, but this seems quite dangerous."

Daniel pulled Marie's hand through the crook of his arm and patted it. "I want to serve, and this seems the best way to do so and still be able to work in my shop at home."

"It seems politically volatile as well," Marie muttered. "All this debate over whether to replace the volunteers with paid firefighters—it's bound to get ugly." She paused for a moment. "Have you told the mothers of your intentions?"

He smiled at her reference to Brenna and Jenny. They were a formidable force combined, and he didn't relish the prospect of telling them he wanted to fight fires. "No. I don't plan to just yet. That would mean *you* remain silent as well." He tweaked her nose when she gave him only a stubborn expression instead of an agreement.

"Why, though, Daniel? Why this?"

He was silent for a moment. "I enjoy the bustle of the city on occasion, and this certainly seems safer than police work. And I . . . I don't know exactly, sweetheart. I like the thought of my Da looking down from heaven and saying, 'That's my boy Daniel! He's rescuing people from danger!'"

Marie's face softened, and she planted a kiss on his arm, shirt and all. "Then do what you must. But promise me you will exercise care."

"I promise it."

"Promise you'll take more care than is actually required."

He laughed. "The most extreme care possible. I swear it. Now *you* promise me that you will refrain from spilling this news to the mothers."

"I swear it," she grumbled. "But if you think *I* am giving you a fight over this, well . . ."

"I know." He grimaced. "This is exactly why I don't want to discuss it with them yet. My mother isn't going to like it. Colin worried her with his work on the rails, and we told her she was upsetting herself needlessly."

"That's small comfort for me, Daniel. Colin died working the rails."

"I know. But . . . I'm not my brother."

"Exactly! Your mother told me once that *you're* the reckless one!"

Daniel laughed and tried to sober himself when he saw how distraught Marie truly was. "Marie, I love you. I love our life together. I just want to do more, that's all."

* * *

Savannah, Georgia
Willow Lane Plantation

"You believe it's time, then?" Anne watched Ivar's face, satisfied to see the bulk of his former health returned. He had gained some much-needed weight—not enough, but it helped, and his hair was growing back. Supplied with a few nice pieces of clothing from Austin's wardrobe, he looked very nearly like his old self.

He nodded. They were sitting under the shade of one of Willow Lane's many beautiful willow trees, near the house. "This time has been nice, and heaven knows I needed it, but I very much would like to return home to Inger."

"I worry that she won't care for me," Anne confessed, twirling a fallen leaf between her fingers.

Ivar laughed. "I worry that she won't care for *me.* She won't remember me. She was but two when I left. Now she's nearly five. We still haven't heard from them—I wonder if they've even received my letters."

"Are you well, Ivar? Lately you've been distant, rather more quiet than usual." Anne broached a subject she'd been avoiding for over a week. With Ivar's improving health, although his spirits had risen as well, he had become withdrawn.

"I've been doing some thinking," he admitted. He spoke so softly she was forced to lean closer to hear. "I've been wondering how you'll like living on a farm. You've lived your life in the city, with money, and I can't help but think you married me because . . . because you might have felt responsible for my condition . . ."

Anne's mouth dropped open. When she could finally form words, she found them tumbling out in a torrent. "Ivar Gundersen, how could you think that of me? I married you because I am so very much in love with you, and the months we spent apart were the worst of my life! As for living on a farm, I don't care if we live in the streets!" She fell silent for a moment and shook her head. "I swore to myself that if I found you—*when* I found you—if you were still alive, I would make you chain yourself to me and I would never leave your side again. Farm, city, an island in the middle of the ocean, I don't care. Knowing you're my husband is enough for me."

He looked up at her through new spectacles. He hadn't smiled or changed expression. "Forgive me for worrying," he said. "Berit . . . she said she wanted only me, that she would be content with me, and she was miserably unhappy."

"Ah, yes. Your first wife." The taste in Anne's mouth was suddenly bitter. How was it possible to be jealous of a ghost? She was envious of every moment the woman had had with Ivar. "Ivar, forgive me for speaking ill of the dead, but Berit was a fool. She also apparently thought she'd find happiness in a city, a place. I've never needed a setting to be happy. I create my own happiness. And truly, the only time in my life I was completely and totally bereft, unable to pull myself up, was when I returned home and left you to the wolves."

"Well, then, I am sorry for comparing you to her. It wasn't my intention." He looked around for a moment and inhaled deeply. "Are you ready for a trip north?"

She nodded. "I owe my parents an explanation, and they certainly need to meet you. I don't know when we'll be able to go to Boston, though."

"We can go now, collect your things, and then go on to Ohio."

"Yes—I suppose once we're up north, travel will be relatively simple. I'm glad you don't mind." Anne hesitated. "I haven't told them we're married."

"You . . . *what?*" Ivar looked at her with an expression of such shock that she couldn't help but laugh. For the most part, Ivar maintained a stoic demeanor. To have caught him by surprise was delightful.

"I want them to meet you in person when I tell them. I want them to see why it was so important to marry you without them there."

His eyes widened a bit, and he looked away as if still reeling. "I hope I measure up to their standards. Mercy, Anne, but you never fail to amaze me."

"I hope that's a good thing."

"It is."

* * *

25 June 1864
Petersburg, Virginia

"You are not going to believe this." Robert found Ben seated in their tent, writing a letter.

Ben looked up from his paper with a smile. "Tell me."

"They are digging a mine shaft."

"A what?"

"A mine shaft! Colonel Pleasants is a mining engineer, and he approached Burnside with a plan—"

Ben held up a hand. "Who is Colonel Pleasants?"

"He's in charge of a regiment from Pennsylvania—a regiment of coal miners. He has an idea to dig a tunnel under the Confederate line and pack it full of explosives."

Ben raised his eyebrows. "And then blow the rebels to the sky?"

Robert sat down next to his belongings and began digging through his bag for a small book he used as a journal of sorts. Ben watched him, swallowing his sympathy as Robert rummaged around in the bag with his one remaining hand. To his credit, Robert didn't complain, but Ben often saw his cousin's frustration as he attempted what should have been simple tasks.

Robert shook his head as he finally found his book and pen. "If they can plan carefully and then exploit their advantage, it has every opportunity of working. If not, well . . ."

Ben watched him thoughtfully in silence for a moment before returning to his letter to Mary. He and Robert were stationed with Grant's army just outside of Petersburg, Virginia. Situated roughly twenty-five miles south of Richmond, Petersburg was crucial to the Confederate supply line. Grant knew that to cut it off meant placing a stranglehold on Richmond much like he'd done in Vicksburg.

Shortly after Cold Harbor, they had moved to Petersburg, but the exhaustion of the men and the refusal of their commander, Smith, to pursue an advantage he'd gained upon his initial attack of the woefully inadequate Confederates under Beauregard gave the Confederates time to regroup and reinforce Beauregard's small force.

Grant had tried twice more to attack but had been repulsed both times. And so they sat, placing the city under siege and waiting, which grew tedious, as did living in trenches. Trenches that were dug out of the ground and fortified with wood and straw defined the lines of both armies. There the soldiers sat and waited to kill each other. Ben would have been hard-pressed to find a reason to be grateful for his and Robert's wounds, but it meant that thus far, they had been allowed to stay well behind the lines and were given the comfort of a small but relatively dry tent.

Ben had told Robert on more than one occasion that he was reasonably justified in asking for an early discharge, given the fact that his arm had been blown off in battle, but Robert insisted on staying with Ben. Truthfully, Ben was grateful for his cousin's company. Robert, a serious young man upon enlistment, had grown only more mature and thoughtful from his experiences. He never failed to amaze with his ability to collect and disseminate information.

Ben focused on the words he'd written to Mary and wondered how she was doing. He had wanted to be with her in person when he proposed, but found he couldn't wait any longer. He poured his heart onto the page and asked her to marry him as soon as she thought she might be ready. Never had he felt so certain about anything in his life. He loved Mary, had known her since his own adolescence and loved the woman she had become. He knew he was rushing things, but his experiences of late had instilled a sense of urgency that made him wonder if he'd live to see the light of another day.

He watched Robert mutter to himself about the potential problems with the "mine shaft" operation and smiled, counting himself fortunate to have had the time and association with not only one but two of his cousins. "Perhaps it will work," he said to Robert, who looked up, distracted.

"I don't know, I just don't know . . ."

* * *

Wyoming-Nebraska

Jeffrey secured the first of their two wagons for the night, checking to be sure the children were safely bedded down. He approached Earl, who had checked on the second, and nodded. "I suppose now we sleep," he said, and Earl smiled.

"It does become fairly familiar," Earl said, "living on the trail. And we're fortunate—we arrived here quickly and with no complications."

"You were correct to take us north and then west," Jeffrey said, clapping Earl once on the shoulder. "The railway served us well."

"Mr. Birmingham, is your wife resting?"

Jeffrey nodded. Sarah had been as bewildered by the move as little Elijah, but she had adjusted well enough. He was also pleased to see that her lapses into coherent thought were becoming more frequent. She accepted his explanation that Bentley was in good hands and seemed at peace when he told her they were going to build another beautiful house in a new place.

Ruth, as always, was the family rock. She kept things organized and moving much as would the most proficient of army generals. Even Earl, who had made the trek a few times on his own, was impressed with her skill. She slept now with Charlotte and the baby in the second wagon, and Clara and Rose had bedded down beneath the wagon, Elijah snug as a bug between them. Sarah slept in the first, and Jeffrey would soon join her, with Earl sleeping underneath, keeping a secure eye on the camp.

They had joined with a relatively small group of eighty people under the direction of trail captain John D. Chase.

They were immigrants mostly, Mormons who were seeking to join with the rest who had already moved to Utah. They were a friendly bunch, and Jeffrey didn't anticipate internal strife; heaven knew it was the last thing he needed. He was anxious to be underway, anxious to arrive in their new home, and anxious about how life would be once settled there.

He climbed into the first wagon and removed his dusty boots. Settling down in the center of the wagon next to Sarah, he wondered if he would last the entire night. There was barely room enough for him, and while Sarah was quite petite, Jeffrey was accustomed to sprawling as he liked while sleeping.

Sarah mumbled a bit and turned over. He could see her face from the light of the moon that streamed in through an opening on one end. He felt a stirring of tenderness for her and wondered how it was that such a strong woman could crumble so completely. Perhaps it was a simple enough thing to be strong when conditions were to one's liking. When those conditions changed, well, that was probably when the strong were truly recognized.

* * *

The next morning dawned much earlier than Charlotte would have liked. The baby fussed until she fed him, Elijah was running about camp whooping like an Indian in an annoying fashion he had learned from Rose, and Sarah kept telling her that if she wanted her baby to grow, she needed to feed him something more substantial, like beef.

She might have been pleased that her mother was communicating with her at all; in some moments, usually quite out of the blue, Sarah sounded a bit like her old self, and then the craziness would return. Charlotte emerged from the wagon, braiding her hair and smoothing her dress. As she thrust her feet into her boots, she gritted her teeth at the amount of dust lodged in the bottom of them and groaned when she got a good look at the hem of her skirt.

It was only their second day on the trail, and already she was miserable. She hadn't wanted to leave Bentley, hadn't wanted to leave South Carolina at all. It was the only home she had ever known, and while she now saw the folly of the Confederate ideas for what they were, she was more terrified of the unknown than certain ruin at home.

Nothing, nothing was the same. Her mother had taken leave of her senses, Richard was dead, William was dead, and Emily lived in Savannah. Cousin Anne had married a prisoner of war who was knocking on death's door, Cousin Luke had gone on to his eternal reward, Cousin Robert was with Ben and more likely than not, the two of them would fall victim to shells, and all of Bentley's slaves were free.

She paused for a moment, her hand on the back of the wagon, and watched little Elijah. Her face flooded with heat for a moment as she considered her thoughts. Bentley's slaves had been *people.* Mary, Elijah's mother, was a *person.* Against her will and entirely unbeknownst to her, some of Ben's and Emily's attitudes about people of color had begun to rub off on her. She wasn't sorry Bentley's slaves were free. She was sorry her own future was so uncertain.

Earl Dobranski rounded the corner then and bumped into her. "Oh, my, I do apologize, Mrs. Ellis," he said in a drawl that certainly wasn't Southern, but had its own lazy quality about it. He was a big man, and she got a crick in her neck from looking up at him.

"Think nothing of it, Mr. Dobranski. I was standing here woolgathering." She knew she had been barely civil to the man since meeting him back at home, and he'd done nothing to warrant her derision. In fact, she probably ought to be nicer to him; he might well be the one thing to keep them alive amidst the marauding Indians and wild animals Charlotte was sure they would encounter along the way. She forced a smile upon her face and added, "Lovely day today."

He stared at her for a moment before finding his tongue. "Yes, yes it is. Nice day to be on the move."

"Mmm." She couldn't make herself go that far. She was saved from further comment when William squealed, seeking her attention. "Excuse me, won't you?" Without waiting for his response, she moved to find her son, whom she discovered standing at the front of the wagon, poised to leap off.

"Well now, there's a boy after my own heart," Earl said as he rounded the corner with her. "Do you mind, Mrs. Ellis?"

Mind? Did she mind what?

Taking her confusion for permission, he held his hands out to the child and said, "Jump!"

Her hand at her throat, Charlotte watched Will jump from the wagon and into Earl Dobranski's hands. It wasn't a big jump, wasn't even that far of a distance from the wagon to where Earl stood, but Charlotte viewed the whole thing with a nightmarish kind of shock.

"I best be about seeing to your father," Earl said after settling the child gently on his feet. He touched the brim of his hat to Charlotte, laughing when the little boy squealed with delight and clung to his leg, begging for another chance to leap into the air. Charlotte snapped herself to her senses and reached down, prying Will's hands from the man's leg. When she had pulled loose her screaming son, Mr. Dobranski turned and was gone. He left before she could give him proper what for about roughly handling other people's children!

With a sigh, she turned her attention to Will, who had started climbing up the wagon wheel for another chance to jump. "No," she said firmly, and pulled him back.

Clara came around from the first wagon then and saw the commotion. Smiling, she signed her hellos to William, and Charlotte had to catch her breath at the beauty in her young sister's face. Traveling and being in constant proximity to the family seemed to have set free a spirit in Clara that was lovely to behold.

The screaming child stopped his complaints and went willingly to Clara, who raised her brows at Charlotte as if asking permission to take him. "Yes, by all means," Charlotte said, glad Clara was proficient at reading lips. She felt a moment of shame that she had never bothered to learn to sign so that she might communicate with Clara.

She watched the young woman carry her child to Rose and Elijah, where she set him next to her nephew on the ground and held his hand while he spun in circles, imitating his cousin. He was finally so dizzy he fell to the ground, laughing, and Charlotte couldn't help but smile.

CHAPTER 25

The work and expectations of almost two months have been blasted. . . . The first temporary success had elevated everyone so much that we imagined ourselves in Petersburg, but fifteen minutes changed it all and plunged everyone into a feeling of despair almost of ever accomplishing anything. Few officers can be found this evening who have not drowned their sorrows in the flowing bowl.

—Major Washington Roebling, witness to The Crater

* * *

5 July 1864
Boston, Massachusetts

Camille sat in her parlor with Abigail, perusing Jacob's notes for articles that would appear in the next edition of the paper. "Reaction to Congress's increase to the Internal Revenue Act," she snorted. "I wonder if any of it is favorable."

"Ha," Abigail said, her head bent over an article that seemed to have captured her interest. "People will generally support the war so long as we're winning battles, their own family members aren't dying, and the government isn't taking money out of their pockets. Giving up three percent of a person's income to support a war when we're losing battles isn't going to make anyone happy."

Camille knew it wasn't just income, either. The government was taxing everything! There were sin taxes on alcohol and tobacco, luxury taxes on yachts and jewelry. Congress had seemingly gone mad with the power of the tax. "Did you know that two years ago when they first began printing the greenbacks, we were spending two point five million dollars per day on the war? Jacob and I were talking about it yesterday."

Abigail looked up from her article. "That much money is enough to make one ill."

"Jacob says that Salmon Chase resigned as treasury secretary. This time Lincoln accepted the resignation."

"Was it a dispute over the Internal Revenue increase?"

Camille shook her head. "I don't believe so. Something about a problem over a particular appointment to the Treasury Department. Many women are working there now, isn't that amazing? Since Chase has been the secretary, the number of clerks employed has risen from four hundred to two thousand. Can you imagine going to work in an office each day?"

Abigail smiled. "Sometimes I wouldn't mind it."

"Abby, you have all the money you need."

"But nothing to fill my time."

Camille eyed her friend in sympathy but remained silent, as any appeal about Abigail's good points and her volunteer work would be mistaken as pity. Instead, she motioned to the paper the other young woman held in her lap. "What do you have there?"

Abigail's brow furrowed in a frown. "Some disturbing details about Sherman's attack on Kennesaw, Georgia. We suffered nearly two thousand casualties. A direct frontal assault." She shook her head, reading. "It seems unnecessarily risky to me. Is that in character for Sherman?"

Camille cocked a brow. "I don't believe he's known for his gentle approach, but perhaps he misjudged the situation."

The sound of the front door opening halted further conversation as Jacob entered the home and a few moments later, the parlor. He smiled at the women, but there was a grim set to his mouth that Camille recognized as worry. "What is it?"

"A man can't come home at the noon hour for something to eat?"

"No. Not like this—there's something wrong."

He sat next to Camille and took her hand. "Not wrong, necessarily, just . . . interesting. Abby, I knew you would be here today, and I wanted to tell you in person before the paper prints the information . . . about your mother's death."

Abigail slowly placed the paper she'd been holding on the coffee table and folded her hands in her lap. "What about my mother's death?"

"Helena Smythe. She was the person who hired the man to run your mother down in the street. She knew of Dolly's walking habits and selected the time and place for the 'accident.'"

"This is supposed to come as a surprise?" Camille couldn't hide her disdain. "I could have told the police a long time ago that she was behind it. In fact, I think I *did* tell them, right about the time she arranged to have this house burned to the ground!" Camille paused in her tirade long enough to glance at Abigail's face. She was pale and tense.

Camille reached over and clasped her friend's fingers. "I'm sorry," she murmured.

Abigail shook her head. "Don't be. We knew all along." She turned her attention to Jacob. "What will happen to Helena?"

"She was arrested this morning at the Sylvesters' house. It seems she had hired men only recently to arrange for others to be involved in similar 'accidents.'"

"What others?" Camille asked.

"I don't know for certain. Others."

"You *do* know, but you're not telling us." Something in his tone made her wary. He was hiding information, probably to protect her feelings.

"Your parents," he said reluctantly. "She had hired someone to hurt or kill both your mother and father at separate times."

Camille was silent then. "I had to know," she finally mumbled. "I made you tell me." Anger surged through her mind, and she nearly shook with it. "I'll scratch her eyes out! I should have when I had the opportunity!"

"It's done, love. Finished. Don't keep thinking about her or she'll harden your heart."

"It's not done, Jacob. She's only one of millions who hate the cause, who hate abolitionists. What if we're never safe?"

"It's not just abolitionists. It's everywhere. All the big cities are seeing trouble from small quarters of people who are bent on terrorizing the Union in favor of the Confederacy." Jacob rubbed a hand across his eyes, and Camille noticed for the first time just how tired he looked. He had been working long hours at the newspaper office, and he needed a rest.

"Jacob, thank you for taking the time to tell me personally. I know you're busy." Abigail still sat, composed, but her face showed her shock.

"Think nothing of it, Abby. I was grateful for an excuse

to stretch my legs. The place is all abuzz with news from Horace Greeley's office in New York. It seems he received a letter from some Confederate delegates in Canada who want to discuss an end to the war."

"Will Lincoln send representatives, I wonder?" Camille asked.

"I'm sure he will, but I doubt much good will come of it. Lincoln will demand that they agree to return to the Union and accept abolition as part of the peace plan." He sighed and rose to leave. "Not likely to happen." Jacob kissed Camille and patted Abigail on the shoulder, said his good-byes, and left.

Camille turned her attention to Abigail, who sat still as though feeling numb. "Are you really so surprised, Abby? I knew that Aunt Helena was a bad person from the first moment I laid eyes on her."

Abigail sighed and leaned back a bit in her chair, her shoulders slightly slumped. "I'm not surprised. I suppose I wanted to believe that it really all was just an accident. Someone hated my mother enough to kill her. I loved her. She was everything to me." A tear escaped Abigail's eye and trailed down her cheek. She wiped it slowly and examined the moisture on her finger, rubbing it absently.

Camille's heart twisted, and her anger surged afresh. "You know, I've never understood the fascination with public executions, but I swear by all things holy, if this woman is hanged, I will be there."

* * *

28 July 1864
Washington, D.C.

Isabelle Webb looked out the window of her hotel room at nothing in particular. The sun was rising again on another day, and she found herself tired. She was ready to be finished witnessing war. She wanted to settle down a bit, if not with a husband then at least with her sister at home in Chicago.

Still matters dragged on, however, and because she had been with Pinkerton as an operative for so long, she wasn't sure how to stop. She wasn't even sure she wanted to stop, really. She would love to go back to Chicago and do the investigative work Allan Pinkerton had originally hired her to do.

Isabelle had lost track of the few people she could name as friends, most significantly Anne Birmingham. The last she had heard, Anne was deep in the South, looking for a man she'd known in the army. Belle couldn't even count Lucy Lockhart among her casual associates anymore; Lucy had died only a month before from complications of an intestinal illness she'd contracted while they were under siege in Vicksburg.

I feel so very . . . alone. Most men were threatened and repelled by her occupation, others by the force of her personality, and women tended to eye her with mistrust. Belle didn't consider herself a classic beauty in any sense, but she knew how best to capitalize on her assets and make the best of what she had.

She turned from the window and walked to the small desk situated in a corner of the room. Taking a seat next to it, she opened the small book she'd been using to record her thoughts.

I have no friends, only you, my diary. There are a handful of people on this earth whom I implicitly trust, and none of them are accessible to me now.

I grow weary of this war. Sometimes I find myself so frustrated with the Union reluctance to press advantages and finish this thing that I could scream. I'm tired of Washington, tired of traveling so much, tired of the hotels and the parties where I pretend to be someone I'm not. I'm tired of lying to people, of lulling them into a false sense of security so they'll tell me their secrets, political or otherwise.

I do have hopes that lie in Generals Grant and Sherman. "The Butcher" people are calling Grant because of his willingness to sacrifice so many lives in order to force the Confederacy to also sacrifice theirs. How quickly the court of public opinion turns. Not long ago people lauded Grant as the Union's savior. Now they are angry with him.

Sherman's style is similar. He's willing to fight to take ground and grind the supporting citizens into submission. He seems to know that if he cuts off all sources of support for the troops by destroying peoples' resources, the South will eventually choke and die. He takes an effective approach, one that would turn the stomach of civilized folk.

His men were recently attacked by John B. Hood just outside of Atlanta, and Hood sustained heavy losses that he could ill afford. I wonder if Jefferson Davis now regrets replacing Joseph Johnston with John Hood. The Confederate soldiers loved Johnston—word has it those boys would have followed him to the ends of the earth, but Davis had a personal dislike for the man. General Sherman is now circling Atlanta, cutting rail lines and roads and effectively blockading the South's last remaining stronghold.

Even closer to home, the winds of battle have knocked at the door. Confederate Jubal Early reached the outskirts of the District of Columbia, but Union general Lew Wallace slowed him down. Once our reinforcements arrived to help Wallace, Early withdrew. It was too close for my personal comfort.

I've given Pinkerton my word that I'll remain here; my position as a woman affords me access to places Pinkerton and the men cannot go, and I remain as valuable to him as ever. I just wonder, really, if this is all my life will ever be about. As much as I would feel utterly stifled to be somewhere mending socks and washing bedsheets, I must admit there are times when it sounds awfully tempting . . .

* * *

30 July 1864
Petersburg, Virginia

Robert walked back to Ben, shaking his head, his face hidden by the darkness. "I don't know about this," he was muttering.

"What are they doing now?"

"Drawing straws to see which regiment will lead the way through the hole."

"They already have a regiment—trained and ready to go."

"A black regiment," Robert said, looking back over his shoulder at the commanders who stood in a circle.

"So . . ." Ben looked at his cousin in confusion.

"General Meade is worried that if the black regiment suffers great losses, it will look as though he valued the life of the Negro less than the life of the white soldier. They're replacing the original regiment, the one that's ready to do this, with one that hasn't been trained."

Ben groaned, a feeling of deep unease settling into the pit of his stomach. As they watched the circle of commanders, one drew the straw signaling that his men would be the first to breach the Confederate line once the explosion in the tunnel underneath the enemy had been set off.

"Who is it?" he asked Robert, who was also watching the men.

Robert rolled his eyes and removed his cap, scratching absently at his hair in frustration. "James Ledlie."

"Is he any good?"

Robert shook his head. "He's a political general. He's best known for his ability to hold hard liquor."

"Oh, that'll be useful."

"I can't watch this, but I don't dare turn away. Are you coming with me?"

Ben rose with a sigh. "I don't suppose I have anything better to do."

Around them, activity ensued as the men prepared for the explosion. Earlier in the day, the tunnel had been packed with four tons of black powder, out of which ran a ninety-eight-foot fuse. The men had then packed dirt back into the last thirty-four feet of the tunnel so the blast wouldn't come back out of the entrance.

Ben yawned. "Three and a half in the morning—what a beastly hour to be awake. Until we hear differently, we're not obligated to participate in this thing. Are you sure you want to stay up for it?"

Robert nodded. "I can't not watch this. You go back to the tent, though. I'm fine."

"No, I'll stay." Ben was reluctant to leave his cousin's side, and had been ever since Cold Harbor. Whether it was for Robert's comfort or for his own, he couldn't say.

"The fuse is lit—nothing's happening."

"Who lit it?"

"Pleasants." Robert squinted, trying to see in the darkness. "I wonder how long they'll wait before checking it."

Fifteen minutes later, Ben pointed to the right. "Two volunteers to check the fuse," he told Robert. The two men ran into the night and returned moments later, running as if there were hounds on their heels. A scant few minutes later, an explosion rocked the earth.

Robert looked at Ben, his eyes wide. "It worked!" He looked around, watching for the newly appointed regiment to begin their charge.

An hour later, Ben and Robert sat on overturned barrels, still watching for the regiment to make a move. The chaos was so profound; the troops had only just received their orders to move. "I would understand if the rebs are facing this much disorganization right about now," Robert muttered. "They've just been blown into the clouds. But *this?*"

"We may be called in to follow eventually," Ben said, and stood. "Let's get some rest while we can."

They were indeed awoken when the morning had progressed a bit, the sun rising over the horizon, but not for the reasons they had supposed. Talking outside the walls of the tent alerted both men, who had become light sleepers.

"There was a crater in the earth that must have been a good thirty feet deep and nearly two hundred feet across. An entire regiment was buried when that explosion went off."

Robert raised himself up and looked at Ben. "That's General Grant," he whispered.

Ben nodded and put a finger to his lips.

"Instead of running around the crater, though, they ran *through it.*"

The voice that answered was one that Ben recognized—a personal aide to Grant. "Through it? But why?"

Robert scooted himself over to the tent opening and peered out to see Grant, looking extremely tired, shaking his head. "They weren't the men who had been trained for it. And because they took so long getting there, the rebs had time to regroup and reinforce."

"And what of Ledlie?"

"He sat in a shelter four hundred yards off drinking rum."

The aide let loose an expletive before asking, "How many men?"

"Over four thousand total. Eleven hundred as prisoners. Shot our boys like fish in a barrel. They couldn't get out of the crater, of course. Thirty-foot walls, and they didn't have ladders. It was the saddest affair I have witnessed in the war."

Robert moved back to his bedroll as Grant and his aide moved along. He buried his face in his pack and groaned. "How *could* they have been so stupid? They must have just followed each other like sheep."

Ben laid his head back down and stared at the walls of the tent. How much longer would it drag on? If his and Robert's luck held, they would go home in October. But when would the war end? Another year? Two years? How much more could they stand to lose?

The tales of the horror grew worse during the course of the day as men who had survived and made it back to Union lines shared firsthand accounts. There was one in particular that haunted Ben until he finally fell asleep that night. "We were trying to surrender, hundreds of us, black and white both. The rebs yelled, 'Take the white man!' I tell you, I've never seen such an awful thing in my life. They attacked the colored troops—used their bayonets or clubbed 'em to death. Just isn't right," the soldier had finished, "when a man's trying to surrender."

Will it ever be right? Ben prayed that night. *Will the hatred ever go away?*

CHAPTER 26

Grant is a butcher and not fit to be at the head of an army. He loses two men to the enemy's one. He has no management, no regard for life. . . . I could fight an army as well myself.

—Mary Todd Lincoln

* * *

1 August 1864
Devil's Gate, Wyoming

"Not really much of a gate, is it?" Rose asked Earl as they looked at the unique landscape that stretched before them.

"Not really," Earl agreed with the young woman. He wondered how she felt to be moving away from the South, breathing free air. Such a shame it was to think that she would have spent her life in slavery if things had not changed so drastically. He turned his attention back to the gate. "It's just two steep cliffs with a river in the middle. If Mr. Birmingham agrees, I don't see why you and Clara can't climb up the side and look down. I did when I was younger—it's so high I felt dizzy."

Rose went off to find Clara, and after securing Mr. Birmingham's approval, the two began climbing up the steep side of the cliff. Earl turned as Charlotte shouted to the girls, "Don't get too close to that ridge! You'll fall right off!"

He smiled. For all of Mrs. Ellis's admonitions and occasionally gruff demeanor, he saw the effort she was making to contribute and do her part in making the trip efficient and uneventful. She was concerned for the children, though—all of them. She became the small group's unofficial worrier. If there were snakes, insects, or any kind of perceived danger nearby, she scrambled to gather the children to her side.

"They'll take care, Charlotte," Ruth said to her as she passed, moving to hang a cooking pot on the side of the first wagon. "They're smart, the pair of them."

"I know they're smart, but they could fall off that cliff!" Charlotte snapped her irritation, but Earl sensed something more dangerous behind it. He was no good at handling women who cried, and he prayed Mrs. Ellis wasn't about to.

Ruth glanced Charlotte's way and commented, "Did you get your rest last night?"

"Oh! Am I not allowed to be anxious that those girls are risking life and limb? It doesn't mean I'm short on sleep!" The last came out on a suspiciously shaky tone, and Earl stepped back a bit, wanting to avoid the inevitable flood.

As it turned out, he didn't have to leave; Charlotte did it for him. She stomped to the back of the second wagon and disappeared. Ruth sighed a bit and looked at Earl. "I believe she's a bit tired," the woman said, looking weary herself. "I'll see to her."

"No, let me, Miss Ruth." Earl couldn't believe his own ears, but he'd said the words. His brain tried to follow along as his feet moved of their own volition and followed Charlotte's trail. When he found her, his fumbling mind caught up with his mouth, and he wasn't sure that was an improvement.

"Mrs. Ellis," he began. "I know it isn't an easy thing, crossing the plains like this. We're nearly there, however . . ."

She waved a hand at him slightly and sniffed, clearly embarrassed. "I'll be fine, I just need a moment."

He reached into his pocket and pulled out a relatively clean if somewhat dusty handkerchief and handed it to her. She took it with a murmur of thanks and dabbed her eyes. He stood there for a moment and barely resisted the impulse to shift his weight back and forth from one foot to the other. Finally, deciding he had little to lose, he chose the honest route and spoke from his heart.

"Mrs. Ellis, this may not make a difference to you, but you should know that I realize you're from a life of privilege. In the time I have spent accompanying people along this trail, I have seen women with much less beauty and poise, money and manners, behave in a very spoiled way. Your behavior on this trip would have led me to believe, had I not known better, that you'd been born to move about and adapt." He paused for a moment as her tears ceased, and she looked up at him with a sniffle.

"I don't know if I'm saying it right," he continued, "but given where you come from, I would have expected you to fight this trip tooth and nail. I'm very impressed with your strength. My mother would be impressed as well, and there's not any that I respect more than her."

"I . . . uh . . . thank you very much for your kind thoughts, Mr. Dobranski," Charlotte murmured in her

Southern tones, still looking as though she weren't sure how she should interpret his comments.

"Please know I meant them as compliments, Mrs. Ellis."

"Uh . . . yes. Again, thank you." She clutched his handkerchief, and he didn't have the heart to ask for its return. As he stepped back to leave, she said, "Please, it would be so much easier, that is, if you'd like, to just call me Charlotte."

He nodded his head once and touched the brim of his hat. "With your permission, then, I'll gladly call you Charlotte."

"Yes. Yes, you have my permission." She flushed slightly and smoothed a stray hair that had been blown free of her braided bun.

"And you have permission, should you choose, to call me Earl." He smiled at her, wanting to ease her tension. She was so very proper!

"Earl." She nodded back at him. "It's a very nice name. Is your mother British, perhaps?"

"Oh, no. Her grandfather is Irish, and her grandmother a Cherokee. My father's family emigrated from Poland. I have seven brothers, each of our names beginning with *E*."

Her mouth formed a small O. "I . . . see. And is there a reason for all those *E*'s?"

"Well, my mother's name is Ellen, my father's, Eli. They wanted to continue the fashion, I believe."

Again, the O.

He thought of something he'd wanted to say to her but had avoided because he knew there had been some bad feelings between Ben and his family when he'd left home nearly ten years before. "I'd like you to know how much your brother Ben means to me. When he arrived in Utah, I was a young teen, my father gone off to proselyte. He met Ben near your home, of course, and after baptizing him, sent him our way when he needed a place to go. Ben took care of me, rather like a brother would. As I had only younger ones, I appreciated his attention."

Charlotte nodded slightly, her expression giving nothing away. "I'm happy to know he was able to make good friends. The atmosphere at our home when he left was . . ." She turned her face into the breeze and squinted, looking at something far away. "It was strained."

"Well," Earl said quietly, some of his former nervousness returning, "I just thought you might like to know."

"Thank you." She turned her face back to his and smiled. "Thank you for your consideration."

"You're most welcome, Charlotte." Still she smiled at him, and he returned it. "And now, if you'll excuse me, I'll see about getting those girls down from the cliff."

Charlotte closed her eyes, looking rueful, and nodded. "Thank you. But perhaps if they're enjoying themselves, we might give them another minute or two."

* * *

It was much later in the evening when Earl finally managed to sit down and relax. The camp was secured for the night, the people under his care resting. He sat back for a moment and looked upward into the vast heavens, feeling small but secure. It was after a few moments of silent contemplation that he noted a soft murmur of voices coming from nearby.

He rose to seek it out to be sure all was well and found Ruth and Jeffrey seated together against one of the large wagon wheels. They looked up at his approach, and he felt a bit sheepish. "I apologize for interrupting," he said, holding up a hand. "Just checking."

"No, no, Earl," Jeffrey said, and motioned next to him on the blanket. "Perhaps you'd join us for a moment. Ruth and I are wondering what we should expect from our new home. Perhaps you can enlighten us a bit."

Earl made himself comfortable next to the pair on the ground. "What would you like to know?" he asked with a bit of a grunt as he stretched his legs.

"Well," Jeffrey began, "many of the other folks in the wagon train are Mormons."

"Yes."

"Are they . . . is Utah . . ."

"Predominantly Mormon?"

"No, I expected that to be the case. We're not, though, obviously, and I suppose we're wondering how we'll be . . . received."

Earl smiled a bit. "You'll find that most will treat you very kindly indeed. You might be ready for some interesting views on the war, however . . ." He looked up for a moment, gathering his thoughts. "Many of the Saints believe that the war is a result of the martyrdom of the Prophet Joseph Smith."

Jeffrey and Sarah regarded him with identical expressions—eyebrows raised, with no further comment.

"They are not particularly fond of either the North or the South. You must remember, though, the conditions under which the original body of Saints left their homes."

Ruth nodded. "They were driven out."

"Yes, they were. And toward the end, with the written permission of a governor. There are many who harbor a small amount of resentment."

Jeffrey cleared his throat. "But we're not Mormons. How will people feel about us?"

"I expect you'll be treated right kindly. We are Christian folk, and you'll find that the good majority are wonderful people. There may be those who won't understand how you can live so near to the truth and not embrace it yourselves," Earl said with a smile, "but one of our credos, our beliefs, is to allow others the privilege of worshipping how, where, and what they may. It's what we want for ourselves; we certainly expect nothing less for others."

Both Ruth and Jeffrey seemed to relax a bit. There was a new set to the shoulders of both that hinted of relief.

"Also," Earl continued, "bear in mind that we are all immigrants. The oldest natural-born citizens of Salt Lake City are sixteen, maybe seventeen years old. We're all newcomers who have fled to the place either for freedom, to be with others who share the same faith, or perhaps to try a new life. There are many, many folk from not only the States but from the British Isles and other countries as well."

"Well, thank you for your enlightenment. It sounds like just the sort of place we want to be then," Jeffrey said, almost to himself.

"That's fortunate for us, isn't it?" Ruth asked, her mouth quirked into a smile. "Especially since we're nearly there."

Jeffrey tipped his head back and laughed softly. "I suppose it is. I admit, I didn't give much thought to the destination itself, only that we needed to get away from home."

"It's as good a place as any to accomplish that," Earl said, smiling and feeling a natural affection for Ben's father.

Funny, but Ben had always talked of his family in frustrated tones. "I do believe Utah will agree with all of you."

* * *

7 August 1864
Boston, Massachusetts

The comfortable silence around the dinner table as the Birmingham family ate lacked the strain of which Anne had been worried. Her parents had taken the news of her marriage in stride, not seeming any more surprised than if she'd come home and told them she'd misplaced a shoe or a handbag. They, by now, expected the extreme from her, and she never failed to deliver.

Camille, on the other hand, had shown considerable more emotion—first frustration that she'd missed the small ceremony, then delight when she conversed with Ivar and found him a suitable match for her sister. She and Jacob sat at the table as well; otherwise, there would have been only James, Elizabeth, and Jimmy dining together. The family structure had changed, and every now and then Anne noticed a far-off look in Elizabeth's eyes that spoke of her distraction.

The one-year anniversary of Luke's death had come and gone, and though they all missed him, for the most part they were able to reminisce about him without becoming emotional. They even laughed at some of the memories, the smiles lingering instead of dissolving into tears.

Anne glanced at Jacob, who had placed a gentle hand over Camille's, occasionally tucking a stray hair behind her ear and looking at her when she spoke to others. Anne was glad to see him so completely devoted to her sister. He and Camille were good for each other, and their mutual affection was evident.

Later that evening, Anne and Ivar completed packing the rest of her belongings that would be sent to Ohio ahead of them. As she looked around her old bedroom, she thought of the young woman she had been and of the person she had become. Ivar was seated on the edge of the bed, and he patted the spot next to him.

"What are you thinking?" he asked as she sat and wrapped both of her arms around one of his. "Will you miss it?"

"No," she said, still looking around and thinking. "Well, perhaps a bit, but only for nostalgic reasons, really. I'm ready to move on. And I'm glad," she said, giving his arm a squeeze, "that you're so likable. My family thinks you're wonderful."

He winked at her. "It's because I'm so chatty."

She laughed and rested her head against his shoulder. When her laughter subsided, she said without lifting her head, "Are you doing well? Do you feel well?"

He rested his chin on her head, and she closed her eyes. As long as he was healthy both in body and mind, she could face anything. If he wasn't, then she would make it her mission to heal him. He took a deep breath and said, "I'm getting better. I find it difficult, though . . ."

She tried not to press him as he trailed off, but could only hope if she were patient enough, he'd finish his thought. She'd found it didn't do to dig for information. He would only share what he was willing to share, and that was that.

"I still think of that place," he said. "I still see the faces of the dead and the walking dead. I think of the battles too. Sometimes in my sleep I hear that bloody rebel shriek and I wake up, certain I'm there."

Anne's eyes, already closed, now squeezed hard. "I do too."

"I know you do. I've heard you cry out in your sleep."

She smiled and opened her eyes. "Well, we're quite a pair then, aren't we?" Raising her head to look at him, she said, "Will it ever go away, do you suppose?"

"I don't know. But I love you."

* * *

News at the breakfast table the next morning centered on Admiral David Farragut and his capture of Mobile, Alabama. It was the last port through which Confederate blockaders were still escaping, and it was considered a major Union victory.

Besides James and Elizabeth, Jimmy, now nearly thirteen, was the only other person at the table. "Maybe the war will go on long enough for me to enlist," he said, and Elizabeth looked at him as though trying to ascertain whether or not he was serious.

"I don't think so," Elizabeth said.

"About the war or my enlistment?"

"Both." She speared a strawberry with her fork and bit into it. "Allow a poor mother at least one untouched child."

"What else will I do? Luke enlisted, Robert enlisted, and even *Anne* enlisted. The only one who hasn't seen battle is Camille."

"Camille creates her own battles," James said, still looking at the paper.

"Jimmy, you're going to give me a headache," Elizabeth said. "No more talk about you going off to war."

The boy cleared his throat a bit and said, "Do you suppose we might address something else then?"

James put his paper down and looked at his son. "Absolutely. What is it?"

"I'd like to be called Jim from now on, not Jimmy. I can't go by my given name, which is the same as yours, because people will become confused."

James glanced at his wife, who was looking at her son, strawberry still poised at the end of her fork. "Well," he said, "I don't see why we shouldn't call you Jim. It suits you rather well. Doesn't it, Liz?"

"Yes, yes it does. Jim it is, then. Jim."

"You don't need to say it a dozen times each meal, really, I just wanted to . . ." The boy rose from the table. "I believe I'm finished eating. May I please be excused?"

"You may." James nodded at him and watched as he left the room.

"Oh," Elizabeth said, placing her fork down. "My baby is going to leave too."

"Not yet, he isn't. Not for a few years."

"The years will fly by. It was only yesterday that Luke was thirteen. Already active in the Society by then, he was." She shook her head. "I miss that boy."

* * *

12 August 1864
Outskirts of Cleveland, Ohio

"I think I'm going to be ill," Anne whispered to Ivar as they approached the front porch of his parents' home. "Do they know we're coming?"

"Yes, they know we're coming." Ivar stopped walking and turned to his wife. "You're not going to be ill. Anne, you have been engaged in battle and faced the devil himself to save my life." He paused. "They are two elderly people and one five-year-old girl."

"I know," she all but wailed, and Ivar was amazed. He'd never seen her so nervous. "But if they don't approve of me, if they don't like me, your relationship with them will be affected, and they won't want to spend time with us, and if Inger doesn't like me, she'll cry to her grandmother that you've brought home someone awful."

"Anne." He set his suitcase down and grasped her by the shoulders. "Stop."

"I will."

"You're composed?"

"Yes."

"Good. Now then, how do I look? Am I too thin?"

She winced a bit.

"Tell me the truth."

"Yes, you're thin, but you look nearly like you did when we first met."

He sighed. "I'll be content with that, I suppose. I don't want to worry my mother."

"Sweetheart," she said, laying a hand to the side of his face, "she'll be happy just to have you home."

With that, he turned and picked up his case and grasped Anne's hand. They made their way to the front door, each looking at it as though it might suddenly bite. Shaking himself a bit, he reached forward and knocked on the door firmly.

When it opened, the woman on the other side gasped and rushed forward into his arms, beginning to tremble. "My Ivar," she said, and pulled back, touching his face.

"My sweet boy, you're alive and home." She had reverted to her native tongue, and Ivar swallowed at the familiarity of the Norwegian lilt. It had been a long time since he'd heard it.

"Mama," he murmured. "Are you well?"

"Yes, yes," she nodded. "And your father is still surviving, he just moves slowly." She laughed then through her tears. "But you mustn't tell him I told you so."

Ivar embraced his mother again and then reached toward Anne, who was standing to the side, chewing on her lip. "Mama, this is my wife, the woman I wrote to you about. This is Anne."

"My, but you look Norsk," Amanda Gundersen said to Anne in English, and she wiped at her tears, extending a hand toward her daughter-in-law. "Welcome, welcome."

"Thank you," Anne said with a tentative smile, grasping the woman's hand. "I . . . I'm so sorry we didn't wait to be married—we wanted to be with both families, but Ivar was . . . was . . ."

Amanda shook her head. "I understand, Anne," she said, and Ivar smiled at the Norwegian pronunciation Amanda gave his wife's name. It came out sounding like *Ah-neh.* "I'm glad my son has found someone who will love him. His last wife was a shrew of a woman."

Anne blinked, and Ivar placed a hand on her back. "Mama, shall we go inside?"

"Oh, yes! Yes, yes, come inside. Someone is very anxious to see you."

Ivar followed his mother and Anne into the house, and as the two women stepped aside, he spied a young girl with enormous blue eyes and short, curly blonde hair standing in the hallway, one hand behind her back and one foot placed atop the other. With her free hand she scratched at the door frame in tiny circles as she looked at him.

My child. His eyes burned with tears, and he dropped to his knees in front of her. "Inger? Do you remember your papa at all? I haven't seen you for so very long . . . I understand if you don't know who I am."

She pulled her hand from her nervous exploration of the door frame and reached up to touch his spectacles, just as she had when she was an infant. He laughed softly through his tears. "You remember the glasses?"

She nodded and drew her lower lip into her mouth, chewing on it much as Anne had been doing outside. "I see myself," she whispered, touching the lens lightly with her finger.

"Do you think I might have a hug?" he asked her.

She nodded again and put her arms tentatively around his neck. He squeezed her gently, marveling at the difference three years had made. She was no longer a baby, but a child. When Inger pulled back, she looked up uncertainly at her grandmother, who sniffled next to Anne.

Amanda reached for Inger's hand, pulled her to her side, and pointed to Anne. "This is your papa's new wife," she said. "Anne, this is Inger."

Anne squatted down so that she was level with the little girl's eyes. "Inger," she said, extending her hand, "it's a pleasure to meet you."

Inger hesitated, then placed her hand in Anne's, and Anne gently moved her hand up and down. "Your papa loves you very much, and he's told me lots of things about you. Good things. But it's been such a long time since he's seen you, and I've only just met you, so we're going to have to get to know you all over again. Do you think that will be fine with you?"

"Yes," Inger said softly. She cleared her throat and said again, "Yes."

"I have a bit of a problem," Anne said to the child in a conspiratorial whisper. "You see, I don't like to stay indoors very much—I would much rather be outside. And your papa tells me you have many animals here, is that so?"

Inger nodded, rocking slightly on one foot.

"Well, perhaps sometime you might show me around outside so that I don't grow too restless indoors? And we can look at the animals? I'm from the city, and we didn't have anything other than horses."

Inger nodded, her eyes taking on an interested spark. Ivar looked down at his wife and wondered what she'd been so nervous about. She knew the path straight into a child's heart. He leaned in closer to hear Inger's response. "My bestemor made me special bloomers to play outside." Inger further lowered her voice and spoke from behind her hand. "They're like breeches! She says I can wear them only when the other neighbors aren't close by."

"Oh, dear girl," Anne said, a wistful expression on her face, "I do believe we're going to get along just fine."

* * *

Ivar slowly entered his father's study and allowed his eyes to adjust. There was one lamp burning, and a small one at that. Combined with the fact that the drapes were drawn, the little light didn't do much to dispel the darkness in the room. "Papa?"

Per Gundersen sat in his favorite chair near the lamp, his head bent over a book. He looked up at Ivar's voice, his face registering his surprise. "Ivar! Your mother didn't tell me you had arrived."

"Only just," Ivar said, and moved to his father's side. Per was attempting to rise and having a difficult time of it. "We only just arrived," he said, and urged Per to take his seat. He reached his arms around the older man and held him quietly for a moment, forgetting how much his father's spirit was like a calm in the storm. Just being in his presence was soothing.

"I am so glad to have you home safely," Per said, his voice gruff. He clasped Ivar's shoulders as Ivar kneeled to the side of the chair. "We were concerned when we didn't hear from you for so long, and then your letter explaining where you'd been had your mother in fits."

Ivar smiled. Per always blamed excessive emotion on Amanda. Chances were, Per had been in fits too. Per ran his hands down Ivar's arms as though checking for a broken bone or another obvious sign of distress. "Are you well, then? You're too thin."

Ivar nodded. "I did lose some of my weight. It's returning slowly."

"And did you catch an illness? We read in the papers about so many soldiers spreading diseases . . ."

Ivar mentally despaired a bit at Per's worried tone. He wanted desperately to be able to put his father at ease. "I'm well enough, Papa. Nothing that time won't heal."

"I'm glad for that, then." Per sat back a bit in his chair. "It is a good, good thing to have you home."

"I'm very glad to be here. And how are you? How is your leg?"

Per shrugged slightly, and Ivar knew from asking Amanda before he'd approached his father that the leg pained him worse every day. "It's still a leg."

"And your eyes?"

Per grunted. "Your mother has been telling you stories."

"Ah. That's why you're sitting in here with the drapes drawn. She said too much bright light hurts your eyes." She'd also told him that Per's eyesight was failing and that it frightened his father more than he would admit.

"She worries." He waved a hand in dismissal. "Where is this bride of yours? She isn't with you?"

"She's here. She's in the parlor with Inger. I'll bring her in to meet you in a moment."

"I'm glad you've found someone special."

"I am also, Papa. Very much."

CHAPTER 27

Now that war comes home to you . . . you deprecate its horrors, but did not feel them when you sent car-loads of soldiers and ammunition, and moulded shells and shot, to carry war into Kentucky and Tennessee, to desolate the homes of hundreds and thousands of good people who only asked to live in peace . . . under the Government of their inheritance.

—General Sherman in a message to the Atlanta City Council

* * *

7 September 1864
Petersburg, Virginia

"I do believe I beat you to the news," Ben called to Robert as he walked across the encampment, dodging shells. He jumped down into a secured trench and grinned at his cousin. "I finally have something to share with you."

"We'll see about that. What do you have?" Robert asked as he cleaned his gun.

"Sherman ordered the evacuation of all civilians from Atlanta today. He's going to go through the city and destroy every piece of military support he can find."

Robert snorted. “I’ll bet there were hardly any civilians left to evacuate. I heard most of them fled before he even took the city.”

“That is entirely beside the point. The point is I heard the news before you did.”

Robert grinned at Ben. “Congratulations.”

“I wonder how long it’ll be before Sherman burns the place to the ground.”

Robert shrugged. “Probably wants to give his men a chance to rest first. They’ve been going full steam ahead for months.”

“Fine, then, Great Predictor, where will he go next?”

Robert looked up from his weapon. “Well,” he said, “I heard he plans to march to Savannah, and from there upward through the Carolinas to join us here. Grant initially wanted him to come by sea from Savannah, but Sherman told him the men would rather go by foot.”

“I can just imagine why,” Ben said, settling his back against the earthen wall of the trench. “They probably want to plunder the whole of it.”

“I think they’re saving the bulk of their vengeance for South Carolina.” Robert turned his attention back to his gun. “It’s a good thing indeed that your father packed up the family and left.”

Ben nodded. “He sent a letter from Nebraska when they joined the wagon train. I think he hopes things will be better away from Bentley.” He tossed a rock across the trench. “Too many ghosts in that place.”

“It’ll most likely be burned to the ground. Don’t you regret that even a bit?”

“I really don’t care. I could never live in it myself, and to go back and visit would only bring to mind ugly memories.” He tossed another rock. “That whole system was built on the backs of slaves. I can't forget it. I'd rather just rebuild somewhere else."

The pop of continual shells and gunshot had been firing so consistently for so many days and weeks on end that the soldiers didn't even notice it anymore. They walked calmly across the encampment as Ben had done, acting as if nothing out of the ordinary were happening. "I think this siege is going to last forever," Ben said to Robert, and retrieved his own weapon to clean. "You and I are going to grow old sitting in this trench."

"You're probably right. We could do like Sam down there and carve our headboards."

"That's rather morbid. When did he do that?"

"This morning." Robert scratched his nose as a shell exploded behind them. "Carved in his name and birth date. Left the death date blank."

"Does he think he'll need it?"

"Nah. He just said he wanted something to fill the time."

"You know, they said that when the men were ordered in at Cold Harbor after the original assault, they wrote their names, addresses, and next of kin on pieces of paper and pinned them to their backs so that their families could be notified upon their deaths."

Robert blew powder residue from his fingers. "I'm not surprised. Sometimes you just know going into it that it's not going to be good."

"Did you feel that way when we went in?"

"At Cold Harbor?" At Ben's nod, Robert also nodded slightly. "I had a bad feeling about it."

"It was a well-placed bad feeling, for certain." Ben leaned back again on the bank.

"And yet . . ."

Ben turned his head toward his cousin, his brow raised in question.

"We lived. Two out of thousands."

Ben regarded him thoughtfully for a moment before turning his attention back to the opposite bank of the trench. Sometimes Robert shamed him with his insight. Ben was supposedly the religious member of the family, and somehow Robert always managed to grasp a higher meaning, highlight a deeper sense of gratitude. He was missing part of his arm, for heaven's sake, and just the other day he'd joked about the ease of washing his hands now that he had only one to worry about.

"Robert, I'm mighty glad you're here," Ben said, not wanting to look at his cousin and risk becoming emotional, embarrassing the both of them. "You help me remember what's important."

Robert glanced up and smiled, opening his mouth to reply. His comment was cut off, however, by a shout from down the trench. He leaned forward and looked to see several men pulling a fellow soldier down into the safety of the trench, but from the appearance of his limp body, it was too late.

Ben leaned forward also, and crawled down a bit to see who had been hit. When he returned to Robert, his face was grim.

"Who was it?" Robert asked him, frowning.

"Sam."

* * *

Washington, D.C.

The most unbelievable things are occurring, I can scarcely believe it myself, Isabelle wrote in her diary in her solitary hotel room. *Sherman has taken Atlanta. What an amazing feat! Atlanta is the Confederacy's last true stronghold—it is a hub for travel by rail and extremely vital to the rebels' continued survival, and now it falls to Union hands. Lincoln is happy, as one would expect he would be. He has compared Grant to a man who holds a bear by the hind legs, and says Sherman is the man who skins it. While I know him to be a man of certain compassion, I do not think Grant relishes in the suffering of the souls in Atlanta. I believe he sees Sherman's continual advance as a spot of light on what has been a very dark horizon.*

As for myself, I have great hopes that the fall of this great city will spark the end of this war. I grow weary of it, and as callous as I found myself at its onset, I worry over the condition of the women and children who are struggling in the South, with no men to help them till the land, and with Union troops consuming what they do manage to produce.

Throw down your arms, you rebels! Go home! Let our boys come home and cease this insanity! For over three years now this conflict has raged, and there isn't a soul living in this country who isn't impatient if not desperate to see it come to an end.

I've seen the battlefields myself; I've lived with the citizens under siege. Where I once thought myself strong, happy, and immune to the suffering, I now find it haunts my thoughts day and night.

I want to go home—I tire of the endless round of social events that are given all too much importance in this capital city. Women wear their furs and jewels and behave as though naught else matters but their belongings and who will be attending their teas and soirees.

I have come to the conclusion that too much money is a curse. Too little money is also a curse. How fortunate for me, then, that I find myself somewhere in the middle. Oh! Some of my humor and arrogance returns! Perhaps there is something good in the air after all—perhaps the fact that Sherman has invaded Atlanta and virtually destroyed all roads leading to it and coming from it is a sign that this madness of war will soon be at an end and we can all return to the quarters from whence we came. We'll sleep in our own beds and eat food kept in our own pantries.

No more hotels, no more sights of gore and horror on the fields of battle. No more starving people. No more enslavement. No more fear . . .

* * *

15 September 1864
Jacksonville, Florida

Joshua Birmingham leaned against a tree, his eyes closed, enjoying the shade and a few moments of peace. He breathed deeply, as Ruth had taught him years ago, and concentrated on nothing save the rise and fall of his chest. It wasn't long before his heart slowed, his thoughts cleared, and even the tremor in his left arm ceased.

He was exhausted in body and mind. They had fought a few battles, certainly not as many as some of the other colored regiments, but following each encounter he lived with a sense of unease, as though he needed to continually look over his shoulder for the enemy. He found it impossible to relax, even during the long stretches of time when all they did was fortify their positions, drill, and sleep.

As thoughts of battle sounds crept uninvited back into his head, his heart thumped and sped up, and his arm trembled. He imagined Ruth's voice. *Breathe in, breathe out. In, out.* Ruth—he wondered how she was doing. He had only ever known her at Bentley, and he found it difficult imagining her in any other setting. She would flourish, though, in the West. She always flourished, regardless of circumstance.

It was ironic that his enlistment had returned him to South Carolina's shores. The buzzing talk among the men was that when Sherman finished with Georgia, he'd surely march north into the hotbed that had started the whole infernal war. When that happened, Joshua knew his regiment would be called in as reinforcements.

God forgive me, he often prayed, *but I look forward to watching Charleston burn.* He wondered if his soul would burn as well for wanting to see such a grisly demise to the region. His anger often flared when he thought of it—three and one-half long years of fighting that had begun at that very place, out in Charleston Harbor.

How smug the people had been, how certain that they were only going to have to produce a small show of force to drive the Union out. How eager they had been to form their own government that, according to the administration, was founded on the principle that the Negro was inferior to the white man.

These thoughts now attempted to creep into his mind, but he shoved them aside, still clinging to the memory of Ruth's voice. *In, out. Breathe in and out.* She was the only mother he had ever known, and he missed her desperately. Just for one moment he wanted to be young again, to look up into her wise face and know that she would somehow take care of everything that was amiss.

Please, God, please bless her. Bless her and keep her.

* * *

20 September 1864
Utah Territory

Ruth gratefully took advantage of the clean water Ellen Dobranski supplied her and bathed away the dirt of the long, hard trail. She was tired to her bones and imagined that, if left alone, she could probably sleep for a week. They had arrived in the Salt Lake Valley late in the afternoon, and Earl had taken them promptly to his family home, where they were welcomed with generously open arms.

Ruth had helped Sarah clean up, taking satisfaction in her former mistress's insistence that she could care for herself. Perhaps there was hope for a substantial recovery yet. She had then helped the smaller children, washing Elijah while Charlotte washed Will. It was finally her turn to take a few moments of her own to relish the peace and quiet and *clean.*

Ruth was nothing if not an honest woman, and she made it a rule to never lie to herself. She was nervous, she admitted now. She had focused on the rigors of the wagon train, throwing herself tirelessly into the work of simply arriving at their destination with her whole heart and soul so that she wouldn't have to think overlong on what she would do with her life once she arrived.

Time enough for that later, she admonished her worried mind, and tried to relax and simply enjoy the moment. She was a free woman in free territory. Jeffrey had given her papers stating that she was no longer a slave, and he had pulled her aside on their arrival and paid her a staggering amount of money. "Wages for a lifetime of service," he had told her, and when she had but stared at the large bag of gold coins she held in her hand, he had closed her hands firmly around it. "It's yours. You deserve it and you know it."

So why was she not more at peace? More likely than not it was fatigue that clouded her thoughts. She was tired and in a new land where people professed to be kind, but how would she know for certain? She was a black woman, and there were very few other black folk in this particular region. How would she be received? Would she be hated? Resented? Ignored?

Ruth finished scrubbing her skin and toweled herself dry. Dressing in fresh clothing graciously supplied by a woman from a local church, she returned to the rest of the family who were gathered in the backyard of the Dobranski home. The air was pleasant, with just the beginnings of a nip to it, signaling fall was imminent. She'd never experienced a drastic change of season. In so many ways she was as innocent as Clara and Rose.

She smiled as she looked them over, satisfied to see them cleaned up and also dressed in fresh clothing. My, but they would all sleep well that night! Where they would go after the next few days when their stay with the Dobranskis was at an end was still an unresolved issue. She would discuss Jeffrey's plans with him in the morning, she supposed. For now, she would be a fool if she didn't just sit down and relax.

Taking her great-grandson by the hand, she found an empty seat and pulled him into her lap. He leaned his weary head against her chest and yawned. It wasn't long before his eyelids fluttered closed. Seeing him so still was an odd thing indeed. If the boy wasn't sleeping, he was up and running.

She ran a hand over his curls and leaned down to kiss his forehead. Looking around herself, at the kindness of Earl's family and the tired but happy faces of her loved ones, she felt a sense of peace. *Certainly I will be with thee . . .* The scripture from Exodus came to her thoughts and provided comfort against her churning emotions. She answered the gentle reminder with a renewed sense of hope.

Then I suppose I can get through just about anything . . .

* * *

Charlotte walked around to the side of the Dobranski house, bouncing little William in her arms and wishing he would stop crying. He was irritable and exhausted, and she was tempted to go to Mrs. Dobranski and ask her where she would be bedding down for the night with her son. It was early evening yet, however, and the others seemed to be enjoying the night air and company so much that she didn't feel comfortable interrupting just yet.

"Will, please, just for a moment stop fussing," she moaned. "Are you hungry? Do you want some more to eat?"

The child threw his head back and screamed his refusal of more food. Just when she had determined the only thing to do was to put him on the ground and let him properly throw his tantrum, Earl appeared at her side and wordlessly took the child from her aching arms.

"Will," he said in his deep voice, "you're going to make your mama very sad if you don't stop that." He held the boy close, and William, still recovering from the surprise of having been taken into someone else's arms, quieted his crying.

"Come with me," Earl said to Charlotte when he took a good look at her face. She was awfully near tears herself.

He led her into the house and to a room on the second floor at the end of a hallway. There were three twin beds in the room, and next to the one nearest the door was a small, toddler-sized bed.

"I brought that down from the attic while you were having your bath," Earl said to Will, pointing at the small bed. "I slept in that when I was just your size. Of course, I was half your age, but I suppose that doesn't matter."

Charlotte looked up at him and managed a smile for his attempt at humor. Earl carried the child to the bed and sat down on the floor next to it, holding Will in his lap and not attempting to place him in the bed yet. "I'll just tell you a bit of a story before you lie down, does that sound nice? Which story would you like?"

"Bears."

"Ah, yes. The one about my pet bear."

Charlotte sat on the nearest twin bed and watched as Earl told her son a bedtime story that he'd related many times on the trail. She marveled at his gentleness, seemingly at such odds with his size. She yawned, leaning back a bit on the bed. Perhaps if she just were to lie down for only a moment, she could rest and then have energy enough to handle Will should he decide he didn't want to go to sleep after all.

She lay atop the quilt fully clothed and rested her head against the soft pillow. A groan of delight escaped her lips. How long had it been since she'd slept in an actual bed? Nearly three months! Three months sleeping in a hard, wooden wagon.

A breeze blew into the room from an open window, and it wafted upon her dry, sunburned skin. As she watched her son's eyelids begin to drift closed, she allowed herself to be lulled by the gentle rhythm of Earl's voice and thought that maybe, perhaps it would be all right if she closed her own eyes for a moment. Just a moment, and then she would get up from the bed and take William.

She vaguely noticed someone covering her with a blanket and tucking it under her chin later—it might have been minutes or hours—and she sighed deeply.

* * *

Ellen Dobranski awoke early the next morning and began the task of preparing food for her visitors. The house was quiet still, an amazing feat with eight sons and eight temporary boarders. She hummed quietly, enjoying the light glow from her kitchen window that soon enveloped the whole room. When she and Eli had built the home, she had insisted the kitchen face east, claiming that as she arose in the morning, she wanted to feel the sun on her face.

There was a buzz in the air, and had been since the night before. Ellen had always been sensitive to things, things of which others were often not aware. Something special was occurring in the life of the family she currently sheltered under her roof. Great strain had been evident on their faces upon their arrival, and it was simple enough to see that the stress was not due to the wagon trek alone. The Birmingham family harbored many hurts, many that were evident to Ellen, and she wondered at it as she prepared breakfast.

For some reason she was unable to fathom, Ellen's gaze had continually been drawn to Mrs. Birmingham. She said nothing the entire evening, merely sat by her husband's side and looked about with a blank expression. There was more to the woman beneath the surface, however, and

Ellen frowned a bit in concentration, wondering what it might be.

"Father," she murmured as she often did when she was alone in the mornings, "What wouldst Thou have me do for this family? They are hurting. The woman, she is hurting . . ." She fell silent for a moment, continuing her work and humming, waiting for the answer that she knew would eventually come.

Love her, came the impression. *Welcome her to the fold. She has wandered from the ninety and nine . . .*

Ellen nodded once to herself and patted the bread dough she'd been kneading for baking later in the day. It came as no surprise when Mrs. Birmingham wandered down to the kitchen, dressed for the day with her hair neatly in place. "Hello, Sarah," Ellen said, taking liberties by using her given name. "I was just wishing I had some help in here."

She moved forward and grasped Sarah's small hands, drawing her gently into the kitchen. "I can always use an extra pair of hands, and yours are perfect for this dough."

Sarah looked at her for a moment, and Ellen saw something in the woman's eyes flicker. She nodded again, more to herself than to Sarah, and said, "You're going to be fine, you are. You just needed to back up a few steps, that's all."

CHAPTER 28

Clover . . . would have been entitled to discharge in a few days. . . . [He]went out gaily [to bring in the wounded] and was shot in the knee by a rebel sharpshooter; consequence, amputation and death. . . . He kept a little diary, like so many of the soldiers. On the day of his death, he wrote the following in it, "Today the doctor says I must die—all is over with me—ah, so young to die." On another blank leaf he penciled to his brother, "Dear brother Thomas, I have been brave but wicked—pray for me."

—Walt Whitman, who served as an unofficial volunteer nurse during the war—in a selection from his memoirs, Specimen Days

* * *

25 October 1864
Petersburg, Virginia

Ben and Robert shook hands with fellow soldiers and officers as they were officially discharged from the Union army. Ben exchanged smiles and comments of goodwill, appreciating the friendliness and sense of cautious optimism, but concerned only that he and his cousin be on their way. Before Luke died, Ben had been relatively active in his efforts to communicate with the other men and build friendships. Since Robert's arrival, however, he had kept mostly to himself, socializing only with his cousin. He had watched too many men die, and the less he knew of their personal lives, the less it hurt when they fell.

"What are you most looking forward to when we get home?" Robert asked him as they packed their belongings on their horses and headed north.

"Palatable food. I've had enough lobcourse to last me a lifetime." Ben thought of the soup made from hardtack, salt pork, and anything else the soldiers could manage, and shuddered.

"I particularly like the baled hay," Robert said.

Ben groaned his dislike of the stuff. The army, in an attempt to ward off scurvy that affected so many of the men because of the lack of fresh vegetables in their diets, created dehydrated cakes of carrots, beans, onions, and other vegetables. "It's worse for the rebs, I hear," Ben said. "They don't have teeth dullers, but they make cornmeal cakes that are even worse for attracting weevils than the hardtack."

Robert grimaced. "It's good to be going home."

Ben glanced at his cousin. "What will you do?"

"I don't know. I've thought of various things, but . . . I don't know." He showed the first signs of unease over his injury since it happened. "I'm not sure exactly what I'm suited for anymore."

"Robert, your strength has been and always will be your mind. It's as clear as ever, and you've learned things in the last year that will help you."

Robert shrugged and kept his gaze trained on the road ahead. "We'll be fortunate if we're not shot for deserters."

Ben thought of the times he and Robert had taken their turns patrolling for stragglers and deserters. "We never shot anybody."

"We were nice. Are you leaving for Utah right away, then?"

"As soon as Mary feels she's ready."

"Has she accepted your proposal?"

Ben nodded, a genuine smile for the first time in a long while crossing his face. "She's worried about what others will think, how they'll react, but she did say yes."

"Congratulations. How is the climate in Utah for . . . acceptance?"

Ben sighed a bit. "Tolerable, I suppose. There are many whose roots in slavery ran deep, and there have been some who moved to the territory still as slaveholders. There are a handful of black people living there now in freedom—I have hope that people will be supportive of us. They knew me and cared for me before."

"People can be fickle."

"I know. But I don't dare think on that too much right now."

"Well," Robert said, "Mary's a beautiful woman, inside and out. And although it shouldn't matter, perhaps the fact that she also has white blood and lighter skin will be to her advantage."

Ben nodded, hating to admit that he was right.

"Have you considered staying with her in Boston? At least there you would find many who would be supportive and accepting."

Ben wrinkled his brow in thought. "I did consider it, but Ruth and the rest of our families are there. Mary said she wants very much to be with them. We must at least try to live there. If it becomes obvious that it won't work, perhaps we'll come back this way."

"And you'll keep your temper in check?"

Ben glanced at his cousin to see Robert smiling slightly at him. "I see my reputation precedes me," Ben muttered. "I have been calm and collected during this time with you, even in battle. What would give you the idea I have a temper?"

"Your temper is legendary in this family, my friend. Luke regaled us with stories of your hasty departure from Bentley and then shared some of your letters from Utah."

"Well, I've much improved since then."

"Yes, you have. I can only imagine, though, how difficult it might be to hear others malign your wife. My advice to you would be to think of her welfare first and foremost. Watch that, as you seek to protect her, you don't make the situation worse for her."

Ben shook his head. Robert sounded much like Luke. "And how is it that you're so wise at such a young age?" Ben said it lightly, but in truth he hoped Robert had an answer for his question. The boy was only now nineteen years old.

"I watched my father . . ." Robert mumbled. "My mother told us from when we were young to watch him, that if we followed his example we would have peace in our marriages."

"Mmm. Your example of a marriage was slightly different than mine. Amazing in some ways that they're brothers."

"I'd say your father has made some changes of late."

Ben nodded, reluctantly. "He has. He's making things right. Now then, tell me what news you uncovered this morning. I haven't had my daily dosage."

"Very well, let me think for a moment. Well, you knew that Fremont withdrew from the presidential race? That was several weeks ago. He worried about splitting the vote among Republicans and allowing McClellan the win."

"Yes, I'd heard. Sounds like the first unselfish thing he's ever done in his life. Go on."

"Oh! Sheridan finally defeated Jubal Early in the Shenandoah Valley. They've been going at each other for a month now—just a few days ago Sheridan drove him out. Sustained awfully heavy losses, though."

"That's unfortunate. It's a good maneuver, however. That valley was one of the last remaining supply sources for the rebels, was it not?"

Robert nodded. "May take a few more months yet, but I believe that dreaded siege we just left behind may actually serve its purpose. With Shenandoah cut off and Petersburg as well, Richmond will be starving before long."

"I'm amazed it's taken this long as it is. They've been starving in Richmond for quite some time."

"Now then," Robert said, taking a breath, thinking. "More news." He looked over the countryside they traveled, but Ben knew he wasn't seeing anything but the inner workings of his own mind. "Roger B. Taney, Supreme Court justice, is finally dead. Eighty-nine long years he walked the earth."

"Good riddance. Next?"

Robert cast him a quick grin. Ben had never forgiven the chief justice for his notorious Dred Scott decision many years back that had initiated a precedent for slavery that was just one more stumbling block in the way for emancipation. "This will raise your spirits—Maryland has just adopted a new state constitution that abolishes slavery."

"That is good news. How wide a margin of victory?"

"Slim."

"Not surprising. Anything else?"

"The Nevada Territory is about to become a state. They're calling it the Battle State because it's joining during the war." Robert lifted his shoulders. "That's all I have."

"Very good. Thank you, once again. You're better than a newspaper. What will I ever do without you?"

"Stay in Boston." Robert looked at him without humor. "I'll miss you dreadfully."

"Chances are I may return, Rob. Time will tell."

* * *

Robert lay in the bed of the small hotel room in Washington that he and Ben shared for the night. It wasn't comfortable as far as beds went, but it was better than the dirty trench. The men had both taken advantage of the hotel's bathing facilities, and Robert felt cleaner than he had in a year.

He had been amazed when they rode into the capital city at the sense of *normalcy* that seemed to prevail. He had been living on nasty rations and in filthy, dangerous conditions for so long that he found it incredible that outside all of that, the world still continued and people's lives still went forward. The contrast between Washington and the cities he'd lived near during his time in the army was astounding. Richmond and Petersburg were scraping by at extreme poverty. Washington and, he suspected, the big cities in the North, were living at a level he hadn't imagined. The strain of war still showed, but it was nowhere near that of the Confederacy.

His enlistment had passed quickly, and Robert didn't feel like the same person who had left Boston determined to fill his dead brother's shoes. Although he was relieved to be alive at the end of it and grateful to be sleeping in a building with a bed, a small corner of his mind wished he were back in the trench.

As a soldier, he didn't have to explain to anyone why his stomach constantly clenched in pain, why he coughed sometimes as though his lungs would come up, and why he had only one arm. He unconsciously felt with his hand the portion below his elbow where his left arm ended. It was healing, although he still kept it bandaged, and he supposed he should be grateful it hadn't turned gangrenous and required even further amputation. He was lucky to be alive; he had cheated death on more than one occasion, and he knew it.

Perhaps he should have extended his enlistment. Maybe, after all this time, his childhood spent in fascinated study of the military, it was his destiny to be a soldier for life. Men made careers out of the army—it certainly wasn't unheard of. As he considered the possibility, though, it didn't make him happy.

The trouble was that he couldn't think of *anything* that would make him happy. He had absolutely no idea what he was going to do once he returned home. Nothing appealed to him, nothing stood out as a viable option. He tightened his grip on the end of his wounded arm, his stomach churning uncomfortably as he thought of the looks he would certainly receive; the pitying glances, the shock, the inability to meet his gaze. The men in his regiment—those who had survived—had been ecstatic to see him still alive. That he was missing an arm was of no consequence whatsoever. Many of them were missing various limbs as well.

He sighed and tried to sleep. He supposed life would take care of itself as it happened—it always had before.

Releasing his arm, he let it fall to his side and rest against the bed, his hand coming instead to lie on his shirt pocket. The crinkling sound of paper at his touch brought a small smile to his lips. Camille had finally written to him. She would look at his arm, and after initial exclamations of horror, or at least intense concern, her practicality would prevail and she would tell him it was barely noticeable.

It would be good to see his family, he decided as his mind began to drift. They would help him sort through his confusion.

* * *

The travel back to Boston from Washington was swift, and a few days later Ben found himself in the Birmingham parlor. He and Robert had been given a hero's welcome each, with endless hugs and tears, and yet he sensed that behind the cries of delight, there remained a lingering thought or two about the one who hadn't come home. And now the family had cleared out of the room to leave him a moment with Mary.

"I'll tell her you're here," his Aunt Elizabeth had said, and he noted the sweet poignancy of it. His relatives were exceptional. Not only were they going to allow a servant to socially see someone in their parlor—and he a relative, at that—but that servant had also been a slave. Liz hadn't told him to go to the kitchen to visit Mary, hadn't been scandalized at their growing affection for each other, but had told him to wait, that Mary would soon see him.

It was with these thoughts swirling in his head that he spied her coming around the corner. His breath caught in his throat. Mary wore a simply cut but beautifully soft dress of baby blue trimmed with white lace. Her hair was pulled up in a charmingly braided bun at the crown of her head, and her face was radiant, her expression clear and her eyes in sparkles.

She ran to him, her eyes brimming with tears of joy. He caught her up into his arms and held tight, never wanting to let go. She laughed finally and pulled back. "There were times I wondered if you'd live," she admitted. "Especially once we heard of Luke." Her smile dimmed a bit, and she sobered. "Ben, I'm so sorry. I know how much you loved him. We all did."

"I know." Ben caught one of her tears with his thumb. "And thank you." He took her hands in his and guided her to a sofa, dropping to one knee as she sat. "But before we discuss anything else, I must ask you in person . . . will you marry me?"

Rather than laugh her delight as he expected, indeed *hoped* she might, she winced.

"Ben, there's something we must talk about first."

His heart began to pound in his chest, and he felt a fear he hadn't experienced since the battlefield. His throat was hoarse, and he wondered if he were about to fall over. "Is there someone else?"

"No, no. But I have something to tell you, and then you may decide you'd rather not marry me, and I do understand. I willingly release you from your commitment to me."

"Mary, nothing will change my mind."

"Not even the news that I have a son?"

His pounding heart nearly stopped. "So there is someone else," he murmured. "Or was."

"No, Ben. There was never anyone else."

"But then, how . . ."

"I didn't bear the child by choice. I didn't conceive the child by choice." Mary pulled her hands from his and rose, walking slowly to the window. As he watched her, the meaning of her words sinking in, he heard a roaring in his ears that threatened to deafen him. It was only as he viewed her pain, obvious in the clenching fists she shoved into the fabric of her skirts, that he managed to calm himself.

"Who is the man that did such a thing to you?" he asked, his voice low. "I will call him out and I will kill him."

"You can't. He's already dead."

"When did this happen, Mary?"

"At Bentley. Over three years ago."

Someone at Bentley had forced himself on this sweet woman? "Who? Who did it?"

"Is it so important?"

"I want to know all of it. I do not want any secrets between us."

Mary took a deep breath and released it on a shuddering sigh. "It was Richard."

"Richard?" *My own brother?* His voice rang with the disbelief he felt. He slipped from his knee and sat flat on the floor. He thought he would choke on the pain and the fury. Emily had hinted at some things through the years after he left Bentley—things about Richard, but she had never told him this.

"Why didn't you tell me?" he whispered. "Why didn't Emily tell me?"

Mary stared out the window, still as a statue. "I begged her not to. I didn't want you to know."

"But *why?*"

"I loved you. I thought you would hate me. I understand if you do now. I would never hold you to something you felt under false pretenses."

Ben found his way to his feet and moved to Mary, wrapping his arms around her from the side. He dropped his head forward, resting his forehead on the top of her head, his tears falling into her hair. He soon shook with the force of his pain for her, and in the back of his mind he heard her murmuring as though to quiet a child. Had he not had her arms trapped in his embrace, he didn't doubt that she would smooth his hair and pat his cheek.

"How could you think I would hate you? Mary, it wasn't your fault! Oh, I could *kill* him! I want to kill him!"

"You're too late." He felt Mary smile, and she turned her head, looking at him. "And that is probably a good thing. I'm learning to release the anger, Ben, and so also must you. It will tear at you inside."

"You sound like Luke," Ben said, releasing her and wiping at his face, embarrassed at his display of raw emotion. "Mary, I'm so sorry, I'm so very sorry my brother did such a thing to you. If I had been there, if I had only stayed . . ."

"Ben, you couldn't. You would have been dead. Nobody is responsible except for Richard, and I expect he is getting his just reward."

"And your child? Where is he?"

"With your family. In Utah."

"Did you raise him then?"

"No." Mary's face remained emotionless. "He was sold to the Charlesworths not long after his birth."

Ben closed his eyes briefly and then pulled Mary back over to the sofa. When she sat, he pulled her close under his arm. Tucking her head gently under his chin, he said, "Please, please say you'll marry me. I can manage anything then."

"I will, Ben, if you're certain it's what you wish."

"I'm certain."

"Then yes, I would love to marry you." Her voice had grown extremely soft, and he felt warmth on his shirtfront. A few sniffles accompanied her tears. "It's a dream," she murmured. "A dream come true for me. I've loved you all my life."

* * *

Much later that evening, Ben left the Birmingham house by the front door, closing it quietly behind him. He began to walk but didn't know exactly where he wanted to go. His mind echoed with Mary's words from earlier in the day, her staggering news about her son. His mind continued to reel in shock, perhaps nearly worse than anything he'd experienced. To know that his brother had raped, *raped* Mary had induced a fury inside his head that had nearly made him physically ill. He had kept his temper for her sake, had managed to stay calm throughout the evening with the family, but now he felt an angry energy so restlessly building inside him that he began to run.

He ran until he was well outside the city proper, slightly limping because of his lingering wounds, trying to hold the anger inside. When he finally stopped running a good twenty minutes later and found himself standing alongside a vacant field, he finally gave in to the intense anguish and screamed his rage to the heavens. Tears coursed down his cheeks as he thought of Mary having borne his nephew, and entirely against her will.

He tried to slow his breathing and began moving again, this time at a slow walk, begging the Lord shamelessly to help him calm his heart for Mary's sake and find a more constructive way to consider the situation. He was of no use to Mary and certainly no use to little Elijah if he couldn't pull himself out of his rage-induced stupor. He was simply so angry at Richard, so hatefully angry that his own brother would do something so hurtful, and that the target of Richard's attack had been the woman Ben had come to love—*the woman who would be his wife!*—it made him all the angrier.

A restful spirit worked its way into his heart as he finished his mumbled, heartfelt prayer, and due partly to a raging headache and exhaustion, he somehow found a way to focus only on Mary and the child. Mary was in agony over the fact that she couldn't be with Elijah sooner. She didn't ever want him to look back on his life and think there had been a time when his mother had been able to be with him but had chosen not to.

"I wrote you a letter about Elijah not long ago, but I couldn't bring myself to send it," Mary had admitted quietly to him after dinner. "I wanted to tell you in person."

She still had the letter, she admitted to him, and had given it to him at his request. He now pulled the paper from his pocket and unfolded it, scanning its contents by the light of the moon through gritty, swollen eyes.

I don't mean to burden you with my problems at a time like this, she had written, *but I want you to know the truth about what happened while you were away, and I hope you will not judge me harshly for it. I did not choose to have a baby. I did not choose to* conceive *a baby. I also did not choose to give him away. Yet these are the circumstances, and now that life is changing, perhaps I have a say in what becomes of my future.*

You mentioned once that you plan to come to me in Boston when you are discharged; I hope this is still your intention. If not, however, I do understand your reticence. Should you decide to continue with your original plans, however, and find that you would like to eventually return to the Utah Territory, I would very much appreciate it if you would allow me to accompany you there so that I might meet my son.

His throat constricted in pain for her. It hurt him to think she would find him so shallow as to hold her responsible for the actions of someone bigger, stronger, and intent on doing no good. Taking a deep, shuddering breath, he slowly folded the letter and placed it back in his pocket. He turned around and, feeling spent and yet somehow purged, began walking back toward the city.

* * *

Utah Territory

Construction was well underway on Jeffrey Birmingham's new home. The legion of workers he'd employed at Earl's suggestion were making quick work of the design Jeffrey had laid out for them. They seemed to feel it would even be inhabitable before the snow fell.

The smaller town of Ogden appealed to Jeffrey when he had gone riding with Earl trying to find the perfect location to plant his new family. Salt Lake was big and bustling, and while he enjoyed the structure and friendly faces, he felt the need to take Sarah away from it. He looked down the street and smiled. Ruth's home was very near completion as well. After some careful consideration, she had decided to build near Jeffrey and Sarah, and, using some of the money he had paid her, funded a place of her own. Since their arrival in the territory, he had officially "hired" Ruth to help him care for Sarah. He paid her a salary regularly, taking satisfaction in the fact that Ruth's shoulders were even straighter in their customarily firm posture.

The family had settled into a comfortable if temporary rhythm. They all lived together in a rented home on the same street as the new homes. Clara and Rose attended school in the neighborhood, Rose acting as Clara's interpreter when necessary. They were adapting well, and to date the youth in the area accepted the girls, much to Jeffrey's relief. Charlotte and little William also lived with Jeffrey and Sarah. Charlotte complained little, but Jeffrey saw the effort it took for her to refrain. She was homesick for a routine with which she was familiar, and every now and again in the evening when she was in her room, door closed, he heard her crying.

Ruth was as solid as ever, but he sometimes wondered at the confusion he sensed in her. She seemed to be grappling about for her new role, and he hoped she would find it once her home was complete and she had settled in. Perhaps the brightest spot in all of their lives was Elijah; the child was a ray of delight, happy in nearly every situation.

As he strolled around the side of the new house, examining the progress, he felt someone behind him. He turned and, to his surprise, saw Sarah also looking up at the house. He approached her, glad to see her out and about of her own free will, but concerned. What would happen to her if she chose to leave in the middle of the night or wander off when nobody was with her or paying particular attention to her?

"It's coming along nicely," she said.

Jeffrey eyed her with some caution. It was the first time she'd given any indication she was aware of what was going on around her with respect to the future. "It is," he said. "Shouldn't be too much longer before we can move in."

She wandered slowly back to the front. "I see you've designed a nice, big front porch."

"Yes, yes I thought you might like that."

"Reminds me of home."

"That was my intention." He studied her face, looking for clues as to where she was in her mind. "What do you think of this new place?"

"It's . . . different. I feel as though we've come to the ends of the earth."

"Sarah, do you know where we are? This isn't Bentley."

She turned to look at him. "I know."

* * *

As Sarah looked up into her husband's face, the morning light glinting off his black hair that was now streaked with gray, she squinted a bit. Who was this man, her husband? She hardly knew him anymore. She looked back at the new home, still in its raw form, and the wide front porch. In her mind she saw Bentley as it had been in its glory days.

Bentley had been more important to her than anything else in her life, and it had crumbled. It was destructible, and she had no doubt that before the Confederacy came to an end, her childhood home would be burned to the ground in righteous Union fury. Bentley had failed her, and it was the one thing to which she'd given all of her love. And then word had come that Jeffrey was lost at sea, and Sarah remembered that day as clear as a bell.

She reached her hand out, trembling, to her husband, and felt her knees buckle. She fell then, and he caught her just before she hit the ground. Gripping his lapels with her small hands, she squeezed them until her knuckles were white. Her tears came, accompanied by great, gulping sobs. She felt as though she were coming out of a fog—memories of the recent past blending in her mind with memories from when she was young and her father had been her whole world.

Sarah cried as Jeffrey rocked her gently back and forth, sitting in front of the new home he was building for her. That he was by her side was a miracle. She had treated him with little more than disdain and apathy during their lives together, and if he were a man of lesser character, he might well have left her at Bentley where he'd found her upon his return. She thought of her children, people who had grown into lives of their own—people born of her own flesh and blood—in whom she had taken barely a secondary notice.

Everything, *everything* had come second to Bentley. And without slavery, without a good economy, without political stability, Bentley couldn't survive. But her family had survived! The people she had created and then largely dismissed had survived when her beloved plantation had slipped. Charlotte was a mother to a beautiful young child, and Charlotte herself had softened and allowed herself a vulnerability that would in time make her a better person.

Emily had married a good man and now had a life with him and her baby—and she was happy! Emily was happy. Sarah would never have believed it possible. And Clara, what a beautiful young woman she had become. Sarah had always assumed her hearing loss would be a devastating liability, and had despaired at such an imperfection when Clara was a toddler, but the girl was succeeding in spite of it.

And Ben. Ben, possessing all the character and strength of the greatest men who ever lived, had followed his intuition and his heart to fight for what he knew to be right.

She missed him so much it hurt. What a wonderful young man he'd been, so handsome and full of life and compassion. And she and Jeffrey had stomped on the flames of his beliefs and thrown him from their home.

Her shoulders heaved as she remembered selling Elijah, her own grandson, to the Charlesworths. Had Jeffrey not come home when he had and purchased the child back, who knows where fate might have cast him. Sarah remembered everything about the trek west, everything that had happened since their arrival. She thought of her young grandsons with a sense of joy. Their happiness was infectious, their matching green eyes so very expressive.

And Jeffrey. As she sat with him, rocking slowly in his arms, she wondered how she had ever been fortunate enough to choose a man who would come into his own and care for his family when the world around them crumbled. He was so infinitely tender with her, so patient, and he spoke with her daily as though nothing were amiss. She barely remembered the time at Bentley after she had been informed of his apparent demise, but she remembered now events that had occurred since his return.

She glanced up from her grief to see Ruth running down the street toward them, and her heart lurched further. *Ruth.* Her childhood companion. She had known Ruth the bulk of her life, and had always looked, albeit unconsciously, for her support and approval. She knew Ruth was smart, had always known it, and as a teen had resented it. Perhaps that was why she had been only too happy to thrust Ruth completely into the role of subservient slave. Ruth had frightened her with her intelligence and capabilities, and she supposed it was that fear—and the knowledge that her way of life was therefore flawed—that the crack in her resolve had begun to erode away her strength.

Jeffrey loosened his hold on Sarah as Ruth flew to her side, catching her in her arms and holding her tight. "Ruth," Sarah gulped. "Ruth!"

"Shhh, Sarah, it's all right. It will be fine." Ruth settled next to her on the ground and held her close, rocking her in much the same manner as Jeffrey. "You'll see. Everything will be fine. Your new house will be beautiful, and you'll be so happy in it. Ben will come home soon too, and I will help Jeffrey take care of you."

"Oh, Ruth." Still the tears flowed, and Sarah choked, thinking she might be sick. Ruth stroked her hair and murmured comfort in her ear. "I don't know what to do! What will I do with my life? Bentley is gone. It's all I've ever known . . . I lost so much, wasted so much time . . ."

"We start over, Sarah. You and I and all of us. We begin again."

"I don't know how. I don't know how to do anything but Bentley! I don't know what to say to my children. You've been their mother, Ruth, because I was too busy."

"They care for you, Sarah."

"They hate me. You know they do. And why shouldn't they?" To give voice to her worst fears, to acknowledge aloud her worst qualities and deeds—it was awful. She hated speaking of the things she had shoved deep down inside, hated the feeling that she was opening wide her chest for bullets or arrows or swords to pierce through, killing her spirit as she knew they could. To finally admit that Ruth, a black woman, a slave, was a better person, a more capable person than she, was the hardest thing she had ever done. She pulled back, her whole body shaking, and looked into the woman's deep brown eyes. "You are twice the woman I will ever be, Ruth. I have wronged you for a lifetime, and no amount of apology will ever make it better."

There. She'd said it. She'd completely laid bare her soul, all the ugliness and fear and insecurity. She could now face God and tell Him that she'd been completely honest at least one time in her life, and had given another soul her respect.

Ruth wiped Sarah's tears with the hem of her crisp, white pinafore. The dress she wore beneath it was a vibrant apple green, and it brought a light to her face Sarah had never seen. She had only ever, *ever* seen Ruth attired in browns. "Sarah, Sarah," Ruth murmured, her expressive, wise eyes bright with moisture. "What a long way we've come." She paused. "Sarah, I forgive you." The last was whispered, and the tears fell from her eyes.

Sarah choked on another sob and allowed Ruth to pull her forward again into her embrace. How had she known what Sarah had needed to hear? She splayed her fingers across Ruth's back, knowing of the thin scars that crossed it, scars that Sarah herself had caused. "How can you? How can you forgive me?"

"I do it for the both of us. They are words I need to say." Ruth pulled back again and smiled, dissolving into gentle laughter. "Aren't we a sight? What will the neighbors say?"

Sarah laughed then, feeling as though she had been under water for a very long time and a strong arm had reached down to pull her up. She looked around the street, her laughter increasing as she imagined the neighbors peering out through their windows at the spectacle. "I suppose it's a good thing that there aren't too many houses on this street."

"Would you like to walk down a bit and see my new house?" Ruth asked her, and Sarah suddenly remembered how it had been when they were young girls. She now knew why watching Rose and Clara often brought such a sense of nostalgia.

Sarah nodded and wiped at her nose with a lacy handkerchief that Jeffrey had tucked into her sleeve that morning. As they stood, they noticed him standing to one side, watching the proceedings with a moist eye. Ruth laughed and said, "Would you like to join us?"

Jeffrey offered his arms to both women, one on either side. As they began a slow walk down the street, he said, "We'll fit in just fine like this. Did you know that some of the men here have more than one wife?"

CHAPTER 29

In all his efforts he was ably seconded by his men, not one flagged. Neither sleep nor rest was thought of, and every moment was devoted to the great work they had in hand.

—New York Times *article lauding the efforts of chief of detectives John Young and his police force*

* * *

5 November 1864
New York, New York

Daniel O'Shea entered through the Greek-style portico of the Astor House and made his way toward the front desk, passing the expensive shops that lined the street level of the five-story hotel. Wasting no time, he asked to speak with the proprietor of the hotel on official business for the New York City Fire Department chief John Decker. The clerk looked at Daniel for a moment as one might inspect a flea.

"The fire department?" The young man was tall and thin, with an aquiline nose that he seemed to take great pleasure in looking down on.

"Yes, the fire department. Or if that isn't good enough for you, perhaps the fact that I also come here at the request of police chief of detectives John Young will suffice."

After one more definitive sniff, the clerk excused himself and turned away. Daniel used the time to peruse his surroundings. The hotel was the grandest of the grand, and only those who were most wealthy and influential stayed within its opulent walls. It boasted 309 rooms, each with individual locks, and the amazing feat of running water in each room. The hotel also contained luxurious bathing rooms that were the talk of the town and had been during the hotel's thirty-year existence.

Daniel forced himself to unclench his jaw and relax. The arrogant reception he'd received from the clerk was an example of one of the reasons Daniel had come of age in New York such an angry young man, full of resentment and disgust for those who looked down upon one for reasons of money or stature. Those angry feelings, coupled with a desperate sense of loss over the death of his only brother, had led Daniel to a life of fighting in bars for money as a way to release his frustration over society and the misfortunes of his own life.

He was older now, however, a man of thirty years who had a loving wife and a small, cozy home. He was surprised at how quickly the old ire rose up in him, and it was only by thinking of Marie's probable reaction that he was able to take a deep breath and feel some of the anger abate.

By the time he had calmed himself sufficiently, the clerk returned with a distinguished-looking man who greeted him with a sense of civility if not outright friendliness. "May I be of some assistance?"

"Yes, sir. I come on official fire department and police business. It has been brought to the attention of fire chief

John Decker that there is a Confederate plot afoot to set fire to much of New York City, striking the biggest hotels as their targets."

The man's eyes widened slightly and he moved from around the desk to take Daniel by the arm. "I wonder if we might come over here to discuss this matter," he said, and walked with Daniel to a quiet corner of the lobby. "What do you know?" he asked when they were alone.

"The information Chief Decker has received thus far seems to indicate that the rebels plan to strike on Election Day. They are apparently hoping to incite disturbance similar to the draft riots of last summer and encourage the copperheads here to come out in a show of support."

"And they're hoping to gain . . ."

"It's believed they want to claim the city for the Confederacy and operate as a separate city-state."

The hotel proprietor exhaled and shook his head. "What does Mr. Decker propose we do?"

"He suggests that you set double watches throughout all the halls and examine each room thoroughly, regardless of the occupant." At the man's nod, Daniel continued. "Should Election Day pass uneventfully, Chief Decker feels it would be beneficial to still maintain vigilance."

"Very well. And your name, in case I should have further questions?"

Daniel told him and left the man, exiting the building. Stepping back onto the busy street, he wondered if his suggestions would be followed. Since joining with the volunteer firefighters, he had trained and associated with the other volunteers in a way that helped sate his yearning for adventure and also build a sense of community with others. Before his enlistment, he had been a largely solitary individual. Now that he had returned home and had a wife he loved and sought to protect, he found himself wanting to become more involved in the community.

The recent threats, provided to Chief Decker by a tip from a Confederate sympathizer, were sobering and were being treated very seriously. The fire department was well trained, and the use of the horse-drawn, steam-powered fire engine was an infinite improvement over the formerly used hand-pumped versions, but unless the hotel proprietors heeded the advice, the fire department couldn't possibly hope to reach all the intended targets in time to avert disaster. And if enough hotels went up in flames, the entire city would be soon to follow.

* * *

Marie perused the paper two days later while Daniel worked in his wood shop that stood adjacent to the home. She wandered into the shop, still reading the paper, and said, "They are still suggesting the rebels may attempt their plan, although Election Day came and went uneventfully." She looked up at her husband and moved to his side, placing a hand on his back.

Daniel nodded and paused in his activities. He was working on a rocking chair that Marie secretly wished could stay in the house rather than be sold. It was a thing of beauty, and she marveled at Daniel's talent with tools. "Supposedly, many of the conspirators left New York with the news of Sherman's departure from Atlanta. Young received a tip, though, that at least eight remain," he said.

Marie turned the paper over and looked at the front page. "'Sherman Burns Atlanta,'" she read aloud. "Those eight might think to exact revenge if nothing else."

Daniel nodded and ran a hand over the back of the chair. Finding a rough spot, he retrieved a small file from the workbench and smoothed it down, blowing away the excess shavings. "I suspect they might."

"And what has Mr. Decker suggested the fire department do? How are you to know when they might strike?"

"We don't, but there are those who feel the rebs might try to do their worst on the twenty-fifth of this month."

"Why the twenty-fifth?"

"It's Evacuation Day. Eighty years ago the British evacuated New York during the Revolution."

"Ah. The perfect statement then."

Daniel touched the tip of Marie's nose with his finger. "Yes, indeed."

"Well then, I'm thinking we may need to travel into the country over the twenty-fifth. A nice vacation, perhaps."

He smiled at her and shook his head. "Marie, you mustn't worry so. You'll make yourself sick. I'll be fine."

He said he'd be fine, but Marie had seen him after thugs in New Orleans had beaten him. Since then, she'd been unable to banish the thought that if he continued to place himself in extreme situations, eventually his luck would dissolve and he wouldn't escape unhurt. It was useless for her to tell him this, though, so instead she swallowed any further comments on the state of his health and turned her attention to the article on the front page.

"It seems Sherman ordered that all military and train affiliates be burned as they left Atlanta," she read. "The fires spread to other buildings—businesses and homes—and before long the city was leveled."

"And where are they going now?"

"He's calling it a 'March to the Sea.' They're headed for Savannah, burning and looting everything in their path. They've cut themselves off from the Union supply line, so they're living off the land, consuming the local harvest and livestock, and destroying or killing whatever they can't carry with them."

"Hmm," Daniel said, again inspecting the back of the rocking chair. He paused for a moment, reflecting. "When I was stationed in New Orleans, there was a sailor who bunked next to me. He was a tiny little fellow—couldn't have been more than seventeen years old." He stretched a bit, reaching his arms high into the air. Marie smiled, anticipating Daniel's comments. He told stories with a flair that made her laugh.

"At any rate, this little fellow used to read all the time. Said he wanted to be informed in the art of war. He read a book, a translated book called *On War,* by a Prussian named Clausewitz. The author fought in the French Revolution and in the Napoleonic Wars, and I'll never forget his name because Peanut—that's what we called the sailor—quoted the book continually. 'Clausewitz says this or that,'" Daniel imitated, raising his voice an octave.

Marie smiled, and he continued. "One thing he said was that this Clausewitz wrote on the necessity of 'total war,' of war on an entire population, not just military targets. He said that it becomes necessary to break the will of the enemy, to destroy the resources and the support of the people behind the lines in order to dismantle the troops."

Marie sighed and drew her brows together in a frown. "It's . . . harsh."

Daniel nodded and leaned against the bench behind him, crossing his arms over his chest. "It is harsh. But then

Sherman said all along, even before the war, that it's a bloody, brutal thing. There was a time, according to the stories, that early on in the war he was very near collapse, distraught and thinking the war would never end. Some of the soldiers thought he was truly going mad. They say that Grant buoyed him up, and then later on Sherman supported Grant through his bouts with alcohol. They've been thick as thieves ever since."

"So Grant will support Sherman's concept of this 'total war'?"

"It sounds as though he does. There's one thing I admire about both men, though. While they may take drastic measures, neither one enjoys doing so."

"I don't suppose the citizens of Atlanta would agree with that. I imagine they think Sherman is chortling all the way to the sea."

Daniel nodded. "Most likely." He paused. "Do you ever miss home?"

"Sometimes. But the memories there . . . I miss my father so much . . ."

He laughed, but it was hollow. "I understand. I never imagined we'd have that in common."

"Nor did I." She moved closer to him for an embrace. "I do miss the beauty and climate of New Orleans, but I'm happy here. I don't want to be anywhere else."

* * *

16 November 1864
Boston, Massachusetts

The Birmingham family sat gathered in the parlor following dinner, and Robert felt odd but at ease. In some ways it was as though he'd never gone, but then a glance at the space where his left hand should have been reminded him of exactly how long it had been.

His family had reacted as he had known they would. He had warned them by mail of his injury so their shock wasn't excessive, but his mother had shed tears and hugged him, and his father had shown his sympathy through the gruff manner in which he cleared his throat and clasped Robert's shoulder. Jimmy, "Jim," had reacted with curiosity; Robert was amazed at the amount his younger brother had grown in one year.

Camille and Jacob were also present. Camille had cried and fumed at him, saying if he'd never gone in the first place he'd be fine, but then had told him it wasn't such a bad thing, that if he tucked the cuff of his sleeve into his pocket then nobody would be the wiser.

Ben and Mary sat side by side on a sofa near the hearth, Ben's hand possessively over Mary's. She had waited until Ben's return to inform the family of their engagement, and even as she sat by Ben, whose eyes rarely left her face, she was obviously nervous about people's reactions. She needn't have been; the only friction she encountered was over the fact that she had dared keep the engagement a secret from them.

Perhaps the person whose attention drew Robert's the most was Abigail. She sat a bit apart from the family, and although she seemed happy enough, her presence was a reminder of the one who wasn't with them. The space next to her where Luke should have been was made even more pronounced by the fact that he would never return. There was a look about her eyes that seemed lonely; he ached for her and cursed the fact that his schoolboy adoration of her obviously hadn't abated during his absence.

"Lincoln's election was a great defeat in the electoral college," Jacob was telling Ben, "but not with the general populace."

Elizabeth shuddered. "Can you imagine if McClellan had won? Heaven help us all."

"I heard there was a riot of sorts planned in New York on Election Day," Ben said.

"I suppose Sherman's victory in Atlanta, not to mention the fact that he left it in flames, helped to diffuse some of the conspiracy." James shook his head. "There was much at stake with Atlanta. Many feel that Lincoln would have lost the election if Sherman hadn't been victorious."

"So Sherman gained Atlanta, cut off the Confederate supply lines, and saved the presidency." Robert rubbed a bruise on his thigh. He and Ben had ridden long hours to return home, and his soreness caught him by surprise; he had thought himself accustomed to such time spent in the saddle. "Now he wages total war."

Robert felt his father's gaze on his face. "You don't approve?" James asked him.

He massaged his eyes with his hand, suddenly feeling extremely tired. "It's not that I don't approve, exactly, and I understand his reasons. I suppose it will bring a quicker end to the war than we might have seen otherwise." He paused, feeling the sympathetic eyes of his family resting upon him. "It's a very ugly thing," he murmured, and glanced at Ben. "It's a horrible thing, really. I never imagined how it would be, not even after Bull Run."

He looked at Camille then and saw her eyes filling with tears. Her heart was bigger than she wished it to be—he knew she ached for him, and he loved her for it. "Perhaps time will soften the memories," she said. "And if you will recall, I told you not to go."

"I had no choice, Camille. I needed to do it. I've studied it my entire life, and needed to see it firsthand."

"Did you learn what you hoped to?" James asked.

"I'm not certain."

"Much of it he already knew," Ben interceded. "Your son has a grasp for details like nobody I've ever seen. I think he came for me, and I'm grateful." Ben glanced at Robert. "He brought me safely out of it."

Robert shrugged and looked down at his hand. He suddenly felt very self-conscious. Ben gave him too much credit, as if he could have brought him home from a war by sheer will alone. The very thought was silly. That he had felt a measure of responsibility for his cousin, however, he couldn't deny.

Seeking to turn the conversation away from himself, Robert asked Ben, "What are your plans? How long will you stay in Boston?"

"Well," Ben said on a sigh, "we'll have to stay out the winter. It's too late to head out across the plains now, so when the wagon trains start moving again in the spring, we'll move. As for our immediate plans, we'd like to be married as soon as possible."

"Wonderful," Camille said, clasping her hands together. "A little joy in the midst of such heaviness is a very good thing."

"I must be selfish for a moment and bemoan my loss of an excellent seamstress," Elizabeth said with a smile at Mary. "We'll talk later and perhaps I can convince you to work on some projects in your new home."

"That sounds nice," Mary answered, her shoulders relaxing a bit. "I appreciate very much your kindness to me—I can never repay it."

"Nonsense," Elizabeth said. "You've been wonderful company for us, and you've also provided us with a service we needed. We'll miss you very much when you leave Boston entirely."

"Speaking of which," Ben said to James, "have you heard from my parents?"

"I have, as a matter of fact. Only just last week we received a letter. Your father and mother are building a new home north of Salt Lake City, as is Ruth."

"Ruth is building a home?" Ben's eyes lit up with pleasure and amazement.

Mary nodded, smiling at him. "Your father has officially employed her and also paid her 'back wages,' he calls it."

"I'll be . . ." Ben said, shaking his head. "I would never, *ever* have dreamed such a thing."

"Your mother is doing much better as well," James continued. "The children are all sound, and Charlotte seems to be growing accustomed to her new surroundings."

At the mention of the children, Mary sat up a bit, a nearly indiscernible movement that bore evidence of an awareness. "Elijah is well, then? That's very good," Ben said, directing the last to Mary.

She nodded slightly and murmured, "Ruth tells me so."

Wanting to ask about Elijah but sensing Mary's discomfort, Robert remained silent on the subject. Ben turned his attention back to James and said, "I must thank you for your intervention on behalf of my father. He might well still be languishing as a captive somewhere in New York if not for you."

"Think nothing of it. He's my brother. I've enjoyed renewing the acquaintance."

* * *

Later that evening, Robert sat in his old bedroom, looking around at his things and wondering what he was to do with his life now that he was home again. He had fought the self-pity he'd felt encroaching time and again after losing his arm, but it had been easier then because he'd been in an interim place—a place that was temporary and required no thoughts on the future beyond surviving to live one more day.

Now he was home and reminded of all the things he'd dreamed of someday doing. Paramount among those dreams had been thoughts of a career in the military. His fright at Bull Run three years back had stemmed some of those imaginings, but they hadn't completely gone away. After serving out his year of enlistment, however, he was fairly certain that the life of a soldier wasn't something he wished to continue.

He walked to a small table that contained several figurines, pieces of one of his collections of military miniatures. He picked up a likeness of a general and ran his thumb over the smooth surface, spying the parts where the paint had chipped during the years he'd maneuvered it, playing at battles and drills. "I don't have a moral objection to the military," he said softly to the beloved piece as though he owed it an explanation. "I just don't want to be the one to do it anymore." He replaced the piece and selected another, this one a lowly foot soldier. As a child, he'd always imagined himself the general. In reality, he'd been the one on the front lines, ducking and running, firing and reloading. Killing and scrambling for his life.

Holding the piece in his hand, he walked to his writing desk and sat down, withdrawing a piece of paper from an inner drawer. He set the wooden soldier near the head of his paper and grasped his pen, the one he'd taken over a year before from this very desk and carried into battle.

Organizing his thoughts into compartments that allowed him clarity, he began to write about his experiences.

CHAPTER 30

The plan was excellently well conceived, and evidently prepared with great care, and had it been executed with one-half the ability with which it was drawn up, no human power could have saved this city from utter destruction.
—New York Times

* * *

25 November 1864
New York, New York

"Who was that at the door?" Marie asked Daniel from the kitchen at the back of the house.

"It's happening," Daniel said as he shrugged his arms into his coat. "They've just sent word. I must go." He kissed her cheek and paused as she grabbed his coat lapels. She didn't have to say anything; her expressive eyes were full of fear. "I'll take care," he said, and kissed her again. "I don't want you to worry. In fact," he said, "get your coat. I'll drop you by the mothers'."

She looked at him as though she would like to have argued but in the end allowed Daniel to help her into her coat and picked up a basket of handwork on her way out the door. When he helped her down from the back of his horse, she clutched his coat one more time.

"Marie," he said, "everyone has prepared for this. I doubt the fire department will even be necessary."

He couldn't know how true his statement would be. As he made his way to the LaFarge House, he found that the employees of the hotel along with several of the patrons had taken matters into their own hands and extinguished the blaze that had been set in one of the third-floor rooms. He made his way to the center of the smoking room, taking stock of the heap of bed clothing and furniture that had been piled together. An empty bottle lay atop the smoldering mess, and Daniel told the staff in the room to leave it as it was until the police force arrived.

It wasn't long before the fire engine arrived out front, and Daniel went outside to meet it. As he was explaining the situation to the other volunteers, a roar went up from the theater adjoining the hotel. He ran inside the building, following the noise until he found utter chaos and bedlam erupting in the stage area.

The chief had warned them that the crowd attending the theater that night might prove to be a problem should the LaFarge be targeted. The crowd was unusually large; it was one of the few nights the famed Booth brothers would be performing together on the same stage. As Daniel watched, trying to make his way to the stage, Edwin Booth yelled to the crowd that the danger was past, that stampeding toward the exits would do more harm than good.

Daniel shouted to the crowd to listen to the actor who stood with his brother, John, on the stage. Other volunteers in the crowd who had followed Daniel into the fray were yelling likewise, begging the crowd to be calm. Another man rose in the dress circle and yelled for quiet.

At his commanding voice, some of the din began to recede, and a man Daniel recognized as Judge McCunn shouted of the folly of scrambling about in fear, especially as the danger had passed.

Eventually, the fevered pitch inside the building dropped, the awful panic and fear dissipating with it, and a good majority of the patrons resumed their seats. Finally seeing that the situation was manageable, Daniel and the other volunteers left the building and moved back toward the fire engine.

"We're going to the river," a shout carried over the noise outside. "There are several hay barges on fire."

Climbing aboard his place on the wagon, Daniel held on as the horses were snapped to attention and began running at a full gallop through the streets. The few minutes that it took to reach the river were exhilarating for Daniel, who turned his face into the cold night wind with relish. It was refreshingly crisp, with a hint of snow in the air, and Daniel was glad to be out in it.

Upon reaching the river, it wasn't long before the burning barges were in full view. Moving quickly to draw on the river as a water source for the steam engine, the men took to their positions and began to work on the blazing hay. The multiple fires were quickly extinguished, and as he looked back over the city, Daniel noted with satisfaction that nothing seemed ablaze. The acrid smell of smoke hung heavy in the air, but thanks to their words of warning and the unflagging effort on the part of the police department, New York had not gone up in flames.

The men spent their time gathering as much information as they could obtain and joined with other investigators and volunteers at the fire station a few hours later. Daniel listened with interest as the details began to come together; all told, thirteen hotels had been targeted, some in multiple rooms, but because of the quick reactions of the hotels' staff and patrons, some with their own internal firefighters, the blazes were contained with minimal amounts of damage.

"We believe it to be either phosphorus or possibly Greek fire that was used to set these blazes," the chief was saying to the men gathered. "Greek fire is," he explained to the police investigators present, "the mixture of sulfur, naphtha, and quicklime that bursts into flame when exposed to the air. One of the reasons these fires didn't blaze the way the Confederates obviously hoped they might is because all of the rooms that were targeted were also tightly closed. The arsonists had apparently hoped to avoid detection, so they left the windows and doors locked. In fact," the chief said, glancing down at his notes, "at the Fifth Avenue Hotel, the fire didn't flame until a porter opened the door."

After informing the group assembled that the fifteenth precinct would provide the news to the papers in the morning, most of the volunteers made their way out of the station and toward home. Daniel joined them, sharing in some of the conversation until he reached his horse and mounted, bidding the others good night.

When he reached his mother's house, Marie met him at the door. "You smell like smoke," she said as she grabbed him close. "Are you hurt? What happened? It's nearly three in the morning!"

As Daniel submitted to the anxious ministrations of the women in his life, he felt . . . content. It was with a profound sense of gratitude that he fell asleep during the wee dawn hours, holding his wife close in his arms.

* * *

Marie left for the orphanage the following morning with her mother and mother-in-law, and she was feeling decidedly irritated. Daniel had returned home the night before, telling them in great detail about his experiences as a firefighter. She was as proud of him as she could be, and yet a part of her, a little corner that she didn't want to acknowledge, felt annoyance at the fact that he was happy doing something that distressed her so much.

There were nights in her sleep when visions of her burning home lingered with her long after she awoke, and she was hard-pressed throughout the day to shake the feeling that something disastrous was about to happen. But then nothing ever did, and she wondered if she wasn't losing her mind.

So much had been taken from her in three short years, however, that it was little wonder she felt as though at any moment the rug would be ripped from beneath her feet. That Daniel was choosing to live a life that placed him in danger on a regular basis was frustrating. Things were only now coming together for them, and she didn't relish the thought of joining the mothers' ranks as a widow.

When she reached the schoolhouse, she felt the fist around her heart relax a bit, and by the time she had entered and was seated with the children, listening to their adventures and sharing in their simple joys, she had forgotten her irritation completely. She loved the children, and with a pang of guilt, she realized that Daniel had found something he also loved.

It isn't fair, though, she thought as she listened to the children. *The work that I do doesn't endanger my life. How likely is it that I'll be killed one day in teaching these children?*

It was no use, she decided the more she thought about it. She hadn't known Daniel intimately when they married, but she had known a few basic things about his character. She had known that he possessed a great desire to help others who couldn't help themselves, and she had also known there was a side to him that craved adventure. To curb that would be to squelch a part of him that had attracted her to him in the first place.

She would have to support him in his love of firefighting and pray each day he went out with the engine and the other volunteers that he would return home safely.

* * *

30 November 1864
Savannah, Georgia

Emily sat in her parlor, sipping tea and eyeing her neighbor with barely disguised disdain. She had promised Austin, however, that she would behave herself. What she truly wanted to say to the woman was, "Your awful husband is the reason my husband was forced to enlist, and now he's missing a leg!"

The unsuspecting Mrs. Mandalay was blissfully unaware, however, of her husband's blackmailing enterprise, and so Austin wished it to remain. "My life is my own, and my destiny my own, Emily," he'd said. "I will control what I can and handle the rest." Austin's idea of "handling the rest" meant ignoring the neighbors who had discovered his slave-freeing activities in order to protect those whom he had helped escape.

"They're far away now, Austin, and things are changing. Those men deserve to be punished," she had argued with him earlier in the day.

"And who would punish them? The local authorities? No, Em, we leave well enough alone. At least I'm alive."

And so it was for her husband that she sat silently, listening to the woman chatter on about how despite the war, her family still had wealth in stored cotton, property, and a good harvest. *You are so very sure of your position,* Emily thought as she examined the woman over the rim of her teacup. *You are blue-blooded aristocracy, and you are soon to fall.*

"It's such a shame, isn't it, about Hood's army in Franklin, Tennessee? I hear he lost over six thousand men in that battle, and he had only twenty-seven to begin with!" Emily shook her head. "Just bodes no good for us to have our commanders throwing their men into such ill-advised attacks."

Mrs. Mandalay regarded Emily, her jaw slightly slack. Before she could bluster a reply, though, Emily continued. "You are aware that Sherman is on his way? If he treats Savannah as he did Atlanta, I daresay the whole lot of us are in for a surprise."

Mrs. Mandalay's face turned a mottled red. "How can you discuss such vulgarity so casually? You don't think you would suffer?"

"Now, now then," Emily said, and reached over to pat the woman's hand. "I'm sure we'll all be fine. After all, it isn't as though Sherman burned *everything* in Atlanta. I hear he left a handful of houses still standing, and given the fact that *ours* are the most beautiful in all of Savannah, perhaps he'll merely use them to shelter his troops."

The woman stared at her, clearly unable to decide which would be worse—her home burned to the ground or Union troops inside it. After a few more moments of idle and distracted chitchat, the woman thanked her for the tea, mumbled that they must do it again sometime, and that next time she would be sure to arrange a tea before stopping in on Emily so suddenly.

As Gwenyth showed the woman to the front door with a ghost of a smile upon her lips, Emily stood and began clearing the tea things. She had been flippant with Mrs. Mandalay, but in truth she was apprehensive. She doubted very much that General Sherman cared one way or another that Austin had freed slaves and that he and Emily were sympathetic to the Union cause. Sherman was bent on destroying the South so that the Confederacy had no support, and Willow Lane was very definitely a Southern resource.

When Gwenyth returned to the parlor, Emily set the tray down on a side table and turned to her. "Gwen, what do you think of General Sherman?"

The black woman wrinkled her nose. "I suppose he's the best man to bring a quick end to the war."

"But?"

"I don't know that I like him much as a person. I've read things about him, things he's said . . ."

"What kind of things?"

"He thinks black people are good for digging trenches and following base orders, but doesn't trust them to fight. Doesn't think them capable. Says he would never give one a gun."

Emily nodded slowly. "Not much of an abolitionist then, is he." She pursed her lips, hands on her hips.

"Why do you ask?"

"Well," she sighed, "I would very much like to see Willow Lane emerge unscathed from Sherman's sweep. I want to understand the way he thinks to see if there isn't something I can do . . ." She waved a hand at Gwenyth. "I don't know. I'm just thinking aloud. By my best estimate, we have a few weeks before they arrive."

"Do you still want to see the price comparison sheet? I finished it this morning."

"Oh dear, I'm not sure I want to look. How bad is it?"

Gwenyth gave her a wry grin and picked up the tray Emily had set down. "Awful. Come and see."

The list Gwenyth had made sat innocently on the kitchen house table, but as she looked it over, Emily sucked in her breath. "Mercy," she whispered. "This is worse than I thought. You know, I owe you an apology for 'allowing' you to do this on your own. I've been so consumed with Austin and Mary Alice that I've left the running of this place entirely in your hands—oh, and then I was gone for so long at Bentley . . ."

"Emily, stop. You've turned your attention to people who needed you. I've been doing just fine."

"But the stress of trying to make this all work! I don't know how you've slept at night!"

"We've done well enough with our resources here. You'll notice meat has been on the menu sparingly, but the harvest has stayed consistently good."

Emily turned her attention back to the paper in her hand. Gwenyth had made two columns, one detailing the cost of food in the year 1861, the other the current cost, four years later. "Bacon used to be twelve and a half cents a pound," Emily read, "and it now costs eight to nine dollars a pound." She lowered the sheet and looked in shock at the housekeeper.

"Yes," Gwenyth said. "I'm sure you've noticed we consume more beef these days than pork." She gestured toward the paper, and Emily read on.

"Beef was twelve and a half cents a pound, now two dollars a pound. Flour was six dollars per barrel, now anywhere from one hundred twenty-five to *five hundred dollars a barrel?*"

Gwenyth nodded and began cleaning the teacups and plates, one of which held half of Mrs. Mandalay's small open-faced cucumber sandwich. "Give me that!" Emily grabbed the sandwich and stuffed it in her mouth. "At five hundred dollars a barrel, we are not wasting one crumb," she said, her full mouth muffling her words.

Gwenyth's mouth had dropped open in surprise, and she now laughed, her mirth increasing so much that she was soon forced to hold on to the side of the sink.

"And furthermore," Emily said, swallowing the sandwich, "the next time that woman stops in uninvited, we are not feeding her one blessed thing!"

"That's scandalous, Emily," Gwenyth said, wiping the corner of her eye with her apron, still laughing. "To not serve tea . . ."

"No. That's not scandalous. That's war." Emily glanced at the big wooden table. "What's in that bowl?" she asked Gwenyth, whose laughter subsided as she turned back to the dishes.

"It's leavening for the bread," a voice from the doorway replied. Janet, Emily's cook, entered the room and deposited a large bowl of flour on the table. Emily eyed the white powder as though it were an enemy.

"We might as well be eating gold," she muttered, and turned her attention back to the leavening compound. "You've been mixing your own?" she asked Janet.

The cook nodded. "The regular hasn't been available for some time, so some of the other cooks in the area created this particular concoction."

"What do you put in it?"

"First I burn red corncobs in a pan over a bed of coals. The corncob becomes a white ash. Then I add water and leave it to stand until clear. After that, I mix it with sour milk, two parts to one part."

Emily wrinkled her nose. "Very inventive." She glanced up at the woman, who smiled and began gathering other ingredients for placement on the large table. "I'm glad you two are so resourceful," she said to both Janet and Gwenyth. "All this time I had no idea we've been in such dire straits. I should have just left well enough alone. We might have reached the end of the war and I would never have felt a thing."

She winked at Janet and smiled. "I'll leave you to your work and check on Mary Alice. She's probably awake by now." The women bid her farewell, and she made her way back to the main house on legs that felt slightly weak. She'd been deliberately avoiding the truth about the state of the economy in Savannah. She knew it had been bad, but the bold facts were painful to see. How much worse would it become before it got better? How much longer would the war drag on, continuing to pull the economy down with it—the Southern economy, anyway? From all she'd heard, the citizens in the North were all but living with barely a skip in the rhythm.

To make matters worse, Sherman was on his way, and she wondered if they'd even have a house to live in by the time he was finished. For all of her bold talk in years past about wanting to see the South suffer because of its insistence on slavery, she found she was extremely averse to the idea of wandering the streets with her husband, trying to find shelter for her child.

* * *

Utah Territory

Earl Dobranski walked the distance from the newspaper office to his home with his head slightly bowed. News out of Denver wasn't good; some citizens had attacked a peaceful Indian camp on Sand Creek, killing five hundred Arapahoe and Cheyenne, sparing no thought for man, woman, or child. The territories in the West had been rife with friction between white settlers and Indians for years, but each time there was news of slaughter, whether of the Indians or the white man, it sat heavily in Earl's heart.

He didn't look forward to sharing the news with his mother. She was part Cherokee, and she was proud of her native blood. Nothing escaped her eye, however, and sooner or later she would learn of it.

Earl reached his home and reluctantly told his parents what he'd heard. Ellen took it with a stoic face, but following dinner with her rowdy boys, she retired to the parlor without saying much. Eli looked at Earl thoughtfully, an understanding passing between them, but he refrained from comment, choosing instead to follow Ellen into the parlor. Earl entered the room after his father and looked at Ellen in concern.

"Are you all right?" he asked her.

She nodded, knitting in her lap. "Of course," she said. "Just feeling a bit tired."

Earl watched her for a moment, knowing full well she wouldn't be willing to say anything further unless she felt compelled to do so, and when it came to matters of concern or worry, she usually didn't. He frowned a bit, feeling entirely selfish that his own personal news probably wasn't coming at an opportune time.

"What is it, son?" Eli asked. "You've had something on your mind for days."

Earl sat down on a chair near his mother. "I've been informed that local law enforcement is looking for a sheriff," he said.

"Oh?" His mother looked up from her knitting.

He cleared his throat. "Yes. I'm thinking of pursuing it."

"Local, you say?" she asked, returning to her knitting.

"In a manner of speaking."

"It wouldn't be north of here, would it?"

"Yes, actually. Ogden."

She glanced up again, her expression bland. There was a spark in her eye, though, that he recognized as a good sign. "You've been spending much of your time up that way lately. I wondered how long it would be before you would seek to make it a permanent arrangement."

Earl shrugged. "No more time than usual, really . . ."

Eli laughed, and Earl looked at him. "Son, to my knowledge you've not ever spent much time in Ogden. Since roughly September or so, however . . ."

"I felt it important to help the Birminghams settle in, make sure their laborers were good folk. And they wanted to be into their home by winter if possible, and I knew it would be close . . . Mother, you've spent nearly as much time up there as I have!"

Eli held up his hand. "Say no more. You wouldn't be so helpful because of a certain widowed young lady, though, would you?"

Earl felt himself blushing. Blushing! For heaven's sake, he was nearly twenty-three years old, and here he was feeling like he needed to ask his parents for permission to move out on his own and embarrassed because his father knew he was sweet on a woman.

Ellen sighed. "I had rather hoped you would fall in love with a Mormon girl, Earl. It's not an easy thing to live separate lives when it comes to religion."

"Mother," Earl said evenly. "I never said I was in love with anyone. And if I were, it's early yet. Furthermore, I wouldn't know, if I were in love, if my feelings were returned. I merely wanted to tell you and him," Earl said, jerking a thumb in his father's direction and ignoring the resulting chortle, "that I will be pursuing the position of sheriff. In Ogden."

He rose from his chair and looked down at his parents, both of whom regarded him with expressions of amusement. "Say hello to the Birminghams when next you see them," Eli said. "It's time they came again for a visit."

Earl nodded his head and left the room, his hackles raised at the whispers and laughter that followed behind him. They were acting as though he were still in short pants, coming home from school to tell them a girl had kissed his cheek! Just because they were right about his intentions to pursue work in Ogden was beside the point. Charlotte Birmingham Ellis was a beautiful woman who could choose herself a husband out of many willing applicants. He had no idea if she returned his affection and certainly didn't plan to ask her.

It didn't hurt to live near her, though. When he wasn't missing her company, he was missing her son. The boy had wormed his way into Earl's heart and didn't show any signs of leaving. In the morning he planned to ride to Ogden for an extended stay to see what he could learn about the job. Of course he would see the Birminghams while there, and of course he would help with the construction on their house. It was already snowing, but not so much that if they worked hard, the crew finishing both Jeffrey's and Miss Ruth's homes couldn't finish within a matter of weeks.

They were good people, all of them, and he wanted their lives to be better now than they had been before. He didn't know many details about them; even though Ben had lived in Utah for a good five years before returning back east to enlist, he had never said much about his parents or siblings. Earl knew that they had needed a fresh start, however, and he was happy to see that they got it.

Charlotte Ellis was another matter altogether . . .

CHAPTER 31

Darkest of all Decembers
Ever my life has known,
Sitting here by the embers
Stunned, helpless, alone.
—Mary Chesnut

* * *

I beg to present you, as a Christmas gift, the city of Savannah, with 150 heavy guns and plenty of ammunition; also, about 25,000 bales of cotton.

—William Tecumseh Sherman, in a telegram to President Lincoln

* * *

15 December 1864
Cleveland, Ohio

Anne and Inger sat on the log fence that surrounded Per and Amanda's property. "Look at this one," Inger said, and puffed her breath out, hoping to create a ring in the air. "I just can't make it hollow like Bestefar's."

"Well," Anne said, puffing out a ring of her own, "I think it's a little easier with pipe smoke. But perhaps we just don't know how to do it correctly. We should ask your bestefar if he can make smoke rings outside with the cold air."

"Do you think the pigs can make smoke rings?"

"Hmm. I've never seen a pig smoke a pipe."

Inger laughed and tipped her golden head up to the sky. "No, silly! I mean smoke rings with the cold air!"

"The pigs? Smoke rings with cold air? Well, Inger, that would require a very clever pig. Shall we ask them?"

Inger nodded and, taking Anne's hand, hopped down from the railing. As they walked over to the pigpen, swinging hands and Inger skipping, Anne looked down at the child with a surge of affection. They had been in Ohio for nearly four months, the first four weeks of which she and Ivar had spent, day and night, at Per and Amanda's house.

Inger had been nervous, despite her natural affection for her father and Anne, to leave the only home and parents she could ever remember. Despite Ivar's disappointment, which he managed to patiently hide from his daughter, Anne and Amanda decided it would be best for Inger to grow comfortable around her new parents before moving out of her grandparents' home. Anne and Ivar moved into his house, therefore, and Inger still slept at Per and Amanda's. She saw her father and new stepmother every day, and much to Amanda's relief, Anne gradually took over in caring for the child. "I love the little one," Amanda said, "but these bones are growing old."

As for Anne, she couldn't remember a time when she'd ever felt more content. She was extremely relieved that her in-laws had proven themselves to be accepting and generous people, willing to grow accustomed to Anne and her personality as it blended itself into the family. Inger was a precious child, full of wonder and questions, and she possessed a feisty spark that Anne felt a kinship with.

Her love for Ivar grew daily, and the only dim spot in her life was his recurring bouts with the intestinal illness he had acquired at Andersonville. He had relaxed more in the time they'd been home than at any other time she could remember. Of course, she realized, the only times she had known him were encamped with the regiment and going into battle, followed by a harrowing several months in a horrid prison camp. She didn't suppose most people were relaxed under those circumstances.

She glanced up at the sound of his voice as he approached, having finished his duties on their neighboring farm for the afternoon. Their lives had fallen into a comfortable routine. Ivar had dismissed the young man Per had hired to take on the responsibilities he could no longer manage because of his deteriorating health, and in the mornings Ivar saw to the animals on both farms. He then completed the tasks requiring immediate attention on his parents' property, followed by those on his and Anne's farm. Afternoon usually signaled a lull before milking time came around again.

Anne smiled as he approached and, when he reached her, kissed his cold lips. He then reached down to nuzzle Inger's ear, and she giggled as he tickled her. "What are you two about on such a cold afternoon?" he asked them as he did each afternoon. As much as they could, Anne and Inger spent time out-of-doors. It was a boon for the both of them, and much of the time, Anne carried along a small notebook in which she and the young girl drew pictures. The only part of Ivar's opening question that ever changed was the state of the weather; as the heat of autumn had lingered, he had asked them, "What are you two about on such a warm afternoon?"

Inger now bounced up and down on the pigpen railing, her hands holding the upper log, her feet on the lower. "We're watching to see if the pigs can blow smoke rings."

"Smoke rings?"

"Yes," Anne said. "We caught the pigs using Bestefar's pipe." Inger burst into gales of laughter that had Anne and Ivar chuckling along with her.

"Yes," the little girl said. "They were choking on the smoke!"

"Look," Anne said as small puffs of steam left the pigs' noses. "Inger, I think they make better rings than we do."

"Their noses are rounder," Inger said, and hopped down from the gate. "I'm going inside to tell Bestemor I'm ready to go home with you," she said, looking up at the pair of adults who stared back at her, speechless. She blew them a kiss and ran to the house, blonde curls bouncing with each step.

Ivar looked at Anne. "Just like that? After all this time she's suddenly ready? What did you two talk about today?"

Anne shrugged, her eyes wide. "Smoke rings."

Ivar pulled Anne close and placed a kiss on her cheek. "Will you mind? We've had the house to ourselves, but you're a mother now whether you wanted it or not. I never thought to ask you, although it wouldn't have made much of a difference anyway, but . . ."

Anne placed her mittened hand over his mouth. "You're babbling, my sweet. You never babble. And no, I don't mind. She's a delightful child, and I enjoy her company. Why do you think I've been working so hard every day to help her be comfortable around me? She needs to be at home, with us."

She removed her hand from his mouth and he kissed her. "Thank you." He moved toward the house, pulling her along. "I have something for you inside," he said. "It's an early Christmas present—I don't want to wait another week for you to see it."

"Are you certain? This doesn't sound like you. What is it?"

"You'll see." He grinned like a little boy, and Anne found herself grinning back at him. Once inside the house, he made her sit at the kitchen table while he went into the parlor at the front of the house. Anne looked at Amanda and Per, who also sat in the kitchen, smiling from ear to ear.

"So Inger is ready to go home," Amanda said with a nod. "That is a good thing." She bounced the child up and down on her knee, and Inger began pestering her grandfather about whether or not he could blow smoke rings just by using his cold outside breath.

Ivar appeared in the kitchen doorway, holding something behind his back. "Close your eyes," he said to Anne, and she obediently shut them, wondering what he had that couldn't wait until Christmas. "Hold out your hands," he murmured, and Anne heard him shifting his weight, rustling something against his shirtfront.

When she extended her hands, Ivar placed something heavy and solid in her arms. She opened them to see the large box of a camera before her. Her mouth dropped open and she sat for a long moment, blinking at the camera and searching for words.

She cried, then, thinking of the time she had spent with the camp photographer in their regiment, immortalizing the faces of the wounded and dying as well as the vitally alive on film. She had loved learning the process of picture taking and developing, and had wanted desperately to be able to continue at some future date. That Ivar had remembered touched her beyond words.

She looked up at him, noticing that his eyes were also red-rimmed behind his glasses and suspiciously moist. "Oh, Ivar," she said. "This is beautiful! How did you ever find it?"

He shrugged, looking sheepish. "I found it at a shop downtown. It's been used already, but the proprietor assured me it's in good working condition. We can even make a developing room in the house," he said, motioning over his shoulder to their property. "One of the extra rooms will work nicely, I think."

She nodded, overcome. "This is such a wonderful gift," she murmured. "You sweet man, thank you so much."

Anne wiped her tears and examined the camera with excitement. Inger, meanwhile, looked at her grandmother in some confusion. "I don't think she likes it very much," the child whispered in a loud voice.

Anne laughed and motioned for Inger to come close. "Look at this! I love it—and it does the most amazing things. I'll show you tomorrow, all right?"

Ivar nodded and pointed toward the parlor. "The plates and the rest of the equipment are in the front there."

"It's wonderful. Ivar, thank you." She looked about herself at her new little family with a satisfied smile. "What a perfect Christmas."

* * *

22 December 1864
Savannah, Georgia

"Well, here they are," Emily murmured to Austin as they stood to the side of the wide street, watching

Sherman's army march into town. "They just keep coming!" There were hundreds of men, thousands, in smart blue lines.

Austin leaned on his new false leg, trying to adjust his weight. "Do you want me to take her?" Emily asked, pointing to Mary Alice.

"No," Austin said, his eyes on the troops. "I'll be fine." His gaze was wary as it traveled down the line, and Emily knew he was wondering about their fate, as was she.

The token band of Confederate soldiers guarding the city had fled in the face of Sherman's troops, leaving Savannah open and defenseless against the invading army. Emily had made great sport of mocking the fleeing Confederates when she'd heard the news until she looked at Austin, his gaze a mixture of amusement and annoyance. "Must I remind you that *I* was once a 'gray-coated coward'?"

"You were never truly gray-coated," she answered, poking his ribs, "and you've never been a coward. I'm a caustic person, Austin. You must allow me to have my fun."

"I don't blame the poor men," Austin had said. "They're tired and hungry and they want to go home. I think I'd have run too."

All traces of good humor had fled from Emily's heart as she viewed the troops now filling the streets of the city she'd come to consider her own. She had once assumed she would welcome the Union army with open arms; indeed, she *would* be if she were certain she would have a home left by the time they made their exit.

She fidgeted a bit until Austin asked her, "Are you cold, love?" Emily shook her head and tried to still her movements but found that unless she were moving, even a little bit, she felt extremely vulnerable.

"Serves me right for calling them 'gray-coated cowards,'" she muttered under her breath. "The gods of the Confederacy are having their revenge on me."

"What?"

"Nothing. What should we do? Go home? Stand here?"

"Emily, pull yourself together."

"I can't!" Emily walked a distance away from the side of the road and paced, hands on her hips, looking back at the men in blue. Sherman had led their advance, straight in his posture, unswerving in his purpose. The flags of the Union, though a welcome sight to her heart, caused it to beat rapidly.

Austin looked back at her, holding Mary Alice close in one arm and leaning on a cane with the other. Her heart lurched at the sight; she'd been so smug as a girl when the war had broken out! She had wanted the people of the South to suffer, every last one of them. She hadn't imagined what it would be like to be one of the innocent caught in the wake of a dangerous duel, hadn't known how it would feel to have so much to lose.

She walked to Austin's side then, quickly, and wrapped her arms around his waist. He balanced his cane against his leg and wrapped his arm around her shoulders, pulling her close. "What is it?" he whispered against her hair.

"I love you, and I'm very, very frightened."

"Emily, I have lived in the literal fires of hell. I am not going to let anything happen to us, do you understand me?"

She nodded and allowed the tears to fall, feeling a bit better at their release. Mary Alice babbled and grabbed Emily's nose, squeezing it with her little fingers. "Ow," Emily gasped as one of her child's sharp fingernails dug into her flesh.

"There, you see?" Austin said. "Your daughter doesn't like to see you upset."

Emily poked at Mary Alice's tummy until the little girl laughed and grabbed at her mother's hand. In that moment, close to her husband's beating heart and hearing her daughter's laughter, she could have stayed forever. It was almost possible, for a fraction of an instant, to believe that all was well, that there was no war, no slavery, no misery, that she and her husband were living a fairy tale.

"He's going to talk," Austin whispered, and leaned forward to hear what the people around them were saying about General Sherman. It took several minutes, but word eventually traveled back down the line that Sherman intended for the city to stay intact, that he wanted to establish Savannah as a supply base for the Union, especially as it was directly on the water. He would have ships sent from the North to provide relief for the populace as well.

Emily raised her brows in surprise. "That's all of it? He isn't going to burn it down?"

Austin released her and reached for his cane, moving forward among the throng of blue-coated soldiers, calling over his shoulder to Emily. "Come with me, and stay close."

"Where are we going?"

"To offer our house."

"What?" She ran to catch up with him.

"They mean us no harm, Emily," he murmured, "and they need places for their men to stay. In return, I'm hoping for leniency."

"Well, for heaven's sake, don't tell Sherman what you did for a living before the war. It won't win you any favors with him, even though he fights for the Union."

"He's a fair man. All he asks for is allegiance to the United States, and we're more than willing to give it."

"True," she grumbled. Austin wasn't rash; every decision she'd ever known him to make had been done with considerable thought. She imagined he had well considered this possibility long before the troops had reached Savannah's gates. Trusting in his instincts and hoping desperately that he was right, she followed her husband as he made his way to the front of the lines to speak with the Union officers.

* * *

Boston, Massachusetts

James paced outside Robert's bedroom door, wondering how he could tell his son that he'd been prying into his personal space. He didn't have long to ponder on it, however, because the door opened and Robert stepped out, dressed for the day and apparently ready to go out. He stopped short when he saw James, his brows lifting in surprise.

"Robert, I was hoping to see you soon," James said, internally wincing at the silliness of his comment.

"Oh?"

"Well, yes, there was something I was hoping we could discuss."

"All right," Robert said. He led the way back into his room and motioned to two chairs situated near his small hearth.

"I've been meaning to ask you about this, but the time just never seemed right to admit I've been . . . well, I saw . . ."

Robert leaned forward slightly, his eyes focusing on James's face.

"Robert, I was passing by your room one day and I stopped to ask you a question. I knocked, but you weren't here. Your door was open, and I spied your desk there."

James pointed. "There were papers on the desk and, well, I suppose curiosity got the better of me and I came inside to take a look."

"You did?"

"I did. I'm very sorry for invading your privacy in such a manner, but it was the content of your writings I was hoping to address with you."

Robert sat back in his chair, his expression suddenly guarded. "Father, you should know that I would gladly have shown you the papers had I known you wanted to see them, but if you've a problem with the content, I'm afraid I'm not going to change it."

"A problem with the content?" James shook his head. "Robert, I was amazed at the content. We seem to be developing a family of writers in this house, and son, your memoirs are incredible. I believe they're worthy of publication."

"I . . . I don't know. It's rather personal, it's not exactly fit for public consumption with all of the detail . . ."

"But I believe the public should have the option to read it. If you were to agree, that is. It's amazing, son, the things you and Ben experienced, and the citizens of this country need to know the price our men are paying to secure its continuation."

Robert sat for a moment, speechless. "If you feel so strongly," he finally said, looking a bit bewildered.

"I do. Will you allow me the liberty of looking into publication?"

"Yes, I'd be honored."

"Good." James paused, feeling much more at ease. "Do you have plans for the day?"

Robert shrugged lightly. "Nothing definite, really."

"I'm taking Jim on-site today. You're welcome to join us if you'd like."

Robert looked as though he might decline but then apparently thought the better of it. With a sense of pleasure, James saw the moment when his son changed his mind.

"I do believe I will," Robert said. "I haven't been onsite since I was quite young."

* * *

Ogden, Utah

Jeffrey watched out the front window as the children threw snowballs at each other. They were joined by some of Earl Dobranski's youngest brothers, who hurled them firmly at each other but spared the girls some of their enthusiasm.

Through the newspapers and general gossip, he followed the happenings on the eastern end of the country with a close eye, watching for the day when South Carolina would be invaded. He knew it was close; Sherman was preparing to leave Savannah and march north into the hotbed of emotion that had started the whole thing.

He was uncertain at times how much news he should share with Sarah. He had read of Hood's defeat at Nashville earlier in the month, of how over four thousand men had been captured and another fifteen hundred had been killed or wounded. Hood's force now numbered fourteen thousand, as opposed to Thomas's fifty thousand.

It was staggering, really, in a sad way, how very much of itself the South had hurled at the Union. The Confederacy was nothing but a hollow shell and was doomed to certain failure soon. So much of his life, of Sarah's life, gone in an instant. And yet, when he truly pondered the matter, he realized it had been coming for a long, long time.

Sarah was regaining her mental strength, and her physical body was following suit. There was a color to her cheeks that was returning, and she seemed to enjoy the new home. Every now and again he noticed a faraway look in her eyes and knew she was somewhere else entirely. Bentley had been such a part of her identity that she seemed lost, at times, without it.

She seemed to flourish especially in the company of Ruth and Ellen Dobranski. Ellen made it a habit to visit at least once a week, and Jeffrey was grateful for the woman's willingness to travel the fair distance to their home. Ellen had drawn both women into her circle of compassion and was helping them adjust to their new lives.

As for himself, for the first time in a long time—maybe ever—he was happy. He had made a decision concerning the welfare of his family and he had acted on it, caring for them as he'd always longed to do. Regardless of the challenges the future might hold, as he watched the children hurling snow at each other, he had hope.

CHAPTER 32

It was very touching to see the vast numbers of colored women following after us with babies in their arms, and little ones like our Anna clinging to their tattered skirts. One poor creature, while nobody was looking, hid two boys, five years old, in a wagon, intending, I suppose, that they should see the land of freedom if she couldn't.

—Union officer, witness to the crowds of black people who followed Sherman's army

* * *

27 December 1864
South of Charleston, South Carolina

Joshua struggled through the underbrush, wincing at the pain in his shoulder and feeling panic as delirium came and went. He was lost to all hope if he couldn't keep his senses about him. His regiment had been caught in a skirmish that proved to be deadly for many of the men he fought beside. A lead ball had struck him in his shoulder, and shrapnel that had hit a tree and splintered sent wood and metal into his leg.

His own regiment had all but disappeared, and several of the men in the regiment to which they had attached themselves had been taken prisoner; Joshua had escaped the same fate only by moving quickly and hiding in the thick foliage, barely detecting notice time and again in those first crucial minutes after the fighting ceased. He moved now, knowing it meant his very survival. Black soldiers taken as prisoners of war were, at best, sold into slavery. More often than not, they were tortured and killed outright.

His only hope lay in his ability to pick his way along the coastline and reach Savannah. Sherman was there with his troops, as were Emily and Austin. The minutes dragged into hours as he worked his way south, moving under the cover of darkness and racing along as best he could, his shoulder burning with pain and his leg protesting every step.

It was a difficult thing, knowing who to trust. Sherman was no guarantee, even though Joshua possessed the credentials and smart blue uniform of the Union army. Sherman knew that bands of freed blacks and liberated slaves followed his troops, moving along with the gargantuan army columns in parallel lines, hoping by virtue of their association with Sherman that they would find their way to safety. It was also common knowledge, however, that Sherman wasn't necessarily pleased with their presence unless they managed to secure more goods and supplies for his men.

At any rate, Sherman would be on the move soon, moving upward to Columbia, and then to the birthplace of the current conflict, Charleston herself. Joshua had debated staying in one place and trying to wait until the troops showed themselves, but something urged him forward, an instinct warning him that he needed to be quick on his feet.

The daunting prospect of one hundred miles between his current position and his destination nearly had him giving up in despair, but he kept plodding along, one foot in front of the other, dodging in and out of shadows and trying to stay out of the moonlight.

The sound of a horse nickering in the night came to his ears like an answer to prayer. Provided the horse was riderless, he was in luck. To his immediate left he spied a small farmhouse and stable. Circling the house, he crept to the stable and cautiously opened the door, freezing at the resulting creak.

When nobody else seemed to hear or be alerted to the noise, he snuck inside the building and allowed his eyes a moment to adjust to the interior, which was completely dark without the benefit of the moonlight. Three horses stood in stalls, looking at him as though they had been sent straight from heaven. Walking slowly inside, he ran a gentle hand over each head, enjoying the feel of the breath on his palm. It had been a long time since he'd worked with horses. He was surprised to realize he missed their companionship.

He looked behind himself and found a saddle and blanket, and with an experienced hand, he chose the largest of the three horses and prepared it to ride. "I'll return you someday soon," he whispered to the animal as though it understood his intentions. As he slipped the saddle over the large back, a wave of dizziness nearly brought him to his knees.

He finished his task by leaning against the sturdy animal, cinching the buckles tight and securing everything into place. "Now," he whispered as he led the animal to the door, "I need your help." Quietly, he led the horse from the stable and out into the moonlight, hoping with all he was worth that the inhabitants of the house remained asleep. He detected no lights or anything that would lead him to believe he had awoken anyone.

Leading the horse some distance from the house before mounting, he found a large rock near a stream that wandered through a patch of thick vegetation. Standing on the rock and using his good arm to hoist himself into the saddle, he settled into place with an ease born of many years of experience.

He clicked his teeth together, gently nudging the horse's flanks, and urged the creature onward, following parallel to the main road and keeping the ocean to his left. Stopping only long enough for the horse to rest and find food, he kept at his goal throughout the night. When the rosy hues of morning covered the sky, he found shelter in an abandoned shack near a river.

He didn't sleep well all day, dozing in and out of a fitful rest that was plagued with dreams of torture and death. The horse he kept with him, tying his ankle to the saddle with a length of rope. It was with a feeling of intense relief that he watched night fall, grateful that it was December and not the middle of July.

He mounted again, this time with increasing difficulty, and couldn't subdue the pain that shot through both his wounded leg and his shoulder. Leaning low over the horse's neck, he clicked it forward and again followed the line of the ocean, staying as hidden as he could manage, shying away from the sound of voices and other horses.

He was forced to repeat his routine when morning again rose, but this time he didn't have the fortune of an abandoned shack as shelter. Rain fell a good portion of the day, and by the time night approached again, he was soaked to the skin and shivering. *If I don't make it tonight, I don't think I'm going to.* He told himself to remain focused, to shy away from thoughts of failure and capture, but they crept in on him continually throughout the night until he thought he might either go completely mad or announce himself to the enemy merely to end his mental anguish.

As dawn approached yet one more time, he began to recognize the lay of the land. It filled him with a renewed sense of hope, and he urged the tired horse onward as they neared their destination. It wasn't hard to find Willow Lane—it was close to downtown Savannah—and he had learned the city well in the time he'd lived with Austin and Emily shortly after their marriage. As he approached the large home, however, he noticed the unmistakable presence of the army. There were piles of equipment outside the house and a handful of soldiers patrolling the grounds.

He dismounted and fell to the ground, allowing himself a moment to feel his legs again before trying to rise and walk on them. The horse nickered and nudged his wounded shoulder, and surprisingly enough, the spurt of pain urged him to his feet. He patted the horse's rump and led it in the direction of Willow Lane's stables. Once he spied it, he again slapped the horse and sent it toward the building, knowing that a riderless horse might arouse suspicion, but that at any rate, the horse would be cared for.

Joshua watched with eyes that felt gritty and sore as one lone soldier passed around the back of the house. With a soft step, he followed the young man until he reached one of the smaller outbuildings, the one he knew to be the kitchen. Slipping inside undetected, he leaned against the wall and breathed a sigh of relief. His safety might be temporary, but for the moment, it would do.

He found a loaf of bread wrapped in a cloth on the table and he tore into it, mentally apologizing to Janet for eating her food without permission. When he felt he couldn't eat another bite, he stumbled to the pump and gulped down some water. He slowly straightened and looked around himself, feeling a surge of relief. He may not live much longer, but at least he'd made it to Willow Lane.

Dragging his feet upon the stone floor, he moved to a far corner by the hearth, where he collapsed in a heap, hoping with all of his might that it would be Gwenyth and not a soldier who would find him in the morning.

* * *

Ogden, Utah

Ruth wandered from the bedroom of her new house and down the stairs to the parlor. Something was wrong with her, and she couldn't ignore it any longer. For weeks on end she had had a nagging cough that never completely went away. That morning as she coughed into a handkerchief, she had coughed up specks of blood, and it had sent a thread of alarm down her spine.

She had seen people die of consumption, had tried to care for them herself, but the most she had ever been able to do had been to prolong their lives. She had yet to come across a physician or healer who could point her in the right direction in terms of healing the illness.

Why now? she wondered as she walked into her dark parlor? Why when she had achieved her grandest dream would it all be taken away? Was she truly to die now that she finally had almost everything she wanted?

Perhaps, though, she thought as she slowly sat down on a sofa under the front window, death wouldn't be such a bad thing. Her husband was waiting for her, of that much she was certain. She'd seen him in her dreams, smiling at her, waiting for her to finish her journey on the earth so that she could join him for the next phase of life. Maybe it wouldn't be such a hard thing after all.

There were things, though, that were unresolved. There were people she loved dearly who still had problems she felt she needed to offer comfort for. Her relationship with Sarah had returned to the innocence and happiness they had shared when they were very, very young, and it was a bright spot in her life she hadn't ever expected to see. Sarah was still regaining her strength, however, and trying to find her place in her new world, and Ruth wanted very much to be able to see Sarah make the transition.

The girls still needed her too. Clara and Rose were, for all intents and purposes, her daughters. They lived with her, although there was plenty of room at Jeffrey and Sarah's new house. They were comfortable with Ruth and were loath to leave Elijah's side.

Charlotte and Will lived with her parents, and Charlotte was slowly, slowly releasing her hold on her former home and trying to find happiness in a new place. She hadn't reached it yet, however, and she relied on Ruth's judgment and conversation.

Mary and Ben. The names came to her in the darkness, and she rested her head on the back of the sofa. Perhaps they were the two who held her to earth more firmly than all the rest; she had yet to see Ben and Mary reunited with Elijah, happy together and at peace.

Please, dear Lord, she prayed, her lips moving noiselessly with the words in her head, *please let me live to see my children, all of them, happy. Don't take me just yet. Let me stay for just a bit longer . . .*

* * *

Boston, Massachusetts

For Christmas, Ben had taken Mary to a church and made her his bride. It was the very thing she had wanted most for as long as she could remember, and even now she wondered if it wasn't all a dream. They rented a small home in an abolition-supporting neighborhood, and Mary felt such joy she wondered if her heart could contain it all.

The sun was creeping over the horizon and Mary rose, placing a wrapper over her nightshirt, and walked into the little kitchen. She brewed a pot of herbal tea for herself and Ben and sat at the table, thinking. It was a few months yet that they would stay in Boston, and when the snow melted, they would travel west to a land she'd never been, and she would meet her child.

According to Ruth, Elijah was besotted with the family, and for that Mary was grateful. She wondered, though, what kind of role she would play in his life. Was there even a place for her in it? Suppose he didn't care for her, didn't want her to be his mother? She cupped her chin in her hand and absently chewed on the inside of her cheek, wondering how she would go about winning the heart of her own child.

She turned her head as Ben entered the room, rubbing his eyes and yawning.

"Why are you awake so early again?" he asked her, and pulled out a chair next to hers.

"I don't know. I can't sleep lately after the sun comes up. When I lived at Bentley, there were mornings I'd have given my left eye for a couple of minutes' extra sleep. Now I can't *make* myself."

Ben reached his hand up underneath her hair and massaged her neck. "You toss and turn in your sleep too."

"I'm sorry."

He smiled. "I don't mind. But I've noticed you do seem restless."

"I'm nervous about going west," she told him. She hadn't said it to him before in so many words, and it was a bit of a relief to finally have shared it with him. "I'm worried about how we'll be received, and I'm worried about living near your mother—what she'll say when she discovers we're married. I'm worried about Elijah. I miss Emily dreadfully. I miss Ruth too."

"I believe you'll find everything will work itself out for the best. If my mother has problems with our marriage, we won't see her."

"I don't want that."

"Mary, I *left* my mother. She has no hold on me."

"And what of the religious differences? What will people think when they learn you married a black non-Mormon girl?"

"Sweetheart, there are very few people whose opinion I cherish. Some of those people are Emily and Ruth and my family here in Boston. Others are the Dobranskis. They will or already do accept you with open arms. I couldn't care less what others think of your religious affiliation."

"But what of *you?*"

"I don't understand. You know I love you."

"Yes, but what if I decide never to join your church?" Mary gnawed on her lip again. The thought had troubled her since their marriage. What if Ben decided he needed a wife who shared his religious beliefs? Would he cast her aside? There wouldn't be many who would blame him, likely thinking him crazy in the first place for marrying a black woman. A former slave!

"Mary," Ben said, rubbing a finger across her knuckles. "I've not pressured you to be baptized. I know you have reservations about Joseph Smith. I found it odd at first also. All I ask is that you eventually read the Book of Mormon and pray about it. If you do this and still don't feel a need to be baptized, I'll just be happy you're at my side."

Her dubious expression must have spoken for itself because he shook her hand a bit. "Truly."

"I don't know, Ben. I think it will become a wedge between us."

"It *could* become a wedge, but I'm confident it won't. I love you and I accept you for who you are. I am blessed to be with you, and I will always respect your wishes."

A knock at the door interrupted him, and he frowned. "Who would be here at this hour?" he wondered aloud, and rose to answer the door. When he returned to the kitchen, his face was pale with worry.

"Camille's having some sort of trouble," he said. "Jacob is sending word to the family. She wants me to come and say a prayer for her . . ." Ben left the kitchen, and Mary hastily removed the teakettle from the heat and followed him into the bedroom, where he was pulling on his clothing.

"I'm coming with you," she told him, and he nodded. "We need to hurry."

* * *

New York, New York

Marie turned over in the bed and reached for Daniel.

When her hand touched the cold sheet where he should have been sleeping, she sat up and shoved her hair out of her eyes. Where was he? With a sinking heart, she remembered he had been called out to answer a fire alarm at three and a half that morning.

She rubbed her eyes and looked over at the small clock mounted on the wall. Daniel had made the clock, carving it out of a beautiful piece of oak and taken it to a clockmaker for the inner workings. She noticed she had slept late—it was nearly half past nine.

She rose from the bed with a frown, wandering to the kitchen and out of the door that adjoined the wood shop with the house. He wasn't working. She reentered the kitchen and glanced around, wondering if perhaps he'd left her a note explaining where he'd be. When a quick perusal of the kitchen and parlor didn't turn up anything satisfactory, she went back into the bedroom and changed her clothes.

She reached the mothers' house a few minutes later and banged on the door. "I can't find Daniel," she said when Brenna opened it. "He was called to a fire in the middle of the night. Have you seen him yet this morning?"

Within minutes Brenna had a horse harnessed to the carriage, and the three women rode into town, none speaking much. The city was largely quiet the morning after New Year's festivities. A few stragglers on their way home from parties walked along the streets, soon to reach their homes or rented rooms and fall into a satisfied slumber.

Marie barely saw them. She was focused on reaching the fire department, and when they did, she jumped down from the carriage before it had rolled to a complete stop. She ran into the building, looking for someone who could give her some direction.

"Have you seen my husband, Daniel O'Shea?" she breathlessly asked the first man she came across.

He looked decidedly uneasy. It was then that she noticed the smudges of black on his face, arms, and hands, and the gritty, red-rimmed appearance of his eyes. "We fought a bad one last night," the man told her. "O'Shea was in a bit of an accident."

Marie felt faint and heard the man's words as though they echoed at her through a long tunnel. When she refocused on his voice, she heard him telling her Daniel was at the hospital . . .

She walked from the fire station and approached Brenna and Jenny. Climbing up into the carriage next to Brenna, she repeated what the man had said to her, her voice sounding rather flat even to her own ears. The quick ride to the hospital near the scene of the accident went by in a blur; Marie couldn't have retraced the route if she'd tried.

A series of questions and ten minutes later found Marie at Daniel's bedside, a bandage wrapped around his head, covering his eyes. He was filthy, his hair blackened and singed on the ends. She gripped the hands of the mothers, one on either side, and held tight as Brenna began to cry.

* * *

Boston, Massachusetts

Camille's eyes were filled with tears, and she rocked on the bed, curled in a ball and clutching Jacob's hand. He kneeled near her head, brushed the hair from her forehead, and tried to calm her fears. "I didn't know I was carrying," she cried as another intense wave of pain ripped through her abdomen.

"Sweetheart," Jacob said as she clenched her teeth, "how long do you suppose it has been since, well since . . ."

If she weren't in so much pain she would have been supremely embarrassed to be discussing such a delicate matter with her husband. "I don't know," she moaned. "Three months . . . maybe four . . ."

She hated the stunned look on his face, hated that she had been the one to put it there. "No, you don't understand," she said. "I wasn't keeping anything from you. I've always been that way, my whole life. We could set a watch by Anne's monthlies, but mine were always so inconsistent . . ."

"Honey, that can't be. You're still as thin as a rail. If you were four months along with child, I think we would have noticed." Jacob looked at Camille's white nightgown that was stained red with blood. He blanched and tried to hide his worry from her, but she saw it in his face.

She wanted to comfort him, tell him she would be fine, but another wave of pain ripped through her midsection, and she cried out in agony. "I'm fine," she gasped as it passed. "I'll be fine. Don't look at me like that—you're frightening me!" Her voice rose to a fevered pitch, and Jacob leaned forward, placing his lips on her forehead.

"Shhh, sweetheart, of course you're fine. Your mother's on her way, and so is Ben. I sent word that you wanted him to come over and pray."

"I think it was a good idea. Don't you think it was a good idea?"

"Yes, yes, it was a good idea." He lifted his head. "In fact, I think they're here now. Someone's knocking at the door. I'll be right back."

"No!"

"Sweet, I'll be right back. I have to let them in." Jacob pulled his hand from her grip and ran out of the room and down the stairs to the front door, returning in moments with Ben and Mary. Mary immediately entered and took Camille's hand, beginning a perusal of the young woman's condition to ascertain the problem.

"Have you sent for the doctor?" Mary asked Jacob over her shoulder.

"Yes. I sent messengers to your house, to James and Elizabeth, and to Dr. Child."

Camille reached her hand toward Jacob, who kneeled and clasped her fingers. "Ben," Camille said as Mary rose and looked about the room, moving to the wardrobe and retrieving a folded sheet from within. "I want you to say a special prayer. I'm so very afraid."

Ben moved next to Jacob and crouched down low next to her head while Mary climbed on the bed behind her and began to attempt to staunch the flow of blood. "I'll place my hands on your head; is that all right with you, Camille?" At her nod, he gently touched her head and said, "I'm going to give you a blessing."

The moment Ben began speaking, Camille felt her fear abate. The cramping in her lower abdomen was so intense she felt that death might well be a relief, and in that moment she wasn't afraid of it. She listened to the cadence of his voice and felt a light in the room, a presence of love and comfort.

She gripped Jacob's hand tighter until she was certain she might snap his bones, and she felt him rest his forehead against her fist, felt the moisture on the back of her hand. *Please, please let the pain go away . . .* she prayed as Ben continued his blessing. He concluded, and she cried out again in anguish, hurting so badly that she saw stars before her eyes, floating in a haze until they melted together and she sank into peaceful oblivion.

AUTHOR'S NOTES

Chapter 2—Ben and Luke's regiment, the 1st Massachusetts Cavalry, was not actually engaged at Gettysburg until the second day, when they joined with the 6th Corps, and then on the third day as provost guard at army headquarters where they were employed in guarding prisoners. I placed both Ben and Luke at places I wanted the reader to see firsthand, although if I had stayed true to their regiment's history, they wouldn't have actually been there. The battle at Little Round Top with Chamberlain is one of the most amazing stories to me, and I wanted at least one of the men to be there for it. As for Pickett's charge, I suppose I have a personal connection with it, as George Edward Pickett is an ancestor of mine. Even though he fought for the wrong side (I say this with a smile), it was my nod to him as his descendant.

Chapter 5—I also took creative license in chapter 5 by placing Ben and Luke at the New York draft riots. To my knowledge, men from the 1st Massachusetts Cavalry were not in New York at the time, but there were Gettysburg veterans sent to the city to restore order. I knew from the beginning of the series that the draft riots would be meaningful for Luke, so I again strayed from actual regimental history in this case.

Chapter 14—In chapter 14 I mention the battle of Chickamauga and concentrate on the battle at Chattanooga where Grant, from the west, and other reinforcements from the North moved in to act as support to the beleaguered Army of the Cumberland. It was the first time in the war that troops were moved so many miles so quickly. I did take liberties with history here, however, in terms of chronology and the exact number of days. When the troops from the North were sent south to act as reinforcements, the trip took them eight days. They were in place well before the battle of Chattanooga began. Because I wanted Ben and Robert to witness the Gettysburg Address firsthand, I manipulated events so that the men in this book don't actually arrive in Tennessee until November 23 or 24, and, given that the Gettysburg Address occurred on November 19, that moves the miraculously quick journey from eight days to six.

Chapters 17 and 18—In these chapters, we see Ivar set up in the newly created prison at Andersonville, and the date header on chapter 17 places the events in early January 1864. Andersonville was actually completed and opened its doors in April of that year. In chapter 17, Jeffrey tells Anne of his news about Ivar, that he's been moved to a new camp in Andersonville, Georgia, called "Sumter," leading one to believe that the camp might have been named for the fort in Charleston Bay, but Sumter was the name of the county enclosing Andersonville. Andersonville was a small town of perhaps twenty residents, and its name soon became associated with the notorious camp. Now Camp Sumter is referred to merely as "Andersonville." The very name of the place makes me shudder—much as do the names *Auschwitz,* or *Dachau.* No, Andersonville wasn't initially designed to be a death camp, but surely, that's what it became.

Chapter 23—All the details I recounted in this chapter regarding the battle of Cold Harbor are true, up to and including the fact that for seven days after the beginning of the battle, the dead and dying lay between the two armies with neither side making a move to retrieve them. According to some sources, the stench became unbearable and a temporary truce was called—roughly two hours worth—while they collected and attempted to bury their dead. They found two, *two* survivors among those thousands spread over the five acres. I took license in this book by stating that those two were my fictional characters.

Chapter 24—You will have noticed, in reading this book, that I did not spend extensive time detailing the Birminghams' trek west. The LDS reader is largely familiar with the walk across the plains, so I chose to keep the story moving along at its quick pace. I enjoy stories about life on the wagon trails, and I know many do—therefore, I hope the reader will forgive my light treatment of it in this novel.

Chapter 27—I relate an incident in this chapter of a young soldier who carved his "headboard," or headstone, with his name and birth date, simply looking for something to fill the time. He did die soon after, most likely while walking through the trenches and encampments, which were under constant attack during the Petersburg siege. The continual gunshot was reportedly so commonplace that the men finally took to literally *strolling* through, shots flying about them, as if they were taking a walk through a park. Most often, they moved from one place to the next unscathed, but occasionally the bullets found their marks and the men fell.

Chapter 30—The incident described in this chapter concerning a Confederate plot against New York is true. Also true is the fact that the famed Booth brothers were sharing a stage that night at Winter Garden Theatre. John Wilkes Booth was indeed one of those brothers who would play a significant role in the course of events not five months down the road.

BIBLIOGRAPHY

Axelrod, Alan. *The Complete Idiot's Guide to the Civil War.* New York: Alpha Books, 1998.

*Author's note: Regardless of how the title of this book, included in this list, reflects upon my intellect, I have found it to be an excellent source offering a clear, concise reference detailing a broad overview of the Civil War.

Ball, Edward. *Slaves in the Family*. New York: Ballantine Books, 1998.

Bowman, John S. *The Civil War Day by Day—An Illustrated Almanac of America's Bloodiest War.* Greenwich: Dorset Press, 1989.

Davis, Kenneth C. *Don't Know Much about the Civil War.* New York: Avon Books, 1997.

*Author's note: See above comments on the Axelrod book. The same apply here.

Davis, Burke. *The Civil War, Strange and Fascinating Facts.* New York: Wings Books, 1980.

Davis, William C. *The Soldiers of the Civil War.* New York: Quadrillion Publishing, 1993.

Douglass, Frederick. *Narrative of the Life of Frederick Douglass, An American Slave.* New York: Dell Publishing, 1997.

Hackwell, Grace-Marie Moore, owner and creator. "1st Regiment Massachusetts VolunteerCavalry." http://hometown.aol.com/Shortyhack/1stmass.html.

Long, E. B., with Barbara Long. *The Civil War Day by Day, An Almanac 1861–1865.* Garden City, N.Y.: Doubleday, 1971.

Long, E. B. *The Saints and the Union—Utah Territory during the Civil War.* Champaign: University of Illinois Press, 1981.

Lyman, Darryl. *Civil War Wordbook, including Sayings, Phrases and Expletives.* Pennsylvania: Combined Books, 1994.

McPherson, James M. *Battle Cry of Freedom.* New York: Ballantine, 1998.

McPherson, James, and Mort Küntsler. *Images of the Civil War.* New Jersey: Gramercy Books, 1992.

Miller, William J., and Brian C. Pohanka, *An Illustrated History of the Civil War.* Alexandria, Virginia: Time-Life, 2000.

Varhola, Michael J. *Everyday Life during the Civil War: A Guide for Writers, Students and Historians.* Cincinnati, Ohio: Writer's Digest Books, 1999.

Ward, Geoffrey C., Ken Burns, and Rick Burns. *The Civil War.* New York: Knopf, Inc., 1990.

Wheeler, Richard. *Voices of the Civil War.* New York: Penguin, 1976.

EXCERPT FROM LAND DIVDED

Jerusalem, October 1841

Elder Orson Hyde walked out of Stephen's Gate and stared up at the city wall. Though he knew these were not the same walls Jesus had looked upon anciently, he felt awed at the sight of their harsh, firm beauty bathed in the light of a nearly full moon. They had seen hundreds of years of war and turmoil, peace and promise, and much more was yet to come, for there was much prophesied about Jerusalem and its role in the world. These walls would yet see the final destruction of the wicked and the coming of the Son of Man.

He walked down the poorly maintained road into the Kidron Valley, across the stone bridge, up a winding, rock-strewn path, and through an old gate in a wall of stone. Here in the Garden of Gethsemane, he delayed briefly, his thoughts on Christ and His sacrifice. Shedding a few tears, he took a small branch from one of the trees and climbed to the crest of the Mount of Olives.

It was from here that the Lord ascended to Heaven and, according to prophets older than the walls of the city across the Kidron, the place where Jesus would come again to save His people from their enemies one last time.

And he was here. To the west he could see the distant Mediterranean Sea; to the east, the Dead Sea valley. It was not an unfamiliar sight. He had seen it all in a vision eighteen months earlier—witness that he was to come, witness to the need to begin something new for the house of Israel.

He sat down on a large rock and watched the city come to life as the sun rose behind him. Over the last few days he had mingled with Arabs in traditional bright colored garb, Turks in their conical hats and loose pantaloon trousers, and Jews in more European attire. It was a city of twenty thousand people with dingy, narrow streets, each emitting a thousand different smells. It had all been strange, but then most of his trip had been that way.

Taking out a piece of paper, he smoothed it flat and dipped his pen in an inkwell he had brought and began writing his prayer. Now he must do what he had come to do. He cleared his mind then began to write the prayer God had revealed to him.

"O Thou! Who art from everlasting to everlasting . . ."

His greeting petitioned God to listen to his words. Then he consecrated the land under and around him for the gathering together of Judah's scattered remnants, the building up of Jerusalem again—though now trodden under the feet of Gentiles—and the rearing of a temple that would honor God's name and work.

Pausing for a brief moment, he thanked God for his safety in the midst of a tumultuous land and asked for that continued kindness on his return home. He then spoke of the promises the Lord had made to Abraham, Isaac, and Jacob wherein He would remember their scattered seed who waited for the fulfillment of these promises. He asked that God grant removal of the barrenness and sterility of the land and let springs of living water break forth to water its thirsty soil that it might flow with plenty to eat when possessed by its rightful heirs, those returning prodigals who would come home.

He concluded his prayer by remembering the Saints at home, especially his family. He then prayed for the Saints and the leaders of the Church who were being persecuted. Finally he spoke words that would bless members of the Church forever. "And let this blessing rest upon every faithful officer and member in thy Church. And all the glory and honor will we ascribe unto God and the Lamb for ever and ever. AMEN."

Standing, Orson piled stones, that by ancient custom established by Jacob and Joshua would witness that he had fulfilled his mission.

As he viewed the city from his lofty position one last time, he knew Jerusalem would never be the same. Slowly but surely the hearts of the dispersed of Judah would turn to this dusty, dry, and sparsely-inhabited land, and it would become "a cup of trembling unto all the people round about, . . . a burdensome stone for all people" (Zech. 12:2–3). Though the entire world would be gathered against them, they would survive this time. They would prevail.

The words of Zechariah came to mind wherein that ancient prophet said that the governors of Judah would reestablish a nation that would become "like an hearth of fire among the wood, and like a torch of fire in a sheaf; and they shall devour all the people round about, on the right hand and on the left" (Zech. 12:6). With only seven thousand Jews in all of Palestine and its ancient beauty all but gone, Elder Hyde wondered how they could become that nation.

He took a deep breath. He did not know, but he knew it would be. Somewhere, somehow—even now—the hearts of dispersed Judah would begin to change until Judah returned like a flood to this land. It would not be pleasant; it would certainly not be without war and mayhem in the lives of both Jew and Gentile, but it would happen. The hardships she would endure to prepare this land for the return of her King would make the Jews shudder if they were able to see them. What lay ahead to bring them home would be as difficult as anything Judah had ever endured in her history. Eventually, she would become a humble nation prepared for the Gospel by the coming of the Lord to drive away both her pride and her enemies.

Elder Hyde started down the slope toward the road. Once on it, he turned south and began a final trip around the city.

November 29, 1947

Silently unfolding the first slip of paper, Assembly President Oswaldo Aranha paused, the heaviness of the impending vote weighing on him. This vote—the vote for partition—would establish separate Jewish and Arab states in Palestine. It had already been delayed once, leading to a three-day break of intense lobbying and promise making. Aranha himself had lobbied hard with the Catholic countries of South America. The moment of truth was at hand.

"Guatemala."

Aranha's heavy silence now transferred to the old skating rink, the improvised assembly hall of the United Nations. For this one moment, the delegates, the spectators, even the reporters in the press gallery, were silent, almost in awe.

Quietly, Dr. Jorge Garcia Granados rose from his seat. As he rose, a piercing cry in Hebrew came from the spectators' gallery. *"Ana Ad Hoshiya!"* O Lord, save us.

"Guatemala votes for partition."

Almost 5,700 miles away, Hannah Daniels squeezed Naomi Stavsky's hand. They stood huddled around an old radio with a number of their fellow outcasts in a small garden in Tel Aviv, concentrating on the most important moment in Jewish history since Joshua crossed the Jordan River to capture the Promised Land.

The United Nations' vote to partition Palestine, if successful, would effectively give them the opportunity to create a Jewish state. It had not come easily. Over the last two years Hannah had watched as Britain had remained intractable in its policy, Foreign Secretary Ernest Bevin insisting that British interests were more closely linked to Arab nationalists than to Jewish Zionism. Most in Israel considered the arguments he spewed forth dirty water—nothing but a cover for a deeply ingrained anti-Semitism. Regardless, much of the world had slowly turned against the British, the United States especially.

"The United States of America votes for partition." There was applause by all those who gathered to hear the news as it blared from the radio in the garden.

"That's nearly enough," Naomi said to Hannah.

Hannah could only nod. It was going well; they were close! She put her arm around her young friend and pulled her in. Naomi had only recently arrived from Europe where she had been a part of the underground for nearly two years now. She and dozens like her had led Jews out of Displaced Persons camps to the shorelines of the Mediterranean where they had put them on boats similar to—and even larger than—the one on which Hannah had escaped, sending them on their way to Palestine. Though hundreds had made it to Israel's shores, many more had been caught by the British and interred on the island of Cyprus where more than fifty thousand waited in camps similar to those they had escaped in Europe. Still more continued to wait in those DP camps hoping the doors of legal immigration would finally open and they too could escape the squalor of the camps of postwar Europe. Though all such people would not come to Palestine, many would, and their ability to do so without further British interference depended on this vote!

She glanced at her young friend. Her hair was lighter, but her eyes dark brown, set to the side of an aquiline nose. Taller than Hannah, she was thin with no sign of any fat, though she had matured in recent years. More noticeable to Hannah was the way Naomi carried the emotional and spiritual growth gained by literally walking thousands of miles over valley and mountain to lead others out of the camps. Smart, determined, and confident, Naomi was a far cry from the self-protective introvert Hannah had first led out of Berlin. She and Hannah had grown close those last few months in Italy, and even closer through their constant letters to one another. Now she was here. It was wonderful!

Hannah would not be in Tel Aviv were it not for Naomi coming in by ship that morning. Her own home was in Jerusalem where she and Ephraim had found a place in the Jewish Quarter of the Old City. It wasn't much, but it was home, and David and Elizabeth were there now, anxiously awaiting Hannah and Naomi's return.

"England abstains."

"Fancy that," said one man cynically.

"Still want to hold on do they. Well, we won't let them," cried another. With that there was applause.

Though Britain had announced two weeks prior that it would withdraw all its troops from Palestine by August 1, 1948, many Jews—especially the leaders—were doubtful they would actually go. Palestine was the most important part of the British Empire's tenuous hold on the Middle East. To walk away might cause them to lose their grip entirely, and few believed that was what they intended. If partition were successful, many Jews were afraid the disgruntled British would allow disorder, either to show their displeasure or to try and force a reconsideration. After all, if Jews and Arabs started massacring one another, someone would have to step in. With the British already here, the UN would surely give them what they wanted—a trusteeship and the freedom to clean out the rebels.

"The Brits at least stayed out of the vote," Naomi said.

"Tonight. Tomorrow they vote with their favors." By giving the Arabs the advantage in the coming fight, the Brits could still beat back any Jewish national home.

"When will Ephraim be back?" Naomi asked.

"In the next few days," Hannah grinned. Just the sound of his name gave her joy. He was the miracle in her life. She missed him terribly, but the Jewish Agency, the representative government for the Jews in Palestine under the British Mandate, had sent Ephraim to contact old friends in postwar Europe to help open the doors for arms purchases, especially planes. Without such weapons, any Jewish State promised by the UN would never become a reality, would never survive the coming war.

War. She dreaded even the thought of it. The Arabs were armed with weapons her people could only dream of. To survive the next few months would be critical. While the British prepared to leave, while the Jews still had some peace, they must buy and ship an array of weapons to Israel or lose their state to the Arab nations the moment they crossed the borders.

Another vote, another celebration. A vote for partition would only open the door for statehood, not guarantee it. The Jews would have to come to a peaceful solution with the Arabs, who would not even speak of peace, or they would have to fight. And if they could not show the world that they had the ability to hold such a state, the UN could reverse its position as easily as it had granted it.

"How much arm twisting did the Americans have to do to push this vote through?" Naomi asked.

"A great deal, and because of it those countries would be glad to have a clear chance to reverse their vote."

"I hear that the President had trouble with some in his own cabinet."

"Secretary of Defense James Forrestal is the most opposed. But there are others, and they are avid Arabists for the same reason as the Brits—influence and oil. Ephraim thinks they've already laid plans for bringing about reversal and may have even secretly promised the Arabs to try." The cry of a baby immediately turned her toward the house as another round of applause greeted words announced by the radio. Inside she found the twins still lying on the bed in her host's bedroom, Jacob wide awake. She picked him up and cradled him in her arms, her warmth giving him immediate comfort.

When planning their marriage, she and Ephraim had wondered if they would ever have children. Who really knew the effects of the Holocaust? She smiled. The twins had been a double gift from God, but a challenge to care for. She glanced at Joseph where he lay on the bed. Alike down to the shape of their nose and the length of their feet, even she had difficulty at times knowing the difference. Only the slight cowlick in Joseph's hairline gave him away.

She pulled Jacob even closer as she returned to the yard. How she loved them!

As she left the house, a clock on the cupboard revealed that it was near midnight. The crowd in the yard had doubled and was overflowing into the street. All were silent, straining to hear the radio. A barrel-chested man with a bald pate turned to her and said hello as she approached.

"Yitzhak, nice to see you." Hannah smiled.

"I see Ephraim has not returned."

She shook her head. "If we win tonight, his work may take even longer."

Yitzhak only smiled agreement. Yitzhak Perlman worked as an arms procurement agent for the underground Jewish army known as the Haganah. Because of those connections, he knew of Ephraim's mission to Europe and how such missions would make the difference between victory and defeat. It would do no good to have the UN resolution if they must fight the Arabs with little more than rocks and sticks.

"What will happen tomorrow, Yitzhak?"

"Haj Amin will start a strike, then a riot, then a war. What else?" He forced a smile.

"Yes, what else," she replied.

For months the Jews had continued to hope for a peaceful solution, but with the Arabs, especially Haj Amin el Husseini, Mufti of Jerusalem and self-proclaimed leader of the Palestinian Arabs, making rash statements about never allowing a Jewish state in their midst, it was difficult.

"He began fanning the flames of passion against Jews years ago. Now his men—his Holy Strugglers, he calls them—train and arm guerillas both here and across the border. He will set them loose on partition, and by their violence, they will make it hard for the UN to resist reversing what happens tonight," Yitzhak said.

"He is a butcher," Hannah said through a granite jaw.

"He is a nationalist, just like you and me. And he hates Jews because we threaten to take what he thinks belongs to him."

"He sided with Hitler in the war, Yitzhak. That makes him more than a nationalist patriot. Do not forget that he called for the absolute annihilation of the Jews and supported the Nazi resolution to the Jewish problem."

"No one said he was a patriot, Hannah," Yitzhak smiled. "He is Mufti, a holy man to all Islam, a defender of the faith who is justified in fighting the infidel and destroying them all. We are next on his list. He has been planning this for years, and even though the British recognize him as the butcher you know him to be and will not allow him into Palestine, he runs things here for the Arabs through the Arab Higher Committee. It is him we have been fighting since 1920, and now he will see the chance he has always wanted. He will not miss it, and it will be him and his beliefs we will have to defeat more than all other Arab Armies. Until we do, we will not have peace in this land."

"I wish all Jews saw him as the danger. They do not see the danger. They think there may be a few events—a riot or two—but the British will stop it, and we will find a way to peace. Because of it, they will not be ready, and many will die."

"Yes, I know. They think this is a great opportunity for Palestinian Arabs as well as for us, and that the Arabs will see it that way. Most will not. They do not like our foreign ways, and they especially do not want us buying their land. Because of this, many will fight us. Others will not. They will wait to see. Many others will run at the first sign of trouble, thinking they can return later. They have done it for generations. They do not realize this time will be different."

"Some will fight Haj Amin," Hannah said.

"Some. We try to make treaties with those who hate Haj Amin or who believe their lives will be better under us, but they are few—most are Christian Arabs. Islam, at least Haj Amin's rendition of Islam, will prevent most from supporting us. Holy War in defense of one of their holiest cities is strong medicine. They will also remember what happened to those who opposed him in 1936–39. Six thousand Arabs died in those years, four thousand of them at Arab hands. Fear of him will be strong." Yitzhak smiled. "I do not wish to be depressing on such a happy night. *Behatzlaka*, Hannah. Be safe." She watched as Yitzhak left the yard and headed toward Haganah headquarters while turning her attention back to the radio.

"Here it comes!" someone said in a hushed voice.

"Where do we stand?" asked another.

"Thirteen against is all I know," answered another.

"How many does it take?" said Naomi as she slipped her arm around Hannah's waist.

"Two-thirds majority vote," Hannah whispered.

"The General Assembly of the United Nations—" the radio broadcaster began. The yard went silent and someone reached for the knob of the radio in an attempt to get more volume. "—by a vote of thirty-three in favor, thirteen against, and ten abstentions, has voted to partition Palestine."

ABOUT THE AUTHOR

A graduate of Weber State University, N.C. Allen has enjoyed a successful writing career for a number of years. She has proven herself as a gifted and prolific writer whose versatility has earned her a large and loyal readership.

N.C. Allen enjoys spending time with her family, reading, traveling, and learning of other times, people, and places. She and her husband Mark live in Ogden, Utah, with their two children.